Margaret Thomson Janvier

The Queen's Body-Guard

A story of American life for girls

Margaret Thomson Janvier

The Queen's Body-Guard
A story of American life for girls

ISBN/EAN: 9783337322823

Printed in Europe, USA, Canada, Australia, Japan

Cover: Foto ©Andreas Hilbeck / pixelio.de

More available books at **www.hansebooks.com**

THE

QUEEN'S BODY-GUARD.

A STORY OF AMERICAN LIFE
FOR GIRLS.

BY

MARGARET VANDEGRIFT.

" The heights by great men reached and kept
Were not attained by sudden flight,
But they, while their companions slept,
Were toiling upward in the night."
LONGFELLOW.

PHILADELPHIA
HENRY T. COATES & CO.

THE QUEEN'S BODY-GUARD.

CHAPTER I.

" Gray distance hid each shining sail
By ruthless breezes borne from me;
And lessening, fading, faint, and pale,
My ships went forth to sea."—GEORGE ARNOLD.

ANY one happening into Mrs. Stanley's cosy back
parlor, on a certain February afternoon, nearly a
dozen years ago, would have doubted, at first, whether he
had interrupted a council of war, or a treaty of peace. Mrs.
Stanley's gentle, tranquil face, with its almost deprecating
expression, offered testimony to the latter theory; but the
flushed cheeks and slightly-raised voices of the rest of the
family were rather suggestive of imminent war. Two tall
girls with brown hair and frank blue eyes sat hand in hand
on the sofa; their bewildering likeness to each other proclaimed them twins, but a close scrutiny revealed a very
decided difference of expression. They had just passed their
fifteenth birthday, and were in all the dignity of their first
long gowns. On a low ottoman by the mother's chair sat
Elizabeth, the oldest daughter of the house; she was three
years older than the twins, paler and graver-looking, but
with a tranquil, determined face, which gave one the feeling
that she might be safely depended upon. Nestling in her
lap was Mary, known only in the family by her nickname,
May; a delicate-looking child, seven or eight years old.

Ernest and Arnold, two sturdy boys of ten and twelve, occupied the hearth-rug, and a tall, broad-shouldered fellow, with an honest, boyish face, leaned upon one end of the mantel-piece. Since Roderick Stanley's father died, five years ago, he had been a tower of strength to his mother and sisters and younger brothers, although he was not quite sixteen at the time. His manner was far from self-asserting, and he was not especially gifted as to mind; but a certain clear integrity of character, which shone through his brown eyes, and seemed to animate his most trifling words and actions, rendered his face a very attractive one, and the most fractious children and animals always made a distinction in his favor.

Mrs. Stanley had just called the meeting to order by rapping gently on the arm of her chair.

"I think it is my turn to speak," she said, smiling. "I have been patiently waiting for the meeting to come to order, because I have a remark to make before we go any farther."

"Poor mamma!" said the youngest, stroking her mother's hand as she spoke; "we are all very rude—all of us but Rod and Lizzie; but indeed we could not help it, Mr. Kemp is so bad!"

"Dear children," said Mrs. Stanley, "it is just about that very thing that I wish to speak. Nothing can be gained by abusing a man who is not here to take his own part, but a great deal can be lost. Mr. Kemp no doubt thought he was acting for the best when he risked our money, and, if all had turned out as he hoped it would, we should be praising instead of blaming him. So now we will drop that part of the subject entirely, and be thankful that he stopped before it was quite gone. What is left will yield us, probably, five hundred dollars a year; the sale of our furniture ought to bring us at least a thousand dollars, and with this we must do something that will make it up to enough for us to live on. We are all well and strong—all, that is, but our little youngest, and it will be a poor story if we cannot take care of her as well as of ourselves. We must give up this house, and make our arrangements to move immediately, so that we may not be obliged to pay another quarter's rent; but the question is, where had we better go? Even if we could find a smaller house here, we could probably live much more economically in a smaller town, or in the country."

" Mamma!" said Roderick suddenly, " did papa ever sell that little farm in Delaware which he bought to help Mr. Park, fifteen years ago? I came across the title-deeds last night."

" No, dear," replied his mother, "and for an excellent reason—nobody would buy it. It is twelve miles from the nearest railway station, and the house on it is not much better than a barn. I am afraid there is nothing to be hoped for in that quarter."

" I was not thinking of selling it," said Roderick. " I was thinking whether it would not be possible, at least for the present, to live on it."

Babel began again at this suggestion.

Elizabeth exclaimed: " But Rod, you'd have to give up the Polytechnic College, and you're all ready to enter!"

The twins remarked, in concert, " Why, it's a howling wilderness!"

Ernest and Arnold shouted, " What fun!" and " It would be too jolly for anything!"

May gave a little squeak of delight, and said, " Oh, mamma! we could keep chickens, and pigs, and all sorts of lovely things!"

Mrs. Stanley waited for the tumult to subside, and when the lull finally came she said, " I don't see, just now, how it would be possible, dear; there are so many things to be con-

sidered, but I will not condemn the plan without a hearing.
Tell me just how far your ideas had gone."

"I got to thinking of it after I went to bed last night,"
said Roderick. "You know papa took me there once—I
must have been about Arnold's age, I think—and I remember the place quite well. Do you recollect how I implored
you and papa to go and live there? I had never seen such
opportunities for fishing, and sailing, and shooting as that
place offered. Now, as I remember it, it stood on a high
bank, above a very pretty little river, and it was so near the
bay that the water was salt. I ought to know, for I fell in
head first, and drank more than I wished for. The house was
a forlorn affair, a great square building with four rooms on
each floor, but the third-floor rooms were not plastered—the
unlimited garret-accommodations had a great deal to do with
my wild desire to live there. There was not a shutter on any
of the windows, and the wide piazza in front and small
porch at the back were both in ruins, but the house itself
was sound, I think, and well built, and there was a great open
fire-place in every room. I remember that there was a well
of delicious water, near the back door, and there were some
very fine trees in front; there was a large barn, too, but it
was a good deal out of repair, I think. Papa said the land
was good, but when he bought it there was no railway-station within twenty miles, and no market in the neighborhood for anything."

"It would be complete exile," said Mrs. Stanley, thoughtfully; "but there are too many of us to dread being lonesome, and if it were not for upsetting all your plans, I almost
think it might be the best thing; but I know how your heart
is set on your chosen profession, dear, and it does not seem
to me to be right to sacrifice you, or any one member of the
family, to the rest. Has nobody anything else to suggest?"

"It occurred to me," said Elizabeth, "that we might keep

this house, and so avoid the expense of breaking up and moving, and then take boarders. If I were to share your room, mamma, and we were to put May's little bed either there or in Kitty and Pauline's room, and Ernest and Arnold in that third-story room that opens on the back stairs, that would leave us seven bedrooms to rent, and the dining-room is quite large enough."

"It is not to be thought of!" said Roderick, quickly; "you would be exposed to all sorts of annoyance and even insult, and if you were able to make the running expenses of the house, you would be doing very well indeed. It would be a pretty story, for me to walk calmly off to college, and leave mother, and you girls, and the children, to fight the world by yourselves."

"Don't get excited, dear," said Elizabeth, smiling; "we would not be the first women to do it, and though the many fail, a few succeed, and I should propose to be among the few. I am a first-rate cook, if I do say it as shouldn't, and I should keep such a delightful table, on such an astonishingly small outlay, that my boarding-house would always be crowded."

"It cannot be done!" said Roderick, even more decidedly than before. "You need not imagine I shall give up my profession, if we go to Delaware—I shall merely postpone matters a little. I can do a great deal of the requisite study at home, and after things are fairly running there, and Arnold is two or three years older, and able to step into my place, I can enter the Senior class, and graduate, in time, if I succeed as I mean to succeed, to give the boys a lift with whatever trade, calling or profession they may choose. We don't bind ourselves to stay there for the rest of our natural lives, by going to the farm—it only seems the best thing to do now; after we are once there, and managing to make a living, we can 'proceed as the way opens.'"

The conference was interrupted here by the postman's ring. There were five letters, three for Mrs. Stanley, one for Elizabeth, and one for Roderick, and the children waited impatiently for the exchanges of information which would probably follow the reading.

"Here are some offered solutions of our problem which had not occurred to any of us," said Mrs. Stanley, as she finished her third letter and returned it to the envelope. "Your uncle George writes that if I will give him Kitty and Polly for three years, they shall share Edith's schooling, and be " finished " when she is, and that Edith is wild with delight over the idea. He says that they shall be made thoroughly able to teach, if they desire it, so that, if our affairs have not improved by the time the three years are gone, they will be able to help, as they are not now."

"Oh, mamma!" exclaimed Kitty, with a piteous face, "do you wish us to go? Ought we to do it! Indeed, we will cost as little as possible, and I think we *could* help, in a great many ways."

"To be sure we could!" said Polly, indignantly. "Uncle George is very kind, but I don't see what he can think of us! Rod, *you* don't think we ought to go, do you? You're not afraid to undertake us all, if we all help?"

"Not a bit!" said Roderick, smiling. "It is very generous in Uncle George, but I shall want all the help I can get on my farm."

"I should not have hindered your going, if you had wished it, my darlings," said Mrs. Stanley, with a sigh of relief; "and perhaps I ought to urge it—I don't know, I hope I am not acting selfishly, but it seems to me that poverty will be an easy thing to bear, if we can only keep together!"

"And we will keep together!" came in chorus from the whole seven, as they all tried to hug their mother at once.

"Then there is no use in discussing my other two letters,"

said Mrs. Stanley, as she straightened her cap; "one is from your aunt Mary, begging me to send her May, at least for the winter, or until our plans are settled, and the other from my old friend Mrs. Webber, saying that she is to be quite alone for several months to come, and that if I can spare her Elizabeth, she shall have all a daughter's privileges, and a small salary beside."

"If she offers a salary, I am afraid I ought to go," said Elizabeth sadly, and the rest of the children looked apprehensive.

"What a goose!" said Roderick, drawing her close to his side; "I am relying upon you to manage my dairy, and governess the children, and be a sort of general forewoman, and do you suppose Mrs. Webber's small salary would make up for all that?"

"You'd need lots of good clothes, Betty," said Arnold, "and you know, when we once get on our farm, and take up the drawbridge, we can dress in coffee-bags and salt-sacks, with sheepskin cloaks for cold weather!"

"I *should* have to dress a great deal better, of course," said Elizabeth, brightening, "so perhaps it would not pay, after all; I will write and thank Mrs. Webber, and tell her we have other plans."

No one had given a second thought to the suggestion concerning May—it had struck each of them as too absurd for consideration, and the child herself had said, simply, "I wonder aunty thought you could spare me, mamma—but please thank her for wanting me."

"My letter is from Mrs. Maxwell," said Elizabeth, when her mother's three were considered settled; "I think it is beautiful of her to make me such an offer—she says that, if I will give the younger children French and German lessons twice a week, I can stay on for another year, as a sort of parlor-boarder, without paying anything at all, and go on with my music."

"Indeed, I am afraid you ought not to refuse so good an offer, dear," said Mrs. Stanley anxiously. "I can't bear the idea of your giving up your music, when you are succeeding so well with it."

"And who will be governess, if I desert my family in such a fashion as that?" asked the oldest daughter, defiantly. "No, dear, we have decided not to break ranks, and this offer, kind as it is, does not tempt me for a moment."

"Any more than this does me," said Roderick, holding up his letter. "You remember old Mr. Branson, mamma— that old friend of papa's? He writes to say that he can put me into a small bank-clerkship, if I can take the position at once; the salary is three hundred a year, and he admits that there is little hope of advancement, but says it will give me a chance to 'look round.' Now if I can't make as much as three hundred a year out of our farm, I'll own I was mistaken, and go and be a clerk, but I mean to try the farm first."

"But you will write and thank him?" said Mrs. Stanley. "It was kind to think of you at all."

"Indeed it was," replied Roderick heartily, "and I will not let him believe me ungrateful."

"If we decide to try the farm," said Mrs. Stanley, "you will be obliged to go first on an exploring expedition, Roderick—it would not be prudent for us all to go down there, with the risk of being obliged to come back; for the journey, taken by such a flock as ours, would be an expensive affair."

"Perhaps," suggested Elizabeth, "it would be as well to leave the decision open until Rod has been, and then we can judge whether or not we should be justified in spending the money which would no doubt be needed to make the place even habitable."

"There speaks the family balance-wheel," said Roderick, laughing; "right, as usual! Such being the case, it seems to me that the sooner the exploring expedition is made, the better it will be for all concerned."

"I don't wish to do anything rashly," said Mrs. Stanley, a little startled by the rapidity with which Roderick's idea had taken tangible form; "perhaps we had better consult your uncle George before deciding."

"But, mamma," said Elizabeth, "he is so warm-hearted and generous, that, even if he should approve the plan, he will be wanting to make the house over, and stock the farm, and furnish us all with outfits, and we shall be hurting his feelings at every turn with our refusals—you know how hard it was to convince him, when he first heard of Mr. Kemp's failure, that it would not be the best thing in the world for us all to go and live with him for the rest of our days! It will all be to do over again, if he should hear of this before it is irrevocably settled."

"Yes, I suppose it will," admitted Mrs. Stanley; "but we might ask your aunt Mary what she thinks of it."

"Dear little mother," said Roderick, kneeling before her, to bring his eyes to the level of her own, "I hate to oppose you in anything, but surely we can best decide upon the right course, without bewildering our judgment with advice from people who, no matter how kind their intentions may be, cannot know all the facts of the case as we ourselves know them. Let me go down there, before we speak to any one. I promise to try to look at everything without prejudice, and if the scheme should seem crazy, after I have seen the premises and neighborhood, we must try to devise something else. But if I think the place will yield us a living for the present, and something more in the future, then let us quietly make our arrangements, and announce our intentions. Anything will be better than to let an impression get abroad in the family that we need help and looking after."

"Had ever anybody such wise children!" said Mrs. Stanley, kissing her tall son as he knelt before her. "Well, my own heart pleads for your wisdom, so I will at least not oppose the journey of discovery—that can do no harm, even if it does no good, and I will not mention the matter before your return. Will that satisfy you, Mr. President?"

"Quite!" said Roderick, springing lightly up; "I will start to-morrow; then I can be back by Saturday night. I want to have at least two whole days there."

"It's a singular thing," said Arnold gravely, "but among all the offers to lease the family in sections, not a single person has spoken for Ernest or me!"

"The only person who would be at all likely to do it would be the proprietor of a wholesale clothing and shoe store," said Kitty with equal gravity, "and unfortunately such a person is not in the family."

"I suppose we can wear leather trowsers and wooden shoes on the farm," said Ernest; "oh! just think of it, Arnold, there will not be a school within reach! Life will be a perpetual holiday!"

"You are very much out of your reckoning there, young man," said Roderick; "there is, or was, a school-house not quite a mile from the farm, and if it has perished, I, myself, will conduct your education, and a terribly strict master you will find me, I can tell you!"

The conference was broken up by an adjournment to the tea-table, but the subject was much too absorbing to be immediately dropped, and bed-time found them occupying an imaginary mansion, luxuriously furnished, and surrounded with smiling fields and fruit-orchards, which, under their skilful management, yielded fabulous revenues. Their "gilt-edged butter," in demand in all the principal cities, commanded whatever price they chose to set upon it; their famous cheeses, too precious for home consumption, were exported to England, for the benefit of the nobility and gentry. Each of them owned a special riding-horse, and a pair of high-stepping bays drew the family barouche. Mrs. Stanley laughed quietly as one improbability after another was added to the wondrous tale, but they did not notice that her fingers were busy with a pencil, until, as they rose to say good-night, she placed her sketch before them—a barn-like building, with tumble-down piazzas and broken windows; on the step, a clever caricature of herself, her face hidden by a cavernous sun-bonnet, and her work—an enormous pair of trowsers—on her knee. Equally flattering likenesses of her children were scattered about the grounds, chopping wood, drawing water, hoeing corn, and feeding alarmingly-thin pigs and chickens."

"There!" she said; "while you have been constructing your romance, I have been busy with the reality!"

She was assailed by all her children, large and small, at once, with laughing reproaches, and the obnoxious sketch was indignantly voted to the fire, but Elizabeth rescued it, saying: "No—don't let us burn it. We will keep it to pin on the drawing-room wall, and then, no matter how dreadful things may be, we can console ourselves by contrasting them with this!"

2

CHAPTER II.

"'But wait a bit,' the Oysters said, 'before we have our chat,
For some of us are out of breath, and all of us are fat!'
'No hurry,' said the Carpenter. They thanked him much for that."

LEWIS CARROLL.

ELIZABETH and Roderick lingered with their mother, after the younger ones were gone, to consult the newspaper about the journey, about half of which was by rail, and half by boat. They found that, in order to make the connection, a distressingly early breakfast would be necessary; the servants were gone to bed, and past receiving any more orders by this time, but Elizabeth cheerfully undertook to call Roderick in time, and supply the cook's place. He demurred, saying that, if she would put him up a sandwich before she went to bed, he could easily get a cup of coffee at the railway station.

"Don't be foolish, dear!" she said, patting him on the head with a motherly air. "We wish you to see the farm with unprejudiced eyes, and you shall not start on a cup of railway-station coffee! Lend me the alarm-clock, and go to bed—that is the whole of your present duty—the kerosene-stove and I will attend to the rest."

It was not quite light, and Roderick was under the impression that he had been asleep about five minutes, when a tap on his door, and a softly spoken "Are you awake, dear?" made him aware that his five minutes had been six hours. He found the table cosily spread for two, the glass and silver shining in fire and lamp light, and Elizabeth, neat and fresh as if it were 6.30 P.M. instead of A.M., seated behind the coffee-pot. There was no hurry, for she had called him in plenty of time, and they chatted merrily over their breakfast.

"I don't know how it is, Rod," said Elizabeth, as she held her plate for another piece of steak, "but in books, when people lose their money, and are obliged to move out of their houses, they are always overwhelmed with despair, and if they manage to smile at each other, it is in a sort of concealed-chasm fashion, to hide their wounded hearts. Now I don't feel that way in the least! I feel just as Dolly does when I am driving her, and give her the least touch of the whip, and then have all I can do to hold her in!"

"Very much the way I feel myself," replied Roderick; "I suppose I ought to be despairing over my blighted prospects, but it is such a magnificent chance to exemplify a theory, that I really can't, you know."

"And the theory?"

"Is founded upon the extensive observation of a man of my age! I have seen so many people step into easy, ready-made places and opportunities, only to slide and shamble out of them, and so many more reaching the places they meant to reach, through all sorts of difficulty and discouragement, that I began to be afraid I should follow the fashion, and was thinking of asking the mother to stop off my allowance, until I should write her that I was on the brink of starvation!"

"I'm *very* glad you feel that way," said Elizabeth, contentedly; "I hope the rest do—or will. I had a sort of guilty, selfish feeling, when I realized that I was actually enjoying the situation instead of mourning over it. You see, it saves me a good deal of trouble—I never meant to sit down with my hands in my lap, when my school-days were over, and I dreaded looking for something to do—I was so afraid people would think I was in search of a 'Career'!"

"And there's something more than that, Betty," said Roderick, as he rose and buttoned on the coat which had hung near the fire; "I can't talk much about such things, but I have a very firm belief that whatever happens to us is the best thing, in the long run, that could happen—if we use it as we should. I can understand people's praying unconditionally for whatever their shortsightedness makes them think best—I think, I hope I only want what will best help me on my journey home, and make me able to help other people."

Elizabeth's eyes filled with tears. "I am trying very hard to look at things in that way," she said; "but I have not gone as far as you have, Rod—you must help *me* on!"

A very earnest hug and kiss seemed a satisfactory answer, and he took up his valise to go, but was stopped in the entry by four flannel-wrappered forms with sleepy eyes, and a chorus of: "We couldn't let you go without saying good-by!" and as he left the gate, two old shoes sailed by him, narrowly missing his head, and a sound between a chuckle and a crow from the window of the boys' room made him look up to see two tumbled heads stretched out. The shoes sailed promptly back, with such an unerring aim that nothing but dodging saved the conspirators, and they shouted after him, "Rash youth! He has cast away his luck!"

"I'll stand in my own shoes, thank you!" he called gayly back, "and you needn't talk to me of luck—'there ain't no sich a person!'"

That day was a busy one in the Stanley family. A house-agent called, soon after breakfast, to say that he was empowered, by the "party" about to rent the house, to buy all the furniture which Mrs. Stanley desired to sell, at a fair valuation. This was good news indeed, and saved so much trouble and confusion, that mother and daughters went cheerfully to work, deciding upon what had better be kept, and marking the rest with the price they considered just; a furniture-dealer, chosen by Mrs. Stanley, was to be the final authority, but they were requested first to name a price themselves. Somehow, every one seemed to be taking it for granted that the Delaware project was a foregone conclusion, and to be choosing and arranging accordingly. It was Elizabeth's suggestion that they would save, or rather make, no inconsiderable sum, by selling the heavy and costly furniture which filled most of the rooms, and buying light and inexpensive articles, which could be more readily and cheaply moved.

Mrs. Stanley hesitated. Nearly everything about the house had some special association of its own, but her judgment told her that Elizabeth was right. Even should their present plan fall through, they would be obliged to move either into lodgings or the smallest house which would hold them with anything like comfort, and in either case the furniture would be quite unsuitable. There would be no present necessity for parting with glass, china or silver; these things, as Roderick had argued, "represented capital," and could be made available at any time. It was just as well to have something in a form which could not be so readily spent as money. Of course this day was only a beginning. They had agreed not to dismantle the house until as near the time of leaving it as possible; there was no need for haste; a month still remained of the quarter which had, as usual, been paid for in advance; they had a good supply of groceries on hand, and nothing would be gained by leaving the house at present. Their mother carefully explained this to the children, and whatever feeling of fluster and hurry they may have had was dispelled by the explanation. They went to work calmly, and with their wits about them, settling upon an orderly course of proceeding beforehand.

"Mamma!" cried May, bounding into the library, where her mother and the three older girls were sorting the books, "We have an idea, Arnold, Ernest and I, but it takes rags—a great many rags! May we have the rag-bag, and all the things in the piece-box that belong to done-with clothes?"

"Certainly," replied her mother, laughing; "an idea which needs nothing but rags for its carrying out, is too valuable to be lost. You can go on awhile without me, dears," she added, turning to the older girls, "while I start this new firm in business."

Arnold and Ernest were at school, and were to continue to go at least until the decision concerning the future should be made; but they were free before nine o'clock, and after two, and Mrs. Stanley was very glad that their wild excitement over the coming change had found so safe an outlet as the rag business promised, so she rummaged closets, drawers and boxes with a success which quite surprised her; gave the new company undisputed possession of a large third-story room with sunny windows, and left May as happy as a queen, in the midst of her rag-fair. She did not inquire concerning the mystery, for she saw that some grand surprise was being planned, so she was discreetly oblivious of the whispered consultations, which, before long, included Kitty and Polly. Scissors were greatly in demand, and every stray piece of twine or stout string was eagerly pounced upon by the committee of five, which invariably sat with closed doors. This state of affairs went on for two weeks; then Arnold and Ernest borrowed the two largest market baskets, and, after a session in the council chamber, walked off with the baskets, carefully covered and evidently full, on their arms. May followed them to the door, with many whispered charges, and waited impatiently at the parlor window for their return, pouncing on them the moment they entered the hall.

" He says it will make at least forty—— Oh mamma! did you hear?" said Arnold, interrupting himself as his mother passed on her way upstairs.

" I heard that it would make at least forty," she answered, smiling, " but I do not know the nature of the forty, nor what ' it' is."

" You should be more careful, Arnold," said May gravely; " it will be no fun at all, if mamma hears it in that way."

To go back a little—a note had come from Roderick, on the Saturday morning following his departure, to say that he would not be at home until Tuesday evening, but that he was quite well, and having a very pleasant time, adding, " I'm looked upon as the guest of the State, and know exactly how royalty feels when it takes a little pleasure-trip through its kingdom. I will not give my impressions in writing, but will save the wondrous tale until I see you."

This put the family on tiptoe with curiosity and expectation, and Roderick's welcome, on Tuesday evening, was calculated to foster, rather than dispel, his Presidential illusion.

He declined to begin his story until after tea, because, he said, he was nearly famished, in the first place, and in the second, the supper-bell would be sure to ring at the most interesting point.

So the family was obliged to curb its impatience until, his hunger fully satisfied, Roderick stretched himself on the hearth-rug, with his head in his mother's lap, and began at the beginning.

" The railway part of my journey was totally uninteresting," he said; " so I will not describe it, farther than by saying that the cars were comfortable, or rather that I was in them, and that we made very good time. I had half an hour to spare in B——, which I employed in eating a very good dinner ; the boat left at four, and as we went down the bay,

I wished you were all with me. I stayed on deck, after supper, as long as I could keep my eyes open, and then went to bed, and slept like a rock. In the morning—this anecdote has been especially treasured for your benefit, Kit—a small girl, one of a group of six shock-headed children, stationed herself in front of me, and took a good look at my head; she then joined her family, and I heard her remark, ' Yes, he must have one, mam, his head's as slick as grease.'

" ' Well, go along and ask him then,' said ' mam,' ' and be quick about it, for the boat's most in.'

"The engaging child came back, and asked, with the sweet confidence of childhood, ' Say, could you please lend us a comb to comb our heads with?'

"Started out of my politeness, I replied, with some abruptness, I fear, ' No, I could not,' but her grieved and disappointed expression touched my heart, and I added, ' But I could give you one,' and I went to my stateroom for my only comb, purposing to buy one at the country store which I well remembered. Alas, my generosity had been anticipated —my comb had vanished, likewise my brush, and likewise, positively, Kitty! my toothbrush. I apologized to my waiting petitioner, but I saw that my word was doubted. We touched at *our* landing at about seven o'clock, and after an hour or so spent in investigation and argument, I prevailed upon the fortunate owner of a mule to ' tote ' me and my valise to Green Point, which, as I fortunately remembered, is the name of our estate. It is ten miles from the landing, and twelve from the nearest railway-station, but the roads are good, and the country through which they pass is charming. My design was to sort of camp out, as it were, in the family mansion; I knew I could find some clean straw to spread on the floor, and did not doubt that some of the natives would be glad to give me food in exchange for legal tender, but I reckoned without my host, literally. I

THE OLD HOUSE AT GREEN POINT.

beguiled the long two hours which the mule considered necessary for the ten mile journey, by asking my driver how near Green Point I could find supplies? and he answered me with gravity, giving me several names and residences. As he did not mention his own, I asked him where he lived, and he said on Colonel Peyton's farm, about two miles beyond our place. He said he belonged to the Colonel 'befaw de wah,' and had been glad to go back and work for him after trying one Northern winter. I found it was so with all the negroes ; the white people there tell me that no negro who leaves the neighborhood ever stays away more than a year, if they have to beg their way back. Yes, I am coming to the house, ladies and gentlemen, but do let me make a good story of my travels and adventures ! I found only the organic remains of a fence surrounding our estate, and the most magnificent crop of weeds I ever saw anywhere grow- ing on the land, but there are fine orchards, apple, peach and pear, which papa's friend must have set out, for they were not there when I was, eight or nine years ago. There is a tolerably good barn and stable, but oh, the house ! The roof and walls are good enough, but there was literally not a whole pane of glass in any window, two or three of the doors had been wrenched from their hinges, and carried off bodily; one of the chimneys had fallen, but not a single brick was to be seen on the ground, and an old darky who pottered up from one of the cabins in the brush assured me solemnly that they 'blowed away,' adding, 'Mighty high winds we has here by de ribber, in de spring ob de year, sah !' He looked so utterly candid that I almost believed him. Not a vestige of either front or back porch remained on the ground, and I have no doubt that only laziness, and the fact that the house was strongly built, had prevented the negroes from carrying it off piecemeal, for firewood. They had not chopped down the two glorious old elms which shaded the front door, but the pump was gone, and the well uncovered, and half full of rubbish. I had a very faint recollection of the inside of the house—I spent so little time in it—but it is larger than I thought it was, and could be made delightful, in time. A wide hall, with the staircase going up from it, runs through the middle, with two large rooms on each side, the same size all the way up, except that the third story ones have a sloping roof. There is a large, light closet in each room, taken off at one side of the great open fireplace. The people there tell me that stoves are unnecessary, even in the coldest weather they have, if one has plenty of wood; and I was glad to find that our farm contained three or four acres of first-rate oak and pine-woods, some of the trees quite old and large. There is no cellar, but the house is raised on brick piles, six or eight feet above the level of the ground. The kitchen is a separate building about half a block from the house——"

"That would never do!" interpolated Mrs. Stanley; "it would be too inconvenient for anything!"

"I think it would be great fun," said Ernest; "we would carry in dinner on our heads, as the strawberry and fish women do with their trays, every day."

There was a general laugh at this liberal offer, but Roderick continued: "I knew you wouldn't like that, dear, but I reasoned that we could perhaps crowd the furniture into three of the downstairs rooms, and the eight upstairs, and use the fourth room for a kitchen—it would be easy enough to partition off a little vestibule between that and the dining-room."

"Oh, never mind that now!" said Polly, impatiently; "go on with your adventures—we can settle about the kitchen afterward."

"Very well," replied Roderick, good-naturedly. "Where was I? oh yes, I had just gone over the house, and decided that, with a little help from a mason, I could make it habitable for less than fifty dollars, when I saw an old chivalry coming up the lane on horseback. He flourished up to the front door, just as I came out, and pulled off his hat, remarking, 'I believe I have the honor of addressing Mr. Stanley?' I told him, modestly, that he had, and therewith ended my scheme for amateur housekeeping. He was so deeply shocked at the bare idea, that I feared our lineage would be forever disgraced if I stuck to it, so I gracefully yielded, and allowed him to send the family coach of the Peytons for me at five o'clock—for it was Colonel Peyton, as you may perhaps have imagined. It seems that my arrival in the neighborhood was regarded as a piece of startling intelligence, and the darky had faithfully reported all he knew concerning me. I soon found that the shock to the Colonel's feelings was caused by the imputation on Southern hospitality which my staying in the empty house would have been. 'Great heavens, sir!' said the old gentleman, as we drove to his house that evening in a coach which must have been made in Washington's time, 'did you think so meanly of the people of Delaware that you believed you would be allowed to carry out your preposterous intention—if I may be allowed the liberty of calling it so?' I told him I knew no one in the neighborhood, and should not have dreamed of any other plan, but for his generous hospitality to a stranger. Then he told me that I was not a stranger at all; that he had known my father very well 'before the wah,' and that if I at all resembled him, the neighborhood might well rejoice at my coming. I was all the more touched and pleased with this, because I had an idea that we should be unpopular, as Northerners; but if the whole South is like that corner of Delaware, all the newspaper talk about ill feeling and suppressed bitterness, is bosh. He is as philosophical as possible about the result of the late unpleasantness;

he said he firmly believed the South was right in opposing tyranny, but that, when a gentleman got the worst of it in a fair fight, he never refused to shake hands. He lives in a beautiful old place, and his wife is charming. The daughters—there are three—were away on a visit; but the son, a fellow about my age, I should think, was at home, and I liked him immensely. They were so cordial, and remonstrated so warmly when I said I was coming home, or rather going to start, on Friday, that I concluded to stay a day or two longer, and pick up all the information I could, while I was about it. And now comes the practical part. I find that labor is very cheap, especially house-service. Mrs. Peyton, who was as kind as possible, and told me all she could think of, that you would wish to know, mamma, said that they had several hangers-on, who were glad to work in the kitchen or laundry for their board, and an occasional gift of food or old clothes. She said she sometimes had rather more help of this sort than she wanted; so the wail about servant-girls is not yet heard in that happy land. I asked Colonel Peyton to tell me candidly whether we could make a living off the farm, in its present demoralized condition, and he said that, after vegetables and fruit began to ripen next summer, he thought we could. The condition of the orchards is the most favorable thing in the whole plan—there will be profit from them almost immediately, and the farmers in the neighborhood have almost succeeded in inducing one of the steamboat companies to run a 'truck-boat' up the river three times a week, during the summer and autumn, so that their crops may reach the markets in better condition than is possible now. Of course I heard a great deal more about soil and fertilizers, and pigs and poultry and cows and horses,—by the way, both the latter are cheap there, but there is no use in boring you all with it. The question is now, whether we are all willing to be more or less buried alive for a few years, for the sake of keeping together and helping each other, or whether we shall scatter on the every-man-for-himself-etc. principle. The decision rests with you, Mrs. Mother, and we all await your fiat."

Nothing that Roderick could have said would have so inclined his mother to this somewhat rash enterprise, as the vision called up of the every-man-for-himself-etc. principle. She saw her girls deprived of their home just when they should be learning how a woman may make home beautiful and gracious; her boys drifting about the world just at the age when a strong anchor and stout cable are most needed to save from shoals and quicksands; herself lonely and sad for want of the bright young faces and voices which made the sunshine of her life.

"It may be foolish," she said; "I don't know, but if you all agree in wishing it, and feel brave enough to face the hardships which it must involve, we will at least try it. I will put it to the vote—all in favor of this crazy project will say 'aye'!"

A perfectly unanimous shout of "aye!" rang through the room.

"'There is no use in calling for the 'contrary,'" said Mrs. Stanley, "the meeting is singularly harmonious in its views. I hope it may be equally so a year from to-night, when it will be held, so far as we can now see, in an old Delaware farm-house."

So it was settled. Whether or not that settlement caused regret; whether it was for good or for ill, is what this story is going to tell. But this much of prophecy may be allowed —the foundations of the new home were unselfishness and love.

CHAPTER III.

" She doeth little kindnesses
Which most leave undone, or despise :
For nought that sets one heart at ease,
And giveth happiness or peace,
Is low esteemed in her eyes."—LOWELL.

AFTER Roderick's return, and the definite settlement of
their plans just recorded, preparations for the exodus
went cheerfully and rapidly on. Arnold and Ernest were
taken from school, partly because they could be useful as
errand goers and general assistants, and partly because they
were too much excited to study with either profit or pleasure.
This excitement culminated, and was fully shared by May, on
the afternoon when, taking turns at the wheel-barrow, they
wheeled home the forty yards of well-woven rag carpet which
was one result of the secret conclaves. Two or three pretty
rugs of tufted silk were proudly displayed by the twins and
May as a farther result of the rag society's labors, and Mrs.
Stanley declared that the most magnificent Turkey carpet
could not have afforded her the pleasure she would always
feel in looking at this evidence of zealous love. It answered
the question which had arisen, as to whether the nearly new
and very pretty dining-room carpet should be kept or sold—
the rag-carpet would be quite in keeping, they agreed, with
the new dining-room, and the sale of the costly one would
add materially to their revenues. The money for weaving
the rag-carpet had been contributed by the five conspirators,
who had all been saving for Christmas, and decided that
opportunities for shopping, in their new home, would be

fully met with the remainder of their funds. The hardest trial was parting with the greater part of a large and well-chosen library. Its transportation would have added too much to the expense of moving, which expense its sale would fully cover. Enough books to fill one good-sized book-case were reserved, and the choice was the most difficult of all their decisions.

To the intense delight of Arnold and Ernest, Roderick took them with him, for several successive days, first to a carpenter's and then to a painter and glazier's, and they learned to handle the commoner tools with enough skill to make them resolve upon stopping nowhere short of perfection. Roderick, who had always been dexterous, drew forth enthusiastic praise from his instructors, and a solemn assurance from the carpenter that he was "a born cabinet-maker, and would be fairly throwing himself away if he didn't learn the trade, and stick to it." He had resolved to mend the broken windows himself, a very slight calculation sufficing to show that the cost of the necessary tools would be much less than that of the work, and the tools would be useful in future emergencies. He had discovered that the general "store" five or six miles from Green Point, contained a poor and high-priced assortment of the small wares which would be needed for their various employments, so work-baskets were well stocked, a supply of stationery was laid in, and the strictly-needful implements for farm and garden bought. It was a venture, when the supply of ready money was so small ; but any business which they could undertake would involve some outlay at the beginning, and they felt the courage which comes with a steady purpose. They had agreed to take for their watch-word the motto of a favorite book—

> " Look up, not down,
> Look out, not in,
> Look forward, not back,
> And lend a helping hand."

When Mrs. Stanley's sister and brother-in-law heard of the contemplated move, they remonstrated with her long and earnestly. Mr. Stanley especially almost shook her resolution by imploring her not to bury her children alive, if she were determined on burying herself. He assured her that his home was open to her whole family, for as long a time as she would honor him by occupying it; that her boys were fine fellows, who would be sure to make their way, and her girls too attractive to remain long unmarried. If she objected to the obligation, she might consider it a debt, to be cancelled when the boys were able to cancel it. When he found that, although she was deeply grateful for his offered kindness, she remained firm to her purpose, he next assailed her on the subject of stocking the farm, and giving the boys "a start"; but she made him understand, at last, that the truest kindness would be to let them learn the lesson of courage and independence which their supposed misfortune could teach them, if it were rightly taken, and he tried to content himself with her assurance that if the experiment failed, and they desired to leave the farm, she would let him know immediately, and accept his help in anything they decided to undertake. She found it even harder to convince her sister that their scheme was anything but the wildest and most unreasonable nonsense. Miss Mackenzie lamented, and even wept over it, as if the place of their exile were to be Siberia instead of Delaware, and then, with startling suddenness, when she found she could not shake Mrs. Stanley's resolution, declared that, from what they said, the climate, she knew, would exactly suit her; she was tired of her lonely boarding-house life, and if they had any charity, they would let her board with them—she could only pay ten dollars a week, the sum she was paying in her present boarding-house, but perhaps that would cover what she would cost them. Mrs. Stanley laughed at the transparency of this device for adding to their income, but she was deeply touched by her sister's eagerness to give up comfort and society for the sake of making their lot a little more easy. She persuaded Miss Mackenzie, however, to wait until the following summer—they would know, by that time, whether or not they should be able to remain on the farm; and so much was needed to make the house comfortable, that Mrs. Stanley felt unwilling to expose her sister to the first and hardest part of the experiment.

The original plan had been that the whole family should start together for the new home, but the longer Roderick thought the matter over, the more averse he felt to letting his mother and the younger girls see the place in its present comfortless condition. So he persuaded Mrs. Stanley to accept her brother-in-law's urgent invitation for "at least a little visit from them all before they consigned themselves to oblivion," arranging that Elizabeth and he should pilot the furniture to the new home, and write for the rest of the family as soon as things were in tolerable order.

Arnold and Ernest begged so frantically to join the advance-guard, promising such unquestioning obedience and vast usefulness, that Roderick pleaded their cause with the mother, and, to their unutterable delight, she gave her consent. The twins were quite willing to wait, as they said, for civilization.

"It's all very well," said Kitty confidentially to her double, "to talk about Robinson Crusoe and the Swiss family Robinson—but its one thing to read in a story about living up a tree, and another to do it! We shall find things quite heathenish enough after Rod and Betty have done all they can to make the place habitable."

Kitty and Polly had undergone a slight reaction, after the plan was fully decided upon. They had just begun to appreciate the value of their various lessons, and were almost

3

tempted to wish that their uncle's invitation had been accepted.

"To be sure," said Polly, "it wouldn't have been pleasant to feel that uncle was paying for everything, but then we would have learned enough to begin teaching, in another year or two, and paid him back all he spent on us; and now, I don't see what we can do to help."

"I must confess that I do," said Kitty, smiling; "I am afraid that my longing after the flesh-pots is partly caused by the knowledge that two strong and healthy young women can do as much general housework as three or four incompetent servants could. But after all, as Rod says, we're not binding ourselves to stay there forever, and you know perfectly well, Polly, that if we were to go to uncle's, and let the rest of the family farm without us, we should be repenting in dust and ashes before a week was over, and feeling too mean to live."

"Yes, I dare say we should," assented Polly; "and perhaps we shall like it, after we get there. At any rate, Rod and Betty are giving up much more than we are, and they don't seem to be a bit sorry for themselves. I do wonder, Kit, if we shall ever be as good and solid as Betty is!"

Arnold was passing the open door as she spoke, and put in his head long enough to quote from his favorite ballad:

> "'I doubt it,' said the Carpenter,
> And shed a bitter tear."

When the last box lid was screwed down and the last 'trunk locked, the oldest brother and sister, with the two boys, started for the new home, in charge of all the furniture, and whatever the rest of the family would not need during the two weeks' visit at Mr. Stanley's. It was early in March, the weather was sparklingly clear, and the two boys were in such overflowing good humor and good spirits that anything like sadness or sentiment was simply impossible. Every one came down to the early breakfast this time, for a long day would be needed by those who remained behind; they were to go to Mr. Stanley's late in the afternoon, and although everything was supposed to be done, Mrs. Stanley knew that more last things would keep starting up so long as they remained in the house. They all felt thankful that no peculiar associations attached them to the home they were leaving. At the time of Mr. Stanley's death, they had been living in a smaller house, which he had owned, and shortly afterward a very good offer had been made for this house and the few acres of land surrounding it, for it was in that part of the town which was rapidly being given over to business. He had the plan ready drawn for a new and larger house, which was to have been begun in a month or two, when he died, but his widow had felt unequal to the undertaking of superintending the building, and, as a large and pleasant house had been offered for renting, soon after the sale of the old house had been effected, she had taken it, and found it so convenient that there had been no talk of changing until the catastrophe took place which obliged them to find a less expensive house.

This journey to Delaware was the boys' first traveling-experience, and their eager delight in everything kept Elizabeth and Roderick amused from the time of their early start until, weary with the long drive, they arrived, on the second day, at their future home. Elizabeth, who was delighted with the green and fertile looking country through which they passed, was surprised by the tone of all Roderick's remarks, as they drove along. He began by saying: "Don't be looking out for a house, Betty—look for a good large barn, with the allowance of windows usually made for a house. Our mansion is utterly guiltless of either paint or white-wash, so far as the outside is concerned, you know, and would pass for a barn very well!"

"We'll fresco it," said Arnold; "outside frescoes will be something new and pleasing. We'll mix a large tank of whitewash, Rod, and then dip out bucketfuls, and color them with indigo, and copperas, and—what is there that would make scarlet? We must have some of that, whatever it is!"

"You know the front and back piazzas fell off some time ago, Betty," said Roderick, returning to the charge, "and there isn't a single whole window-pane in any of the windows, and the plaster is stained on the walls where the rain has beaten in, and the floors are discolored, from the same cause, and in some places great chunks of plaster have fallen off, leaving a ghastly skeleton of laths exposed to view."

"Perhaps we had better turn back!" said Elizabeth, laughing; and Ernest added, reproachfully, "What in the world has come over you, Rod, to make you tell Betty all the disagreeable things you can think of, just as we are almost there?"

"I don't wish to be accused of beguiling her there upon false pretenses," said Roderick, gravely.

They had driven from the wharf in a large wagon, engaged beforehand by Roderick, in order that they might have with them the furniture and bedding, and numerous small house-keeping articles, which would be needful for their comfort on the first night, and it was well that they took this precaution, for the rest of the luggage—fortunately not in an easily portable form—they were obliged to leave upon the wharf, to the more-or-less care of the ticket-agent, until the wagon could make the two or three trips which would be necessary for its transportation. Roderick had calculated upon finding other wagons and horses at or near the wharf, as he had done at his first or rather his second visit to the place, but the oyster season was nearly over; vegetables and fruit were not yet carted to meet the boats, and, had he not taken the precaution of engaging a wagon, they would have been left to choose between spending the night on the wharf and walking the ten miles of sandy road which lay between the wharf and the Green Point mansion. But apart from the anxiety which they would naturally have felt concerning the miscellaneous load which the wagon held, they would not have suffered. Before they had accomplished half the journey, they were met by Colonel Peyton, on horseback, and he insisted that, until they could make their new home habitable, they must "certainly" eat and sleep at his house.

"Don't object, my dear Miss Stanley, don't object, I implore you!" he said, bowing gallantly to Elizabeth; "I will facilitate your arrangements in every way. Our place is only two miles from yours; you shall be driven over every morning, immediately after breakfast, and only sent for in time for our six o'clock dinner; Mrs. Peyton will send you your luncheon, so that you really will lose less time than if you undertake to cater for yourselves. And you will be giving us the utmost pleasure—my girls have come home, and are all impatience to make your acquaintance. You'll not deprive an old man of one of his few remaining pleasures, I am sure."

He was so evidently and thoroughly in earnest, that, although Elizabeth shrank from what seemed to her such a remarkably cool proceeding, she was wise enough to see that she could not refuse this more than neighborly kindness without hurting the warm-hearted old gentleman's feelings; so, with grateful thanks, she accepted the invitation, and the Colonel galloped home, to inform his wife of his conquest, and send the coach to Green Point to collect his guests. The warm feeling which this reception gave Elizabeth's heart disposed her to see everything in its best light; and it was a very lovely light, as any one must have admitted, which shone on the old house as they alighted from the wagon. The sun was near setting; rose-colored clouds filled the sky; the grand old elms in front of the house were beautiful in spite of bare branches, and the grass, already turning green, grew up to the improvised doorsteps of slabs brought from the nearest sawmill, which Roderick had constructed during his previous visit.

"Why Rod!" said Elizabeth, indignantly; "you've been trying to make me believe it was horrible, and it's perfectly and entirely lovely! Just look at those waving boughs and the light on the river, and the green grass—and what a beautiful soft shade of gray the old house is, and what great high ceilings, and big windows, and not a trace of the ruins of the piazza—oh, when we've been here a year, it will be our own fault if it isn't the most charming house in America!"

Roderick laughed, a low laugh full of satisfaction. "My experiment has succeeded beyond my fondest hopes," he said, as he turned the key, and opened the wide front door, just as Ernest and Arnold came racing back from a circuit of the house.

"Oh, behold him!" shouted Ernest, gleefully; "the back door of the hall is gone—has died and made no sign," and he unlocks the representative front door with the air of a proud and happy householder.

"The back door gone!" exclaimed Roderick, looking very much provoked, "now that is really too bad! It was gone when I came here, and the side door too, and I unhung two of the inner doors, and put them in the places of the lost ones, just for the present, and I suppose those rascally darkies have crawled in through one of the broken windows and wrenched them off for kindlings. Boys, you and I must stay here to-night, or there will not be a stick of our furniture left in the morning—Betty can represent us at the Colonel's. Are you willing?"

Were they willing! Such a shout of delight echoed

through the old house, that Roderick could feel no possible doubt on that head. They had brought plenty of canned provisions and crackers, knowing that it would be a day or two before they could obtain supplies from the neighborhood, and the wagon was rapidly unpacked under Elizabeth's supervision. A second story room, the only one with sound window frames and a lock that would work on its · door, was chosen for the temporary store-room, and here the miscellaneous cargo was deposited, with the help of the negro-driver. It was through him that Colonel Peyton had been apprized of the day of their expected arrival; for Roderick had not been certain, when he left Delaware, of the exact time when they could be ready, and had written to the freight-agent at the wharf to engage the wagon.

The carriage had not yet come, and Elizabeth hurried on the preparations for the comfort of the campers, spreading the two beds, as soon as the boys had put up the bedsteads, and unpacking provisions and cooking utensils. They had chosen the room next the temporary store-room for their bed-room, and as soon as the bedsteads were up, Arnold and Ernest scampered off to the wood-lot, returning with two great bundles of dead wood, and hatfuls of dried leaves, and presently a roaring fire on the hearth sent its dancing light over the dreary looking room, changing its dreariness to cheeriness. Comfortables and rugs were hung over the windows, for, as soon as the sun went down, the air would be too chill for such an excess of ventilation, and Elizabeth had just made a neat looking tea-table out of a large packing-box, and set it for three, when the carriage drove to the door, and Roderick insisted on her leaving them to their own devices, rather than delay the Peyton dinner.

"Which, by the way," he said, "has been turned suddenly from supper into dinner since I was here, evidently for our sole benefit."

"I hate to leave you," she said, as Roderick, ceremoniously offering his arm, escorted her down the wide staircase; "it seems very mean for me to go and sit in the lap of luxury while you are roughing it so, but I suppose it can't be helped, and I'll come as soon as they'll send me in the morning. Good-night, dear; I'll forgive you for deceiving me about the house."

"Madame, you deceived yourself," he answered, as he put her in the carriage; "what I said was strictly true—I only omitted the other half, and the moral is a very fine and instructive one—good-night."

The carriage went swiftly along a smooth road for about two miles, and then turned in at a gate, and up a wide avenue bordered by fine old oak-trees. It was too dark for Elizabeth to see the house distinctly, but it loomed large in the dim light, and she went up at least a dozen steps before she reached the hospitably-open door.

The Colonel and his wife met her on the threshold, with a welcome so warm and cordial that she felt as if she must have visited them many times before. Mrs. Peyton led her to a large, comfortably furnished bedroom, where a bright wood-fire blazed upon the wide hearth, and it was not until she had refreshed herself with a good wash, and changed her traveling-dress for her black silk, that she was presented to the younger members of the family. They were standing by the hearth, when Mrs. Peyton, having left her to make her toilet, came back and conducted her to the large parlor. The lamps had not yet been lighted, but the fire was piled with light-wood, and she could see all the faces quite distinctly.

"My oldest daughter, Susan," said Mrs. Peyton; and a sweet-faced woman who looked quite forty years old took Elizabeth's hand and held it for a moment with a kindly pressure, while she spoke of her pleasure at meeting one of their new neighbors.

"And this is Louise, and this is Isabel," continued Mrs. Peyton; concluding with, "and this is our only boy among all these girls, Randolph."

Louise and Isabel were bright looking girls about seventeen and nineteen years old, and Randolph, who was only twenty-two, looked several years older; his face was bright and pleasant, and Elizabeth congratulated herself and her absent family upon these most desirable and neighborly neighbors. She had heard her father speak with sincere admiration and liking of Colonel Peyton and his family, and she was quite prepared to be pleased, both from this fact and from Roderick's account of them, and this favorable prepossession influenced her more than she knew. But she had no reason to change her views, when better acquaintance gave her a chance to compare them with the facts of the case—just as they were that evening, when she came among them a perfect stranger in everything but name, they remained always; frank and friendly, warm-hearted and generous. She found herself, before the cheerful dinner was over, talking with them as if she had known them for years, but she was especially attracted to the oldest daughter, whose gentle and unobtrusive ministry to the comfort of all about her seemed to fill the house with sunshine. She noticed that the rest of the family seemed to turn instinctively to Susan for information upon any doubtful point, for any small help that was needed, and for sympathy when anything went wrong. She had thought it a pity, when she was first introduced to her, that, while the younger girls were quite pretty, the oldest daughter had no claim to beauty, save that of expression; but she soon decided that beauty of feature would have added very little, if anything, to the attractiveness of Susan Peyton's face. The evening went quickly by, in pleasant talk and music, for the younger girls, discovering from some incidental allusion that Eliza-

beth could play, opened the piano—which was a very good
one—and begged her, if she were not too tired, to sing for
them.

"For I know you *do* sing," said Louise; "I can see it in
your face!"

Elizabeth sang one or two songs alone, and then they
found that they all knew two or three part-songs, and
what with laughing rehearsals of these, in which the whole
family joined, and discussions about music and singing, it
was eleven o'clock before any one supposed it was nine, and
the meeting broke up rather hastily, in view of the early
breakfast which Mrs. Peyton had ordered for Elizabeth's
benefit. She suddenly discovered that she was very tired,
for she had not slept soundly the night before, on the boat,
and although stern common sense contended that a mattress
was the proper thing to sleep on, she sank with a long sigh
of pleasure into the great soft feather bed on its old-fashioned, high-posted mahogany bedstead, and left her nest
reluctantly the next morning, when a neat handed black
Phyllis knocked at her door with an awakening cup of coffee.

"I forgot to ask you last night, my dear," said Mrs. Peyton, as they sat down to breakfast, "whether you would take
early coffee or not—so I ventured to send it. We don't
admit the presence of the malaria-fiend, of course; but we
think it as well to be on the safe side, and look upon this as
an ounce of prevention."

Elizabeth was a little startled. In all their discussing of
pros and cons, nobody had suggested malaria, and she
resolved to investigate the subject at the earliest opportunity. It was too late now to withdraw from the experiment, but not too late to learn all its dangers, and be as fully
armed as possible against them. But she knew the boys
would need her help every minute of the day; so, arraying
herself in the neatly made dark calico gown which she had

brought for the occasion, she bade good-by till evening to her new friends, and set off in state for Green Point, in the family coach, driven by the highly respectable old colored gentleman who had come for her the previous evening, and would call for her, Mrs. Peyton assured her, at five that afternoon. She found an ample basket of lunch in the carriage, although nothing had been said about it, and she passed the half hour which the drive consumed in composing a letter to her mother, to be written that evening—a letter which was to descant upon Southern hospitality in general, and Colonel Peyton's family in particular.

CHAPTER IV.

"A little water clears us of this deed."—SHAKSPERE.

"For those that fly may fight again,
 Which he can never do that's slain,
 Hence timely running 's no mean part
 Of conduct in the martial art."—BUTLER.

ARNOLD and Ernest rushed out to meet the carriage before it had fairly stopped, and Ernest said, excitedly: "Oh, Betty! if you'd known what you were going to miss, you'd never have gone!"

"It's a regular sensation novel," added Arnold, "and we're the heroes! Poor Betty, if you'd only stayed, perhaps you'd have been the heroine!"

"What do they mean?" asked Elizabeth, in great perplexity, as Roderick helped her out of the carriage.

"Come in and take a seat, ma'am," he replied; "it is quite a narrative."

"You see," he continued, when Elizabeth was comfortably seated on a roll of carpet, "it must have gone abroad that we were all to spend the night at Colonel Peyton's, and I suppose the bushwhackers around here congratulated themselves on the wagon-load of plunder that would be left unguarded in the house. We made a famous supper—that's the best ham I ever tasted—and then we suddenly discovered that we were very tired. The boys were in bed, and had been asleep for an hour, and I was just beginning to undress, when I heard a little noise at the back of the house. I had hung another of the inside doors there, and propped it with a couple of trunks, for I couldn't make it lock; the fire had died down, and beside, the quilts and things kept what was left from showing, I suppose. I lifted a corner of one of the quilts, and quietly looked out. It was bright moonlight, you know, and I had no trouble in recognizing the fellow that drove the wagon. He had two others with him, and I kept still to hear what they were saying.

"'Sunday dinner for all of us, boys!' says one driver. 'I· smelt dat ham, and I made my mind up 'bout him, dat same minute! You kin take de canned goods, but dat ham b'longs to me!' 'But is you right shuah dey's all gone, brudder Skinner?' says another. 'I don't 'zackly like dis doah 'rivin' heah so sudden!'

"'Shut up, you fool niggah!' says the first man; 'dey's put up de doah, and lef' all safe,' and he gave an ecstatic chuckle. I suddenly remembered the buckets of water we had brought from the spring to be ready for morning, so I waked Arnold as softly as I could; he and I each took a bucket and rested it on the window-sill, and, just as they had succeeded, all pushing together, in opening the door about a foot, we let them have it!"

"And oh!" said Arnold, ecstatically, "I *wish* you could have heard them yell! They ran like deer, until they were out of sight, and I've no doubt that by this time it's all over the neighborhood that the house is haunted by the ghost of a fireman!"

"Don't you mean a waterman?" said Ernest, adding, to Elizabeth, "Weren't they too mean for anything, Betty? They never woke me to see the fun?"

"And he slept right straight through that threefold yell!" chuckled Arnold.

"I think a sixfold yell wouldn't have waked me last night," said Elizabeth, springing up and beginning to make the beds. "Now Rod, what had we better do first? It really seems impossible to tell!"

"I don't like to order you all round," said Roderick, "as if I were a superior being, but I will humbly suggest that the very first thing is to attend to the drawbridges and moats, as it were. I wish I could be in two places at once. I want to drive to that sash and door factory, five miles from here, and try to have the doors made before to-morrow night, and I want to put in all these panes of glass in the sound sashes."

"I do believe the boys and I could put in the glass, if you'd show us a little," said Elizabeth; and the boys confirmed the appointment with "Of course we could."

So as soon as beds were made, and dishes washed, and a supply of wood and water brought into the house, Roderick opened the case of window-glass, and instructed his willing pupils in the art of putting in window-panes. It is not a very difficult art, and he had them established in the business in an hour. Then he left them, to hunt up a conveyance to the factory, and succeeded in finding, much to his satisfaction, a good riding-horse at the farm-house which stood about a mile from their outer gate. The people were plain, unpretending Germans, but they were honest looking, and seemed disposed to be good neighbors, and Roderick was glad to find that he could hire a horse for what seemed to him a very small sum, whenever he wished, except during the busy season. The doors and sashes which he ordered were faithfully promised for the next afternoon, and he rode home in time for the good dinner which Elizabeth spread from the basket and their own stores. He had stopped by the way to engage a man to clear out the well; they could not afford a pump just yet, but they could rig up a temporary windlass, and cover the well, for the spring was several hundred yards from the house, in the woods. While the well was being cleared of rubbish, Roderick and the boys, riding by turns, went back to the German farmer and

hired a wagon, and he, seeing their ignorance, good-
naturedly showed them how to harness the horse, and gave
them exact directions for finding the saw-mill whence the
lumber for the platform and windlass was to come. It was
only three miles away, so that by the time the well was
,cleaned they had returned with their load, which Roderick
had made as large as the wagon and horse would admit, for
the repairs in which boards and beams would be needed
were almost numberless. It was too late to complete the job
that afternoon, but they made an encouraging beginning,
and Roderick gave the boys high praise for the manner in
which they handled their tools. Meanwhile, Elizabeth had
been busy in the house. She had insisted on finishing the
glazing alone, in order to leave the boys free to go with
Roderick, and she became more and more expert with every
window. She was glad to find that only four or five sashes
were broken, and she took great comfort in the fact that the
house, when thoroughly swept, showed only weather stains.
It had not been occupied for four or five years, the neighborhood negroes having preferred their easily warmed cabins to
the large and airy rooms of the great house, and the last
occupants had been the family for whom it was originally
bought, but she had been haunted by visions of negro
squatters, and had only half believed the negro driver's
assurance that "nobody but white folks" had ever lived
there. She consulted Mrs. Peyton that evening about finding a woman to clean the house, now that it was comparatively weather-tight; Mrs. Peyton spoke to one or two of
the house-servants, and before bedtime half a dozen applicants had reported themselves in the kitchen. From these,
guided by Mrs. Peyton's recommendation, Elizabeth chose a
stout and capable looking dame, who promised to be on
hand at Green Point early the next morning. The evening
passed as pleasantly as the one before had done, but Eliza-

beth had come to the conclusion, in the course of the day,
that she could not afford the late start and early departure
which were necessary if she continued to spend her nights
at Peyton Hall; so when Mrs. Peyton came to her room at
bedtime, with motherly kindness, to see that everything was
comfortable, Elizabeth laid the case before her, expressing
the deepest gratitude for the hospitality which had been
shown her, and explaining the disadvantages of her absence
from the scene of action. Mrs. Peyton reluctantly admitted
the reasonableness of all she said, and promised to convince
the Colonel, but insisted upon sending them bread and
other things which could not well be bought, until they
should have a settled servant. She also begged that if her
daughters could be of the slightest service in the way of unpacking and helping to arrange, Elizabeth would not hesitate
to call upon them.

"For you know, my dear," she said, "there are so many
things about a house which only a lady can do properly. My
servants are fairly good, but I do not think of trusting them
with everything."

The Colonel could only be appeased by a promise that all
four of his new neighbors would spend the following Sunday at Peyton Hall. He went with Elizabeth, the next
morning, to deliver the invitation to Roderick in person, and
she beguiled the drive with pertinent questions about the
best methods of farming and marketing. He was very hopeful and encouraging, assuring her that when the boats once
began running, there would be no difficulty in making a
handsome profit every year, beside supplying their own table.
He told her that he had of late turned his attention to raising poultry for market, with gratifying success, marred only
by the depredations of certain lawless and "rascally niggers," who lived comfortably without any visible means of
support, save a shallow pretense of farming.

"There's one thing Mr. Roderick won't fancy any more than I do," he said, as they passed one of the vestiges of a departed fence which still adorned the Green Point estate; "the fence laws are peculiar—we are expected to keep trespassing animals out, and can claim no damages if, through negligence about our fences, they break in and ruin our crops. Every darky in the neighborhood has from two to a dozen razor-backed "hawgs," ill-fed, uncanny-looking creatures, with inherited and acquired skill at making the most of small breaches in boundary fences. If your brother will take my advice, he will build a thoroughly good, strong fence around the farm before he sows so much as a grass seed—it will be the only security. We very seldom have enough frost in the ground to prevent any one from digging post-holes, even earlier than this, and if he can make his fence now, when comparatively little else can be done, it will save him valuable time later, and a world of vexation beside."

Elizabeth replied that they intended to put the farm in thorough order, so far as their means would permit, and begged the Colonel to give Roderick the benefit of his own experiments and experiences, and this he cheerfully promised to do.

A second load of their household goods had arrived from the wharf the day before, and the third and last was to come to-day, so that Elizabeth felt anxious to have the cleaning begun. She found " aunt Judy" waiting for her, and was triumphantly informed by the boys that the new "help" had arrived in time to cook their breakfast, and had made corn-bread and "stunning" coffee for them. Roderick was only waiting to see his sister, before driving off for the windows and doors; the boys could easily finish the well cover without him, and then they were to be at her disposal for the rest of the day. Elizabeth meditated for a minute, and then exclaimed, "Roderick! how much lime would it take to whitewash this house—outside I mean? Of course it will have to be done inside."

"Oh, I don't know," he answered; "three or four bushels would do it, I fancy, and it would look much more cheerful, but we can't afford to pay for having it done, I'm afraid. The way these darkies work, according to the Colonel, it would take them a week or two to do it."

"But we could afford the lime?"

"Why yes, I suppose so—it doesn't cost a great deal—but *you're* not going to do it, Miss, if that is what you are driving at, and I can't take the time just now; perhaps I can after we are settled."

"I did not think of doing it myself," said Elizabeth, laughing at the vision of herself perched on a ladder, with a whitewash brush in her hand, "but the boys are ready for anything, and I do believe they could do it. I brought some dreadful clothes for them, and if you don't mind, they can go with you as far as the store, and bring back a basketful of lime, to begin with, and experiment on the smoke-house. We shall want the lime to-day, anyhow, for aunt Judy says she would rather whitewash before she scrubs the floors, and if they find they can't do it, no harm will have been done. I do so want the place to look it's best when mother and the girls come."

"So do I," said Roderick; "and, as you say, trying won't do any harm. I saw the mason yesterday, and he promised to come to-morrow and rebuild that chimney—the bricks have to be brought from some remote place—and do you know, I am certain I saw the identical bricks that were stolen, as I drove by a shanty about a mile from here. They were worked into a chimney and oven, and had been well plastered with clay, but it had fallen off in places, and I am sure they were from our chimney."

"It's too bad," replied Elizabeth, sympathizingly; "the

things we hear about these bushwhackers seem to me the most discouraging part of the enterprise, and I wish we could find a good dog—that would be something of a protection."

"That's a good idea," said Roderick. "The Colonel has about forty, I should say—perhaps he'd be willing to part with one. Well, I must go now—don't work too hard, my dear—use your intellect, and direct the menial and your two stout subordinates."

The boys hailed the idea of whitewashing the house with wild delight, and drove off with Roderick, taking the largest basket they could find, and returning in triumph with a bushel of lime and three brushes, selected, at Elizabeth's suggestion, by the storekeeper. Aunt Judy shook her head at the idea of whitewashing walls with a brand new brush.

"Oughter been soaked over night, anyhow, Miss," she said, "and not good as an old one, then. If Miss 'll 'scuse me, I'll go home and bring a bresh worth all dese—it won't be lost time, for I kin work it twice as fast."

Elizabeth willingly excused her, and persuaded the impatient boys to let their brushes soak until after dinner, suggesting that, as the axe and saw and wheelbarrow had come, they might profitably try to bring in some more substantial wood than the dead branches which had heretofore been burnt. Arnold was inclined to rebel, but Ernest dragged him off to the wood-lot, saying sternly, "See here, my boy, when the Captain isn't here we're under orders from his first assistant; and we're to obey orders if we break owners!"

They could not, of course, attack any very large trees, but they found a good sized oak which either the wind or some quieter agency had uprooted and prostrated, on the edge of the wood, and attacked it with such vigor, that they had wheeled two or three loads to the wood-house before they were called to make ready for dinner.

Roderick came back just as they were sitting down, with one door, and a good deal of vexation.

"They don't seem to think anything of an engagement here!" he said; "the man evidently thought he had done wonders to have that one door finished for me, and I suppose I shall have to make three or four trips, before the whole order is finished. They must dawdle unmercifully, for they have plenty of hands, and very good machinery."

"Which door had they made?" asked Elizabeth, "the outside one?"

"Yes," said Roderick, "they had condescended to remember that I had emphasized the necessity for that, and they seemed to think me highly unreasonable for being in such mad haste about the rest."

"Oh well," said Elizabeth, soothingly, "if it is the outside one, we *can* be a little patient about the rest—that is so much more important. Is it all ready to hang?"

"Yes," he answered, beginning to look more cheerful; "I'll do it right after dinner, and then I'll wait till Monday to go for the rest, and perhaps he'll have them all done by that time. I am sure I spoke impressively to him, this time, and he was very apologetic."

Lock and hinges were put on, and the door hung, immediately after dinner, and the knowledge that they could now make their castle secure against attack from the outside added greatly to their comfort. Roderick unpacked the box of ready mixed paints which he had provided, and gave the new door its first coat, going on from that to the room which Aunt Judy had finished, and giving a coat of white to the discolored woodwork, with delightful effect. Three of the downstairs rooms had really handsome carved mantel-pieces, and over one of these was an imposing reredos. This room, they agreed, should be the "drawing-room," and they amused themselves with choosing plans for the sump-

tuous furniture which existed only in their imagination. In
the meantime, fresh paint, clean windows, and the light and
pretty furniture destined for it, would make a cosy and
cheerful room enough. In buying their supplies, Elizabeth
had thoughtfully suggested that it would be a good plan to
stain some, if not all of the floors, and that they could have
no better opportunity than now, when the house was only
half occupied; so, while Ernest and Arnold valiantly attacked
the smoke-house with their whitewash brushes, Elizabeth
and Roderick began upon the downstairs floors, as fast as
they were scrubbed and dried, and, after two or three days'
steady work at the old house, it was so transformed that
their delight began to change into impatience for the rest of
the family, and especially the dear mother, to see it. The
boys, after a good deal of unnecessary splashing, had succeeded so well with the smoke-house, that they had been
allowed to attack the "mansion." A ladder apiece had
been easily made, and they worked with such a will, that by
the time all was done inside, the outside fairly shone with
two coats of creamy whitewash. Colonel Peyton had given
them directions as to the mixing, which was different
from Aunt Judy's recipe for the inside walls, and he assured
them that one coat every spring in future would keep it
fresh looking. The sash-factory man, perhaps startled by
Roderick's earnestness, in this easy going land, had finished
his order by Monday, and by the end of that week, all was
done which they meant to do at present. The plaster had
been mended, the chimney rebuilt, most of the floors and
the staircase stained, and Aunt Judy, who owned no rival
in her business, had suggested putting a little color into the
whitewash for some of the downstairs rooms. This had
been most successfully done; the parlor walls were a pale
Indian red, the dining-room a soft shade of buff, and the
kitchen a darker shade of blue. All the ceilings and the

bedrooms throughout the house were white, and when mattings and rugs were laid down, pictures hung, and the windows prettily curtained, the house was as sweet and cheerful a home as anybody need desire. The boys had begged hard for a carpenter, and leave to help him with the front porch and back veranda, but Roderick had wisely decided not to undertake too much at once; they could work out-of-doors now, for the short winter was over, and his first anxiety was about the fences, for they were already greatly annoyed by troops of marauding "hawgs."

"I am sure those creatures have the evil eye!" said Elizabeth, as she came back, breathless, from a desperate chase; "they climbed the bank, just where the gate ought to be and isn't, and positively leered down at me! And this morning I found one climbing serenely up the steps at the front door!"

"Yet they're as alarmingly tame as Robinson Crusoe's desert islanders were," replied Roderick; "and when I get into the Delaware Legislature my first business shall be to reverse these abominable trespass laws."

It was wonderful how the free, out-of-doors life they were leading had already strengthened them all, and made hard work not only possible, but almost easy. Nights of unbroken sleep followed busy days; their appetites were appalling, and a healthy coat of tan adorned all their faces. The two boys were in uproarious spirits, but Elizabeth and Roderick wisely endeavored to direct, rather than subdue, their abundant energy and vitality.

Plenty of work still remained for everybody, but the first feeling of bustle had subsided. The Sunday at Colonel Peyton's had been a delightful interlude. Greatly to the boys' delight, they had been provided with fine saddle-horses, for the expedition of three miles to the nearest church. The ladies had all gone in the before mentioned family-coach, which had evidently been built in the days of boundless hospitality. Already many signs of spring had come, although it was early in March. Willows were turning green, and buds swelling on the later trees, while the grass was thick and green enough for May, in the harsher climate to which the Stanleys had been accustomed. The drive was a very beautiful one, chiefly through winding lanes and private roads, the only inconvenience being the number of gates which must be opened and shut; but to these the cavaliers on horseback attended. Elizabeth was surprised to see the many horses and vehicles gathered about the quaint old brick church when they arrived; she had no idea of finding so large a congregation, in this thinly peopled country, as that which nearly filled the church, but Mrs. Peyton, seeing her surprise, told her that they came from various distances within a radius of twelve or fifteen miles.

The clergyman, a fine, genial looking old man, with thick white hair and pleasant blue eyes, read the service reverently and well, and preached an excellent sermon. The organ had seen its best days, and was somewhat asthmatic from dampness, but it was skillfully played, and there was a very good volunteer choir. Roderick and Elizabeth joined in the singing with real pleasure, quite unconscious of the addition to it which their well-trained voices made.

When the service and sermon were over, a bewildering number of introductions followed, as they slowly made their way back to the carriage. Every one seemed to know and respect Colonel and Mrs. Peyton, and to consider any one introduced by them well vouched for, and so many cordial words of welcome and offers of service were tendered, that, as Elizabeth said afterward, it seemed more like a joyful home-coming after a long absence, than a settlement among strangers. Roderick remarked with satisfaction that the introductions included a number of pretty girls, and only hoped he should be able to remember "which was which" when he accepted his various invitations to "call right soon."

"But I'm not so much impressed with the youthful chivalry, my Betty, as I am with its sisters and its cousins and its aunts," he said next day to Elizabeth, when they were talking over the visit; "there's a sort of want of—may I be allowed to say snap?—in them, but perhaps you didn't observe it."

"Yes, I'm sorry to say I did," replied Elizabeth, thoughtfully; "they nearly all had pleasant, kindly faces, and they were very polite indeed, but they looked lazy, every one of them, and I could tell, by various little remarks that I heard, that we have already raised a general astonishment by our industry; yet they must have known that it would be impossible for us to live at Green Point in the wrecked and ruined state in which we found it."

"No, I don't believe they did know that!" said Roderick, laughing; "I imagine they would have sort of camped down, and intended to make everything right in time, and meantime would have done barely enough to keep the weather out. Did you notice that broken down gate, propped with a fence rail, at the entrance of that very pretty place about half way between here and the church? Randolph Peyton says it was pulled off the hinges by some drunken fellows, a year ago last Christmas Eve, and the owner has been 'certainly' going to mend it to-morrow, ever since!"

"I hope the spirit of the country won't have a bad effect upon the boys," said Elizabeth, anxiously; "we must watch them, Rod—and ourselves too, and never humor any inclination to put off till to-morrow what can be done to-day."

Elizabeth had found, to her great relief and joy, that Aunt Judy would be very glad to come as cook and washerwoman, and could recommend a young niece of her own for chamber-maid and waitress. They both preferred sleeping at home, which was an advantage, for, although the garrets were to be plastered and made habitable in time, Roderick wished to defer this for the more important out-of-doors work. It was as Mrs. Peyton had said—Aunt Judy asked such very moderate wages, that Elizabeth, had she not been forewarned, would have felt constrained to add something to them, and Clara, the niece, was thankful to come for her board and whatever clothes the family might choose to give her.

At last all was in order, the cooking-stove set up, the partition made to screen the dining-room door from a full view of the kitchen, the wide hearths red washed, the deep chimneys polished with stove blacking, and, through Mrs. Peyton's kindness, a pair of brass-headed andirons in every chimney. She had given Roderick the names of two or three families in the neighborhood who had, she knew, stores of old furniture and household belongings, and he had succeeded in buying, not only some half dozen pairs of andirons, but a curious old chest of drawers, and a stately chair with a high carved back, which was to be the Mother's throne at the head of her table.

CHAPTER V.

" There lies no desert in the land of life,
For e'en that tract that barrenest doth seem,
Labor'd of thee in faith and hope, shall teem
With heavenly harvests and rich gatherings rife."—F. KEMBLE.

VERY little had been written to Mrs. Stanley or the girls of the various plans and improvements. This had been by Arnold's and Ernest's express desire. "Let's burst it upon them, Betty dear," said Arnold, entreatingly; "They're expecting a ruin without the ivy, and it will be such fun to see their faces!" Roderick and Elizabeth were by no means too old to enter into the fun of the surprise, so, while they had written freely of the kindness of Colonel Peyton's family, the abundant and cheap service to be had from the negroes, and their own health and high spirits, almost nothing had been told of their daily doings, and this, without being in the least intended to do so, had given the impression that they had found the place more hopelessly demoralized, and more difficult to render habitable, than Roderick had at first supposed. Kitty and Polly had held several rather doleful private conferences, and were feeling more and more martyred at the prospect of their exile, as they appreciated the daily comforts and luxuries of Mr. Stanley's home. Edith, too, with unwise affection, kept entreating them to reconsider their decision, or at least to stay the remainder of spring with her.

" Your wilderness will be more endurable in summer, perhaps," she said; "and when Betty and Rod keep writing how cheap and plentiful servants are, it makes it quite plain that you'll not be needed about the house—it's my belief that you'll be rather in the way than otherwise. Ah, *do* stay! I don't see how I'm ever to live without you, after this tantalizing little taste of you—you know *I* haven't any sister, and my lessons and music and everything seem so much easier since you came."

"We should like it very much, you know we would, Edith," said Kitty dolefully, "for I'm sure, from the way Betty and Rod keep still about the place, that it's even worse than Rod thought; but just think how mean it would be for us to sit down in the lap of luxury and leave the rest, and especially mamma, to fight it out down there! I should feel like a pickpocket, and so would Polly, I know."

"Of course I should," assented Polly, promptly; "and there's another thing, Edie, Rod wouldn't say anything—he's too generous—but I am quite certain he would never respect us much if we were to stay. Rod doesn't talk much, but I feel as sure as can be what he would think, and he's giving up a great deal more than we are."

"I don't see how you make that out," said Edith, a little crossly.

"I should think you couldn't help seeing," replied Polly, with somewhat unnecessary warmth; "there are dozens of fellows who would have let Betty have her way and kill herself taking boarders, or let us all be farmed out, as people proposed, or told us we'd better all come here and sponge on Uncle George; and if we'd done that way, I dare say enough money could have been scraped together to take him through the Polytechnic, and much good it would have done him!"

"Well, I don't care!" said Edith, inconsequently; "I'm going to make you a visit next summer, whether you ask me or not, and then I shall just see for myself whether you're all committing suicide, and if you are, papa and I will make your lives a burden to you till we get you out of that heathenish place."

This promise, thoughtlessly as it was made, consoled the twins not a little. They dearly loved Edith, whose daring spirit and quick, impulsive character made them her faithful followers, and they felt sure that, should the place really prove unendurable, Mr. Stanley would devise some plan for their deliverance.

Their mother remained serenely and smilingly unshaken under all arguments and entreaties ; she had given her word to her boy that the experiment should be tried, and, in spite of all the drawbacks which she knew must exist, she looked forward with a quiet pleasure to the peaceful country home, where she would have all her beloved children within sound of her voice. For she was one of those old-fashioned mothers who are never perfectly happy unless all their bairns are under the home roof; and although she would never have let any foolish sentimentality stand in the way of their well-being and advancement, she would have many a heartache to conceal as they should find and take their places in the outside world. She had consented to let Kitty and Polly remain with Mr. Stanley, should they decide to do so, but they knew very well what the consent had cost her, and so could not bring themselves to take advantage of it.

It was decided that Mrs. Stanley and the girls should go by the boat, for, although the accommodations were not sumptuous, the drive from the landing was so much shorter than that from the railway-station, that it seemed the better way. On the evening before their departure Mr. Stanley suddenly announced that he intended to go with them, and see them safely to their journey's end, but he turned a deaf ear to all Edith's entreaties that she might be allowed to join the party. And, to tell the truth, neither Mrs. Stanley, Kitty or Polly desired that she should, for they felt very doubtful as to the accommodations which they could offer to guests at this stage of the proceedings, and were a little dismayed by Mr. Stanley's kind offer.

The boat had met with several small delays, and it was toward sunset, on the loveliest of spring evenings, when it touched at the Green Point landing. Colonel Peyton had insisted, with a kindness which would take no denial, upon sending his carriage for "the ladies," and one of Aunt Judy's sons had followed it with a wagon for the luggage. Roderick had come in the carriage, and was standing on the wharf, a look of eager pleasure on his face; he had missed his gentle mother and bright young sisters not a little. His hearty and joyful reception of his uncle put Mrs. Stanley's mind at rest upon the score of making her brother-in-law comfortable; she felt now that the house must be at least decent, or Rod could not look so care-free and thoroughly glad to welcome an unexpected visitor.

The drive along the winding country road, through green fields and budding trees, was so beautiful that it did not seem long to any of them. Choruses of frogs made distant music; the air was as balmy as that of June, and the stars were just beginning to come out as the carriage drove through what Roderick assured them was the gateway, although it was still unadorned by a gate.

Lights were shining from all the lower floor windows and from those of two or three of the bedrooms, and a dancing fire of dry boughs sparkled on the hearths of the dining-room and parlor. In the dim twilight the snowy walls seemed imposingly high, and the grand old elms, towering yet higher, seemed to hold the house in their protecting arms.

"Why Rod!" said Mrs. Stanley, in utter bewilderment, as the carriage drew up to the door with a flourish, "surely the man has made a mistake—this *can't* be the house!"

But Elizabeth had rushed to the carriage door by this time, closely followed by Arnold and Ernest, and if Mrs. Stanley had any further doubts, they were dispelled by the chorus of welcome and the eager help which almost prevented her from leaving the carriage. Amazement was a small word for the sensation with which she had seen the outside, and it was quite inadequate to describe her feelings as she was led first into the pretty parlor, and then into the equally pretty dining-room, where, at a signal from Elizabeth to Aunt Judy, a tempting supper was soon on the table. Stewed oysters, clam fritters, the lightest of biscuit, waffles and cup-cake, fragrant coffee, and an offering from Mrs. Peyton of rich cream and delicately preserved peaches. Mr. Stanley had come in for his full share of the warm welcome which had awaited the mother, and, having indulged in far more dismal forebodings than she had allowed herself, had been even more astonished than she was. He was a silent, but smiling and appreciative listener, as Elizabeth, roused to unwonted excitement, took turns with Roderick and the boys in pouring out eager narratives and explanations.

The clams and oysters which formed the solid basis of that delightful supper, came, as the boys proudly declared, "off the Estate"; there was a fine oyster bed in the little river, not a hundred yards from the kitchen-door, and clams were to be had for the digging, in the sandy bank. The long drive which the travelers had taken, and the busy day of preparation which the others had spent, had provided them all with startling appetites, and Aunt Judy's face shone with gratified vanity, as she brought in her tenth plate of delicately browned waffles, and heard Mr. Stanley say that he hoped there was a doctor in the neighborhood, for he hadn't eaten such a supper since he was a boy.

The air had grown chill as darkness fell, and the wood-fires were far from oppressive. One drawback to the pleasure of living on an "Estate" was the fact that, in this particular neighborhood, it was considered unsafe to sit out of doors, or even in an open veranda, after dark. But Roderick explained that, when he had the veranda rebuilt, he meant to have a large vestibule enclosed, with windows at the sides, and an open front; he had noticed an arrangement of this kind at Colonel Peyton's, and found that it was considered a sufficient protection from the dews and chills of evening.

After it was decided that nobody could possibly eat any more supper, a procession was formed to inspect the house, and the four conspirators flushed high with happiness as praises and thanks were showered upon them. It was astonishing, considering the small amount of money which had been spent to accomplish it, to see the transformation which had been wrought in the old house in two weeks. The twins had been in a sort of dazed silence until now, but when they were introduced to their pretty bower, with its white draperies, neat cottage furniture and checkered matting, they found their tongues, and mingled admiration for all they saw with heartfelt regrets that they had missed the fun of helping with the transformation. The cheery little fires, reflected from shining andirons, no doubt lent their glamour to everything, but even without their spell, no one could have denied that a more homelike home would have been difficult to find. All four of the second-floor rooms had been furnished, and there would be no difficulty about giving one of them to Mr. Stanley, for—

"We'll take you in with us to-night, Rod, if you'll behave yourself," said Arnold, grandly, "and allow Betty to shake you down on that cot bed which we said there'd be no use for!"

The inspection was just finished when a knock at the

parlor door called Roderick out to the kitchen, whence he presently returned with a puzzled face.

"Betty," he said, half-laughing, "you've not ordered a cow, unbeknownst to me, have you?"

"I?" said Elizabeth, looking up in great astonishment, which increased when Mr. Stanley said quietly,

"Oh, she's come, has she? I was beginning to think that respectable old uncle must have made off with her—come, children, and make the new member of your family welcome!" and he led Elizabeth by the hand, the rest following, to the back door, where a pretty Alderney cow was patiently standing, her rope held by a serious looking old colored man.

"There, my dear," said Mr. Stanley, putting the rope into Elizabeth's hand; "since you were determined to turn dairy-maid, I thought I would make it as well worth your while as possible—this is your own special cow, for the family cream and butter. I didn't dare to offer flocks and herds to his lordship there, but I thought you would not deny your old uncle the pleasure of giving you this."

Elizabeth gave the "old uncle" a very grateful and loving kiss, and then there was a chorus of thanks and admiration as Roderick and the boys took the "new member" off to the long-disused barn to make her comfortable for the night.

"I saw that cow on the boat," said Kitty when they had returned to the parlor, "and I thought then what a beauty she was, but I never dreamed—— Uncle, how *did* you have her brought here without our knowing anything about it?"

"Easily enough," said Mr. Stanley, smiling; "she came on board before we did, and you were all so busy hugging each other and seeing to your luggage when we landed that I had no trouble in finding a man whom the freight agent recommended, and starting her ladyship off before you were ready to move on."

"Oh yes, I remember now," said Polly; "we passed her on the road, and I wondered where she was going."

"You must stay long enough to eat some of my butter, uncle," said Elizabeth; "Aunt Judy is a famous butter-maker, and is going to teach me all about it."

"Indeed, I am tempted to stay for good and all," replied Mr. Stanley, looking affectionately round the circle of bright faces, and pulling Elizabeth down to his knee; "I came down here as much to make a final effort to persuade you out of this crazy scheme as for anything else, and since I have touched Delaware soil I'm as mad as the maddest of you; I wonder if you could be induced to take Edith and me to board this summer? I've been overworked lately, and mean to take a good long rest."

"You shall come for as long a visit as you choose to make, dear brother," said Mrs. Stanley, "but you must not talk about boarding after all you have done for us."

"Indeed, I will talk about boarding," he replied; "a great business firm you will make, beginning in this un-worldly manner! If you will put up with Edith and me for a month or six weeks—a spoiled child and a cranky old man —you shall at least not be out of pocket by it; if we mayn't board, we will not come—so there! You needn't imagine you have a monopoly of independence, little woman."

"We'll not fight about it yet," said Mrs. Stanley, laugh-ing; "we mean to coax you to stay two or three days this time, and perhaps after that you will not care for the month or six weeks. And now I think we had all better go to bed— this has been a long and exciting day, and judging you all by myself, you are very tired. Dear brother," she added, turning to Mr. Stanley, "if John were here with us, the new home would have a blessing asked upon it; will you take his place in this to-night?" Her voice faltered a little, but her face was calm and sweet as ever; to her the husband and

5

father seemed not far away, but she missed him sadly in the founding of their new home. The evening hymn was sung very sweetly by the six young voices, and if Elizabeth's piano was missed, no one spoke of it. As Mr. Stanley looked round upon the bright, loving faces, all earnest with the purpose which had drawn them even more closely together than they were before, his last prejudice against the "crazy scheme" vanished, and he prayed for a blessing on their undertaking as fervently as if he had never said a word in opposition to it.

Quiet settled down over the old house, and sleep upon all the inmates, excepting Kitty and Polly. Excitement and a sense of joyful disappointment kept them awake for an hour or two, talking in eager whispers.

"I didn't believe it was our house at all when we drove up," said Kitty; "I thought Rod's Colonel Peyton must have made him promise to bring us all there to tea the first night, because our place was so forlorn."

"I never thought of that," replied Polly, "I thought I must be dreaming, and I pinched myself to see if I were really awake. It's beautiful—ever so much nicer than the house we left, and oh, Kitty, if we can *only* have horses sometimes, what rides we can take through all these lovely green lanes and wood roads! But do you know I feel dreadfully ashamed—just think how Betty and Rod and the boys must have worked while we were sitting in the lap of luxury! I'm sure we could have helped like everything if we had been here."

"I don't believe they wanted us, Poll," said Kitty, philosophically; "we should have wanted to make plans and do things our own way, and you know they only consented to take the boys when they had promised to mind. I suppose it's very wrong, but you know Betty is only three years older than we are, and sometimes I feel like letting her know that I think my ways and opinions are fully as good as hers."

"But you know they're not," answered Polly, simply, "for somehow she nearly always comes out right, and I'd much rather have people—the right people, I mean, like Mamma and Betty and Rod—tell me what I'd better do; it saves me so much trouble, for I am never quite certain when I have to decide for myself."

"I am!" said Kitty, laughing, "and sometimes I think—afterward, of course—that the more wrong I am, the more certain I feel that I am right. Don't you ever want to do things just because you know you can't?"

There was no answer, but a sound of even breathing which convinced Kitty that her last remark had been wasted, and then she suddenly discovered that she was very sleepy, and followed Polly's wise example.

The next few days were busy ones. The fact that they were settling into a permanent home made Mrs. Stanley anxious to have every trunk and box unpacked and removed to one of the spacious garrets, for she rightly judged that while any of the unpacking and arranging remained to be done, it would serve as an excuse from the routine which must be kept up, to prevent much harmful dawdling. She had felt some little apprehension about the spirit of indolence of which Roderick had spoken, and she resolved to anticipate it, by a few simple rules and regulations which should give her children a sense of responsibility. So when breakfast and prayers were over, the next morning, and Mr. Stanley had gone out with Roderick and the boys to be shown over "the Estate," she called her girls about her, and unfolded her plans.

"It will make things easier to begin as we mean to keep on, dear children," she said; "and there are certain things about the house which we must attend to ourselves, no mat-

ter how many maids we can keep if we choose! I only want
two, at least for the present; Aunt Judy seems to be a
capital cook, and Clara is very willing to be taught, but, if
we are to use our pretty table service every day, we must at
least wash the breakfast things, and teach Clara carefully
about washing the dinner and tea things. Then, if we are
to keep our parlor and library neat, and have as many books'
and ornaments about as we wish, both in them and in our
bedrooms, we must ourselves do the daily dusting, and
teach Clara to sweep and dust thoroughly once a week.
Elizabeth, with Aunt Judy's help, will take charge of the
milk and cream, but we will all take lessons about it, so that
we can relieve her whenever she would like a little rest from
her dairy work. You know the story of the poor woman
who became rich by carrying the enchanted box into every
room of her house, from garret to cellar, once a day—the
real enchantment which worked the change was the fact
that she saw, and stopped, all the little leaks and rifts that
work so imperceptibly. So my plan is this—I will carry the
box myself every day, unless I should be ill, or unavoidably
hindered; I will give out all the daily rations, and 'lend a
helping hand' wherever I am most needed; you, my twins,
will either share the cup-washing, silver-cleaning and dusting every day, or else divide it, and take week and week
about, as you shall choose."

"We'd rather divide and take turns, wouldn't we, Polly,"
said Kitty, before Polly had time to speak, and she answered
meekly :

"Whichever you like, dear—I don't care!"

"But oh! mamma," begged Kitty, "mayn't we have a few
days first, just to run about and see things, and get a little
used to it all? I'm so excited, I don't see how I can possibly
begin to do anything regularly, and the unpacking will
keep—it isn't as if we had to go away again any time soon."

"No, darling, it isn't," said Mrs. Stanley, "and I think you will find that the longer you make your days aimless and purposeless, the harder it will be to begin a regular and useful life. There will be a little excitement, you know, in deciding where our things are to be bestowed, and in making the house look as if we had always lived in it. You observe that I have said nothing yet about lessons; I am going to give everybody two weeks' holiday, and then, when everything is running as smoothly as I mean it to run, we will arrange about them, and decide whether the boys shall go to school or be taught at home."

"But it's so nearly time for the summer vacation, mamma; hadn't we better wait till fall, before we make a beginning?" asked Kitty, coaxingly.

"The climate is evidently doing its worst for you," said Mrs. Stanley, laughing; "but don't imagine you can wheedle me into partnership with it, lazy girl! Be off at once, and dust yourself sober, while Polly and I wash breakfast things, and Elizabeth sees how many milk pans she is going to want, and 'sets' the milk. Your dear uncle has given the Alderney an 'outfit' of pans, and churn, and butter prints, as if she were a dozen, instead of one."

It was a hungry and happy family which met around the dinner-table, at one o'clock that day. Mr. Stanley had worked on his father's farm when he was young and before he decided to become a merchant, and old memories were pleasantly revived as he tramped with Roderick and the boys over the sadly neglected land, which was already so thickly sown with hopes. They had together calculated how much fencing lumber would be needed, and they were going after dinner to the saw-mill, to see if a bargain could be made with the sawyer, who was also a lumber merchant in a small way, which would save a little ready money. The wood-lot could stand a good deal of thinning, and it had occurred to Roderick to offer some of the fine timber, which could well be spared, in exchange for posts and boards for the door-yard fence. They had all agreed in preferring a moderate sized door-yard, out of which marauding animals could be kept, and in which flowers and shrubs might be raised, to the acre or so, which seemed to be the custom of the country, and which generally served as a happy hunting-ground for all the flocks and herds. The outside boundary was to be marked by the easily constructed "snake-fence," which could be made of roughly split logs. Roderick had made inquiries, and found that their German neighbor was considered an accomplished fence maker, and that he worked for moderate wages; so, as they were all new to the business, he had engaged the German, who rejoiced in the name of Joshua Hummel, to come and lead the enterprise. He had been a little doubtful about putting the boys to such hard work, but they had begged so earnestly to share it, that he had promised to let them try—as they seemed, in their abounding health and spirits, to be equal to anything.

"But you must tell me, honor bright, boys, if you find it too much for you," he said, "for labor is so cheap here, that I should not hesitate to hire two or three of the natives, as it is important to have it done soon!"

"Oh, we'll sing out if we're hurt, Rod," said Arnold, "but I've never felt so well in my life as I have since we came down here, and I don't believe Ernest has either, and when you work so hard yourself, you shouldn't grudge us our share."

"Yes," chimed in Ernest, "we want to show you that we can help with the *real* work, as well as the fancy work—it has been more or less of a lark, so far, but making fence will be a good solid job, and you'll see how we'll go into it!"

Roderick was deeply gratified by this manifestation. Hard as the boys had been working, what Ernest said was true,

and when the older brother saw them return manfully, day
after day, to the monotonous work of fence making, without grumbling or complaint, he felt encouraged for their
future.   He took care that they should have only the lighter
part to do, and should never work beyond their strength,
and as soon as the door-yard fence was finished, he suggested
to them that it would look much better whitewashed.   Mr.
Stanley became so deeply interested in the proceedings, that
he telegraphed from the railway station to Edith, saying that
he would remain until the end of the week.   The arrival
had taken place on Tuesday, and he declared that he could
not go home with an easy mind until he saw the fence
finished, or at least on its way to completion.   It was not
quite done when he left Green Point, early Saturday morning, but the work was going on so vigorously, that it evidently would be, in two or three days more.   He had showed
himself so entirely in earnest about coming to board for six
weeks in the summer, bringing Edith with him, and had
declared so emphatically that, unless they were allowed to
pay at least ten dollars a week apiece, they would not come
at all, that Mrs. Stanley had at last reluctantly yielded, with
a compromise ; she would accept eight dollars apiece from
them, although she considered that too much ; more she
positively would not take.

"But, my dear sister," said Mr. Stanley, speaking quite
crossly for him, "don't you see that I shall be actually
saving, or rather making money, by paying only ten dollars?
I give you my word, that when I took Edith traveling last
summer, our board averaged twenty dollars apiece every
week, for the whole six that we were gone !   I always
thought you a reasonable woman until now !"

Mrs. Stanley laughed.   "But don't *you* see, my dear
brother," she replied, "that if you pay us eight dollars, we
shall be making a scandalously large profit off you ?   We are

going to feed you on corn bread, and milk, and puddings, and fruit, with an occasional piece of fresh meat by way of a holiday feast, and if you can be obstinate, so can I—it is eight, or nothing !"

"Such a family of American eagles I never encountered," exclaimed Mr. Stanley, kissing them all good-by. "I give up—you are too many for me—but I warn you that my courage will rise with every mile that is put between us ; I am not to be lightly thwarted."

CHAPTER VI.

" This many-diapasoned maze,
    Through which the breath of being strays,
    Whose music makes our earth divine,
    Has work for mortal hands like mine.
    My duty lies before me. Lo,
    The lever there ! Take hold and blow !
    And He whose hand is on the keys
    Will play the tune as He shall please !"—O. W. HOLMES.

RODERICK missed his uncle very much—more than
he had thought he would. Now that the excitement
of starting the enterprise was almost over, a little reaction
was coming, and at times he almost doubted whether he had
done right in assuming so heavy a responsibility. To no
one but Elizabeth did he mention these doubts, and her
steadfast disposition and clear common sense were a tower
of strength to him.

"I don't know, Betty," he said one evening, after an unusually discouraging day ; " I'm afraid I have been fool hardy.
I know so little about farming that I feel all the time as if
these darkies who work for me were taking advantage of me;
and they're so abominably slow and lazy, that it's well they
have the grace to ask low wages. The ploughing ought
easily to have been finished to-day, and it is only about three
quarters done."

"But the blackberry and raspberry patches were the most
important, you know," said Elizabeth, cheerfully; "and the
boys and that new man finished clearing them out to-day—
they look beautiful, and while the warm weather keeps off
so, it makes less hurry about the planting. Aunt Judy says
there was a little frost last night. And you wait till we all

tell you you've been fool-hardy, dear, before you decide that you have. Even if the experiment were not to succeed, financially—though I begin to think now that it will—I should not regret that we made it. I have not seen mamma look so bright, and well, and like herself, since papa died, and just see how manly and vigorous the boys are growing, and how blooming May looks; the child is eating and sleeping as she never did in her life before."

"You are a real comforter," said Roderick, squeezing the hand that lay upon his arm, "and all you say is quite true; but I pity the girls—you never seemed to feel so much like prancing as they do, dear, and you make yourself and other people happy wherever you are, but I can see that they are beginning to find it very stupid. Their visit at Uncle George's was a bad preparation for the life they must lead here. I almost wish we had decided that they should remain there."

"I suppose you're talking about us," said Kitty, as she and Polly came into view from behind a tall blackberry bush; "we weren't eavesdropping, Mr. Rod, but we couldn't help catching those last few words, and we're very much obliged to you. It would be so—so nice of us to live at uncle's, and have everything we wanted, without doing anything for it, while you all grubbed for your living here! We mayn't be of much use, but we flatter ourselves we're a little better than nothing."

"Why Kitty!" exclaimed Polly, opening her blue eyes wide, "you *know* you were saying yourself to-day that we might just as well——"

"I daresay I was." interrupted Kitty, coolly; "I talk a great deal of nonsense, Poll, and you ought to have more sense, by this time, than to take it all for gospel, especially when I am dusting, for I loathe dusting, and it makes me ready to say anything. But Rod, I wish you'd believe, once for all, that if I had the magic carpet, this minute, and could go anywhere I liked, I wouldn't go a step beyond the mansion! One week at uncle's, or anywhere else, with you all here, would make me a great deal more wretched than even dusting does!"

The climax of this lofty speech set them all laughing, and as they walked back to the house, Kitty proceeded to free her mind still further.

"You probably wouldn't catch me saying this to-morrow, so you'd better make the most of it. The two weeks' holiday mamma said we might have is not quite over, but I think the sooner we begin our lessons the better, and it seems to me it would be a good plan for us to learn them through the day, and recite to whoever is to hear us in the evenings, for mamma says we're not to accept any evening invitations yet awhile, and if you and Rod are away, we can say them to her—I'd much rather, anyhow! But I suppose you'll teach us French and German, Betty, and Rod Latin, and we'll be as respectful as we can, under the circumstances!"

There was another laugh when she finished, and Elizabeth made a low courtesy, saying, "Thank you very much for my share of the respect! In return, I will promise to be as patient and forbearing as I 'can under the circumstances.' I hope I shall not be tried too severely."

"I don't know," said Kitty, with a mischievous smile; "I'm not always so meek as I am to-day—but I don't think you'll have any trouble with Polly. I do not see how it was that she received all the virtues of both of us, but she evidently did, and I do believe it's more trouble for her to be bad, than it is for me to be good."

To go back a few days—Colonel Peyton's whole family had called the day after Mrs. Stanley's arrival, and the pleasure caused by the visit had been mutual. The Peytons were the Stanleys' nearest neighbors, and were full of kindly feeling, and a cordial desire to make the new-comers feel at home. They had been almost hurt that they had not been called upon for help in Elizabeth's arrangements, and seemed quite to forget the kindness which they had so freely and generously extended to the sister and brothers. An early day was fixed for the whole Stanley family to dine and spend the evening at Rivermouth, as Colonel Peyton's place was called. Mrs. Stanley accepted the invitation for herself and her oldest daughter and son, but Mrs. Peyton begged earnestly that they would *all* come, assuring her that no other guests would be invited, and that the carriage should come for them, and bring them home at whatever hour they chose. The children said nothing, but their wistful faces spoke for them, and their mother, seeing how sincerely the invitation was given, accepted it unconditionally, judging rightly that Kitty and Polly would not consider this indulgence as a pretext for accepting general invitations. The visit had been a delightful one, and if Mrs. Stanley felt a little disturbed by Mr. Randolph Peyton's very cordial welcome to Elizabeth, and the marked attention with which he listened to her most trivial remarks, the uneasiness was diverted, if not dispelled, in the course of the evening, as he transferred himself first to Polly and then to Kitty. Polly's shy and brief replies shortened his interview with her considerably, but Kitty kept him laughing and sparring with her until the carriage was announced, and he said something, as he helped her in, which implied an intention to call at Green Point very soon. Mrs. Stanley did not remark upon this, as they drove home. She saw that Kitty was elated and excited, for in the quiet school-girl life which the twins had hitherto led, this was a new experience; but she knew that under all Kitty's waywardness there was a good deal of common sense, and that by the next day it would probably assert itself. It did; for before twenty-four hours were over, Kitty had confided to Polly that she wondered they hadn't all laughed at her, coming home!

"Why, what for?" asked Polly, looking very much astonished.

"Don't be a goose, Polly!" answered Kitty, rather sharply; "I was dreadfully set up because that gilded youth talked to me a little longer than he did to Betty and you, and of course you all saw I was, and I suppose he did too, and very probably he was laughing to himself all the time, for when I came to think it over I found he had talked nothing but the most arrant nonsense, and you know Betty had told us he was quite sensible."

"I suppose he was trying to make himself agreeable to you," said Polly, innocently.

"That finishes me! Oh Polly, you're worth your weight in bank-notes!" and with a shout of laughter, Kitty ran out of the room.

Other "neighbors," who lived at distances ranging between three and ten miles, had called in the course of the first week, and many of them were very pleasant; all very friendly. But the Stanleys met no one who impressed them so favorably as the Peytons had done, perhaps because the latter had been first in the field with kind words and kinder deeds.

Roderick soon found that, although the yield of fruit promised well, he could not look for large crops of any other kind that year. Weeds had grown unmolested for so long, sowing their seeds year by year, that it would take more than one ploughing to eradicate them. But it was a cheering thing that the fruit was there to begin with, and, now that the place was thoroughly fenced in, there was some comfort in clearing up and putting to rights.

It was decided, greatly to May's delight, to move the outside kitchen to the end of the barn, and turn it into a chicken-house. Mrs. Peyton had suggested to Elizabeth that poultry of various kinds would be almost indispensable in a region where fresh meat was so difficult, sometimes impossible, to procure, and that the neighborhood of the river would make it easy to keep ducks and geese. Two or three respectable looking hens and a dashing red-brown cock had been purchased from their German neighbor's wife, and then Mrs. Peyton took Elizabeth for a delightful drive among the farms, telling her where to go for the different "settings" of eggs which were to be confided to the hens. The day after this expedition Colonel Peyton called, bringing with him a large mastiff and a pretty, gentle looking shepherd-dog.

"I brought these fellows to protect the poultry-yard, Miss Elizabeth," he said; "you'll need them both, for the rascally negroes in the bush about here live chiefly by stealing. Here, Nero; here, Duke; come shake hands with your mistress!"

"But indeed," said Elizabeth, somewhat embarrassed, "I don't like to rob you of these two splendid fellows, Colonel Peyton; it is *very* kind, but——"

"Don't say another word, my dear!" said the Colonel, cheerily. "We've a round dozen left, and my wife was only too thankful to see them go; you're doing us a positive favor by taking them! they've been well trained as watch-dogs, and will be quite content with corn bread for their steady diet and a pan of clabber every day or two. I would advise you to keep them tied for two or three days, and talk to them and pet them every time you feed them; after that, I think, you may safely let them loose at night, for they are young dogs, and will very soon become attached to any one who is kind to them."

The boys and May were greatly delighted with this acquisition, and the dogs must have been stony-hearted indeed, to have resisted the blandishments lavished upon them. It would have been quite safe to loose them at the end of two days, but Elizabeth followed the Colonel's advice. She and Roderick led the dogs to the chicken-house every night, and tied them near the door, and the second night after their arrival the whole family was waked from its first sleep by their furious barking. The three defenders of the family hurried on their clothes and hastened to the chicken-house, but there was no sign of marauders, except the fury of the dogs, who were tugging at their chains, and were only quieted after a good deal of petting and talking to. But the next morning footprints of unusual size were found in the sandy bank by the river, and Roderick felt greatly annoyed, for the chickens were such recent arrivals that it must have been some of their near neighbors whose purpose had been defeated. The rest of the family amused itself with the length of the tracks and allusions to Robinson Crusoe, and Mrs. Stanley made Roderick laugh, anxious as he was, by a clever little caricature of himself, dressed *à la* Robinson Crusoe, gazing, transfixed with horror, at a footprint which, by its proportion to his own pictured feet, must have been at least a yard long. But, although he laughed, the anxious, worried look returned, and after tea that evening she took his arm, and announced that she wished to go and call on the cow. The pretty creature was restricted from wandering into the ploughed land by what Gail Hamilton has immortalized as "the new centrifugal iron fence," viz., a crowbar driven well into the ground, as anchor for a long rope. This could be moved every day, and Bonny, as the children had dubbed the cow, seemed quite content with her shifting pasture, being carefully stabled every night, and given a bed of the soft, fine hay which had been used in packing the china and lighter articles. She had evidently been used to petting, for as they drew near, she went to the end of her rope,

lowing softly, and holding her head down, plainly invited
them to rub it. They caressed and admired her to her
heart's content, and then walked slowly around the farm,
Roderick pointing out to his mother, as they went, the
various improvements which were to come in time. So far,
no fences had been made, save the one enclosing "the
Estate" and that about the barn-yard and door-yard, but
Roderick, acting, as he did in all important matters, under
Colonel Peyton's advice, intended, when the planting was
over, to make a few dividing fences, for the protection of the
crops which would suffer most, should the invading army of
"hawgs" break through or burrow under the outer fence.
The dogs manifested a lively interest in these outlaws, barking loudly if the enemy even approached the outposts, and it
was well that they did, for no fence was thoroughly secure
for any length of time against the ingenuity and determination of these evil beasts.

"I wished to talk with you, dear," said Mrs. Stanley, as
she and her son turned toward the house, "about the school
question—do you think it will be best to send Arnold and
Ernest to that school near here, of which we were speaking
the other day?"

"I don't know, mother," replied Roderick, thoughtfully;
"there's a good deal to be said on both sides. I stopped
there yesterday, as I was passing, and had a little talk with
the teacher, as I told you. I liked his face and manner very
much, but the boys, and girls too, for that matter, were
very rough looking, and most of them older than our boys.
If I thought Arnold and Ernest would catch their rough
ways, I should prefer to teach them at home, with your help,
for I hate the very idea of their suffering, in any way, by this
move."

"Dear boy," said his mother, "I wished to speak of that,
too—you are letting yourself grow morbid upon this subject,

and I want you to take yourself vigorously in hand. You are not responsible—the final decision rested with me, and I assure you that, even should we be obliged to give up this plan, and turn to other things, I shall never be sorry that we tried it, for it has caused a growth, in all of you, of traits which are well worth cultivating, and setting aside all else, the improvement in our little May's health is alone enough to repay me for my share of the effort; so now I wish you to try, prayerfully, to stop this anxious brooding and forecasting, and be your own bright self again."

"I will try, mother," said Roderick, between a sigh and a smile, "but indeed I can't help feeling that, although, as you say, the final decision rested with you, the suggestion which brought about the decision was mine, and if harm should come of it to any of you, I don't know how I should bear it."

"Dear Rod," replied his mother, earnestly, "there is a proverb which says, 'Deeds are ours, results are God's.' We have all acted for the best in this, so far as we could see, and all with the feeling that almost anything was better than the breaking up and scattering of the family. All we have to do is to keep on acting for the best, a day at a time, and, as the Friends say, 'proceed as the way opens.' I have always liked that expression, for the best and wisest of mortals cannot see a day ahead, and it seems to make everything easy. Our Father knows what things we have need of; we have only to trust Him, and keep on."

"I will try—indeed I will," said Roderick, earnestly, and stooping to kiss his mother as he spoke; "my anxiety has made me selfish and you uncomfortable, and it does no good, after all."

"No," said his mother, smiling, "for 'merry heart goes all the day; sad, tires before a mile.' Faith is not faith, if it only serves us in fair weather. We have so much that no

6

ill-fortune can take away, that we can afford to be cheerful.
I feel like Cornelia, 'only more so,' as Arnold would say,
every time I look around upon my children."

"Dear little mother," said Roderick, putting his arm
about her as they walked. "You are a tower of strength to
all of us; I don't see how we *can* be anything but cheerful,
with your untroubled face shining on us."

The gentle face shone with a very loving smile at these
tender words ; nothing seemed hard or wearisome to the
mother, secure as she was in the love and confidence of her
children.

After some further talk about the school question, it was
finally settled that the boys should go to the district school
for the short remainder of the term.   Mrs. Stanley was
induced to make this decision chiefly because it seemed to
her that Roderick was already working beyond his strength,
and she thought that, if it could be avoided, his cares should
in no way be increased. She knew that he had planned and
expected to take up his own studies, so soon as the affairs of
the farm were in running order, but she noticed that, so far,
he had seemed so tired, by evening, that he had not even
unpacked his books. Everything else, excepting winter
clothing, had been unpacked and put away, but he had
begged for an exception in favor of his text-books.

"I really ought not to touch them for at least a month
to come," he had said; "but if they are where I can see
them every day, I am afraid I shall sometimes be tempted to
pick them up, when I ought to be at other things; so I
would rather leave them safely boxed in the garret, until I
can go at them with a clear conscience."

His mother had daily expected him to bring them down,
now that the bustle of their settlement was over, and the
work was assuming a definite shape, but he had not even
spoken of them.

He had just finished posting his account-book, which he kept very strictly, that evening, when Kitty came up behind him, and began smoothing his hair up into little points, saying, as she worked at it,—

"Rod, do you know what you've reminded me of, lately? The old woman who was afraid the bridge she was crossing was unsafe;—you know she said she 'held her breath, and bore up, and she knew she didn't weigh a pound.' You look all the time as if you were holding your breath, and bearing up!"

Rod caught her wrists, and drew her round to his lap. It was rarely that Miss Kitty bestowed upon any one so much, even in the way of a caress, as the whimsical endearment she was now bestowing upon her older brother, and he knew that, under the joke with which she had attacked him there was as much warm feeling as Polly would have demonstrated with a kiss and a tear.

"You're an impertinent young person to your elders, not to say betters," he said, making a pretense at boxing her ears, "but for once in your life, you're about right. I believe I have been under the impression, since we came to this wilderness, that I had you all to carry on my back, as it were, but the mother has convinced me, if I can only stay convinced, that that is not a sensible view of things. So now I am going to try to take life at retail, instead of by wholesale, to use a beautiful mercantile figure, and I hope the result will be more pleasing to my family than my recent state of mind has been."

"Dear Rod!" exclaimed this unaccountable-for Kitty, suddenly throwing both arms about his neck, and beginning to sob—"you make me so ashamed; I'm nothing but a care and a trouble to everybody, and you——" she stopped to cry for a minute, and then, finding her voice again, continued, "Polly and I have done something to-day, and you mustn't

scold—we've made you a dear little study out of the end of
the upstairs hall;—mamma said we might, but it was May
that thought of the place, and the way to do it—she's a nice
child, if she is my sister. We made a great curtain out of
the old chintz bed-hangings, and hung it on a rope—there
were lots of rings—and we've made you a perfectly *lovely*
lounge, out of the biggest packing-box and some other
things, and the boys have made some shelves, and—— but it's
mean to tell, for Polly and May and the boys are waiting up
there for you now—they sent me to call you—come on!"

And seizing his hand, she half led, half dragged him up
the wide stairs, to the cosy little room where the other conspirators were awaiting him. It was as charming a study as
any one need wish for. The one large window, commanding
a view of the river, was hung with white curtains, a thick
green shade beneath them serving to regulate the light. The
"lounge" was broad and low, without head or back, but
with three or four large square cushions to be arranged
according to fancy. A table and arm-chair, contributed
from two of the other rooms, occupied one corner; the
neatly stained book-shelves, filled with Roderick's text-books,
another. He was touched to the heart. In all his unselfish
planning and working for the others, it had never occurred
to him that any special attention should be paid to his own
wants and wishes, and as he looked round the cosy little
room, and saw the beaming faces of the plotters, his fears
and doubts were scattered by a sudden rush of happy
feeling.

"I can't embrace you all at once," he said, dropping on
the lounge as he spoke: "but I'll take you in relays, ladies
first, of course—come on!"

The girls fell upon him with overwhelming affection, and
then the boys followed suit; it did not occur to any of them
that there was anything unmanly in the hearty kiss which

Roderick bestowed upon each of his brothers, and which they returned with equal heartiness.

The faces around the tea-table that night shone with unusual brightness, and it seemed to Roderick that his new resolution would not, under the circumstances, be a very difficult one to keep.

CHAPTER VII.

"Hope rules a land forever green ;
All powers that serve the bright-eyed queen
    Are confident and gay ;
Clouds at her bidding disappear ;
Points she to aught ?—the bliss draws near,
    And fancy smooths the way."—WORDSWORTH.

THE Stanleys were coming now to the real testing-time
of their experiment. The season had been unusually
backward for that latitude, which had made it possible to
plant a good many things for which they had not hoped that
year. Roderick had done nothing of any importance without
first consulting Colonel Peyton, for he had a gift which comes
next to knowledge—a perfect consciousness of his ignorance,
and he was more than willing to take advice. He had hesitated a little at first about troubling his kind neighbor about
his affairs, but he so soon became assured of the hearty
interest which the Colonel felt, and of his eagerness to help
in any way, that he fell in the habit of carrying his per-
plexities to Rivermouth, sure of a kindly hearing, and of
sound and practical counsel. He had been greatly troubled
by the incorrigible laziness and pilfering habits of the
negroes, but, after a number of changes, had at last secured
an honest and industrious "head-man," who was hired by
the year. The Colonel recommended him to engage other
workmen as he should need them, by the week or month, as
there was no danger of any scarcity, and, excepting for two
or three months at most, one capable man would probably
be enough, for, wherever it was possible, vegetables had been
planted in rows sufficiently wide apart to admit a horse and

"cultivator" between them, this leaving but little hoeing to be done.

Wild strawberries grew in abundance along the edges of the wood-lot, and the boys and May had begged a corner of the vegetable-garden and made a strawberry bed, in firm faith that cultivation would in time produce mammoth berries! They had also brought home from the woods, and set in the door-yard, many wild-flower roots, some of which had thriven, while others utterly refused to be civilized, and died in the most abject and discouraging manner. The beautiful Virginian creeper, which the farmers in the neighborhood regarded as a weed, had been planted on all sides of the house, and was thriving well; many roots of the "five-fingered ivy," too, were flourishing, and the two together gave promise of turning the mansion into a bower, in time. The fruit-trees and vines and bushes were looking surprisingly well, considering the long neglect which they had suffered, but the skillful pruning which they had had this year had not been without its effect, and the children were looking forward impatiently to the ripening of the fruit. Even the "grown-ups" acknowledged that they would be very glad of it, for, in spite of light bread, sweet butter, and every variety of corn-bread, from hoe-cake to pone, there was a good deal of monotony in the daily fare, which was too frequently, by force of circumstances, little more than the proverbial hog and hominy, so far as substantials went. Elizabeth varied the exercise as much as she could, with delicate desserts, made from their abundant supply of milk and cream, but even here she did not feel wholly at liberty, for the various expenses incident to starting the enterprise had, as a matter of course, exceeded the estimate made beforehand, and economy was eminently necessary.

"I wish I could 'swap' some of Bonny's milk for groceries, mamma," said Elizabeth, one day, as she bore a great pan of "clabber" from the dairy to the table.

"I wish you could, dear," replied her mother; "but I don't believe even our most accommodating tradesman at the Corners would be willing to make such a trade as that!"

No more was said at the time, but the remark and answer set Elizabeth thinking. So far, they had only made butter for their own use, with an occasional pound, done up in fanciful little prints, as an offering of affection to Mrs. Peyton. Before they discovered exactly how much was needed for the weekly supply, they had once or twice fallen short, and been obliged to purchase a pound or two at the country store. It had been cheap enough for good butter, but so startlingly bad that they had resolved to go without, when they had not their own, and they had been surprised to find that, even at Mrs. Peyton's otherwise well furnished table, the butter was almost uneatable. Elizabeth thought the matter over for a day or two, and then quietly proceeded to gather cream for an extra churning.

"The clabber is quite good enough for you without cream on it, my dears," she said to the dogs, as she filled their pan; and, judging by the way in which it was devoured, they quite agreed with her.

One of the first pieces of work which had been undertaken after the completion of the boundary fence, was a substitute for a spring house, for the need of a cellar had already begun to be greatly felt. With help from Joshua and the "headman," a small building was put up, near enough to the well for a moderately-long trough to convey water to it. The well water was deliciously cold, and excepting in very hot weather, it would only be necessary to renew it twice a day, in the shallow wooden troughs which ran around the inside of the milk-house. These Roderick had made just wide enough for the milk-pans to set in them. He meant in time to dig a sort of vault in the middle of the house, and line it with bricks; but this could very well be deferred, for so far the milk and butter kept very nicely, and the milk-house was found useful for other articles of food. A large tin bucket, hung down the well, was used for keeping fresh meat, when they were so fortunate as to have any, which was not quite so often as they wished. The cold water arrangement enabled Elizabeth to gather enough cream, in two or three days, for several pounds of butter, without at all stinting the family. She took special pains with it, and stamped it with her most ornamental prints; then she lined a basket with freshly washed grape-vine leaves, and packed the butter daintily. She confided her project to Arnold, who willingly agreed to take it to the store for her, and should the store-keeper be willing to "trade," to bring back the result.

He returned in triumph, with sugar, spices, one or two bottles of flavoring extracts, and a dozen lemons, and also with the pleasing information that the grocer would be glad to have as much of "such butter as that" every week. He had allowed thirty cents a pound for it, and said that he might give more, if he found he could command a better price for it than he usually asked. This was good news indeed, for although everything was dearer here than in large cities, the cost of transportation made it useless to send for small supplies. The groceries which they had brought with them were not yet exhausted, but Elizabeth had felt that she ought not to draw on these for desserts and cake, at least until they knew a little better where they stood. She felt quite at liberty to use whatever she could make by her butter-enterprise, to make the table more attractive. The boys and May were growing fast, and had good hearty appetites, but even to hungry people monotony is unpleasant, and Elizabeth did not disdain to make the table one of the attractive features of the house. It was always daintily set, and

adorned with flowers whenever any were to be had, and the
boys instinctively made themselves neat before coming
to it. Mrs. Stanley never would have any hurry about the
meals; pleasant talk often made the family linger around
the table, but the time was not lost; they all went back to
their work, or their studies, with fresh energy, and worked
the better for the rest and change of thought.

Elizabeth announced her new enterprise when she helped
the family to the first dessert which was the result of it, and
every one but Roderick seemed pleased. He looked a little
disturbed, but did not say anything until the next time that
Elizabeth and he were alone together. Then he said—

"I'm afraid I don't quite approve of your butter-enterprise, Betty; you have your full share to do without that,
and I certainly ought to be able to provide what is needed
for the table."

"Now, Rod, don't be foolish!" said Elizabeth, appealingly; "Aunt Judy did the churning; I only worked the
butter and printed it, and that is nothing but fun. I really
enjoy it. And I'd like to know why I shouldn't turn an
honest penny any way I can, if I am a girl. I am going to
insist on 'equal rights' about some things, and you must
not interfere with me!"

"I suppose you'll have your way, in spite of my will,"
said Roderick, with a doubtful smile and emphatic kiss;
"but I shall keep a sharp eye on you, and if I see you sinking under this additional care, I shall find means to put a
stop to it."

"I agree to that entirely," she replied merrily; "I never
felt better in my life than I do at this present writing."

When the butter basket went to the store the following
week, the storekeeper voluntarily offered five cents more on
each pound, and asked if Miss Stanley could not manage to
spare him two or three pounds more every week; he said

he could have sold quite that much, and that one or two people had wished to engage it for every week. Arnold said he could make no engagement without consulting his sister; he had his list, and found the butter money quite filled it ; indeed, the storekeeper said, there was a dollar to their credit.

"Could I have the dollar, then?" asked Arnold; "we don't want anything more this week, and I think my sister would rather have the money anyhow."

"Well, no, sonny," replied the grocer, in apologetic tones; "you see, it's not the custom to do business that way; everything I take from the farmers around, it's understood that *they're* to take it out in trade."

"Then you make a double profit?" said Arnold, laughing; "I see!"

The man laughed too, with easy good-nature, and Arnold turned to leave the store, but, struck with a new idea, he went back and said: "Will you please tell me the names of those people who would like our butter every week?"

"One was old Miss Carroll," replied Mr. Joyce, "and another was Mrs. Summerville—she lives down to the Cove, and takes a few boarders, when she can get 'em—there was another wanted it bad, but I disremember the name—it'll come to me, perhaps. Why, was your sister thinking of serving it round?"

"Not that I know of," said Arnold; "but it seems to me it would almost pay to do it, if she's willing."

"You're a right smart little chap, I declare!" said Mr. Joyce, admiringly, "and I don't blame you; but still, I'd be sorry to lose that butter—it sorter fetched people to the store, and they most always buy something they didn't set out to! See here—you tell Miss Stanley that, seeing it's her, I'll give her thirty cents a pound, money down, and she can spend it here, or not, as she likes. How'll that answer?"

"I'll tell her," said Arnold, "and let you know this week. I don't know which she'd rather do, but I'm pretty sure she would rather have the money than to 'trade.' Good-morning."

Elizabeth was greatly pleased with the result of Arnold's negotiations, but she was not yet ready to go the whole length of his enthusiasm; she thought it would be better to accept the thirty cents cash for the present, and she hoped to put by at least half of it, for, with a little care in the management of the milk and cream, she could make two or three pounds more butter every week than she was making now. Arnold was somewhat disappointed.

"You're not living up to your opportunities, Betty!" he said, impatiently; "here when the gilt-edged butter vision is actually beginning to be realized, you're turning faint-hearted about it! The Dutchman would let me have his horse for fifty cents for the whole afternoon, and I'll bet a hat Mr. Joyce got forty cents for that butter."

"Yes," said Elizabeth, smiling at his enthusiasm, "and Miss Carroll lives five miles away, in one direction, and Mrs. Summerville four in another, and Joshua's horse goes at a rate of about three miles an hour! So you must imagine your time to be worth absolutely nothing, in which I am sure Rod would not agree with you."

"Don't you think Kit and Polly might go, when I have something better to do?" asked Arnold, still unquenched.

"They would doubtless regard it as a magnificent 'lark,' as you would say," answered Elizabeth, "but I'm afraid, mamma and Rod would not agree with them, and I'm quite certain I shouldn't. No, dear; I admire your ambition, and even share it, but I mean to wait until the way opens. When we have a horse of our own, and some sort of con-veyance beside an open cart, and when we have one or two more cows, and can make twenty or thirty pounds of butter a week, I shall be quite willing to join you in the enterprise; but for awhile we must remember that 'he who goes softly goes safely,' and be content with quick returns and small profits."

"I suppose you're right, because you're so disagreeable!" said Arnold, contradicting his words with a hug and kiss, "but you and Rod are getting to be too elderly for anything —I shall be obliged to take up with Kit and Polly."

"You'd better take up with your lessons, just at present," said Elizabeth, "or you may find Mr. Kendall even more disagreeable than I am, to-morrow morning."

The twenty-fifth of July was Elizabeth's nineteenth birthday, and there were various small conspiracies about keeping it among the children, in all of which the mother was a more or less silent partner. It was impossible to make any preparations which involved the outlay of much money, so they all set their wits to work upon home-made presents. Roderick was not "handy with his hands," as Aunt Judy said, so he chose one of his few remaining books for his offering, and Elizabeth accepted it without a remonstrance and with warm thanks—putting herself, by a great effort of her imagination, in his place.

Kitty hated sewing with a frank and cordial hatred, but she had cheerfully joined Polly in working at an elaborate contrivance combining the beauties of a shoe box and an ottoman. She voluntarily hemmed the deep ruffles which adorned the cover, and as she had not yet learned to use the sewing-machine, and was obliged to sew very slowly to make her work neat, it involved no little self-denial. Arnold and Ernest combined the remainder of their Christmas purses, trusting to good fortune for their replenishment, and took a walk of several miles to a neighboring farm, returning in triumph with a beautiful pair of Muscovy ducks. Elizabeth had expressed a wish for them, not knowing that there were any within reach. May had spent all her spare time for many weeks in knitting a silk purse, and the mother had contrived to knit a pretty white shawl, in the times when she was popularly supposed to be taking naps. Even Aunt Judy caught the enthusiasm, and proudly set upon the tea-table a beautiful iced pound-cake, which she had made the evening before, after she had gone home for the night.

"But, Aunt Judy, how did you manage to bake it so beautifully, when you have no stove?" asked Elizabeth, when it had been duly admired and praised.

Aunt Judy laughed the laugh of superior wisdom.

"And doesn't you know, Missy," she said, "dat dere's no sweeter way to bake muffin dan in de kittle, wid good hick'ry coals jist hot enough underneaf? Stoves is handy, dere's no denyin' dat, but for prime bakin', I'll take de coals ebery time."

The perfect evenness with which the cake was baked justified Aunt Judy's prejudice in favor of "kittles" and coals, and her little round, black eyes twinkled with delight as, peeping around the partition, and in at the door, she saw the manner in which her offering disappeared, and heard Elizabeth say gently—

"We must leave a slice apiece for Aunt Judy and Clara— it was so *very* nice of the old aunty to make it."

They were sitting in the wide hall after tea, just inside the front door, discussing plans and prospects. So far, things looked very encouraging. There would be much more fruit, even this first year, than they would need for immediate use, and for putting up for winter; the vegetable garden was beginning to yield nicely, and the pasture was looking rich and green. Arnold and Ernest, with persevering industry and two long, old kitchen knives, had gone over the pasture and mowing-lot again and again, uprooting the weeds as they appeared, and now the reward was beginning to come.

"By your next birthday, Betty, my dear," Roderick said cheerfully, "we shall have the veranda, if all goes well, with the vestibule in the middle, and perhaps we can even venture to give you some imported birthday presents."

"I don't wish any better presents than I've had to-day," said Elizabeth, with a look of great contentment; "I never enjoyed a birthday more, or had things I liked better. After all, I think cheap pleasures are the pleasantest—if one once begins on dear things, there are always others, so much dearer, just beyond."

"Spoken like a philosopheress," said Roderick, and added with a sudden change of tone—

"Hallo! what's all this?"

It was a heavily loaded wagon, which drew up at the door, and the negro-driver, touching his hat politely, said—

"Dis Miss Stanley's, isn't it?"

Upon being assured that it was, he got down, and walked up the steps, saying—

"Hab to hab a little help, Missus—de pianner's powerful big lift."

Roderick went quickly to the wagon, thinking there must have been some mistake; but no, the great packing-case was directed, clearly and fully, to

"Miss Elizabeth Stanley;"

so one of the boys ran to see if their factotum, Moses, had gone home for the night. He had not, fortunately, for it took their united forces to carry the great case up the steps and into the parlor. Everybody stood about in eager excitement, while Roderick brought chisel and hammer, and dexterously opened it. It was a piano, "sure enough," as the children said—not a "Steinway Grand," but a beautiful

little upright one, which harmonized with the furnishings
of the parlor as if it had been made to order. The children
were wild with excitement, and could hardly wait for it to be
set up. As soon as it was in place, the packing-case carried
into the hall, and the driver of the wagon paid and dismissed,
Elizabeth was conducted in triumph to the music-stool ;—
the fact that the latter, and a pretty little music-rack filled
with carefully selected music, had been packed with the
piano, accounted for the size of the box. One old favorite
after another was called for, and glees and choruses followed
each other in rapid succession, while Mrs. Stanley sat happily listening, and occasionally asking for some "number"
which she especially loved. Eleven o'clock struck before
they thought it was nine, and then the mother gently bade
Elizabeth play the evening hymn, and for the first time she
rose and joined her voice with theirs.

No one doubted from whom the gift had come, but if any
one had, a card found in the case would have settled the
doubt. It was one of Mr. Stanley's, and on the back of
it was written :

"For my dear niece Elizabeth, from her loving uncle
George, who wishes all the Green Point eagles to remember
that when they deign to accept a gift, they return it in
the blessing which is promised to the giver."

The "eagles" had said a few words about "too large an
obligation," but this silenced them, and with very happy
and contented hearts, they betook themselves to bed.

CHAPTER VIII.

"The angry word suppress'd, the taunting thoughts
Subduing, and subdued the petty strife
Which clouds the color of domestic life ;
The sober comfort, all the peace which springs
From the large aggregate of little things ;
On these small cares of daughter, wife or friend
The almost sacred joys of home depend."—HANNAH MORE.

IT was becoming very evident that the farm required at
least one permanent horse, and it was decided in full
counsel that the money which was beginning to collect, over
and above the running expenses of the house, since the sales
of fruit had begun, should be devoted to this purpose just
as soon as it reached the required sum. Here again Colonel
Peyton's advice was invaluable, for Roderick knew very well
that any moderately sharp horse-dealer could succeed in imposing on him. The Colonel recommended that the search
should begin at once, for it would be rather difficult to meet
all the requirements, each member of the family having
made a special stipulation.

"He must be *perfectly* gentle and quiet," said Mrs.
Stanley, "and not in the least afraid of the cars—or anything!"

"He must be willing to stand without being tied," said
Elizabeth, thinking of her butter project.

"He must be a good strong draft horse," said Roderick,
thinking of the farm work and the saw-mill.

"He must be a first rate saddle-horse, and used to the
side-saddle," said the twins.

"He must be a hunter, and know how to jump fences,"

7

said Arnold and Ernest, to the great amusement of the rest of the family.

"He must be a low horse," said May, "for I mean to ride him, and I dare say I shall fall off once or twice, while I am learning."

An animal was at last found, that united many of the desired qualities. A beautiful gray, of Norman descent, heavily built and apparently very strong. He was better adapted for field work and driving, than for riding, but he had been ridden a little, and did not appear to object to the saddle. His trot was distantly suggestive of an earthquake, under the saddle, but Roderick and the boys, at least, could stand it, and powers of work and endurance were the first essentials. The money was not quite ready when he was discovered, but his owner, who was anxious to dispose of him, and had had no other offer, promised not to let any one else have him without first informing Roderick.

Elizabeth had a project of her own, for which she was putting by all the butter money which she did not appropriate to the table, and to such little comforts and conveniences as made housekeeping easier. She was determined to buy a second cow, and go into the butter business in earnest. She liked it; so far, Aunt Judy, instead of objecting to the extra work, had taken quite a pride in it, declaring that she never before had seen such butter in Delaware as "Miss 'Lizabeth and me" turned out every week. Once or twice, when her other work had overtaken her, she had called in a small and indescribably ragged boy or girl from "the bush," and, after subjecting her victim to an unmerciful scrubbing and a change of raiment from her own accumulated stock of well washed rags, had set him, or her, as the case might be, at the churning. When Elizabeth had suggested a small specie payment as only just, she had waxed as indignant as was possible to her easy good nature.

" You'll just please to go 'long, Miss 'Lizabeth," she said, on one of these occasions; "he aint had sich a scrubbin as I made him give heself, since he bawn, and I's got a hanker-cher full o' cold cawn-bread ready for him soon as de butter comes—wite folks wouldn't tech it, naterally, but it'll be turkey an' stuffin' to him—*my* cawn-bread will ; it's made outen Bonny's best clabber, a pan I sot a' purpose, no cream ben took off it!"

Elizabeth insisted upon adding some cold wheat-flour bis-cuit and a couple of gingerbread to the "hankercher," and from that time forth, two or three candidates presented themselves every morning, inquiring anxiously if there were any churning to be done. The temptation of the eatables had triumphed over an inherent hatred of soap and water.

Aunt Judy took it good-naturedly for two or three days ; then she arose in her wrath, and "shoo'd" the intruders off the place, as if they had been marauding pigs.

"When I wants help, I'll ask for it!" she screamed, as three pairs of black heels whipped over the top bar of the fence ; "so don't let me see no more of you fool niggers, widout you's sent for."

"Now, Miss 'Lizabeth," she said, coming back breathless and indignant, "you'll know better nex' time. I knowed what I was about, when I on'y gave 'em cawn-bread ; I'd a' had any one of 'em agin, fur askin' ; but now, wid your wite-bread and cakes, we'se gwine to have our lives pestered outen us. Not fur long, dough—dey'll find a stick be-hine de doah, nex' time!"

Perhaps a rumor of this dire threat penetrated the bush, for, although Aunt Judy could always find a churner when she wanted one, no more candidates offered themselves. Elizabeth always washed and worked the butter herself, and took a genuine pleasure and pride in her work. May was her

faithful and ready assistant, and delighted in making the
little butter-balls and dainty pats with which the table was
always adorned. Lessons had been given up, when Mr.
Kendall's school closed. Up to that time, May and Kitty
and Polly had recited to Elizabeth all their lessons, excepting Latin, French, and German ; May only "took" Latin
as an extra, so far; but all three of the girls were learning
the other two languages as well, and the latter was recited
to Mrs. Stanley, who was an excellent German scholar ;
Roderick heard their French and Latin lessons, and cor-
rected their exercises. The lessons were purposely made
short and easy, but Mrs. Stanley required that they should
be thoroughly learned, and when any were missed, the unfortunate who had failed was "kept in" as strictly as if the
school had been a public one, until the lesson had been
learned and said. Neither Elizabeth or Roderick attempted
to exercise any authority over the younger ones, in this or
in anything else; the mother was the head, and all vexed
questions were instantly referred to her. Kitty had given
more trouble than all the rest put together. It was her
nature to defy any and all authority, and it did not suit her
ladyship at all that her brother and sister, so little her su-
periors in age, should have even a semblance of authority
over her.

Poor Polly's life was too often made a burden to her, by
the struggle between her naturally sweet and docile disposition and her blind admiration for her double ; and one day,
when Kitty had been more than usually fractious and unreasonable, Polly, without in the least intending it, had conquered by her tears.

"I don't care!" Kitty had said, excitedly, when she and
Polly were left alone in the dining-room, which generally
served as school-room as well; "I knew that geography
lesson perfectly, this morning, but after I tripped in one

question, Betty looked as if she expected me to miss all the
rest, so I thought I'd just gratify her!"

"Oh Kitty!" exclaimed Polly, piteously, "how *could* you
—when you knew Rod had Joshua's horse and wagon, and
was going to drive us all to the saw-mill, as soon as we'd
said our lessons."

"Bless my heart!" exclaimed the rebel, struck with sudden contrition, "I forgot every bit about that! I suppose
it serves me right, so run along, Poll, and tell Betty not to
worry about my lesson—she can hear it when she comes
back, and I'll darn all her stockings, while she's gone, by way
of penance. There are some truly awful ones; I sorted the
wash this week, and I know!"

"But I'm not going with the rest, to leave you all alone;
it would be too despicably mean," said Polly, beginning to
cry, partly from sympathy with the offender, and partly
from real disappointment, for the trip to the saw-mill had
been looked forward to for several days.

"Now, look here, Pauline Stanley," said Kitty, with sudden fierceness, put on to hide her own feelings and convince
Polly, "I want to look over my lesson in peace, and medi-
tate on my sinful folly while I darn the stockings, and I
can't do either with your woe begone face before my eyes. I
should very much prefer to have you safely out of my way;
so if you really wish to oblige me, you'll stop crying, and
kiss me good-by, and go wash your face and get into the
wagon."

"Are you quite in earnest?" asked Polly, doubtfully, but
brightening perceptibly as she spoke.

"More so than usual," replied Kitty, nodding her head
severely; "so now leave me in peace, and go."

Polly went, lingeringly and reluctantly, but she could not
help enjoying the expedition. Lessons had been said directly
after dinner that day, for a late tea had been bespoken, and

nobody would wish either to hear or recite after that was over, so there was a holiday feeling to add pleasure to the drive. Every one lamented about Kitty, and Mrs. Stanley with difficulty kept her resolution to enforce the rule agreed upon; but just as they were starting, the culprit's face appeared at the dining-room window, and a parcel of ginger-bread, shot with unerring aim, landed in Elizabeth's lap.

"You're all so ethereal," called Kitty, mockingly, "that it didn't occur to you that you would all be ravenous when you were about half way home. You needn't pine about me—I never did care much for saw-mills, anyhow!"

But when they returned, Kitty recited her lesson with ease and fluency, and handed her mother the stocking-basket with every pair of socks and stockings neatly mended. Mrs. Stanley gave an approving smile and kiss, but she whispered to Kitty,

"Was the game worth the candle, dear?"

"Speaking confidentially, mamma, I'll admit that it was quite the reverse," Kitty whispered back.

"Then I wouldn't play it again, if I were you," said her mother; and Kitty answered gravely—

"I wish you *could* be me for a week, mamma; I should so like to see what you would do!"

But from that time she gave less trouble about her lessons, and a look of distress on Polly's face often served to check her unruly spirit; she was beginning to perceive the selfishness of sin—even of those sins which people call small ones.

There was a general sense of relief when the holidays came. So many deeply interesting things were waiting to be done out of doors, that staying in the house seemed like imprisonment. The door-yard was beginning to repay its cultivators with soft, rich grass, and several varieties of flowers. Some few currants, gooseberries and raspberries yet remained to be picked, and wild blackberries of delicious flavor were abundant. The pantry was beginning to show a goodly array of preserves, canned fruit, and pickles; Elizabeth's butter money having paid for the requisite sugar. There would be no difficulty in varying the table supplies next winter, and, with plenty of preserves and sauces, the inevitable pork and ham would not become so tiresome. Still, Roderick meant to have fresh meat more frequently than he had heretofore been able to provide it. He had enclosed a corner of the pasture land, and bought a dozen sheep, although by doing so the purchase of the horse must be a little deferred ; and the chicken yard gave promise of varying the exercises very pleasantly. The care of the chickens and ducks and geese was May's especial delight, and she was keeping a careful record of the number of eggs collected daily, the hens which were set, and the broods hatched. Mrs. Peyton and she held long counsels together on this subject, and exchanges of treasured eggs were frequently made. May's chief pride was a brood of little turkeys—which an unsuspecting hen had hatched, and now led about with great contentment, apparently ignorant of the fact that her children came of an alien race. There were ten of them, and May had them all prophetically disposed of the day after they were hatched.

"We will have one for Christmas, of course," she said, "and one for New Year's, and one for mamma's birthday—that's three ; and we must keep a cock and two of the little hens, so that we may have some to sell next year—that's six ; and I want to send one to Mrs. Peyton, and one to Uncle George, just before Christmas, because they've been so kind —that's eight ; and the other two I shall sell, if mamma is willing, for Christmas-money."

"Mamma is quite willing," said Mrs. Stanley, smiling ; "you have taken all the trouble of them, and shall dispose of them as you like; but although they are hatched, they are not yet grown up, and Mrs. Peyton says they are more difficult to raise than any other sort of poultry."

"Oh, but, mamma, she says they are more easily raised when they have a hen-mother than when they have a turkey-mother," said May, confidently; "and I mean to take such pains with them that I don't see how they *can* die!"

"They can 'die easy,' as Aunt Judy says she hopes to," Arnold put in.

"No; if they die at all, they shall die hard," said May, resolutely.

"Cruel creature!" responded Arnold.

Mr. Stanley and Edith had hoped to begin their visit in the latter part of June, but business had detained the former in town, and his daughter entirely declined his proposal that she should precede him.

"And leave you to the tender mercies of a cook and a housekeeper!" said Edith, indignantly. "I should like to know what you take me for, papa. You'd be eating green cucumbers, and sitting in draughts, and wearing your red flannels instead of your gauze merinos, and dear knows what beside! No; I am going to lie on sofas, and read inoffensive novels—Miss Thackery's, and *sich*—and try to recover the tone of my mind before I go among all those wide awake people. That last examination came near permanently unsettling my reason."

"I wish you'd give up this graduating business, dear," said Mr. Stanley, uneasily. "If your dear mother were living she would know how to have you educated without this high-pressure; I am heartily sorry now that I ever sent away the governess and allowed you to go to that French school. If the last year should be worse than this has been—and I suppose it will be—I don't see how you are going to stand it."

"Oh, I shall pull through somehow, as all the rest of them

do, I suppose," said Edith, lightly. "You must allow a little for my figures of speech, you know, papa; and I am going to spend such a strictly rational summer, that I shall be equal to anything next fall. I have a misgiving that it will be somewhat stupid as well as rational. I wish you hadn't committed us for six weeks."

"I'm not much of a prophet," said Mr. Stanley, smiling, "but I am quite willing, upon this occasion, to risk a prophecy that you'll be begging for an extension, before the six weeks are over, my lady!"

Miss Mackenzie, reassured by her sister's cheerful letters, and dreading the journey, had decided to defer her visit till autumn. Notwithstanding the good reports, she could not help fancying that the place was a sort of modified Siberia; so her resolution to stay all winter, if she should find that she was not adding to their cares, was truly heroic. It was as well, from one point of view, that her visit was deferred, for neither the time nor the money had as yet been at Roderick's disposal for having the garrets plastered, and the four bedrooms would be little enough for the family of ten people during Mr. Stanley's and Edith's visit.

Arrangements were being discussed one evening, just before the arrival of the visitors, and it was proposed that Roderick should occupy the cot, either in his "study" or in a corner of the boys' room, that his room might be given to his uncle.

"I think I will give the study the preference," he said; "my lounge will make a delightful bed, and that will leave the cot for somebody else—it will be needed. Beside, I am sorry to say that my relish for pillow fights and cold-pigging has become dulled with advancing years."

"You don't know what you're missing, young man!" said Ernest, with a grin; "but it's your own loss, so go ahead."

"Then the cot can be put in my room," said Mrs. Stanley. "May can sleep on it, and either Kitty or Polly with me."

The rooms were all large, and a single bedstead for Elizabeth had easily found space in a corner of her mother's room.

"Oh mamma!" said Kitty, beseechingly; "Polly and I had counted on having Edith in our room. Can't the cot be put up there, and let her choose whether she'll sleep on it or the bed? You'd be dreadfully crowded with anybody more in your room."

"Perhaps I should," said Mrs. Stanley, laughing; "and your arrangement certainly makes things more even, so we will let it stand that way, unless I should find that you keep each other awake all night with your talking."

The promised line of "truck-boats" had begun to run in the latter part of June—too late for the strawberries, but this did not affect our farmers, for they had none to send. The boats touched at a small landing about a mile down the river, and so far, Moses, assisted by Roderick and the boys, had managed to carry in baskets on the wheelbarrow, all that could be spared from the place; but it was heavy work, and would be impossible, when the grapes, pears and apples, of which there was fair promise, should be ready for market. The truck-boats had some accommodation for passengers, and Mr. Stanley and Edith had decided to come on one of them, rather than give Roderick the long drive to meet them, either at the railway station or steamboat landing. They only ran three times a week as yet, on Monday, Wednesday and Friday, but Roderick had heard that, upon sufficient encouragement, they would run daily, and he fully intended, by the following season, to do his share of the encouraging. So far, the vegetables and fruit had sold remarkably well, and this was owing to the great care which was bestowed upon the picking and packing. Roderick was amused by discovering, accidentally, that he was popularly reported, among the negroes, to have eyes in the back of his head, and he did nothing to discourage the superstition. His mother often wondered, that summer, at his tireless energy and far-seeing thoughtfulness. He no longer looked worried and oppressed, and he took every opportunity that he conscientiously could to go on with his studies, but he profited by Colonel Peyton's slightest hint, while making careful investigations and cautious experiments for himself. He, in turn, wondered at the perseverance and steadiness of the boys; he did not know how often they encouraged each other with the remark that "it would be a shame to back down when Betty and Rod kept ahead at such a rate!" Arnold was much inclined to put off till the last possible minute whatever he had to do, and this failing sometimes made trouble, but he was fighting the bad habit manfully, and with good success. Taking it altogether, Roderick thought his uncle would be pleased with the result of the experiment thus far, and he and the boys worked over-hours, to have everything in "apple-pie order" before he should come, partly that they might have the more time to devote to him and their cousin.

Joshua's best horse and most respectable wagon were hired to bring the travelers from the landing; carriage he had none, but the wagon was clean and moderately comfortable, and to Edith the delights of novelty, to which she had been looking forward with eager interest, quite compensated for any small sacrifices of ease. In consideration of the luggage, which must also come in the wagon, only Arnold went with Roderick to the landing; the rest were standing, a happy, eager group, just outside the open door, watching the wagon drive through the substantial gateway, as Ernest flung the gate wide open. Mr. Stanley looked about him in pleased surprise, as they drove along.

"Why boys!" he said, heartily; "I thought you did wonders while I was down here, but you've surpassed yourselves since then. The place looks as if you had lived here for years."

"*I'm* disappointed,' said Edith, saucily; "I've been led to expect a wilderness and ruins, and a general scene of desolation, and here's a stately country residence, with well-kept grounds, and such a family of fat and rosy cheeked people that I feel positively ashamed of my leanness and paleness."

"We'll try to make you like the rest of us, dear," said Mrs. Stanley, as she took Edith in her arms; "plenty of out-door air, and good sleep, and good bread and butter and milk will make you show a different face before you go home."

Aunt Judy's delight at having some more "quality wite folks" upon whom to exercise her skill, had made her "explite herself," as she termed it, with the supper.

"Now these are real corn muffins," said Mr. Stanley, as he helped himself to a fourth "such as my mother used to make. The things that cooks of the present day call muffins are little hard cakes with shiny tops—not these melting morsels, and I'll give you a five-pound box of chocolates, Edith, if you can tell me what makes the difference?"

"You don't know yourself, papa!" said Edith, audaciously. "What is it, aunty?" and she turned with an engaging smile to Aunt Judy, who, upon all festive occasions, managed not only to attend to the cooking, but to take a share in the waiting, and so hear the praises of her dainties.

"Dese is baked on a griddle, miss, in rings," said Aunt Judy, with a grin of delight and a deep courtesy, "an' you tuns 'em wid a knife, soon's one side's done. Folks what don't know nuffin 'bout cookin' sets de rings in pans, and bakes 'em in de oven, till dey's all over hard crusses."

"You shall show me how while I'm here," said Edith, "and then I'll teach the cook when I go home."

Nothing could so effectually have conquered Aunt Judy as this tribute. She was Edith's devoted slave for the remainder of the visit, and only an occasional gentle remonstrance from Mrs. Stanley or Elizabeth kept her from a wasteful extravagance in her cooking, by way of showing off her skill.

The evening sped delightfully with talk and singing and planning for the coming weeks, and, but for Mrs. Stanley's gentle authority, would have lasted far into the night. Mr. Stanley was old enough to know that he was tired, and finally began to push Edith to the door by her shoulders, as he saw that there was a fair prospect of their "saying good-night until to-morrow."

"Come, come!" he said, with affected sternness, "'Early to bed and early to rise——''"

"''Makes a man boast in a way I despise !'" finished Edith for him, as she ran upstairs.

Most of the family had fallen asleep, when a loud crash, followed by what sounded like smothered screams, roused them effectually. The sounds seemed to come from the girls' room, and an anxious group, variously attired in hastily snatched-up garments, was soon at the door.

"Girls, what has happened? Let me in at once!" said Mrs. Stanley. Polly's nightly fears of enterprising burglars always made her vigilant about fastenings. The bolt was slipped back, but the door only opened a few inches, and Kitty's face appeared.

"*Please* don't come in, mamma!" she said, appealingly; "nothing much has happened, but Edith's so ashamed!"

"I might have guessed that she was at the bottom of it," said Mr. Stanley, then coming nearer the door. "Edith! tell me at once what you did to cause this uproar."

His voice was so stern that Kitty was frightened, and laid
a beseeching hand on his arm, saying,

"Oh, please, don't scold her, uncle dear; it was quite an
accident, and not her fault at all—she couldn't help it."

"But I insist upon knowing what it was," said Mr. Stanley, a little less sternly, and Kitty hesitatingly answered—

"She said she was so glad to be here, and that school was
over, and all, that she must have a little exercise, or she
couldn't sleep; so she went to the other end of the room to
get a good start, and took a flying leap into bed, and it broke
down—she had chosen to sleep in the cot."

"I'll mend it to-morrow, papa," said a meek voice which
seemed to come from the floor, "and I can sleep beautifully
with the mattress spread on the floor; it will make me dream
I am again a child."

"You'd better dream you are almost a woman," said her
father, trying to speak sternly, but not succeeding very well;
"if there's any more racket in this room, I shall ask your
aunt to give you a solitary cell in the garret."

Mrs. Stanley wished to make some better arrangement
for Edith's comfort than the mattress on the floor, but her
brother drew her away, saying decidedly,

"No, my dear sister, you shall lose no more rest upon her
account; she has made her bed, literally, so now let her lie
in it."

CHAPTER IX.

"She is most fair, and thereunto
Her life doth rightly harmonize;
Feeling or thought that was not true
Ne'er made less beautiful the blue
Unclouded heaven of her eyes."—LOWELL.

IN telling the story of so large a family as that which I am chronicling, it is necessary sometimes to go back a little to pick up dropped stitches. When Roderick had called to investigate the school, he had been, as he told his mother, very much pleased with the master, Mr. Kendall, and he had cordially invited him to Green Point. Several weeks had elapsed before the invitation was accepted. Mr. Kendall's boarding-place was nearly five miles distant from Green Point, and, as he kept no horse, a call upon his new neighbors involved no slight expenditure of time, and time to him, just now, was rather precious. Roderick would have been even more drawn toward him had he known that Mr. Kendall, like himself, was studying engineering under difficulties. He was one of a large family, and his father having, with some self-denial, given him a collegiate education, was able to do but little more for him. But this did not in the least daunt John Kendall in his determination to achieve a profession. When he left college he took, for a year or two, whatever honest work he could find for his head or his hands, and, being used to "plain living and high thinking," he found, before the end of the second year, that, by a rigid course of economy, he had saved enough to warrant him in beginning his studies, if he could find some occupation that would pay his board. Hearing by accident of this remote school, he had applied for it, bringing such excellent testimonials that he was accepted over the heads of several other candidates, some of whom were older and more experienced than himself. He was fortunate in finding a boarding-place not a mile away, where he could be tolerably comfortable, and where, before the winter was over, he was doing several things which served to partly work out his board. The man in whose house he boarded kept a country store, but he had no knowledge whatever of book-keeping, and his accounts were in a perpetual muddle. Young Kendall undertook to show him a simple and exact way of keeping his accounts, but Mr. Downey's head did not seem quite equal to it.

"I'm first-rate at unloading the wagons and lifting the boxes and kags," he said, laughing good-naturedly at his own blunders, "but I never did feel to brag much about my head-piece—but I'll tell you what it is, young man," and his face suddenly brightened, "I'll dock a dollar a week off your board, if you'll kind o' straighten up my accounts every day or two. I can give you the what-you-may-call-ems— the memorandums, every night, slate and all; it don't seem no trouble to you to sort things out."

To this liberal proposal Kendall readily agreed, and when, in the course of the winter, he found that Mr. Downey did not seem to find time to saw and split and stack the great pile of wood which had been laid in in the fall, he offered to do it, a little every day, for a fair compensation. It gave him good exercise while the roads were too bad for any walking excepting his daily tramp to and from the school-house, and put a little money in his pocket beside. He was very popular as a teacher, partly because, while he was teaching, he gave the whole of his mind to it. Many of his scholars were nearly or quite as old as he was himself—between twenty-three and four—and at first he had some little trouble to convince them that he "meant business." But by this

time things were running very smoothly, for the most
unruly ones had found that they gained most by unqualified
submission. He had intended, during his vacation, to go to
a more bracing climate, for the sake of complete change, but
somehow he stayed on. His home was too far away for
more than a yearly visit, and this he preferred to make at
Christmas.

When he mentioned to Mr. Downey that, if there were
no objection, he would remain there for the summer, as he
found the quiet and seclusion of the place well suited to his
plan for studying, and it would save him the expense of
traveling, Mr. Downey expressed his pleasure with becoming gravity, and said that, in his opinion, it was as healthy
a place as his boarder would find anywhere, and nobody
could say it wasn't quiet.

"And as for coolness," he added, "whichever way the
wind blows about here, it comes off salt water, so it's no
chance to get het up."

But as Kendall turned away, his host nodded his head
sagaciously, and with twinkling eyes, remarking to himself
with a chuckle, "Neighbors makes a difference to a neighborhood."

John Kendall had almost succeeded in convincing himself,
by an elaborate course of argument, that the fact that some
unusually agreeable people had come to live at Green Point
had not in any way influenced his decision, excepting perhaps his discovery that he and Roderick were studying the
same profession—that, he admitted, was an inducement, for
each had one or two books which the other had not, and
their talks with each other were always encouraging. It
was just possible, too, he said, treating himself with great
candor, that Mrs. Stanley's motherly kindness and hospitality had its influence; but as for Miss Stanley having anything to do with it, he hoped he was not such an idiot as

8

to indulge in any visions of that sort. He would be doing well if he accomplished his purpose, and made his own bread and butter in the next five years. So, knowing this quite well, and intending only friendship, what harm could there be in seeing as much of her as he could, without neglecting his studies? He came rather more frequently, after his vacation began, and to do him justice, much of his visit was often spent with Roderick in the "study," consulting and talking over their books. But after awhile he fell into the way of coming late in the afternoon, and, upon a small amount of persuasion, staying to tea and spending the evening. Mrs. Stanley's motherly heart was full of pity for his lonely and laborious life, and she was not one of the dreadful women who foresee an "affair" to be either encouraged or suppressed whenever a young man comes within speaking distance of their daughters. All that she saw, in this instance, was a lonely young fellow, hoeing a hard row with courage and energy, and she thought how thankful she would be, under similar circumstances, to any one in a safe and pleasant home who held out a kind hand to one of her boys. So she encouraged him to talk with her about the absent mother and father, and sisters and brothers, and it was not long before she filled a very warm corner of his heart. She had been sorry, and the rest of the family indignant, to see the cool and haughty manner, bordering on contempt, with which he was received by Randolph Peyton and a few other young "chivalries" who sometimes met him at her house. Too many of these young men had no visible means of support but what their fathers chose to allow them, and spent their time in a busy idleness, which profited neither themselves or any one else, and sometimes did very much the reverse.

One evening, shortly after Edith's arrival, the parlor was quite full of visitors who had dropped in, in detachments or

one at a time. Randolph Peyton and two of his sisters
had driven over from Rivermouth; Mr. Kendall had come
between five and six and consented to stay to tea, and two
young men named Reed, recent acquaintances, introduced
by Colonel Peyton, had arrived soon after the Peytons. The
talk, so far, was general, and had turned upon some historical question; there was a division of opinion, and Elizabeth
laughingly turned to Mr. Kendall, asking him to decide the
point.

"Oh, I say, that's hardly fair, Miss Stanley, said the
younger Mr. Reed; "as an instructor of youth, Mr. Kemble
is bound to know such things, and it puts the rest of us at a
disadvantage."

"Yes," chimed in Randolph Peyton, "''tis his vocation.'
I move we leave it to Mr. Stanley."

There was not much in the words, but the covert sneer in
the tones, and the willfully miscalled name, made Elizabeth's
blood tingle. Mr. Stanley, ignoring everything but the
words, said pleasantly—

"I support my niece's nomination. I am fully as rusty
concerning ancient history as the rest of you appear to be.
Mr. Kendall, will you tell us which side is correct?"

Mr. Kendall, without appearing to notice anything but
Mr. Stanley's question, replied modestly, but clearly and
decidedly. His reply was followed, for a minute or two, by a
rather uncomfortable silence, which Randolph Peyton broke
by requesting Elizabeth to sing.

"Oh do, Miss Stanley!" said the younger Mr. Reed, with
much animation; "we have heard so much of your musical,
abilities, that we feel quite left out in the cold until we are
able to add our testimony."

"Thank you," said Elizabeth, with a smile which had no
warmth in it; "but you must excuse me this evening, please.
To-day is my weekly butter making day—you may not know

it, but my butter is in great and increasing demand at Mr.
Joyce's store—and I am more than usually tired this evening. Besides, I should be afraid to display my very moderate
ability to any one who had heard such exaggerated accounts
of it as you must have heard by what you say."

Arnold was sitting behind the table, with his eyes on a
book, but he restrained a prolonged whistle with difficulty.

Randolph Peyton, who was near Elizabeth, said in low
tones—

"You are severe, Miss Stanley; how proud *I* should be of
such a champion!"

Elizabeth felt her face turning crimson; but before
Randolph had time to notice it—as she hoped—Edith,
who was on the opposite side of the room, suddenly exclaimed:

"Oh! was that thunder? I *hope* not. I am so afraid of
thunder storms!"

"If there's a thunder-storm in prospect, we must be on
our way home," said the elder Mr. Reed, rising as he spoke.

"And we must too," echoed Randolph, "or mother will
be worried about the girls. Wait till they put their shawls
on, Reed; our roads are the same for a mile or two."

Affectionate good-nights were exchanged between the
girls, and commonplace ones between the Stanleys and Randolph and the Reeds. Mr. Kendall made no motion to go,
and the others appeared to remember him just in time for a
formal leave taking.

The sound of wheels and hoof-beats had not yet died
away, when Edith suddenly opened the piano. saying:

"Nobody asked *me* to sing, but I feel a sudden inspiration.
I don't believe in dying with all one's music in one!"

She struck a few sounding chords, and then dashed into a
ringing hunting song. It was a special favorite of Roderick's,
and one which Elizabeth almost invariably sang for him

before she rose from the piano, no matter with what she had begun. When she came to the chorus, she said, hastily:

"Sing, all of you!" and all the younger ones, without thinking, joined in.

Mr. and Mrs. Stanley had remained standing at the front door, after the visitors rode and drove away, commenting on the beauty of the night, and wondering whence had come the "thunder sound" which had startled away the Peytons and Reeds. But when the song rang suddenly upon the still air, Mrs. Stanley turned, with a look of distress upon her face, saying:

"Elizabeth must be very much excited; I never knew her do such an inconsiderate thing as that before. I must stop her."

Mr. Stanley followed to the parlor, and when they found Edith on the music-stool they both looked bewildered, and Mrs. Stanley said, "I was *sure* it was Elizabeth's touch and voice." Then, as soon as she could make herself heard, she gently suggested to Edith that it would be better not to continue the song until their guests were out of hearing.

"Why yes, aunty, of course it would," said Edith, innocently; "I ought to have thought of that myself, but you know it was Elizabeth who declined to play, and they did not ask me; I suppose I must look as if I didn't know how."

"We thought it was Elizabeth, as we stood in the hall," said Mrs. Stanley, looking very much puzzled, "yet I never noticed before that your voices were alike."

"There's a family resemblance, I suppose, aunty dear," said Edith, demurely, and searching diligently in the music-stand for something which she did not appear to find.

There was a sudden explosion of laughter from Arnold, which called his mother's attention to the fact that it was nearly an hour past his usual bed time; he passed Edith on his way out of the room, and under cover of an affectionate good-night he whispered, "You see I can't stay to see this little game out—tell me how it ends to-morrow, like a good girl."

"What *do* you mean?" said Edith, quite aloud, and looking him full in the face.

Arnold once more puckered his mouth for a whistle which did not come, and went up stairs, laughing softly all the way.

Mr. Kendall had taken the opportunity, when the rest struck into the chorus, to say to Elizabeth, "You must let me thank you for your championship, Miss Stanley—I think I understood you, although perhaps my thought is presumptuous; I am more grateful than I can tell you now, but indeed, things of that sort do not annoy me, as I can see that you think they do—they only amuse me."

"You are much stronger minded than I could possibly be!" said Elizabeth, looking up with a bright, sweet smile; "I will confess that I am foolishly sensitive to slights and rudeness, even when I feel quite secure of my position and real superiority."

"And yet you subjected yourself to possible scorn when you told them——" began Mr. Kendall, eagerly, but just here the music suddenly stopped; and John Kendall came to the conclusion, as he walked home and thought things over, that it was just as well, all things considered, that it did! He took his departure very soon after the hunting song came to an untimely end, remarking that he had a long walk before him.

"That is a most singular young man!" exclaimed Edith, as soon as Mr. Kendall was well out of hearing. "How *could* he help asking you to sing for him, Betty, as soon as those puppies were gone—he must have known you'd have done it!"

"No," said Elizabeth, quietly; "he knew quite well that I would not have done it, but even if he had not known, he would not have asked me."

Edith raised her eyebrows, remarking, "If I were Arnold, I imagine I should whistle. You and he must have improved the shining hours of your short acquaintance—there's a vast amount of psychological research implied in that speech."

"Not so much as you think," replied Elizabeth, with perfect good nature, and none of the confusion for which Edith had hoped. "It is the obscure characters which require such deep research; I know Mr. Kendall's is transparent, and I flatter myself that mine is not exactly opaque."

"Crushed again!" said Edith, dramatically. "Sing a little song to restore me, dear; something with a nice lively chorus. There's a sort of depression in the air!"

Two or three songs were sung, and then, as usual, a hymn to finish with; prayers were read, and the family began to say good-night.

Mr. Stanley put his arm around his daughter, and, as Roderick closed shutters and bolted doors, he walked with her up and down the hall.

"How was it that you imitated Elizabeth's playing and singing so exactly to-night, dear?" he asked; "was it accidental?"

"Well, no, papa," said Edith, rather reluctantly, and trying to laugh, although her face had no longer the sparkling look of mischief which it wore before prayers; "you know I have a very pretty little talent for mimicry—I found that out when we had private theatricals last winter—and it seemed to me that I saw my way to administering an instructive moral lesson."

"I don't wish to scold you, dear," said Mr. Stanley, gently; he could never forget that for ten years his "little girl" had been motherless; "but I think you must see for yourself, now that the excitement is over, that what you did this evening was a double wrong. You conveyed an entirely false impression, and you put your cousin in a most ungracious light."

"I know it, papa," said Edith, mournfully; "my forethoughts always come afterward, and I saw the whole thing before we had finished the hymn. But indeed, if you'll trust me, I think I can set it straight, in a little while, and I'll try not to be so silly again. I was carried away by my wrath against those idiots! Why, that fine, manly, industrious fellow is worth a gross of them!"

"That is evident," said Mr. Stanley, heartily, "but two wrongs, my little daughter, never yet made a right. Dear child," he added, tenderly, "you can remember your mother quite well—try to think what she would have wished her girl to be."

Two or three bright tears rolled down Edith's cheeks, but she controlled her desire to sob, and said, "I almost forgot, papa, there was another thing; I pretended I thought it was thundering, but I knew quite well it was the noise Aunt Judy made beating her Maryland biscuit—she beats them over night, and again in the morning."

"I don't think anybody was deceived on that head," said Mr. Stanley, smiling involuntarily. "The cavaliers were only too glad of an excuse for going—but I am glad you told me, dear. And now we must go to bed—they are waiting to put the lights out."

Edith did not enliven her room-mates, that night, with the pranks which usually accompanied her preparations for bed, and when she kissed her aunt good-night, she said, "You've so many children, aunty, that one more can't make much difference; so while I am here, I wish you'd mother me too!"

"Indeed I will, with pleasure," said Mrs. Stanley, taking

Edith in her arms as she spoke ; "a home is like an omnibus—'there's always room for one more.'"

"I don't see," said Edith, as she carefully extinguished the candle, "why all you girls—and boys too, for that matter—aren't a great deal better than you are—yes, even St. Elizabeth and Sir Roderick!"

CHAPTER X.

" Give me, I cry'd (enongh for me)
My bread and independency !"—Pope.

THERE would be no wheat harvest at Green Point this year, for the excellent reason that no wheat had been sown, but, thanks to the diligence with which the boys had uprooted weeds, there had been an excellent hay harvest. This was happily over before Mr. Stanley and Edith came, so, excepting for the daily routine, which the boys managed with more and more ease as they became accustomed to it, and the extra work when there was anything to be prepared for market, there was now nothing very pressing to do. Roderick wished to have the garrets plastered before cold weather came, but money was needed for so many more important things, that he was beginning to think they would be obliged to postpone it for another year. His plan for the porch and vestibule must be laid aside indefinitely, for, after the horse should be paid for, next in importance would come two vehicles—a cart for the farm work, and some sort of carry-all which should be decent enough to take the whole family to church.

Mr. Stanley's affairs had been prospering for many years ; his income always exceeded his expenditure, and nothing would have made him happier than to shower upon the widow and children of his dearly loved younger brother all that was needed to make the new home as luxurious as the one which they had left. But he saw that his gifts, unless they were very occasional, and managed with great skill, would give pain, rather than pleasure. Mrs. Stanley, in an affectionately plain talk which she had with him during her visit to his house, had succeeded in making him understand that there were few things which she so much dreaded for her children as that they should grow up in the belief that the world owed them a living, whether they chose to work for it or not.

"My girls and boys," she said, "have taken this reverse—for I cannot call it an affliction, precisely as I hoped they would ; instead of looking helplessly about them for assistance and encouragement, and being distressed at the change, they seem really to enjoy it, even those who are sacrificing most for the general welfare. It has roused them to earnest thought, and thoughtful action, and will have, I feel sure, life-long results for good. But if they begin to trust to, and expect, outside help, the good work will be neutralized, if not entirely undone."

"And do you expect me," said Mr. Stanley, with some warmth, "to stand by and see my only brother's wife and children in want and distress, and refrain from helping them, by way of teaching a moral lesson ?"

"Not at all," replied Mrs. Stanley, with a smile ; "when things come to that pass, I shall expect you to assist us ; I will even promise to ask you to!"

"You're a very provoking woman, if you are my sister-in-law!" said Mr. Stanley, somewhat irrelevantly, and there, for the time, the subject was dropped.

But after Mr. Stanley had been at Green Point a week, on his second visit, he was obliged to admit to himself that his provoking sister-in-law was right; and much as he longed to add comforts and luxuries to the everyday life of the farm, he was sensible enough to deny himself the pleasure of giving, excepting when he saw that there would also be a pleasure in receiving. He saw, too, that the subjects of his anxiety were all genuinely happy—one had only to look in their faces to be sure of that. So he consoled himself with the recollection that Christmas came every year, and that he had always been in the habit of sending gifts for the whole family then, and it also occurred to him that he had been shamefully negligent in the matter of birthdays. It was only by an accident that he had discovered the date of Elizabeth's—so, now, by cautious inquiries, made at different times from one and another, he gradually obtained the wished-for information, and " made a note of it."

A few days after the evening just described, a messenger was sent to Roderick to tell him that the owner of the gray horse had had an offer for him, and that, although he, the owner, should be sorry to disoblige Mr. Stanley, he was in urgent need of the money, and must have a decision at once. Roderick called a council of his mother and Elizabeth. His savings still lacked twenty dollars of the price agreed upon, and it would take at least two weeks to complete the sum, even if he made unusually good sales. Should he ask for credit for the trifling amount that was wanting ?

"No," said Mrs. Stanley; "that would not be fair when the man needs the money so, and has another offer, presumably of ready money. If I thought your uncle would take my request literally, and not insist upon paying for the whole horse, I would ask him to lend us the twenty dollars for a few weeks. But, no ; we made up our minds not to run into debt for *anything*, and I dare say we shall find another horse when we have the money ready."

Elizabeth had been making a silent calculation, and now she suddenly exclaimed:

"Do you know, I think I must have nearly, or quite twenty dollars in my butter money box. We have needed so few extra groceries since the fruit began to ripen, that some weeks I have put in all I made. Just wait till I see !"

and she flew off for the neat little box which Arnold had
made her for a bank; it had a slit in the lid, through
which she dropped the money, and she had meant not to
unlock it for six months, unless some great emergency should
arise.

"I hate even to borrow that money," said Roderick, uneasily. "I know she is saving it for something special,'
although she has not told what it is, and it may be a month
or six weeks before I can return it to her."

" Now I do know what it is," said Mrs. Stanley, cheerfully,
"and you need feel no uneasiness if it is not returned for
two months; it will be longer than that before she can
accumulate the rest, even should she do as well as she has
done lately."

"That makes a little difference," said Roderick; "but
still, I can't help feeling mean about it. I never dreamed of
her undertaking such work as this weekly butter-making,
when I suggested the farm as an alternative."

" But, don't you see, dear Rod," replied his mother, " that
it really adds to her happiness? One of the hardest things
in the world to learn is, that if we would really make people
happy, we must do it in *their* way, instead of in *our* way. I
have never seen Elizabeth looking so well, or so bright, as
she is now."

She came back at that moment, with a triumphant
face.

"Twenty-five dollars and thirty-five cents!" she said,
jingling her box gleefully. "Five dollars more than my
wildest hopes—the horse is ours. Rod, you'd better go for
Joshua's charger at once, and secure the gray !"

Nothing was said upon the subject to Mr. Stanley or
Edith until Roderick returned with his purchase. He was
met with acclamation, and if the gallant gray's head was not
turned by openly expressed admiration that day, it must

have been because he did not understand much of the English language. He really was a beautiful horse: heavily built, but finely formed, and of a deep iron-gray.

"You have a very speaking countenance, Uncle George," said Elizabeth, gaily, when the horse was at last led off to the stable; "and I can see that you are wondering when we became rich enough to buy a horse! We made the money, every bit of it; but you must remember that horses are not such expensive luxuries, here in the wilds of Delaware, as they are in large cities."

"Did I look surprised?" said Mr. Stanley. "I am surprised if I did, and I humbly beg your pardon—nothing that I see here ought to astonish me after what I have already seen. My chief trouble about you now is, that I am afraid the Nation will not consent to elect three Presidents out of one family. Still, there are always consulships in its gift, and perhaps one of the boys might be induced to take one, failing the Presidency, or while he is waiting his turn. But may I be permitted to ask what that stately steed is expected to draw?"

"A plow, first of all," said Elizabeth, laughing; "after awhile, a cart; and after another while, some sort of an ark which will contain the whole family. Rod had the good sense to reserve papa's cavalry saddle and two side saddles, when our things were sold, so the gray can be ridden at once, if he is needed; and until we have a conveyance of our own, we can always hire Joshua's wagon, for a trifle— the one that brought you and Edith from the boat, you know—or his cart, as the case may be. It is not exactly beautiful, but with a few cushions and rugs it can be made quite comfortable, even for mamma."

"No, it is not beautiful," replied Mr. Stanley, "and I should say it would require a good deal of imagination as well as a good many cushions to make any one think it comfortable. But I have observed, among other things, that all of you have unusually vivid imaginations."

The next time Arnold took the butter to the store, he and Ernest—who often went with him—returned in a state of wild excitement. But the family, including the visitors, was gathered in the wide hall, with books and work, and the boys managed to restrain their eagerness to tell their news, until Mr. Stanley and Edith were not present. Then they began talking, both at once—

" There's to be an auction next week——"

" Some wagons and carriages are to be sold——"

" There's a red cow——"

" There are some white Brahma chickens——"

" It's only three miles from here——"

" I read the bill of sale *carefully*, and they're going to give ninety days' credit for all sums over twenty dollars——"

This from Arnold, whose business talent was rapidly developing.

" I asked the man for a bill," he added, " but he said he only had that one, and it must stay in the store, so I took down some of the things," and he drew a memorandum from his pocket and read—

" Household goods, farming utensils, the furniture of a dairy, a red cow, very fine milker, horses, cows, pigs, white Brahma and other chickens, carts, ploughs, harrows, a cultivator, horse-rake, steam threshing-machine, with wood-sawing attachment, with other articles too numerous to mention. Sheriff's sale. Peremptory."

When the excited boys at last came to a pause, Roderick said quietly—

" Do you remember the man who said there was a time when he could have bought all Texas for a pair of boots ?"

Nobody seemed to remember this singularly fortunate man, and Arnold asked eagerly—

"Why didn't he do it then?"

"Because," said Roderick, his eyes twinkling as he spoke, "he didn't happen to have the boots."

"Now, Rod," said Arnold, with some annoyance, "you know quite well that's not a parallel case! We haven't sold an apple, or a peach, or a pear, or a grape yet, and you know we are going to begin barreling oysters, and sending them up for sale as soon as the season opens—we can make a rough calculation, at the lowest estimates, and buy as much as we can be sure of paying for at the end of three months. Just imagine our getting that steam thresher, with the wood-sawing attachment! Why, you and I could take it round to the different farms, and make it pay for itself before pay-day comes."

"I don't like to throw cold water on your young enthusiasms," said Roderick, putting his arm about Arnold's shoulders as he spoke, "but when you are as old as I am, you will know that it is not safe to count possibilities among certainties. If all were to go well, without a hitch or setback of any kind, we could doubtless pay a bill of at least two hundred dollars at the end of the three months, but a thousand things might happen to upset our calculations, and it would not be honest to run our heads into a debt which we have no reasonable certainty of paying. I'm as sorry as you are, but if you'll think it over quietly, I am sure you will agree with me."

The boys looked deeply chagrined, but they were already learning to depend upon Roderick's judgment, so they did not rebel, but Arnold said despondently—

"I suppose there's no help for it—but it is too outrageously tantalizing for anything."

That afternoon Mr. Stanley announced his intention of

walking to the nearest "corner," three miles away. It was a mile nearer than Mr. Joyce's, but the goods kept at the store were even less desirable than his.

"I'm only going for the exercise," he said in answer to Edith's wonder "what on earth he could want at that horrid little store." "The truth is that, since I came to this wilderness, I have grown most uncommonly fat, and I mean to take a walk every day, and see if I can train a little of it off. Is anybody pining to keep me company?"

Edith, Kitty, Polly, and both the boys volunteered. They were all good walkers, and nowise appalled by the three miles and back.

Dinner was hastened a little, for Mr. Stanley declared that he would not go until *his* dinner was "settled." At three o'clock he announced himself ready to start, and they set merrily off. Elizabeth and Roderick had declined, the former because she had letters to write, the latter because, he said, he could not afford to waste so unusual a chance for study as the silence of the house would afford.

Mr. Stanley began to groan a little before the store was reached, and to suggest that, perhaps, it would be as well only to go half-way to-day, and keep the other half for another time ; but his daughter and nieces held him sternly to his bargain, promising that, should he be entirely overcome when they reached the store, they would borrow a wheel-barrow, and all take turns in wheeling him home.

"Very well," he said, gloomily ; "I shall probably keep you to that bargain, and then you'll wish you'd been a little more merciful."

"What are you going to buy, papa?" asked Edith, by way of diverting his mind from his fatigue, and beguiling the way.

"I didn't contemplate buying anything," he replied. "What should I buy, pray?"

"Why, you'll have to ask the man to let you sit down and rest in his store," said Edith, "and it will be dreadfully rude if we don't buy something."

"I *did* think I was safe from you down here," her father said, despairingly; "one of the attractions of this place to me—one upon which I counted greatly, was the fact—for I believed it to be a fact—that you couldn't find a single thing in the neighborhood which you would consider worth buying."

"You are justly punished for harboring such a base motive, papa," said Edith severely; "I want a number of things—I must have a gingham gown, or at least a calico one, for I have begun to help Elizabeth with the butter—it's perfectly fascinating work, but when I buttered my new organdie a little, she said I should not come into the dairy again, unless I put on a common gown that would wash, and I haven't such a thing here. Then I must have a large white apron—several white aprons, to save my new gown, and I want a pair of nice, large slippers for Aunt Judy—she told me yesterday her new boots had nearly 'screwed her heart out,' and that she didn't dare to go barefooted, excepting when she was at home, or on the way there."

"Anything else?" asked Mr. Stanley, resignedly.

"Oh yes!" replied Edith; "I promised Clara a ribbon for buttering my organdie, and I want a very large hat—one that will reach out to the end of my nose, and a good way down the back of my neck."

"But Edith!" remonstrated Kitty; "this man doesn't have as nice things as Mr. Joyce does, and he asks more for them—that's the reason we always go to Mr. Joyce, although he is a mile farther away."

"And that's the reason *I* am going to bestow my patronage on the other man," said Edith; "Mr. Joyce is a Monopoly, and I will never favor monopolies! I don't blame this poor other man for charging high prices, if nobody ever buys anything—it at least serves to keep up his self-respect."

"And I am to be made to pay for the other man's self-respect and your lofty principles!" said Mr. Stanley. "I suppose I ought to feel highly flattered and grateful for the privilege."

"Of course you ought, papa!" said Edith, in a tone which left no room for doubt.

Mr. Stanley had ample time to rest, while Edith was making her purchases, for the storekeeper, delighted with so promising a customer, took care that she should discover several more wants. Becoming tired of resting, Mr. Stanley began to walk up and down the store, to see if he could discover anything that he wanted, and presently his eye fell upon a fac-simile of the bill of sale which had so excited the boys.

"Hallo!" he said, when he had read a few words; "here's something Rod ought to see—there are lots of things in his line here, and no doubt there will be bargains."

"Do you think he has heard of it, boys?"

"Yes, uncle," said Arnold, looking confused; "we told him about it—we saw the bill at Mr. Joyce's."

"And he will go, I suppose, of course," said Mr. Stanley. The boys were silent.

Edith having at last decided that she could not possibly think of anything more to buy, the procession turned homeward, each one bearing a share of her spoils. She too had read the bill of sale; but, with her quicker perception, had noticed the confused and downcast look of the boys, and had readily guessed the reason. She had been fond of her aunt and cousins before she came for this visit; but it seemed to her, more and more every day, as she saw the unselfishness and affection which made their daily lives beautiful, that she had never before really appreciated them. Somehow the contrast between her own easy and untroubled lot and their lives of work and self-denial had never struck her so forcibly as it did now, when she saw how very much straitened they must be, if they could not take advantage of this opportunity—one which might never occur again. She was so unusually silent that her cousins declared the walk had been too much for her, and Arnold said that in future, when she wished to go shopping, the gray should be harnessed to the Dutch carriage, and she should go to Mr. Joyce's, whether she would or not.

"No," she said, mournfully ; "I am not tired, not physically, that is—it's mental strain that ails me. I feel that I have committed a blunder, and that, you know, is worse than a crime. I allowed that man to talk me into buying a blue gingham, when my mind was firmly set upon pink, and the moral of it is the worst part; it shows that my mind won't stay set—can't resist the slightest external pressure, no matter how determined I think I am."

"Be comforted, my dear child," said her father, soothingly ; "I have known it to stay set, for days together, and sometimes upon the merest trifle."

"That was when I was younger, papa," she replied; "it is losing its tone—I feel it. When I put on that blue gingham, and begin to work the butter, between the contrast and the reflection, I shall look as if I had jaundice! Girls, why didn't you come to my rescue, when he threw it over his shoulder and said so sweetly, 'But only just look, Miss, how becomin' it is, and if it's becomin' to *me*——!' a word from either of you would have saved me; you might have told him that I 'never was so fair' as he is."

"Why Edith!" said Polly; "he was just the color of new skim-milk cheese. And, beside, he hadn't any pink gingham—the other one was a dreadful green."

After the laugh at Polly's expense—in which she joined—had subsided, Arnold remarked—

" Mr. Joyce has some pink stuff like that ; at least, I'm pretty sure it's the same. He made me take a little piece the other day, ' to show the young ladies.' Wait—I think I have it here in my pocket-book."

" Arnold, you are an angel!" said Edith, enthusiastically, as she looked at the scrap of gingham ; "this is *exactly* what I want—I shall look lovely in it, and to-morrow is butter-day, and you shall buy it for me, enough to make me a beautiful puckered sun bonnet too, shaped like the clam-wagon that went by just now. And Polly, you'll have to take this blue thing, whether you want to or not—*you're* fair enough to wear anything, and it just matches your eyes. Don't break my heart by refusing it."

" I shall like it very much," said Polly, gratefully, and thanking Edith with a kiss ; " it will be so nice and cool, and I sha'n't be afraid of spoiling it, because it will wash."

" I am beginning to feel cheerful again," said Edith ; "and here we are at last—now boys, fetch up a bucket of water from the lowest depths of the well, while we squeeze some of these lemons. Kitty, you've earned two glasses, carrying the sugar ; the rest can only have one apiece."

Mr. Stanley said he felt he had lost two pounds, but he was afraid he should regain it at supper, and he looked so tired, that his daughter, having refreshed him with a glass of lemonade, told him severely that he must go and take a nap until tea-time.

He went, obediently, and she managed to escape from the others, and go to his room a little while before the tea-bell rang. All her gaiety vanished, as she closed the door.

" Papa," she began, impetuously, "didn't you *see* how it was about that sale ? They've just spent all their money for the horse, and they'll have to let all those delightful things go, when probably most of them will sell for next to nothing— they're so horribly proud, that I don't dare to say a word, for fear of hurting their feelings, and I love them so——" her voice trembled, and then stopped.

"Of course," said Mr. Stanley, "I might have known—it was stupid in me to speak of it to the boys; but don't cry, darling, I think I can manage about it. They have common-sense as well as pride, and I shall appeal to that."

"Do you really think you can make them take what they will need, papa?" and Edith's face brightened wonderfully. "I wanted to tell you—I don't think it is at all good for me to have such a large allowance; I just spend it for foolish things——"

"Such as blue gingham, when your complexion only permits you to wear pink."

"Exactly. How wise you are, papa! So I wish you would take half of it from me, and contrive somehow to make the girls accept it. I don't believe they've bought so much as a ruffle since they came here."

"Yet they don't seem miserable—strange!" said Mr. Stanley, adding, more seriously, "I am very glad you feel this way, darling, but I am afraid that what you propose would be impossible. I have thought a great deal on the subject, and it seems to me that if I wish your aunt and cousins to make a concession, I must begin by making one myself. It goes to my heart to talk of *lending* money to my only brother's widow and children, when I would so gladly give them all they need, but I think it is my only chance. I think I can persuade them to borrow a few hundred dollars from me, rather than lose this opportunity, but I should only make them unhappy by trying to give it to them."

"Oh papa!" and Edith was nearly crying again. "It seems too mean for anything—*don't* you suppose we could make them take it if we were to tell them it was all their birthday presents and Christmas presents for this year?"

"I am afraid not," said Mr. Stanley; "but I hope I can convince them that my plan is a wise one, and that they can pay the money just as it suits them, in small installments, or all at once. I think if Rod could secure the 'threshing-machine with wood-sawing attachment,' he could make a very good thing of it, especially if there is no other in the neighborhood. Arnold is so bright and intelligent, and is growing so large and strong, that he could be a great help with it."

The ringing of the tea-bell put an end to the conference, and after tea Edith led the younger ones in a series of gymnastic exercises, which kept every one laughing till bed-time.

CHAPTER XI.

THERE was no opportunity, the next day, until evening came and tea was over, for Mr. Stanley to undertake his rather difficult mission, but when they were at last
all assembled in the wide hall, he lost no time.

"I claim the floor for at least half an hour," he began. "I
wish to be listened to with respect and attention, and on no
account to be interrupted. Betty, my dear, will you and
Rod please sit between those giggling girls, and keep them
quiet until I am done? That's right—now I can hope to be
heard."

"Is it a story, Uncle George?" asked May, drawing a
cushion to his feet, and settling herself with great content.

"Yes, it is a story," he replied; "and I will begin at
once—they can't keep still long, poor things! There was
once upon a time a man who sometimes had bad dreams,
and this was one of them. He thought he was standing on
the sea-shore, with a high surf rolling in, and a little way
out at sea was a small rock, on which were gathered a number of people whom he dearly loved. They were standing
close, hand joined in hand, for the tide was rising, and every
moment lessened the length and width of their foothold.
They had escaped to the rock from a stranded ship, and it
was through no fault or folly of their own that they were in

this dreadful predicament. But the man on the shore had seen them, and was able and willing to help them.

"'I have a rope here,' he cried, 'and a rocket — if I send the rope out, will one of you catch it, and then I can send a life-boat.' 'Not at all!' they all called back; 'we couldn't think of troubling you! When the tide goes out we can easily wade ashore.'"

"Oh uncle!" interrupted May, with breathless interest; "they must have been crazy!" Mr. Stanley merely smiled, and continued his story.

"'But the tide is not yet in!' the man shouted; 'how do you know that it will not sweep quite over the rock? You *must* catch the rope.'

"'If it were our rope, perhaps we would,' replied one of them, 'though even then we shouldn't like to give you the trouble of throwing it; but you see it is *your* rope, and it might be all cut to pieces by the rocks.'

"'And what then?' shouted the man, almost angrily; 'I have plenty of ropes, and to what better use can I put them than to saving precious lives?'

"'But it's not a question of life and death yet,' said the other; 'it isn't pleasant here, but we are quite safe so far; we hope—indeed, we have reason to think—that the tide will turn before we are swept away; and if we find we really can't stick any longer, then we will accept the use of the rope, if you are quite sure you can spare it, in case it should be spoiled.'

"'And meanwhile,' said the man, indignantly, 'I am to stand shivering here and watch you all stand shivering there, and suffer enough to turn my hair white.'

"'Oh, *we're* not shivering!' they all sang out together; 'we're quite warm, and salt-water never gives people cold, you know.'"

"I hope he went home and left them to soak," said May,

indignantly; "I *never* heard of such foolish people; and they were selfish, too, for if they didn't like to use the nice man's rope, it was much, much worse for him to see them in such danger, and not be able to help them."

"They did not think of that," resumed Mr. Stanley, "and he loved them too much to 'go home and leave them to soak,' so he waited, hoping they would yield."

"But why didn't he just send the rope anyhow?" asked Polly, "instead of standing there talking."

"Because he knew quite well," said Mr. Stanley, "that if he sent it without their permission they would not catch it, and so one chance would be lost. So he said everything he could think of——"

"He, and they too, must have had excellent lungs," said Edith, in a low voice.

"They had speaking-trumpets," said Mr. Stanley, calmly. "So he said everything he could think of, and then he stood and waited, with the rope and rocket in his hand, and every five minutes he called out—

"'Will you catch it if I send it?'

"And then they all called back—

"'Thanks, very much; but we really don't need it—not at present, anyhow!'

"He was beginning to sneeze a good deal, and to get pretty hoarse, when, just as he was going to call for the sixteenth time, a huge wave curled high over the rock, and—he was so terribly frightened that he woke up!"

There was an indignant outcry from the audience, most of which had forgotten that it was a dream, and had not guessed that it was an allegory.

"Oh, Uncle George!" exclaimed May, "*please* make him stay asleep a little longer, till we find out whether they did let him throw the rope."

"I don't believe they did," said Ernest; "I think they

kept waiting, and hoping they would not need it, until a big wave came and swept them all off—and served them right, too!"

"*I* think that they weathered it out, and went ashore when the tide went down," said Kitty, mischievously.

" But even if they did," said Polly, "I think they ought to have been ashamed ; they should have thought how very, very miserable they were making the kind man who was fond of them, feel. They were fonder of their pride, and of themselves, than they were of him, or they couldn't have done it."

" My little Polly has found the moral," said Mr. Stanley, drawing her close to his side ; " there are times when generosity consists in receiving rather than in giving."

To Edith's great surprise, her father said nothing whatever that evening about the auction. She was so impatient to have the matter settled that she came very near introducing the subject herself, but fortunately concluded that he must have some reason for his silence, and that " for once " she would try to be patient. She was rewarded when he whispered, as he kissed her good-night—

"Thank you for your forbearance, my little girl ; I think it will be rewarded."

The next morning Roderick and the boys were up early, attending to the picking of the early apples, of which they expected to have several barrels. The trees had been carefully watched and kept free from insects, and, by Roderick's request, all the soapsuds and dishwater used at the house had been saved, and they had poured it about the roots of the trees and vines. He had not left this to chance, but had placed at the back door of the kitchen a large barrel, procured from the store, to which he had fitted a cover and wooden spigot. The kitchen was several steps above the ground, so that, by arranging a small wooden trough just outside the door, he made it easy for Aunt Judy to carry out his directions. He was reaping his reward already; the harvest apples on the neighboring farms were almost a failure, and it seemed probable that the later fruits would be also, for the summer was unusually dry ; but, considering the long neglect as to pruning which the young trees at Green Point had suffered, the fruit crop was truly encouraging.

Mr. Stanley followed his nephews to the orchard as soon as breakfast was over, and, having dressed himself in an immaculate looking "business-suit," which he said was an old affair which he brought on purpose to work in, had insisted upon being provided with a "picker," and doing his share of the work.

"I *must* manage to lose some of this extra flesh," he said. "The two pounds I walked off yesterday have come back to-day, with interest, and before long I shall be like that luckless man in the Bab Ballad, who had

> 'Everything a man of taste
> Could want or wish—except a waist!'"

"I hope you'll not look like him, uncle," said Ernest, instantly recognizing the quotation.

Roderick had made some small leather pouches, and fastened them to the ends of long poles, and with these he proposed to have all the finest of the fruit picked, to save bruising. He expected the price which this culled fruit would bring to repay him for the outlay of time and trouble, and the event quite justified his expectation. The picking was not so tedious a business as they had expected it to be ; they all became quite expert at taking aim with their poles, and long before dinner time the three trees which were ready had been stripped, and the apples sorted, and packed for transportation. Roderick had had his barrels and straw for the packing all in readiness, and the actual work was soon accomplished. A few of the best, and a number of the "mediums" were reserved for immediate use, and these were spread out upon the floor of one of the garrets.

As Mr. Stanley and the boys sat resting under the trees, and "sampling" some of the finest of the apples, Mr. Stanley began, without preface or preamble—

"Rod, my boy, I want to say a few frank words to you, and I want you at least to listen patiently, for the sake of my love for your father, and his love for me—it is what I should say to him, were he here in your place. There are certain things to be sold, at that sale next week, which, if they are in good order, will be of the greatest use to you, and which will probably go for half their value, or less. I want you to go there, and buy freely whatever you like, from the threshing-machine down; I will pay for it, and you shall pay me when, and as, it may suit you best. It would do my very heart good, if you would put all question of payment aside; but I will not ask this, for I know it would be useless. Since I have come half-way, and am willing to let you repay me, can't you bring yourself to come the other half?"

Roderick seized his uncle's outstretched hand, and clasped it warmly.

"You are very kind, very good, Uncle George," he said, "and if my mother is willing, I *will* accept your offer—only, if you would let us give you a mortgage on the farm——"

"I shall do nothing of the kind," said Mr. Stanley, resolutely; "you may give me a written acknowledgment of the debt, if you choose to call it so, but nothing more, and that is folly, under the circumstances. And it must be quite understood that you are not to live on bread and water, and go in shreds and patches, until it is paid—you are to live quite as well as you are living now, and only put by what you can readily spare."

"But that does not seem right," said Roderick, hesitatingly; "I think we could manage on less than we spend, after awhile, and if we can, I think we ought to do it, until this debt shall be paid."

Mr. Stanley looked really hurt.

"My dear boy," he said, "I don't believe you would talk in this way, if you realized the pain it gives me. All I ask you to do is, to imagine the case reversed. Your father was —is still—very dear to me; it would be my happiness to treat you all as my own sons and daughters, for I have but one child, and there is room in my heart and home for a dozen. Think then, what it must be to me, to be treated by all of you, from your mother down, as if I were a well-meaning stranger! I have nothing to say against a reasonable amount of pride and independence, but virtues cease to be virtues, sometimes, when they are carried too far. Don't hold me at arm's length any longer, Rod—I can't stand it— you grow more like your father every day, and I have never had a son!"

There were tears in Mr. Stanley's kind, frank blue eyes, and his voice trembled with feeling.

Roderick was conquered.

"I'm afraid I have been brutal, Uncle George," he said, humbly, "and I beg your pardon. Self-gratification knows how to disguise itself. But indeed, I will do as you say—I will even ask mother and Betty to go with me to the sale, and we will buy whatever we need that is worth buying, for even if it does not sell much under its market value, transportation to this place costs a good deal."

"Now I feel as if you belonged to me again," said Mr. Stanley, warmly; "we will make a picnic of it, and all go —we can get Joshua's carry-all, and one of his horses to go with the gray, and tell the girls to put us up a magnificent lunch. What day is it to be? Thursday? This is only

Saturday, so they will have ample time to prepare. We will go early, so as to have a look at the things before the sale begins."

Mr. Stanley's proposition caused a general and joyful excitement. Mrs. Stanley had yielded her consent, when Roderick told her how deeply Mr. Stanley would feel her refusal, although she agreed with her son that they would have preferred letting the opportunity go, to contracting a debt. They had been firm in their intention to buy nothing for which they could not immediately pay, and although this was not exactly on a par with a butcher's or grocer's bill, still it was a debt, and they knew they should be sensible of a weight upon their minds until it could be paid.

The advantages of securing the threshing-machine, should it prove to be in good order, were great and undoubted; the farmers had already begun their threshing, and to buy a new one that year, and pay for it, would be utterly out of the question; whereas, if Roderick could secure the threshing from three or four of the large farms in the neighborhood, it would probably pay for the machine, bought at second hand, and he would be prepared for his own work next summer. For he had already made up his mind to put the larger part of the farm in wheat the following year. Colonel Peyton told him that it had once been the richest wheat-growing farm in the neighborhood, and that, with judicious manuring, he thought it would still yield a crop more profitable than one which would require more cultivation. Roderick had intended to perform his duties on the farm thoroughly and conscientiously; he had no idea that he would come to feel the real interest and pleasure which it now gave him. He and the boys were studying chemistry together, with a view to applying it to their farming operations, and Ernest showed an unusual aptitude for so young a boy. One of the large, unplastered garrets had been given up to their work, and they had made a long, light table, and several benches. Roderick had been greatly interested in this study while he was at school, and his father had furnished a small laboratory for him, very completely. This furniture now came into use, and many rainy afternoons were beguiled away, both by boys and girls; for the three younger girls, having been invited once or twice to see something "specially thrilling," had manifested such a flattering interest in the proceedings that a gracious permission had been accorded them to come up whenever they liked, if they would not "chatter," or touch anything without permission. Ernest's special interest settled upon assaying, and one corner of the garret was filled with a set of shelves, upon which were specimens of soil and rock from every part of the farm, each carefully labeled, and awaiting its turn for a critical examination. Nobody but May was in the secret—to her Ernest had confided his belief that he should discover either silver or gold upon "the Estate"—gold was preferable, of course, but silver would be a long way better than nothing. She had implicit faith in this vision, and had added largely to the collection. They were looking forward eagerly to the next rainy day—some of the recently found specimens had such a very promising appearance!

Mr. Stanley had taken Edith into his confidence, and asked her to look carefully over the "household goods," on the day of the sale, and point out whatever she thought would be useful to the family, for no furniture had yet been bought for the garrets, and if these things should prove to be in good order, a very great saving might be made by purchasing them. Edith joyfully accepted the commission, although her joy was a good deal damped by the knowledge that her aunt would ultimately pay for whatever was bought.

"And as a commission for your services," Mr. Stanley had

added, "if you see anything which you consider valuable on account of its extreme age—for I believe that is the standard now—and which would not be useful to your aunt or cousins, you may buy it for yourself."

"Thank you, papa," replied Edith, "but I don't feel as if I deserved it; it makes me sick to think how I have been spending money on myself all these years, and how little there is of me, after all—I should think you'd be dreadfully disgusted with me, when you contrast me with my cousins."

"You have only spent what I gave you, dear," said her father, putting his arm about her as he spoke, "and I am not disgusted. My little girl has needed a mother's care, but I think her heart is in the right place."

"Dear papa!" she exclaimed, without the least intention of quoting, "you have been father and mother both——"

"And uncle, all in one," said Arnold, who had come in while she was speaking; "the rest of the babes are going to the wood for blackberries, ma'am, and they sent me to find you, for a person who objects to quoting when other people do it——"

"I wasn't quoting!" said Edith, indignantly; "I was talking to papa, and I was quite in earnest—I don't know what you mean."

Arnold began reciting "The Babes in the Wood," but before he reached the verse which Edith had unconsciously quoted, he found himself obliged to use all his breath for running, in order to keep up with his fleet-footed cousin.

"Hold on!" he panted; "I haven't any apples in my pocket, and they've not started for the woods; they're waiting at the back door."

"Why couldn't you have mentioned that sooner, instead of stopping to quote poetry?" said Edith, turning back, and "beating" him to the house easily.

10

CHAPTER XII.

"John Gilpin kissed his loving wife ;
    O'erjoyed was he to find
That though on pleasure she was bent,
    She had a frugal mind."—COWPER.

IT was well that Roderick spoke to Joshua in good season
about hiring the horse for the day of the sale, for he
found that Joshua intended going himself. The good-
natured Dutchman, however, unwilling to disappoint his
neighbor, for whom, by this time, he felt a great esteem,
said he would so arrange his farm work that day as to have
his other horse "vacant," and at Roderick's service.

"But can I have the carry-all too ?" asked Roderick, "or
will your wife want it that day ?"

The Dutchman smiled a smile of conscious superiority, as
he said—

"My wife, she mostly wants what I wants her to want,
Mr. Roderick! If she doan't like my nice little cart, mit the
sunshade up in front, all she got to do is, stay at home and
cook her dinner."

All Roderick's objections to giving Mrs. Joshua a possible
annoyance were answered by variations upon this sentence,
and he finally gave it up, and arranged to ride the gray over,
and bring back the other horse and the carry-all, on Wednesday evening.

Edith insisted upon helping with the preparations for the
vast luncheon which was to be put up for the occasion.
She had a special fancy for beating Aunt Judy's Maryland

biscuit, declaring it to be "the most magnificent exercise, with the one thing which exercise usually lacked—an object."

"I mean to make them every day, when I go home," she said; "just observe, if you please, how splendidly the muscle of my arms is developing!"

"But Edith," said Polly, in gentle remonstrance; "who in the world will eat them, if you make them *every* day? Even here, where there is such a lot of us, Aunt Judy only makes them twice a week."

"I shall eat a great many myself," replied Edith, gravely; "and I shall instruct the cook to give them to all the beggars who come to the back gate for 'cold victuals.' And I shall hand them to people instead of cake—they're infinitely more wholesome, and it will be a novelty beside. I shall be besieged for the recipe, no doubt."

"They're very good," said Polly, doubtfully, "when they're quite fresh, and when one is quite hungry; but I don't believe people will like it much, if you *always* hand them instead of cake."

Edith stopped her "magnificent exercise" long enough to give Polly an ecstatic hug, exclaiming as she did so—

"Polly, you are the joy of my heart; the light of my eyes! How have I ever lived so long without you?"

There had been an opportunity to buy some fresh beef the day before; it had been promptly roasted, and was to form the basis of the collation. Aunt Judy had been permitted to make one of her special pound-cakes, baked over the coals; there was unlimited gingerbread, and some of the best of the harvest apples had been saved. Edith had made a pilgrimage to Mr. Joyce's, attended by Arnold and a basket, and had returned with lemons and sugar and a large bottle of pickled cucumbers. The lemon-juice, squeezed upon the sugar, was carried in a jar, with the hope of finding cold water in or near the pretty wood where they proposed to picnic, either during or after the sale, as the case might be. It was, of course, entirely uncertain as to whether the articles advertised would be worth buying, but it was "an excellent excuse for a spree," as Arnold observed. They were all, or at least all the younger ones, sorry that the place was so near—a longer drive would have been quite to their liking; but three miles was better than nothing.

There had been much speculation concerning the weather, and many fears that it might be such as to keep every one but Mr. Stanley and Roderick at home; but the day turned out to be all that could be desired—it was what Aunt Judy called "seasonable weather," warm but with a good air going, and without the remotest threat of rain.

They were early on the ground, as they had intended to be, and had time to make a pretty thorough examination of the things offered for sale before many other people arrived.

There was a good deal of trash, of course; but there was also much that would be well worth buying. The threshing-machine was nearly new, and apparently in perfect order. The horses and cattle looked sleek and healthy; May went into ecstacies over the beautiful white Brahma chickens, and Elizabeth admitted that with the "red cow," in addition to her Alderney, she would have all the butter-making she could manage.

The furniture had evidently been carefully kept, and it seemed a pity that it should be sold so far from the large cities, where much of it would have brought large prices. There were several of those high chests of drawers, with claw-feet and brass handles, which have recently become so dear to the hearts of amateur antiquarians; all the chairs, with the exception of those which had been used in the servants' quarters, were of the much coveted "lyre-backed" variety;

there were two handsomely carved mahogany bedsteads, and a number of three-footed and one-legged candle-stands, also of mahogany. Fresh treasures were discovered as the party went from room to room.

"Oh, papa!" said Edith, seizing her father's hand and drawing him aside; "there's the *loveliest* tall clock in the next room, with a carved case, and a moon, and a ship—I never saw such a perfect one—and a Franklin stove, a *real* one, and I don't know how many pairs of andirons, all over curlyqueues, and a lot of brass-headed shovels and tongs, and *will* you buy them for me, if aunty and the girls don't want them?"

"I suppose I must," said Mr. Stanley, resignedly, "after my promise, and I think you can be pretty sure of the clock, for your aunt has one, and of the curlyqueued andirons, for there is a pair in every room at Green Point; but might I be allowed to suggest that your home does not contain a single open chimney?"

"Oh, but it's going to, papa!" she answered, confidently; "I shall have the chimney in the library and the one in my room done as soon as we go home; they shall be tiled, with high wooden mantel-pieces above them, like the one in the parlor at Green Point—I mean to paint the tiles for mine, and get Minton for the other. But I think aunty had better take one or two more pairs of andirons—she'll want them when the garrets are made habitable."

"I hope you haven't set your heart upon one of those carved mahogany mausoleums," said her father, not stopping to discuss the open chimney question; "it would just about fill your room, and you'd have to put the rest of the furniture out in the entry."

"But don't you think one would be very stately and stylish for the spare bedroom, the large one, you know?" she inquired, coaxingly.

"To be quite truthful, dear, I don't," he replied; "we shall probably never be called upon to lodge the Kentucky giant, and anybody of smaller dimensions would feel lost in one of those mighty structures."

"Well, I mean to buy all the candle-stands aunty doesn't want," said Edith, cheerfully; "I always did doat upon candle-stands, and I never had such an opportunity as this before."

"I wonder how any family in its senses can permit such treasures to be sold," said Kitty, returning from a general tour of inspection; "they can't be wild enough to imagine that these things can ever be replaced, I should think, or that anybody who is likely to be here to-day will give half their value for them."

"There's nobody left but the widow and two of her step-children, miss," said a pleasant faced country-woman, who had been standing near enough to hear Kitty's remark, "and she can't help herself."

"But, couldn't the children have helped it?" asked Kitty, deeply interested.

"Oh yes, miss," replied her new acquaintance, "*they* could have helped it, easy enough; but they didn't want to —it's their *contrariness* that's brought it about. You see," she continued, pleased with Kitty's attention to her narrative, "one of 'em's the second wife's, and the other the third's ——"

"Why, how many has he had?" interrupted Kitty, in astonished tones.

"This one's the fourth," returned the narrator, much gratified with the sensation she was producing; "and the first thing them two girls ever was known to agree about, was hating their step-mother. Not that she give them any reason—she laid herself out to please them from the start— but you can't satisfy folks that's made up their minds beforehand that they won't *be* satisfied, and they do say that them two girls led that poor woman a life!" .

"I should think she deserved it," said Kitty, indignantly; "the idea of marrying a man who had had three wives!"

"Oh, nobody but the girls thought anything of that! You see, he was a warm hearted, affectionate dispositioned man, and he couldn't get along without a wife at all! He always waited a full year before he even courted anybody; and I don't believe he'd have married at all, this last time, if the girls had made him any kind of a home. But they were as jealous as they could live, and all the time squabbling about the house, and the money, and him; so at last he married again for the sake of a little peace and quietness, but my! things was worse than ever. He'd been sort of ailing for some time—he come of a consumptive family—and they do say that the racket them girls kept up kind of hurried him off. He was all the time talking about making a will, for he knew well enough how things would go if he died without one, and I hear he made one every time he married, except this last one. His wife was dreadful fond of him, and she took on so when anybody told her she ought to speak to him about it, that finally they let her alone. I don't know how it is, but it seems as if, somehow, no matter how long beforehand folks begin to die, it comes kind of sudden at the last. The very day before he went, I hear, he says to Martha—that's his present wife, or widow, as I should say—he says to Martha, 'I'll have that lawyer here to-morrow evening, and make things all straight for you, my dear, in case anything should happen.' But laws! by the next evening he was where even a lawyer couldn't reach him. And he wasn't fairly buried, before them girls let the widow know that she wouldn't get a cent but her thirds, and the few things she'd brought into the house. You see, she was teaching for her living when she married, and it's

my belief she earned it a good sight harder afterward ;
but that's neither here nor there! Instead of having a
pleasant settlement, and dividing things equal, them girls
stuck to it there must be a sale, or it wouldn't be a fair
division.   The widow, she wanted to buy in some of the
things she cared most for beforehand—such as the bedstead
he died on, and the last chair he ever set up in; but my !
they must 'a' bribed the appraiser, for he put such a price
on everything, that she gave it up.   She's not a fool, however, generally speaking; and if I'm not much mistaken,
she'll get even with 'em to-day.   I see a man outside here
—a sort of a distant cousin that was always a great friend
of hers ; he's no money to spare to buy on his own account,
and it's my belief she's given him his orders, and that she'll
get most of what she wants.   You see, there's not many
folks about here with more ready money than they know
what to do with, and its likely things will go low.   There's
them girls now !   I reckon they mean to be on hand and
keep a watch on her."

By this time, the rest of Kitty's family were gathered
about the narrator, listening with manifest interest and
suppressed amusement.   They turned in the direction of
her nod, and saw two gaunt, angular women, apparently
between forty and fifty years of age, stalking about the next
room, and eyeing keenly every one who came in.   The hour
announced for the sale had just sounded from the old
clock which had so excited Edith, and a portly and important looking man was mounting a horse-block at the gate
of the farm-yard.   The men who had been scattered over
the premises were slowly gathering around him, and it was
evident that the sale was to begin with the "stock and
utensils."

" Come on, Rod, and you too, boys, if you like," said Mr.
Stanley ; " if we don't look out, the crowd will keep us too

far off to see well." So they hastened away, while the
mother and her girls made themselves comfortable among
the old fashioned furniture, congratulating themselves that,
if the things should really be sacrificed, they need feel no
compunction, as the loss would fall on "them girls."

"But mamma," said Polly, with a puzzled look, "if the
poor woman is to have a third of everything, won't it be less
if the things sell low?"

"Of course it will, dear," replied her mother; "but don't
you see that this will probably be more than counterbalanced,
if she wishes to buy much of the furniture, by her getting it
for less than its value? It's 'all so broad as it is long,' as
Joshua says."

"Oh yes, mamma! I see now," said Polly, looking very
much relieved; "and I do hope she will get what she wants
—we must watch her cousin, and not bid against him."

The monotonous drone of the auctioneer's voice, sounding,
at that distance, like an immense bee in an immenser bottle,
drew them to the window. Mr. Stanley and the boys had
secured good places, and the former was standing in front,
with a look of boyish eagerness on his face which made
them all smile.

"Dear papa!" said Edith, affectionately; "he looks years
younger since we came here, aunty—don't you think he does?"

"Yes," said Mrs. Stanley, "I do—I have been delighted
with the change that has come over him; he looks almost
as I remember him when I first met him, thirty years ago—
his coat of tan is very becoming. But do look, children—
they are bringing out the red cow. What a pretty thing
she is!"

"I wonder if she is really all the appraiser's fancy painted
her?" said Edith; "she don't look as if she had either an
Alderney or a Jersey on the remotest branch of her family-
tree, does she, aunty?"

"No," said Mrs. Stanley; "I must confess that she does not; but I have heard a good many farmers say that the common red cows were among their best milkers, and that they preferred them to imported stock, because the milk they gave was good for something after it was skimmed, whereas the Alderney milk, after skimming, was almost like water."

" Papa's bidding!" said Edith, excitedly; "there's one of 'them girls' right behind him, and I'm pretty sure she's bidding against him for the cow."

The auctioneer's voice droned on a few minutes longer; Mr. Stanley nodded once more, and then the hammer fell; by this time the younger girls, including Edith, had their heads out of the window, and Mr. Stanley evidently saw them, for he waved his hat triumphantly toward them.

"Oh, I wish we were down there!" said Edith, dancing up and down; "we could keep on the outside of the crowd, and still hear the fun—mayn't we go, aunty?"

"Certainly, dear, if you wish to," said Mrs. Stanley; ' but don't get mixed up with the people—keep at a little distance, and come away before they begin to scatter. You go too, if you would like to, daughter," she said to Elizabeth, who remained at the window when the rest started.

"Thank you, mamma," she replied, "but I really don't care to—I can see and hear all I wish to from this window, with the added advantage of having that delightful old claw-footed sofa within reach, when I am tired of standing."

The next animal put up for sale was a fine looking dark-brown horse.

"He matches our gray in everything but color," said Elizabeth, looking at him attentively; "and see, mamma— uncle is speaking to Rod, and Rod is shaking his head—how dreadfully in earnest uncle seems to be! And now he is bidding again! But somebody else is in earnest too—the auctioneer is nodding right and left, like a Chinese mandarin. There! his hammer has fallen, and I am pretty sure he looked at uncle last—oh, I wonder how much the horse was! I am afraid it will be years and years before we are able to repay uncle."

Mrs. Stanley sighed.

" I almost wish this sale had not taken place," she said. " Rod has been so bright and cheerful, and things were going so nicely, and now I am afraid he will be insensibly weighed down by this debt, kind and generous as your uncle is about it."

" I ought not to have said that, mamma, dear!" Elizabeth exclaimed, penitently. " We must remember our favorite old woman of the bridge—no doubt we shall find a new one when we come to the place, and meanwhile, we will *not* fret! Do come to the window—I can't think what Arnold and Ernest are about!"

The two boys had withdrawn a little from the crowd, and were earnestly consulting over two small pocket-books which they had pulled from their pockets. The sale of live-stock was going on, but it did not appear to interest them.

" I made Arnold begin to take a share of the butter-money, last week," said Elizabeth; " he never would before, but I just told him decidedly, at last, that if he would not share the profits, he should no longer have any of the labor —the boys ought to have a little money at their absolute disposal—don't you think it is better, mamma?"

" Yes, dear, I do," replied Mrs. Stanley; "at least, I think it is better for such boys as ours—there might be cases where it would have a bad, rather than a good, influence— but I am not afraid for Arnold and Ernest; they know that Rod does not consider himself too old to talk the day's doings over with me every night, and while he keeps on

with it, there is no fear of their stopping. Dear Rod! how
like a father, as well as brother, he is to them!"

The boys kept on with their consultation, until the various
vehicles under the sheds began to be drawn out, and offered
for sale. Then they returned to the crowd, placing themselves well in front, and looking so important that Mrs.
Stanley and Elizabeth laughed, and the latter said: "They
are going to bid for something—what in the world can it
be?"

"I can't imagine—oh yes I can," said Mrs. Stanley; "they
have been lamenting that we had no whip but a long
trimmed switch, and no doubt they are hopeful of buying
one at a bargain; very probably they may do it; I'm sure
I hope they will, dear little souls."

"If Ernest has not spent it, he must have a little money
too," rejoined Elizabeth, "for he has dug and carried to the
store several baskets of soft-shelled clams, lately, and I
think Mr. Joyce gives him ten cents a basket. He asked
Rod if he might do it several weeks ago, and Rod was delighted with such a manifestation of enterprise. How Ernest has improved lately, mamma—he hardly ever defers or
forgets his work now, and Rod says his aptitude for chemistry is simply amazing, for so young a boy."

A roomy, old fashioned chaise, hung very low, and looking, as Elizabeth suggested, like the grandmother of the
latter-day phaeton, had been put up first of all, and on this
Mr. Stanley unhesitatingly bid, without consulting Roderick.
It was faded and mournful looking, but quite sound, and
with fresh paint and new curtains could easily be made respectable, if not stylish looking. Mr. Stanley secured it, with
so little opposition, that his sister and niece concluded that
it must have gone at a very low price—which was the case;
it was knocked down at twenty-five dollars, in spite of the
auctioneer's flowery eulogium upon it. Then a large, well-

built market-wagon, set upon high springs, which had evidently been arranged with a view to its use as a family coach, drew forth the liveliest bidding they had yet witnessed. One by one, however, the bidders fell off, and Mr. Stanley secured it for not more than half its first cost. The next vehicle drawn out from the shed excited a general laugh—it had once been a light, two-seated carriage, and the body and wheels still appeared sound, but three of the posts supporting the roof were broken short off, most of the curtains had been torn away, and the cushions had been removed. Altogether, it was a most melancholy looking wreck, evidently the result of some dire accident. The auctioneer, expatiating upon the fact that the body and wheels were sound, tried to start it at five dollars; whereupon the laughter increased, and he was asked why he didn't say five hundred. With many remonstrances, he slid down, by halves and quarters, until at last he said desperately, " Twenty-five cents did I hear? Will none of these gentlemen start her up at twenty-five cents? Why she's worth that much for kindling-wood! Twenty-five cents, twenty-five cents ! "

Arnold stepped forward a little, and nodded; some one else nodded also; Arnold said thirty, and the bids went up, ten cents at a time, until finally the prize was awarded to Arnold, having been run up to one dollar.

Mr. Stanley and Roderick had looked on with great amusement at the eager faces of the boys, and Mr. Stanley said :

" What *can* they intend doing with it, Rod ? It would cost nearly as much to put it in order, as it would to buy a new one."

" I don't know," replied Roderick; " I can see possibilities in it, and I dare say they can, too—you know they have both become very clever at carpentering; I am often surprised at the work they turn out. Did you see the inlaid chess-table they have on hand at the shop ? "

"I did," said Mr. Stanley, "and it surprised me—it looks like the work of a skilled cabinet-maker."

"My father used to say," continued Roderick, "that he heartily approved of the Quaker plan of teaching every boy a trade—it is not so general now, I believe, as it was in his time, but he thought all boys should know thoroughly some one sort of handiwork, by which they might support themselves, should head-work fail, or become impossible. It has guided me in my care of the boys, and I am glad to find that they both have a good deal of mechanical skill."

"It's a first-rate idea," said Mr. Stanley, "and I think it is just as applicable to girls as to boys—so many women who are obliged to work for their living don't know any one thing thoroughly, and so are miserable failures. I intend Edith to learn either dress-making, millinery or telegraphy, as soon as she stops going to school—she may take her choice, but I wish her to really learn one or the other. Are you sure you don't want anything more here, Rod, except the thresher? They're going to bring that out now."

"Yes, I am quite sure," replied Roderick, "and, uncle, please let me say that if the thresher goes for more than twenty-five dollars, I would rather not have it."

"It is nearly certain to go for more than that, Rod," said Mr. Stanley, with some impatience, "and I thought the question was finally settled."

Roderick said no more, and the bidding began, but it was not brisk; very few of the men who were present knew anything about the management of a steam-engine, while most of those who had large farms owned threshing-machines worked by horse-power. Only two men seemed really in earnest, and first one of these dropped off, then the other; no one capped Roderick's bid of twenty-two dollars, and the machine was his. He could not repress a feeling of exultation, as he examined his purchase; he was confident, for the moment, that he would make it pay for itself, with a handsome surplus, before the year was out.

"We may as well go back to your mother and the girls," said Mr. Stanley, "if you're sure there is nothing else here that you wish. Didn't some one say they were going to sell the standing crops next? I do wish you'd reconsider about the wheat—it looks very fine, and is just ready to cut—do oblige me by bidding for it; it seems likely to go cheaper than you could get it elsewhere in the fall, and after it is ground."

"'In for a penny, in for a pound,'" said Roderick, smiling; "I will promise to bid for it, uncle, if I find it is going to be a real bargain; but you know it must go very cheap, to cover the expense of cutting, threshing, and grinding, and yet leave a margin."

"You're abominably clear headed for your age," said Mr. Stanley, half laughing and half annoyed, "but come—there is enough at the barn to keep them going for another hour, and I think we might dispose of our luncheon while they are occupied there—I am fearfully hungry!"

The girls joined Mr. Stanley and Roderick as soon as they were clear of the crowd, and there was a singular unanimity among them upon the lunch question, but when they told Mrs. Stanley and Elizabeth, the former suggested an adjournment to the wagon, instead of to the woods; the day had become quite warm, but the wagon was standing in a shady spot, and the woods were a quarter of a mile away; they must either walk, carrying the heavy baskets, or put Roderick and the boys to the trouble of harnessing the horses, which had been taken out and tied under a tree. There was a little remonstrance at first from the younger girls, but the sale was going briskly on; something which it would break their hearts to lose, according to Edith, might be disposed of in their absence, and as to waiting until all should be

over, not one of them admitted such a possibility. They
were all "simply ravenous." So there was a prompt adjournment to the carry-all, and the feast was distributed, amid
much harmless joking and laughter, and was barely finished
when the auctioneer passed from the contents of the barn
and stables to the standing crops, beginning with the wheat.
Nearly every one present had planted more or less wheat
this year ; few among them cared to take the risk of buying
it as a mere speculation, and the bidding was so languid
that Roderick did not remonstrate when Mr. Stanley, taking
the law into his own hands, broke the solemn pause which
followed the last venture any one seemed willing to make,
with an offer that secured it. The bidding for the other
crops was better, and went on quite briskly, and when the
last of these had been disposed of, the auctioneer turned toward the house, and began with the articles which had been
set out upon the wide veranda. Mrs. Stanley and the girls
had remained in the upper room, amused by the comments
made on the furniture, and the scraps of conversation, as
various people strayed in and out again. Three sunburned,
overworked looking women had seated themselves on the
broad sofa, and opened a conversation in low tones, but
presently the interest of the subject caused them to forget
everything else, and raise their voices so that what they said
was quite audible to every one else in the room.

" You don't say ! Well, that *was* sudden."

" Will they take her home ? "

" Have they got her on ice ? "

" Perhaps they'll embalm her ! "

" No, 'tain't likely—I heard her brother said they'd take
her home if they could do it reasonable, but that the livin'
was to be thought of first, and they do say it costs awful to
embalm anybody—and I shouldn't think nobody'd *want* to
be done that way, if they'd ever been to the *Museum,* and

seen them remnants of old Egyptians. It's enough to give you the nightmare just to look at 'em. For my part, I want to be buried where I happen to die; I've been drove from pillar to post all my life, and I don't care to keep on at it after I'm dead. See there—they're comin' towards the house; let's go down."

"It's a shame to laugh," gasped Edith, laughing helplessly as she spoke, when the women were safely out of the room, "but oh, girls! *did* you notice that one's face, when she said, 'Have they got her on ice?' I thought she was talking of something to eat."

"I fully agree with the one who had no ambition to be like 'them remnants of old Egyptians,'" said Kitty; "I've never quite recovered from the 'turn' a little mummied hand in the Boston Museum gave me. I don't know why, but it seemed to me the most horrible thing I had ever seen."

"I don't think it was half as bad as the heads," said Polly; "I see one of those grinning at me whenever I have a bad dream."

"Oh, girls, for pity's sake, stop!" exclaimed Edith. "We shall be screaming at each other all night if we keep on, and beside, they really have come in, and I hear them beginning to sell things—let's go down and see the fun."

"But we didn't want anything in the parlor, did we?" said Mrs. Stanley.

"I'm not quite certain, aunty," replied Edith; "there were one or two useless but delightful old things there, which I couldn't resist, if they were to go very cheap."

"Then you'd better stay up here, out of the reach of temptation," said Elizabeth, smiling.

"No, I don't think so—if I should hear afterwards that those old girandole frames went for twenty-five cents apiece, my heart would be broken."

11

"But, Edith," said Polly, "the gilding is all worn off, and they haven't any glasses in them."

"Perfectly correct, my dear, but I'm a practised hand at gilding, and I know a bank wherein, if the glasses don't exactly grow, the equivalent for them does; yes, I must see about those girandole frames; restored, and hung in the parlor at home, they will turn countless people green with envy."

Just then the two younger boys rushed in, Arnold exclaiming:

"Oh Edith, didn't you say you wanted a fender? There are three in the parlor, that we quite overlooked, each one handsomer than the other two. Come on—I'll bid for you."

"You lovely boy!" cried Edith, as she followed him; "I thought we had seen everything there; how could we have missed them?"

"They were under that pile of carpet which we thought was solid," he replied; "they and some more andirons; I think this family must have used andirons for mantel-ornaments and mural decorations, from the number and variety about the house. Ernest and I are going to buy some, if they are very cheap, and send them to the great metropolis for sale; Rod says he saw a much commoner-looking pair than any of these, in the window of a second-hand store, marked ten dollars."

The sale of the furniture and household belongings lasted all the rest of the afternoon, and Edith, carried away by the cheapness of everything, went on accumulating treasures, until at last, in reply to her father's mild inquiry as to where they were to be put at home, she announced that she meant to refurnish her little morning-room entirely with antiquities, and that this opportunity was too good to be lost. To her great delight, the widow's agent, as they had decided the man suggested as such to be, manifested no desire for the tall clock, but "them girls" did, and the competition was lively. Edith, carried away by excitement, kept nodding to Arnold to outbid them, and finally secured it at fifty dollars. She looked round at her father, with a deprecating smile, when her name and the price were called out ; he shook his head at her, trying hard to frown, but he had been very much pleased with the clock himself, and had intended securing it if she had not cared for it, so he only said—

" It is to be hoped the ship on your new purchase will come in soon, if you mean to ruin me at this rate; don't buy *all* those fenders, for I want one myself ; I have set my heart on giving it to your aunt for the parlor at Green Point."

The Stanleys wondered at the indifference of most of the people who were present to the curious and beautiful articles of old fashioned furniture which were offered for sale, not realizing that all the houses of any consequence in the neighborhood possessed similar relics, whose value to their owners lay wholly in association ; intrinsically, almost any one of them would have prized more highly the most modern inventions in damask and rosewood.

The sale was over at last, and the accumulated treasures of the Stanley family were piled into the newly purchased wagon, filling it very comfortably. Roderick hunted up Joshua, and engaged his services for the following day to help take home this load and the threshing-machine, and also to help him tie the shafts of the " phaeton," as Edith insisted upon calling the old chaise, firmly to the back of the carry-all ; the harness needed mending, or the new horse would have been utilized to take it home; as it was, Roderick rode the horse bareback, by way of lightening the load ; for Arnold and Ernest, in the face of laughter and unmerciful jokes, insisted upon fastening their vehicle to the back of the chaise, and in this order the cavalcade marched slowly home.

CHAPTER XIII.

" Awake in me a truer life !
    A soul to labor and aspire ;
    Touch thou my mortal lips, O God,
    With thine own truth's immortal fire."—S. J. CLARKE.

EDITH'S treasures were carefully stored in one of the garrets for the present ; her father indulged a faint hope that before they were packed to go home with her she might discover that she did not care for some of the more cumbrous ones, such as the claw-footed sofa and a heavy round mahogany table, with one leg and three claw-feet, beautifully carved, and with a polish which is only attained by years of wax cloth and brush, and can never be counterfeited by oil or varnish. But when he meekly suggested that it would be a troublesome and expensive affair to have her miscellaneous cargo boxed and sent home, she was so distressed and seemed so disappointed that he assured her she should take what she liked, if it only belonged to her. Roderick had not consented to the buying of much furniture, although he had with difficulty restrained his uncle when things went for less than their value. There was no hurry about providing furniture for the garrets until there should be a more immediate prospect of having them plastered. and his mother and he had agreed that their purchases should be confined to articles for immediate use.

Arnold and Ernest had secured three pairs of andirons for a mere trifle, compared with the prices asked at the city stores. but their capital was exhausted, and they were obliged to wait until some more earnings should come in before expressing their treasures to the nearest place where they could be profitably sold. Both boys declined firmly to reveal to any one but their mother what was their design concerning the wreck of a carriage. There was a tumble-down cart-shed leaning feebly against one end of the barn; this they managed to "shore up" until there was no immediate danger of its falling, and here they deposited their treasure, closing the front of the shed from too curious eyes with some old quilts lent them by their mother, and cutting a small window at the back of the shed, too high up for outsiders to look in through it, to give them light for their performances. Here they now spent much of their spare time. Arnold's next allowance of butter money was devoted to the purchase of black paint and varnish, and stains began to appear upon the hands, and even the faces, of the artists, which, in a measure, betrayed the nature of their occupation. Edith declared that she would not leave Green Point until the mystery was revealed, and the boys, upon this, threatened to keep it on hand indefinitely, and so secure her permanent residence on the Estate. The six weeks were already gone, but Mr. Stanley, ably seconded by his daughter, had begged leave to remain two weeks longer; they were both happier and healthier, he said, than they had been for years, and he wished Edith to lay in a stock of strength for the coming ordeal of that last year at school, which she herself dreaded more than she would admit, and which he dreaded for her more yet. She would not be persuaded, however, to give up her design of graduating, and he, knowing how bitterly she would be disappointed should he withdraw her from the school, resolved to watch her closely, and oblige her to care for her health in every other way possible. No one who saw only the light-hearted carelessness of her everyday manner would have guessed how ambitious of success in all that she undertook she really was.

She stood very high in her classes, and even had she been much more conscious than she was of the injury she was inflicting upon her physical health, she would not have withdrawn now, on the eve of her graduation. Mr. Stanley had a half formed plan in his mind, and a half hope that it would draw her away from her object, and, failing that, help her to recover from the effects of the strain which would be put upon mind and body in that last year. The farm which lay next to Green Point had a large meadow fronting on the little river; the ground was slightly elevated just there, several well grown trees were upon it, and, altogether, it was a charming site for a dwelling-house. The strip along the river front, however, was not deep enough for both lawn and garden, according to his ideas, and the ground directly behind this strip was part of the Green Point farm. When Mr. Stanley found how intelligently and systematically Roderick and the boys were laying out their campaign for the following year, and how their plans included every foot of available ground, he hesitated about making his proposal, but the longer he waited, the more attractive his project appeared to him, and he finally introduced the subject a few days before Edith and he returned to their city home, by asking Roderick if he thought the owner of the adjoining farm would be willing to sell him an acre along the river-front. Roderick was very much surprised by the question, but replied that he thought it highly probable. He knew that the man in question had been very much impoverished by the war, and was still a good deal straitened for ready money to carry on his farm; the lot which Mr. Stanley desired to buy had lain fallow for some time, and was only valuable for its oyster beds; but, as the owner had land on the bay shore, he could afford to part with this, presumably.

"You don't ask me what I want with it," said Mr. Stanley, smiling, "and I am very anxious to tell you! I am thinking of building a summer-house for Edith and myself here——"

He was stopped by a shout of delight from all the younger members of the family, and Edith, springing up, seized his hands, exclaiming excitedly—

"Oh, *papa!* Do you really mean it? Are you quite in earnest?"

"I do really mean it, and I am quite in earnest," he replied, drawing her down on his knee; "whether or not I can carry out my earnest meaning depends quite as much upon your aunt as upon the next door neighbor. Would you be willing, Louise," he continued, turning to his sister-in-law, "to sell me an acre from your place, to add to that which borders on the river? My idea is to have a deep lawn, and a good sized garden behind the house, and one acre will not satisfy me."

Mrs. Stanley hesitated.

"I should be quite willing," she said at last, "if Roderick is, and if—are you *sure*, George, that you would wish to buy that other acre, if it belonged to Mr. Logan instead of to us?"

"I will try to keep my temper," said Mr. Stanley, resignedly, "but really, Louise, you are incorrigible! Yes, I am perfectly sure, and, as an evidence of my good faith, Colonel Peyton shall act as referee, if he will be so kind. He shall value the land impartially, and I will offer you the price he fixes upon it, no more and no less. Will that satisfy you?"

"Yes," she replied, "it will entirely, and you must not be angry with me, dear brother; it was no evil deed of which I suspected you, and you must admit that you have given us ample cause to suspect you of good deeds."

"I may have tried to," he said, half laughing and half-vexed, "but you have taken good care that I should not succeed. However, 'I forgive you, and you can't help yourselves.' And now, Rod, what do you say? Will it interfere materially with your deep laid plans, to let me have that acre of land?"

Roderick had been thinking the matter over, while his mother and uncle were discussing it, and he answered frankly—

"No, uncle, I cannot see that it will. The lot of which you speak is part of the land which I had intended sowing with wheat, and I was beginning to be afraid that we could not afford to put so much ground in good condition this year. It will need a large quantity of phosphates to bring it into order again. If Mr. Logan will let you have the other acre, you may count upon the one from the Estate, and the idea of having you for a neighbor is so delightful that I can't quite take it in yet."

"Thank you, my boy," said Mr. Stanley, cordially; "I will see Logan to-morrow morning, and try to conclude the bargain with him before I go away. If this coming winter should prove as mild as the winters, according to the natives, usually are here, there is nothing to prevent me from having a beginning made at once, and I am determined to have the house ready for occupation by next summer, if it be possible. Edith and I have wasted our holidays, year after year, gadding from place to place, not staying long enough anywhere to have any real enjoyment—will you think it stupid, Pussy, to keep house for me in the summer as well as in the winter, after you leave school?"

"Papa, you are fishing for a compliment," she answered merrily, "and on this occasion you really deserve to catch one. I've had the best time this summer I ever had in my life, and the whole plan is too delightful to be true. I don't see how I am going to wait until the house is built."

They all gathered around the parlor-table after tea, and amused themselves with drawing plans for the new house. As each one was finished, it was submitted to Mr. Stanley for his inspection, and he declared that Edith's plan consisted chiefly of bay-windows; Mrs. Stanley's and Elizabeth's of kitchens and closets; and that the others made no provision for either staircases or windows of any kind. Randolph Peyton came in while they were in the midst of these performances, and expressed a proper amount of pleasure upon hearing of Mr. Stanley's intention ; but Edith observed, with a good deal of pique, that it was only a proper amount, and that an expression of doubt, almost of perplexity, rested on his face during the remainder of the evening. She had no feeling beyond a cordial liking for him, but she was used to admiration and attention, and he had not yet rendered her exactly the amount of homage which, in her heart of hearts, she considered merely her due. As for him, he could not have told whether he was glad or sorry that she was coming to live in his neighborhood, for since he had become tolerably well acquainted with her, he found himself in a curious state of divided allegiance. He was beginning to be captivated by the beauty of Elizabeth's character, quite as much as by her sweet and attractive face, before Edith's arrival, but the small advances he had made had met with absolutely no encouragement. Elizabeth's manner to him had been frankly kind and cordial, as it was to his father, and the very novelty of this reception, although it mortified his vanity, made him the more anxious to win at least her friendship, for his handsome face and rather dashing manner had secured for him, so far, a flattering amount of regard and attention from the young girls in the neighborhood, with most of whom he had been more or less intimately acquainted since his childhood.

He had been deeply annoyed on the evening when Edith

had so successfully mimicked Elizabeth's singing and playing. He had already observed that there was a shade of
difference between Elizabeth's manner to Mr. Kendall and
to him—an added respect, a sort of freemasonry of mind,
which increased his prejudice against the "Yankee schoolmaster." But to do him justice, his annoyance on this
occasion was owing quite as much to the fact that Elizabeth
stood convicted of intentional rudeness, a thing of which he
had believed her incapable, as to the favor denied him, and
shown to the schoolmaster. He had absented himself from
Green Point for rather more than a week, but had then
persuaded himself that he really ought to call, to avoid
exciting remark from his mother and sisters. It had so
happened that Edith had found no opportunity to undeceive
him about the music which he had heard and which had
given him such offence. She had decided that it would seem
to attach too much importance to the matter, should she
deliberately explain it to him, so she waited her opportunity
to allow it to explain itself. As to the other two victims,
she felt perfectly indifferent ; but her promise to her father
made her resolve to undeceive them, if they called again
before her departure. Elizabeth had been troubled about
the whole affair, but she would not exculpate herself at
Edith's expense, and had said nothing, fearing she should
say too much, were she to speak at all.

Randolph could not resist the temptation to try his hand
at a plan, and it was so much better than any of the rest,
that Mr. Stanley expressed a good deal of surprise, and asked
him if he had studied achitecture. He admitted that he
had, although it was several years ago, and that when he
first left college, he had almost decided to be an architect.

"Oh, then it's no wonder your windows and doors came
where they belonged, and your house had a visible means of
getting upstairs in it!" exclaimed Edith. "I don't think

that was playing fair; you ought to have told us, and not made us all feel crushed by what appeared to be your natural superiority."

" Your standard as to 'playing fair' is high, Miss Stanley," he replied, with a scarcely perceptible lifting of his eyebrows; " would you consider my question too personal, were I to ask if you always live up to it?" I can't help feeling interested to know."

It flashed across Edith's mind that he must, in some way, have discovered her device on that unfortunate evening, and she felt, to her great annoyance, that a warm wave of color was mounting to her face.

" I don't think that any of us fully live up to our standards," she answered, somewhat abruptly, "but it seems to me it is better to have a high one, even if one sometimes falls short of it, than to have a low one—or none at all."

" That sounds well, Miss Stanley, but will it bear inspection? Repeated fallings-short, it seems to *me*, have a tendency to blunt one's perception of right and wrong, so that in the end the effect must be bad."

" I can't argue," said Edith, impatiently; "I 'never could, you know,' but although that argument is specious, it doesn't seem to me to ring true. If one is to have no standard at all, pray what is the alternative?"

" That is your question," he said lightly, " not mine—it is a good deal like the Wonderland riddle, to which there was no answer; was there not a debating-society, once upon a time, with a rule that whoever asked a question to which he did not know the answer was liable to a fine?"

" It must have been a frightfully stupid affair," she responded. " Where is the use of asking a question, if one already knows the answer?"

" People have been known to be infatuated enough to do it," he replied; " but I admit that it shows a want of wis-

dom. However, my present object in mentioning that
frightfully stupid society, was merely to convince you that
you owe me a forfeit—I have asked you to sing for me, I
believe, every time I have called since you rose upon this
horizon—you need not turn your head away, if you wish to
make a face at me, for that flower of speech, Miss Stanley—
and you have always found some plausible excuse. You are
going to leave us in darkness soon, to continue the figure
which so evidently gratifies you, and I am being driven to
one of two conclusions : either you would sing if you could,
or you can, and will not. Which is it ?"

"It is neither," she answered, bending over the music-rack
as she spoke, and beginning to hunt among the songs;
"you seem abnormally fond of allegories and similes, and
'flowers of speech,' as you gracefully designate them—you
will perhaps recall, when you hear me, the young woman
who bespoke bracelets, and was obliged to take them mixed
with shields."

"Is your voice—your singing voice—such a terrible thing,
then ?" he asked, as she arranged a song upon the rack.
"How little one would imagine it from hearing you speak!"

"You must have had a great deal of practice," she said,
with mock gravity ; "pray, consider my youth and inexperience, and do not turn my little head."

Without giving him time to reply, she struck the opening
chords of the hunting song which she had sung in Elizabeth's best manner a few weeks before. Her imitation of
her cousin's touch and voice was as perfect now as it had
been then, and he listened with a bewildered feeling, which
was amusingly visible on his face. She finished the song,
and began another, before he had found anything to say,
singing the second one simply and unaffectedly, in her own
voice, which was far sweeter and more powerful than Elizabeth's. It had, beside, that scarcely perceptible tremor, on

certain notes, which is so effective when the words and air
sung are pathetic, and with the coquetry which was natural
to her she had chosen a ballad which brought out this quality of her voice. Randolph had listened to her first song
with a feeling of strong and growing indignation, and he
was vexed with himself to find it melting away, as her soft
voice floated and trembled through the words of a song which·
he had always styled " silly" when his sisters sang it.

At her concluding, " Won't you tell me why, Robin ?
Won't you tell me why ? " she turned her eyes appealingly
toward his face, and he wondered that he had ever thought
they were black—why, they were a clear, deep brown, just
the color of cedar-swamp water. And surely, her lips were
trembling, as well as her voice.

" Thank you," he said, with as much significance as he
could express in voice and manner; "you have done me a
double favor, Miss Stanley, but at the same time you have
made me feel that I owe your cousin an abject apology, and
that, in future, I will not take even the evidence of my
senses against her."

Now this should have been very satisfactory, but Edith
was more piqued than she chose to show. Had he any idea,
she wondered, what it had cost her to clear Elizabeth of the
comparatively trifling charge of rudeness, by admitting that
she herself had played a spiteful little trick ? Her face must
have betrayed her thought, for he hastened to add, with a
look of open admiration—

" Believe me, I appreciate what you have just done—it is
so much easier to obey an impulse, than it is to face the
consequences of having obeyed one. You can well afford to
talk of a high standard, Miss Stanley."

Perhaps this was rather too much of a good thing—at any
rate, it caused a sudden revulsion of feeling in Edith's mind,
and a mental comparison of herself with Elizabeth.

"Don't make me feel smaller than I need," she said, lightly; "there is no treatment which equals over-praise, for making one see one's self in a painfully truthful light. Where did you put your plan? I would like to see it again, please."

And she crossed the room, and joined the group about the table, before he could offer a remonstrance.

"She is certainly more volatile and less sweet-tempered than her cousin," mused Mr. Peyton, as he allowed his horse to walk comfortably home, "and somehow, I doubt if she is as thoroughly sincere. And yet—how confoundedly pretty and bewitching she is. Well, at least I mean to find out whether or not she is flirting with me, and if she is—why, that's a little game at which two can play admirably."

CHAPTER XIV.

"And now I see with eye serene
The very pulse of the machine;
A being breathing thoughtful breath,
A traveler between life and death;
The reason firm, the temperate will,
Endurance, foresight, strength and skill."—WORDSWORTH.

MR. STANLEY had been as much pleased with the
Peytons as his sister and her family were. He and
Colonel Peyton had many subjects of conversation in common, and enjoyed meeting each other very much, and the
frank and kindly spirit of hospitality which seemed to per-
vade the house made it a charming place at which to visit.
Mr. Stanley was not long in discovering how greatly the
comfort of the home depended upon the oldest daughter,
quiet and unobtrusive as she was. He missed her if she
happened not to come into the parlor during one of his calls.
He found himself, after he had seen her a few times, confiding to her his hopes and fears concerning Edith, and her
gentle sympathy was very pleasant to him. She had shared
the care of her younger sisters with her mother, and, although she did not venture upon any suggestions with
regard to Edith, he saw that she quite understood his per-
plexities. He began to think to himself how good it would
be for Edith to have the unobtrusive influence of this good
and lovely woman cast about her; how it would change the
entire atmosphere of their home, were she at its head; she
would know by instinct how to deal with his little daughter,
in all the cases which so perplexed and troubled him, and
the beautiful example of her daily life would be the best pos-

sible safeguard against certain hoydenish tendencies which he saw and lamented in Edith, but which he felt he was inadequate to correct. Edith was not obtuse, and she soon observed, with a mingled feeling of pain and amusement, which way her father's thoughts were tending. She had no intention of mentioning her discovery to any one, unless it should take more palpable form; but, as she once said of herself, if it were necessary to keep silent upon any subject, the only really safe place for her would be a desert island, adding— "and an absolute dearth of stationery and bottles; for, if I had no other chance, I should write my views in full, seal them up in a bottle, and launch them in that way, with the hope of having them fished up and read."

The evening on which she had undeceived Randolph Peyton about the singing, she was particularly wide awake, and she kept Kitty and Polly laughing and chattering for an hour after they all went to their room. They had been discussing the new house, and the delights of neighboring with each other, and Edith remarked—

"I only hope we shall not all get tired of each other. That is the sole danger which I apprehend, and if I see the faintest symptom of it, I shall insist upon papa's taking me to Europe at once, for an entire change of air and scene."

"That's all very fine for you, miss," retorted Kitty, "but what are we to do about it? We can't insist on anybody's taking us abroad, or rather, we can if we like, but nobody will do it. We must have some protection. I know what I shall do, individually—most fortunately, this house has two doors; as I see you coming to one, I shall 'softly and silently vanish away' out of the other. If you come three times in succession, and find that I am not at home, you may take it as a sign that, long suffering people as we are, you have worn out your welcome."

"Oh Kitty!" said Polly, very much shocked, "how *can* you say anything so rude? You couldn't wear out your welcome, Edith dear—she does not really mean it, I am sure."

As usual, when poor Polly made "one of her speeches," Edith and Kitty were both laughing before she had finished.

"I'll never get tired of *you*, you darling!" exclaimed Edith, catching Polly up, and whirling her about the room in a waltz which almost took her breath away. "Other people may become monotonous, age may wither, and custom stale them, but you will always be fresh as the morning, and when we live next door, I shall borrow you whenever I am blue, no matter how high the interest on you may be."

"I did that to conceal my real feelings," she panted, as she at last released Polly and sank, breathless, upon the foot of her bed. "I am in a complicated state of mind, one which utterly defies analysis, and if I were not truly and phenomenally amiable, I should be taking heads off all round, just for the abstract pleasure of it."

"How well you conceal your 'real feelings!'" said Kitty, with mock admiration; "I don't think your worst enemy would accuse you of phenomenal amiability! But what, may I ask, is the cause of this tempest in your soul?"

"If you haven't noticed it, you don't deserve to be told," she answered, perversely.

"Haven't noticed what?" asked Polly, wonderingly.

"I know what you mean," said Kitty, nodding her head wisely, "but I didn't mean to speak of it, until, or unless you did. I feel as if we were all turning into a three-volume novel, and I do so wish to know how it is going to end!"

"I can't quite take your abstract view of it," said Edith, with a little grimace; "I hope I'm not utterly selfish, 'but oh, the difference to me!' if anything should come of it. You see, I've been playing at keeping house for papa, ever

12

since I was eleven or twelve years old, and whether or not I could stand it, to begin playing second fiddle now, when I've led the orchestra so long, remains to be seen."

"I wish you'd *please* tell me what you are talking about?" said Polly, plaintively. "You don't really mean that you've been leading an orchestra for concerts and things, do you, Edith?"

"It was a figure of speech, my child," said Edith, her gravity giving way to sudden laughter; "and the plain English of it is, that I don't feel confident that I have the amount of grace which is required by persons of my age who reside with their stepmothers."

"Oh!" said Polly, opening her blue eyes wide. "Is Uncle George going to be married? Will it be soon? Is it to anybody we know?"

"You are hard to ignite, my Polly," said Edith, "but when you do go off, what a conflagration you make! I don't think papa has gone the length of seriously asking anybody to marry him just yet; but there's music in the air which is suggestive, to say the least of it."

"But who is it?" persisted Polly, wonderingly. "I can't think of anybody good enough for him that isn't a great deal too young. Is it somebody down here, or in B—— ?"

"Now, Polly," said Edith, suddenly becoming serious, "if I talk to you about this, you mustn't chatter. I don't mean that you must not tell aunty, of course; no doubt she has seen it as plainly as Kitty and I have; but you mustn't talk of it to any one else, you know. It's that dear saint, Miss Susan Peyton, and if I could stand anybody, I could stand her, for she is as lovely as possible; but the question which arises is, could I stand anybody?"

Polly was silent for a minute or two, thinking it all over. Then she said:

"But what put it into your head, Edith? I don't believe

it, at all! I never was with anybody who was falling in love, to be sure, but I've read stories, and Uncle George and Miss Peyton arn't behaving as lovers do, in books, in the least. He talks a great deal more with Louise and Isabel, and they're both prettier, too."

Edith shook her head.

"You are dealing with glittering generalities, my child," she said. "Papa has taken to lamenting, of late, my prospective loneliness, when I shall leave school, and wishing that he were better able to help and advise me. He has asked me if I have observed what a beautiful and unconscious influence Miss Peyton exerts in her home, and how much more important loveliness of character is than mere prettiness of face. He has said how glad he should be to dismiss the stately dame who undertakes to order the household and matronize me, but that he is afraid the whole care of the house will be too much for me. Then—perhaps it's mean, but I can't help watching him when we are at Rivermouth—he keeps looking from me to her, and from her to me, with an anxious, investigating expression, as if he were trying to see whether or not we match."

"Well," said Polly, resignedly, "perhaps that's the way *old* people go on when they're in love, but they'll have to do more than that before I shall believe in it! And anyhow, Edith," she added, brightening suddenly, "perhaps, even if he wants her, she will not have him."

"I suppose you mean to be consoling, dear," replied Edith, "and I'll accept the intention, but I should be so angry at anybody who had the presumption to refuse papa, that I should be dangerous for weeks. No, if it really comes to anything, I shall try to behave myself, for his sake—he's been too lovely and good to me, all my life, for me to turn again and rend him now, no matter what he may do. And he really might do worse! If it's to be anybody, I would

rather have her than any one else I can think of just at
present, and I'll try not to be more disagreeable to her than
I am by turns to all my family. But remember, not a word
of this is to be mentioned to anybody but aunty! I don't
think it is observable yet to outsiders, and I won't have
papa's affairs gossiped over."

It was quite true that Mr. Stanley, attracted by the
beauty of Miss Peyton's character, was revolving in his
mind the possibility of which his daughter spoke. Since
he had been thrown more with his nieces, he had noticed
more than ever the small ways in which Edith showed the
want of a mother's care. She had a warm heart, and generous impulses, but she lacked stability, and was too ready to
be led by impulse, rather than principle. She was careless,
too, in little matters of "dress and address," to an extent
which sometimes annoyed and troubled him very much, and
yet it was impossible, obliged as he was to leave her to herself for the greater part of every day, for him to correct what
he saw amiss in her. But much as Mr. Stanley felt his
daughter's need of a mother's love and care, and much as he
was attracted by Miss Peyton, he had no intention of taking
any decided step in the matter without consulting Edith's
feelings and wishes, for he knew that, should it happen to
annoy or offend her, no good result to her would come from
it, and he was far more anxious for her happiness than he
was for his own.

It was an amusing side of the matter, that it had not once
occurred to Edith, until Polly suggested it, that Miss Peyton might possibly decline the honor of being Mr. Stanley's
wife and Edith's step-mother, even should it be offered her.
Kitty and Polly were almost as fond of him as his daughter
was; and in spite of Polly's remark, they felt not a doubt
that he would be successful in his wooing in any quarter,
should he choose to woo. He would not have been the

frank and simple-minded man he was, had he shared this feeling; he had very grave doubts as to whether he could induce Miss Peyton to be his wife, but he was not a coward, and he meant, if he found that the idea did not displease Edith, at least to try. He did not dream that she had guessed what was going on in his mind, and rather dreaded the explanation which he intended having with her before saying anything definite to Miss Peyton. His surprise, when she stopped him almost at the first word with a wise nod of her head, and a quiet "Yes, I know, papa; I have seen it coming for some time," was very great.

"Then you must be a witch," he said, laughing, greatly relieved, "and my only safety will be to have you burnt, or sewed up in a sack and anchored in the bay! Surely I have neither said nor done anything which betrayed my thoughts on this matter—how could you guess them? Has any one suggested it to you?"

"My dear little father!" said Edith, in tones of grave reproof, while her eyes sparkled with mischief, "it was you yourself who told me, in my early youth, of the ostrich who hid his head and imagined that nobody could see him. You have behaved very properly—I have no fault to find with you; but, in future, if you wish to conceal anything from me, let me recommend you to wear a mask."

"I suppose it is my own fault that you have turned out such a piece of impertinence," he said. "I should have been more severe with you in that 'early youth' of which you speak so feelingly—I am afraid it is too late to begin to tame you now."

"Nothing is your fault, my darling!" she said, suddenly clasping her arms around his neck. "You have never been anything but good to me, and if I have not turned out well, it is my doing, and not yours."

Edith had fully intended, when the present opportunity

should come, to use whatever influence she possessed with her father against his making a second marriage, if she found, as she expected to find, that he thought it would be for her good as well as his own. But, when the time came, she was governed, as she so often was, by the impulse of the moment, and she presently found herself assuring him earnestly, and with perfect sincerity, that she loved Miss Peyton dearly; that she thought her one of the loveliest women she had ever met, and would not in the least object to having her for a stepmother.

"You see, papa," she continued cheerfully, "it will make it so much easier to get rid of Mrs. Crawford; we should have to do that somehow, before long. It's a perfect bore to have her at the table, when we want to talk to each other—as we always do; and it is my belief that she grows stiffer and primmer all the time. It would be sort of awkward to tell her in so many words that we are tired of her, and would like her to go, but if you marry Miss Peyton, she will see for herself that her remaining would be a work of supererogation."

"In any event," said Mr. Stanley, smiling at this ingenious plea for his marriage, "she need not remain after you leave school, if you are willing to devote a little time every day to giving orders and seeing that they are carried out. If our plans succeed, and we are settled in our new house, this time next year you will have your aunt close at hand, and can always go to her for advice."

"But you don't mean to live here in winter as well as summer, do you, papa?" asked Edith, a little doubtfully. "I should like to see a little of the madding crowd before permanently retiring from it."

"Don't be alarmed," he replied; "we shall spend our winters in B——, and you can go there for a visit whenever you feel inclined; but I have always thought that people

who have country homes reverse the order of things—they
generally come into town in September or October, just when
the country is most attractive, and go out so late as to miss
all the beauty of the spring. My plan would be to board at
some quiet hotel from the first of December to the end of
March, and to spend the rest of the year in our country
home."

"Then what would you do with the house in town,
papa?" she asked. "We should no longer have any use
for it."

"I should move the furniture down here," he replied,
"and either sell or rent the house. But if you would prefer
to keep it for our winter home, dear, I am perfectly willing.
I suppose you will be 'coming out' in a couple of years or
so, and perhaps it would be better, at any rate for your first
society winter, that you should have your own home to entertain in."

"May I think it over before I answer you, papa?" she
asked, with unusual thoughtfulness. "I should like to hear
what Aunt Louise says about it."

"Certainly, dear; it must not be decided hastily, and
there is no one whose judgment I would so readily trust as
your aunt."

"Except, you mean, papa,——" she began, mischievously,
but he interrupted her with—

"I make no exception. Your aunt's judgment is founded
on well used experience."

CHAPTER XV.

"Kindness by secret sympathy is tied ;
For noble souls in nature are allied."—DRYDEN.

BEFORE Mr. Stanley and Edith left Green Point, several things were settled. Mr. Logan was found to be quite willing to sell the acre of land upon which Mr. Stanley desired to build, for he was sensible enough to see that a residence such as the one proposed would, by its neighborhood, increase the value of his own property. Many of the landowners in the vicinity had for some time desired to sell a few building-lots, and see the country more thickly settled, but, until the line of boats recently established began to run, the difficulty of access had proved an effectual bar to enterprise of all kinds. Now there was a more hopeful feeling ; it was confidently expected that real estate would increase in value, and that there would before long be a demand for it.

Mr. Stanley wished Roderick and his mother to accept the price which Mr. Logan had asked, and which he considered very reasonable, for their acre, but to this they would not consent, reminding him that they had agreed to ask Colonel Peyton to appraise the land, and be governed by what he said. Nothing was said upon the subject, but Mrs. Stanley and her children greatly hoped that the price set upon the land would cover the indebtedness contracted at the sale ; it weighed upon the older ones, as they had feared it would, and they all had a feeling that nothing which was not absolutely necessary must be bought until it was paid. The appraisement was made, and, to their great joy, amounted to what they owed, with a few dollars to spare ; Mr. Stanley begged them to let the debt stand, and take the money to carry out the plans concerning the house and grounds which he knew were awaiting an opportunity, but here they stood firm. Mrs. Stanley expressed her gratitude for his kind intention warmly, but assured him that they felt more than ever that their wisest course would be to "pay as they went," and to take the sound advice given to the anxious inquirer who asked, "But suppose I can't pay?" "Then don't go!" They were well provided now, thanks to his kindness, she said, with everything necessary to carry on the farming comfortably and successfully, and as for the adornment of and additions to the house, nothing was wanted which could not readily be waited for until they had succeeded in laying by the money to pay for it. Mr. Stanley was disappointed, but he was wise enough to see that it was quite useless to argue the matter, and he tried to be satisfied with their very evident satisfaction. About one thing, however, he carried his point. He represented to Roderick that it would be impossible for him to leave B—— often enough, during the fall and winter, to attend satisfactorily to the building of the house, and that his nephew would be doing him a real favor by acting as a sort of general overseer, making sure that the work was faithfully done, and only good material used. Roderick readily consented, until Mr. Stanley added that he must of course be compensated, as any one who undertook the matter would be, for his time : then he demurred, saying that he should have more leisure in the winter than he had now, and that the hour or less which he would devote to the inspection of the work every day would not be worth reckoning.

Mr. Stanley thought a moment, then he said : "Very well, we will leave it this way; if you find your inspection

has had no visible or tangible result; if you have no blunders to prevent, or mistakes to correct, I will admit your
proposition, and accept your services for nothing, although
that, as you may imagine, will scarcely be more pleasant for
me than my proposition would be for you. But if, on the
other hand, you find that things would have gone wrong
but for your presence, I shall pay you ten dollars a week,·
from the time the house is begun until it is finished. As
you are so confident that the inspection will be a mere form,
you will, of course, agree to this ?"

Roderick was confident, for he knew that his uncle was
going to employ a first-rate architect to draw the plan of the
house, and a well-known master-builder from B——, who
would bring his own corps of workmen with him to carry it
out, so he smilingly agreed to his uncle's proposal.

"But mind, my boy," added Mr. Stanley, "you are to keep
a note-book, and carefully record anything that may occur,
such as I have mentioned. There is a curious stupidity
about the building of houses, and I am very anxious that
the plan should be exactly carried out. To give you an
instance : you know I built the house in which we now live
in B——, I was very busy at the time, and unable to be
there more than once or twice a week, but I had perfect
confidence in the master-builder, until a series of blunders
destroyed it. One of his feats was permitting every inside door to be hung on the wrong side of the doorway;
where it did not make too much difference, I allowed it to
remain, for I was anxious to have the house completed, and
annoyed by unexpected and unnecessary delays, but at least
half of them had to be changed. You can see for yourself
that it is worth a good deal to me, both in time and money,
not to speak of needless wear and tear of temper, to have
such things prevented."

Roderick admitted that it was, and promised to keep a

faithful record, if he found anything to record, but his private opinion was that he would not.

Edith had succeeded so well in convincing herself that it would add to her own happiness, as well as her father's, if Miss Peyton would consent to marry him, that it was with real disappointment, and no slight indignation, that she heard that his proposal had been gently, but very firmly, declined.

"There is no cause for anger about it, my little girl," said Mr. Stanley, with a somewhat forlorn smile; "Miss Peyton had never given me the slightest reason for thinking she would accept me—indeed, she was very much surprised, for I do not think such an idea had crossed her mind. I am not ashamed to own that I am disappointed, but I admire and reverence her even more than I did before—she is quite right in thinking and saying that, if people cannot give each other the deepest and most whole-hearted love, they do wrong to marry."

"But I don't see why she *couldn't* love you with all her heart, papa," said Edith, still unappeased; "I wonder if she wants an angel!"

"She has convinced me that she does not want any one," he replied; "but she has promised, with perfect sincerity, to be my friend and yours, and perhaps, after all, it is better so. No one could ever fill your mother's place in my heart, my darling, and I had no right to expect such a woman as Susan Peyton to be content with any but the first place in the heart of her husband."

Much had been said, in the frank and friendly talk which followed Mr. Stanley's proposal to Miss Peyton, which he did not repeat to Edith. She had admitted that Edith's motherless condition, and winning character and manner, tempted her to accept Mr. Stanley. She had the real mother heart, which is so often bestowed upon women "whose children are all dream children," and when she learned from Mr. Stanley that Edith not only was submissive in the matter, but earnestly wished his success, she wavered. Ought she not to take this duty upon her—to embrace an opportunity for doing so much good? She could not help acknowledging that much in Edith's future would depend upon the influences which should surround her for the next few years, and she longed to take the young girl to her heart and give her every help and encouragement within her own power. Then, too, she heartily liked and respected Mr. Stanley—more, rather than less, for the perfect candor with which he told her that his dead wife would always keep her place in his heart; and that his love for his child had strongly influenced him when he decided upon this step. To the vanity of some women this would have been unpardonable, but Miss Peyton was utterly free from vanity, and she recognized the chivalrous honesty which would let no false pretense plead for it. But she only wavered for a moment; one thing was quite clear, and this decided her. All that Mr. Stanley offered, or asked, was sincere respect and friendship, and much as this was, it was not enough. Only love, pure and perfect, could, in her eyes, justify marriage, and no reasoning with herself, however specious, could change this belief. She never yet had seen any one who had waked this love in her heart, and she did not now expect to, but she would as soon have tried to perform a "rolling organ harmony" on a penny trumpet, as to fill its place with anything less or lower.

"And the worst of it is," said Mr. Stanley, ruefully to himself, as he thought over their conversation, "that I quite agree with her. She would despise me if she were not so angelically charitable. I believe I am much nearer being 'in love' with her now, bless her! than I should be if she had accepted me."

Edith rather frigidly declined making a farewell call at Rivermouth, and her father did not urge it. He was amused, but a good deal touched, also, by her resentment of the wrong which she fancied had been done him. But he trusted to time and her own good sense to efface this impression, and thought it better not to deepen the feeling by too much opposition. He felt not a shadow of anger or resentment himself, but a real regret that he might not have the companionship of this good and sweet natured woman, and her influence over Edith.

There was an endeavor made to settle a plan for Christmas, but no conclusion was arrived at. Mr. Stanley urgently invited the whole family to spend not only that day, but the whole of the holiday week, including New Year's day, with him; he said that his own family would seem so ridiculously small after the tableful of bright faces with which he had been surrounded three times a day, that they really ought to take compassion on him; but Mrs. Stanley said it would be too vast an undertaking to transport such a crowd in the middle of winter, and that it would be much better, in every way, for him to bring Edith to Green Point. Neither side having exhausted its arguments, the question was left for future settlement—there was plenty of time, for as yet it was only September, and Mr. Stanley expected to return in a month or two to see how the house was progressing. Both he and Edith were full of interest in it and plans for the following summer, in all of which the other family shared. It seemed quite probable that the present visit would once more have been extended, had it not been for the re-opening of Edith's school, which would take place now in a few days. She was nervously anxious not to miss a single day; she knew that it would require unceasing effort on her part to pass such an examination, at the end of the term, as the one prepared for the graduating class. She

learned quickly and readily, but her memory was not reten-
tive, and reviews were her special dread. She tried, however, not to let her father see her apprehension, for she
feared that, should he imagine that it or overstudy were
affecting her health, he would remove her from her school
at once. She consoled herself by thinking that, with the
pressure upon her which this last year at school would bring,
she would at least have no time for loneliness. After the
busy cheerfulness of a large and active family, she dreaded
the silence and loneliness of her home. Mrs. Crawford, who
attended to all the real business of the housekeeping, while
she amiably permitted Edith the little airs of importance
and the seat behind the urn at table, which were her chief
share in it, had been in charge of Mr. Stanley's house since
the death of Edith's mother. She was a good woman, and
faithfully and honestly discharged her duties, quite recognizing "her mercies," as she termed the liberality and kindness with which Mr. Stanley invariably treated her. But
she was dull and formal, with little interest in anything
beyond her daily routine, and Edith had long since given
up all attempt at companionship with her. Mr. Stanley,
considering her long and conscientious service, and the fact
that any change of administration would probably be a
change for the worse, counseled Edith to be patient, and to
remember how impossible it would be, at least while she was
still attending school, to carry on the housekeeping herself.
But neither of them could help silently noting the contrast
when, on the evening of their return home, they sat down
to dinner, and Mrs. Crawford, after a few half interested
inquiries and common-place remarks, had relapsed into the
stiff silence which was her usual condition, and which somehow had the effect of making all that was said seem, as Edith
put it, like "talking into a vacuum." Mrs. Stanley's sweet,
bright, interested face at the head of her table acted as an

inspiration to her children, and Edith had more than once threatened to take notes of the lively talk which flashed about at meal times. Perhaps the very fact that the family, by reason of the different employments of its members, was seldom all together, excepting these times, was accountable for the flow of conversation, but Mrs. Stanley had always made the table a pleasant place for her children, and she tried, without seeming to try, more than ever to do so, now that they were cut off from so many other pleasures.

"If she were only deaf and dumb, papa," said Edith, dolefully, as she drew her father into the library, when the silent dinner was at last ended, "we could stand it perfectly well, and talk across her quite cheerfully, but there is nothing so utterly suppressing as a person who hears and does not speak!"

"Oh well," he replied, good-naturedly, "you must remember that for the past two months the poor soul has been obliged to be silent, for want of some one to talk to, and so is in the habit of it—perhaps she'll brighten up a little, when we have been at home a few days. And you must admit that the house is in most spotless order, and she did not bother us once while we were gone, although she tells me she was obliged to hunt both a new housemaid and cook."

"That's just it!" said Edith, perversely. "One has not even the satisfaction of finding fault with her. It would make a little excitement to attack her, and have her defend herself. But no—our faintest wishes are consulted, and she appears to have absolutely none of her own. The monotony is fearful. Papa," she added, suddenly, "*do* you suppose that Colonel and Mrs. Peyton would allow Isabel to spend the winter and go to school with me?"

"I don't know, dear, but we might try," he replied, with the cheerful interest which he always showed in any of her plans or wishes, which were not too wildly unreasonable.

" She's a very sweet girl, I should think, from what I saw of
her, but isn't she a little old to begin school again ? I heard
her say she was nineteen, one day when we were there, I
think."

"That's just it!" said Edith, all her listlessness vanishing
in a moment. "She told me how sorry she was to leave
school—it wasn't a very good one, I judged from what she
said—and how much she would enjoy another term, if she
might take only the things she liked best, German and
Italian, and music and singing. She couldn't find a better
place than Madame's for all of these, and it would be so
delightful to have her here to study, and walk and talk
with. *May* I write and ask her ?"

"Of course you may, dear!" he replied, heartily. "It
can do no harm to ask, whatever comes of it. But try not
to set your heart too much upon it, until the answer comes,
for I am afraid the trouble will be that they cannot afford
it, and even if they can, Isabel's mother may not wish to
spare her for so long a time."

"I will try, papa, but I am afraid my heart is pretty well
set already. And surely they can afford it—they could not
live so comfortably, and entertain so much, if they were
very poor."

"Mrs. Peyton is a capital manager, dear, and nearly all
the furnishing of their table comes from the place; but from
little things the Colonel has said, I think they have not
much ready money, and if I know Isabel at all, she would
not secure this advantage at the expense of the rest."

"Oh papa! Don't you think we might manage, without
offending them, to let them know that you would pay her
bills as well as mine ?"

"No, my child, I do not!" and Mr. Stanley spoke very
decidedly. "They will of course understand that we wish
her to be our guest for the winter, and I am afraid their

pride will scarcely submit to that. They would be hopelessly offended, should I suggest the other."

"It is very hard!" said Edith, mournfully. "I don't see why people who have things may not give them to people who haven't!"

"They may," said her father, smiling; "but there are ways and ways of giving, and, as you will probably have a good deal of money to spend by and by, it is high time you were beginning to study the art in all its branches. Money itself cannot always be offered, and ought not always to be accepted; but money's worth, given with tact, and in ways that show that time and thought have been given too, rarely offends or hurts any one."

"I think that must be an apothegm, papa," said Edith, gravely, "and you'd better write it down for me. But may I write and ask Isabel at once—this evening?"

"It seems to me," replied her father, "that it would be better, in every way, for me to write to Mrs. Peyton, and to ask her not to mention the plan to Isabel, unless she is willing that it should be carried out. That will save disappointment, if it cannot be; and you will not think me vain, I hope, ma'am, if I say that I think the invitation might have more weight, coming directly from me."

"I dare say you are right, papa," said Edith, a little reluctantly; "but I thought that, if I were to write to Isabel, and her heart should be *very* much set upon the plan—as I think it would—they might be more inclined to consent to it, because they would not like to disappoint her. Don't you see?"

"Yes, I see," he answered, smiling at this transparent plotting, "and I don't know that I ought to lend myself to any such deed of darkness; but, if you are willing to risk Isabel's disappointment, you may write a note to her, and I will enclose it with mine."

13

" Thank you, papa—that is much better," she exclaimed joyfully, and started up to bring her writing-desk.

The rest of the evening was devoted to composition ; each of the scribes made several attempts, before they were satisfied, but both at last nodded approvingly, first at their own, and then, exchanging copy, at each other's productions. The results of their labors were as follows :

Mr. Stanley to Mrs. Peyton.

"MY DEAR MADAM—

" You will, I hope, pardon the liberty I take, if it is a liberty, in writing to ask of you a very great favor. My little girl is feeling by contrast, as she never felt before, the silence and loneliness of her home, and has a very earnest wish for the companionship, this winter, of your daughter Isabel. If there are any branches of study which Miss Isabel would like to pursue, she would have excellent opportunities at the school which Edith attends, and her presence in our home would be a real pleasure to both of us. Should you consent to entrust your daughter to our care, we will do all in our power to make the winter both pleasant and profitable for her, and bring her back to you in the spring, or early summer, when we go to take possession of our Delaware home, one great attraction of which will be the fact that we shall be your neighbors.

" We shall both be greatly disappointed, should our request be refused, but I hope that you will see no reason why it may not be granted.

" Believe me most respectfully and sincerely yours,

" GEORGE STANLEY."

Edith to Isabel.

"MY DEAR ISABEL—

" Papa is writing to your mother, but I, of course, cannot be satisfied without putting my oar in as well. We want you to come and keep us from stagnating this winter. I am realizing, as I never realized before, the fact that only daughters are a mistake. Mrs. Crawford is more automatic than ever. The house resembles that tomb which was 'not even a receiving tomb, you know,' and I feel like Marius among the ruins of Carthage. But we will change all that, if you will only come. You shall have every opportunity to improve your mind. Mine will be stretched this winter to its utmost capacity, and it will be encouraging to have yours stretching in company with it. Seriously, you could find the best possible chances at Madame Marotte's, for perfecting yourself in those branches of which you were speaking the other day. You would be quite able, I am sure, should you wish to do so, to take the whole course for the final year, and graduate. And if you could only understand, dear Isabel, how lonely and forlorn I feel, after those few happy weeks with my aunt and cousins, I am sure you would take pity on me, and give me the great pleasure which this visit would—no, *will* be to me.

"I shall be dreadfully impatient for your answer, so do not keep me in suspense any longer than need be. And if you can come, do not wait for any preparation. You know I am a competent dressmaker, and a brilliant milliner, and our sewing woman has not half enough just now to keep her busy. Beside, the distraction of a few pomps and vanities will be good for my about-to-be-overtaxed intellect. I can think of no more arguments, or I would use them ; but surely, these are enough. Give my love to your mother and father, and remember me kindly to the rest of your family, and tell Mrs. Peyton to put herself in my place, before she decides.

"Believe me, affectionately yours,

"EDITH STANLEY."

Edith's resentment toward Miss Peyton had softened a little, but her father smiled at the wording of her messages to the family; it was evident that she did not yet feel equal to sending her love to the offender. He was not sorry that the matter had ended as it had, after all. He dreaded change of any kind, and was already half repenting his decision and prompt action about the new home, and doubting whether the keen enjoyment of country-life, during his visit to his sister, which had helped to induce him to make the change, would last over three-fourths of the year. It was too late, however, to draw back now, and he consoled himself with the thought that it would be infinitely better for Edith, than the unsettled summers which they had spent for the last few years. He was particularly desirous not to expose her to the influences of hotel and boarding-house life for the next few years—years which would, in so large measure, decide her future. He said nothing to her of his misgivings, and listened indulgently to all her plans and suggestions about the house. The architect was engaged upon the plan, and it was to be submitted to Edith, before being finally decided upon. This fact, and the brilliant ideas which were constantly occurring to her, served to beguile the time, and, in a measure, make her forget her impatience during the week which elapsed after the letters were sent, before Mrs. Peyton's answer was received. But she appealed to her father so frequently to know whether or not her suggestions were practicable, that he finally, in despair, threatened to turn her and her suggestions together over to the architect, and let her "fight it out" with him. He had no expectation of being taken at his word, but she was delighted with the idea, and said with decision—

"That will be the very thing, papa. Ask him to spend an evening here, and *he* will tell me whether or not a three-story bow window is possible, and if we can't have a veranda wide enough to set a table in."

"Are you serious?" asked Mr. Stanley, in astonishment.

"Perfectly, papa," she replied. "Don't I look so?"

"Very well!" he said, resignedly; "I will ask him."

CHAPTER XVI.

"Men's looks are nigh as often gay
As sad, or even solemn:
Behold, my entry for to-day
Is in the 'happy column.'"

"HERE it is, papa! Our answer has come, and I thought you'd never come home to read it," cried Edith, running eagerly into the hall, as her father opened the front door.

"I am half an hour earlier than usual to-day, Miss Impatience," he said, stooping to kiss her; "but open the letter while I take my coat off—there is a note for you from Isabel inside, probably."

There was, and Edith tore it open, while her father, in more leisurely fashion, unfolded Mrs. Peyton's letter to him. It was as follows:

"MY DEAR Mr. STANLEY—

"You will, I know, excuse the slight delay which has attended my answer to your very kind and generous proposition. The question was too momentous to be decided in haste, but now that it is decided, I hasten to let you know the result. We accept, with great pleasure, your invitation to our daughter, feeling that it would be selfish to refuse it: for, apart from the enjoyment which this visit will give her, it will afford her an opportunity which she has greatly desired. She and I are quite agreed in thinking that it will not be best for her to attempt to pass the examination which would be necessary were she to graduate; the endeavor to perfect herself in the variety of studies which she must in that case pursue, and the anxiety she would feel, would divert her mind from the special branches in which she has had so little opportunity. Other things she can more readily continue alone; but in languages and music good instruction is all important. We shall miss her sadly, but it would be selfish to deprive her of such advantages as you offer on that account; and believe me, we feel very grateful, both to yourself and your daughter, for this evidence of your friendship. I will not praise my girl to you; I will only say that if you like her now you will be very sure to love her before the winter is over. In accordance with your desire that no time may be lost, she will leave home on Wednesday of next week. Her father cannot just now be absent conveniently, but her brother will see her safely to your house, and bids me say that he shall be very glad of the excuse to spend a few hours in the society of your daughter and yourself.

" With kindest love to Miss Stanley, in which my daughters beg to join, I am gratefully and sincerely yours,

"SUSAN R. PEYTON."

" P. S.—Colonel Peyton begs to be kindly remembered to Miss Stanley and yourself. S. R. P."

Isabel Peyton to Edith Stanley.

"MY DEAR EDITH.

" You must not imagine me ungrateful or negligent because I have left your letter unanswered for three days. There were so many pros and cons to discuss that it was impossible to arrive at a conclusion any sooner. I can't tell you, in writing, all I think of it—I don't write readily at any time, and least of all when my heart is full. But when I see you, as I hope to do next week, I hope I can make you understand at least a part of my feelings about this. I have greatly wished to teach since I left school; indeed, I wished it long before that, but I could not feel that I was competent to undertake it with the very imperfect education which I had been able to command. With this golden opportunity it will be my own fault if I cannot, by a few months' additional study and practice after I return home, fit myself to make a beginning, which is always the hardest part. I will not go into my reasons for wishing to teach now, when I am to see you so soon, and talking is so much easier than writing. I am wondering all the time what made you choose me, when you must know so many girls who would have done greater credit to your choice. But you could have chosen no one who would have been more truly glad and grateful than your loving   " ISABEL."

Edith waltzed entirely round the room by herself when she had read both letters; then she held out her arms imploringly, saying,

"Papa, just one turn! I feel positively explosive—nothing but exercise will save me."

He caught her in his strong arms and gave her the "one turn" with such rapidity that she breathlessly begged for mercy, and they dropped upon the lounge together panting and laughing.

"At your age, papa!" she said, holding up a reproving finger. "Do you wish to give me heart disease and yourself apoplexy?"

"Forty-seven is not very old, you arrogant creature," he answered, laughing; "you needn't imagine that you have a monopoly of youth because you are barely seventeen; but pray, don't mention to Mrs. Crawford that I know how to waltz—she might not believe that I reserve the practice of the accomplishment solely for you."

"I'll not tell her so long as you *do* reserve it for me, sir," said Edith, graciously; "but oh, isn't it lovely? I had almost worried myself into the belief that they would not let her come. Next Wednesday—and this is Saturday—I shall have to dynamite Mrs. Crawford, or we will not be ready."

"Pray, what revolution do you propose making?" inquired Mr. Stanley; "I was under the impression that we had two or three spare rooms in the house, any one of which might answer for Miss Isabel."

"Why, *of course* we must have adjoining rooms, papa," said Edith, in tones which carried conviction, "and the little room behind mine is not good enough for Isabel—it only has two windows, and the carpet and things are sort of faded."

"If that's all, why not get new ones? There will be plenty of time, and Mrs. Crawford can attend to it."

"Please don't interrupt, sir. The nicest room, the one I want her to have, is the south room, on the other side of the entry. She loves flowers, and I can put stands in two of the windows, and still leave her one to sit by. I'm sorry to move away from next door to you, dear, but you'll not know I am gone when you are asleep——"

"Any more than Isabel will know that you are next door to her, when *she* is asleep."

"Papa! you are incorrigible. She will be a little homesick at first, of course, and will want me near her; but if you'd really rather not have me go, of course I will not."

"I was only joking, little daughter. Take any room you please, and you'll please me."

"That's a dear father. Well, I shall put my new lounge in the south room, and take back my old one out of the little room—it will do quite well for another winter with a new cover——"

"Oh! I understood that it was 'positively disgraceful'; that you would 'rather have none at all'; that——"

"It was all that, and more, papa; but you see it never occurred to me that I might have it covered, until after the new one was bought. You should not have such an alarmingly good memory, dear. There ought to be some book-shelves, and a table large enough to hold a desk, and books and papers, I think, in Isabel's room; for, of course, she will sometimes wish to study there. Do you think you can afford them, papa, if I turn my winter bonnet?"

"I'll try, my daughter. You can come to meet me on Monday afternoon, and we will go and choose them. Tell me of anything else which you can think of, which would make the room prettier and more comfortable—we must show Miss Isabel that we appreciate the favor she is doing us."

"There isn't any very comfortable chair in that room, papa," said Edith, after a few moments of deep thought; "and there is no denying that the carpet is ugly—it was Mrs. Crawford's choice, you know, when we were away last summer; she said she thought it was lovely, so don't you think—would it be very extravagant to put it in her room, and get a new one for Isabel? She has darned her carpet within an inch of its life, but I don't suppose the washer-woman would object to it."

"That is a far reaching and excellent arrangement," said Mr. Stanley, smiling at the ingenuity of it; "we will choose a carpet on Monday, as well as the table and chair. Must there be new curtains to match the new carpet?"

"Oh no, papa," said Edith, virtuously; "that would be sheer extravagance. The curtains in that room are the love-liest shade of blue I could find in the whole city. I don't believe I could get anything half so pretty in the short time we have, so I will make the other things harmonize with them."

" Like the lady who tried to live up to her dado ? "

" Exactly. How brilliant you are this evening, little father. My goodness! there's the dinner-bell, and you've never washed your face nor smoothed your hair! Run, run, or you'll be late, and the Monument will say mildly, but chillingly, 'I'm afraid your soup is cold, Mr. Stanley—it does not improve by standing.' "

The tone and manner were so exactly Mrs. Crawford's that Mr. Stanley could scarcely control a smile, but he was troubled about the talent for mimicry which Edith had lately developed, and he said gravely—

" My little girl must remember that women have no more right to carry concealed weapons than men have."

" I know it, dear," she said, penitently; " I'm always sorry afterward, but it's a terrible temptation."

" And so much the more worth overcoming," he said, as he left the room to " make himself tidy," an expression of Mrs. Crawford's, which was one of Edith's favorite quotations.

The good woman showed a mild and proper amount of interest in Edith's triumphant announcement concerning Isabel, but her share of the preparations was promptly and faultlessly carried out. She was evidently much pleased with the arrangement which gave to her room the carpet of her choice, although her conscience obliged her to enter a faint protest against giving the much-darned specimen on her floor to the washerwoman.

" It could be laid by, Miss Edith, my dear—it would be quite safe from moths, wrapped in newspapers with plenty of camphor, and it would do perfectly well for the servants' attic, when their present carpet is worn out. The end of one breadth, the one that has been under the bed since its last turning, is perfectly good. Wealth is no excuse for wastefulness."

"But there's no wastefulness in giving it to the washer-woman," said Edith, impatiently. "I am ashamed to offer her such a rag ; but she told the cook she'd be thankful for anything, so I am taking her at her word."

Both Edith and her father greatly enjoyed the shopping expedition on Monday afternoon. Mr. Stanley was sorely tempted to add a new lounge to the purchases, but he had been so pleased with the little sacrifice Edith had proposed to make for her friend that he compelled himself not to spoil it. A pretty, low rocking-chair and a little wicker sewing-chair were chosen; but when it came to the writing-table, he said that he thought a Davenport would answer the purpose much better, and he made Edith choose one as nearly like her own as could be found. This was delightful, and she went with him to the carpet store in such overflow-ing spirits, that he begged her to think of something un-pleasant, so that she might not subject him to the suspicion of being the keeper of a harmless lunatic.

The chair was blue, to match the curtains, and Mr. Stanley inquired if the carpet was to be blue also, adding that he saw but one difficulty before them—they would probably have some trouble in finding a cake of blue soap! Edith, ignoring the latter part of his remark, said that she was a little uncertain about the carpet—she was afraid a blue one would fade, and so much blueness would be "trying" to any but a faultless complexion.

"And you know I shall be in the room frequently, papa," she said ; "so if I can find it, I'll take a harmony instead of a match—it will be more soulful and suggestive, you know."

Fortunately, the "harmony" was found without much trouble—a pretty Brussels carpet, in soft shades of wood-brown and pearl-gray—"cheerful, but not obstrusive," as Edith said. As the walls of the room were tinted a light blue, the effect would be much prettier than if the carpet had been blue also.

"We have still half an hour, dear," said Mr. Stanley, looking at his watch as they left the carpet store; "would it not be a good idea to stock the Davenport with useful and ornamental stationery? You can attend to the flower-stands and flowers to-morrow; it will be better not to have them sent in until Wednesday morning, after everything else is ready."

"Papa, you are an unrecognized genius!" cried Edith, delightedly; "I should never have thought of that, but it is a beautiful idea. Come, let's walk a little faster, so that we may have more time."

She decided, as they walked home, that choosing the stationery had been the best part of the altogether charming expedition, and Mr. Stanley, happy in her happiness, did not even hint that the supply would be quite adequate, were Isabel's visit to extend over years instead of months. It had given him heartfelt pleasure that Edith had expressed no wish for anything for herself in any of the shops which they had visited; she had been entirely absorbed in her plans for Isabel. This would not, he knew, have been the case before her visit to Green Point, but the daily lesson of a home where "each esteemed other better than themselves," had not been wasted.

School had begun on the day of the shopping expedition, and Edith was obliged the next morning to leave the scene of the preparations, and be absent until nearly three in the afternoon. She did it with extreme reluctance, after heaping directions and injunctions upon Mrs. Crawford, to all of which that long suffering woman replied with a moderate smile, and a quiet, "Certainly, Miss Edith."

It was with great difficulty that Edith kept her mind upon her lessons that morning, but her ambition was wide awake again, and she resolutely turned her thoughts from carpets and furniture, curtains and flower-stands, to geometry, Latin, physical geography, and literature. But she hastened home when school was over for the day, in spite of all entreaties to stay and talk over the new teachers and the probabilities for the opening session. She could scarcely be induced to eat her lunch when she found that the carpet had not only arrived, but was actually being tacked down, but Mrs. Crawford's quiet voice stopped her at the foot of the stairs with—

" Your papa left a special request that you would attend to nothing until you had lunched, Miss Edith, my dear ; and he has sent home some birds, which are waiting for you."

An impatient exclamation rose to Edith's lips, but she checked it, thinking, remorsefully, " The idea of my being provoked with anything papa does, when he is so good, so lovely to me !" and going meekly to the dining-room, she resolutely devoured two of the birds, with bread and butter " accordin'."

By the time she had finished, the tack-hammers of the two experts who had come with the carpet had ceased their marvelously rapid tattoo, and she was at liberty to help Mrs. Crawford with the other arrangements of the room. Her father had undertaken to order the flowers and flower-stands, on his way to the counting-house, and had received special injunctions to have them sent "not *sooner* than five, papa, nor *later* than six ;" she had wished to attend to the matter herself, but he quietly took it out of her hands, saying, " You know it takes a highly trained rider, my dear, to ride more than one horse at a time without getting a fall."

She began to reply with a puzzled—

" What *do* you mean, papa ?" but his significant glance at the pile of books in her book-strap on the table, enlightened her.

"I am glad for you to have the pleasure of arranging the rooms, my little girl," he said, "but I wish to spare you all needless trouble. My conscience is uneasy about this school-business, so you may set down all my unusual acts of solicitude as so many sops to Cerberus."

"I am very much obliged to Cerberus," she answered, gaily, "not to mention you, papa. And I can trust to your taste in ordering the flowers, without any misgivings."

It was nearly six, and she was beginning to express her fears that "something had happened" about the flowers, when they arrived; two half circular stands of light wire-work, set in zinc trays, several inches larger, so that the plants might be freely watered. But beside these there was a porcelain flower-pot on a bronze tripod, filled to over-flowing with a luxurious maiden-hair fern. The plants for the two stands comprised several varieties of roses, a calla-lily, heliotropes, white "lilies of the saints," and red and white carnations.

Edith went into a fresh ecstasy over each plant, as it was placed upon the stand. She dearly loved flowers, and her pleasure in them never lost its freshness.

"But where is this lovely, lovely fern to go, papa?" she asked, when the stands were at last arranged to her liking, and the man who brought them had driven away. "It likes a north light, you know, and I'm afraid even this west window will have too much sunshine for it."

"I was thinking of a 'north light' in the next room, when I bought it, dear," said Mr. Stanley; "here, we will carry it in, and see how it goes there."

"Oh, you darling!" she cried, falling upon his neck, regardless of imminent peril to the fern; "it is just like a piece of the woods—how *do* you always know just what I want?"

"Perhaps because, with the exception of the fragment

necessary to the carrying on of my business, I 'give the whole of my mind to it,' " he answered, holding her fast for a moment.

Although neither of them was quite conscious of it, the threatened separation between them, slight as it was, which Mr. Stanley's marriage must inevitably have caused, had resulted in a sort of revulsion of feeling, which had drawn them even closer together than they were before.

Neither of them was given to analyzing moods and feelings, but Edith had a half conscious desire to spare her father the anxieties which had made him so earnestly wish for a mother's care for her, and he, on his part, was trying as he had never tried before to fill the lost mother's place.

Edith's manner was growing gentler, more womanly and gracious, and though her father was partly right in attributing the change to the influence of her aunt and Elizabeth, it was not wholly caused by this. She had begun to think.

CHAPTER XVII.

"Our doubts are traitors,
And make us lose the good we oft might win
By fearing to attempt."—SHAKSPERE.

RANDOLPH PEYTON seldom had any very long-sustained motive for his actions, but in deciding to take his sister to Mr. Stanley's, he had been influenced by an underlying thought of which he was not exactly proud. The fact that Edith was a mere school-girl, and that, even should her father be ultimately brought to consent to her marriage to a young man who had no visible means of support except his father, there must first be a delay of several years, was not so appalling to his indolent habit of mind, as it would have been to a more energetic person. He was wont to say that time never hung heavily on his hands—that he did not see how it could hang heavily, to a man fond of manly sports, and with "literary tastes." He hunted once or twice a week, wrote a little, read a good deal, smoked, and if the painful truth must be told, slept, rather more than he read. He was as free from vices, apparently, as he was from virtues—virtues, that is, of an active kind. In passive ones he was not lacking. He was an affectionate and dutiful son, a chivalrous brother, and a warm friend, excepting when the requirements of either of these things involved too much exertion, and when they did, had the faculty of delegating, or slipping out of his duties, in such a manner as to avoid giving offence, or even annoyance. Perhaps the adoration which he received at home had something to do with his unquenchable complaisance, but a good deal of incense was

14

burnt before him, in other places beside his home, and he
performed the difficult feat of inhaling it gracefully and
with apparent unconsciousness. He had been not a little
piqued by the gradually made discovery that the family at
Green Point put an estimate on him which somehow differed
from that of his other friends. He could not help seeing
that, kind and courteous as they always were to him, the
welcome they accorded Mr. Kendall was of a more flattering
sort than that accorded to him. He nearly succeeded in convincing himself that this was because "they were all Yankees
together"—but not quite. He happened once or twice to
hear Elizabeth and Roderick talking with eager interest to Mr.
Kendall about the latter's plans and prospects, and it dawned
upon him that possibly their comparative lack of interest in
him was because he had no definite object. At one time he
had fully intended to be an architect, and had even begun
to study in something like earnest, but unfortunately for his
loosely held purpose, his eyes had become troublesome, and
had put a stop to his studying, or even reading for a few
months. When he recovered the use of them, he found it
very difficult to rid himself of the desultory habits into
which he had fallen ; it was easy to persuade himself that he
was not strong, that he was still young enough to delay a
little, that he had perhaps not chosen his profession wisely.
About this time he developed a talent for verse making,
which inclined him to the belief that authorship was his
true vocation. Heartless editors and publishers failed to
sustain him in this idea, but a good deal of time was wasted
before he could bring himself to accept their verdict, and
when he did at last become convinced that it was useless for
him to make any farther attempts in this direction, he was
by no means convinced that his work had been properly
appreciated.

All this time he was gradually assuming little duties about

the house and farm, which endeared him to the hearts of
father, mother and sisters. He spared his father many
small troubles and fatigues about the farm ; he was always
ready to go on an errand for his mother, or ride or drive
with his sisters. He was invaluable when visitors were in
the house—which was quite half the time—and while his
family still cherished the belief that he would study for a
profession, as soon as he could decide upon the one which
would give fullest scope to his genius, and that his indecision
was owing rather to "that rarest of all gifts, a perfectly-
balanced mind," than to any want of energy or character,
he had drifted into a mode of life which suited him exactly.
It would have been well for him if there had been an absolute
necessity that he should earn his own living, but a small
legacy which had come to him when he was of age was sufficient to clothe him comfortably, if not very elegantly, and
he was quite free from anything like foppery. For his
board, it had never occurred to him that he was under any
obligation. The warm hearted hospitality of the house,
which made even strangers welcome, was partly responsible
for this, but, even had the matter come into his thoughts,
he would probably have concluded that he made himself
sufficiently useful to cancel a much larger debt. Since he
had become intimate with the Stanleys, an uncomfortable
feeling of doubt as to the manliness of this course had attacked him, but he evaded it pretty successfully, and more
than once enticed Elizabeth into an argument, in which he
endeavored to prove that the prizes of life were not worth
the struggle which must be undertaken to secure them.
But it annoyed him to find that, thoroughly as he might
succeed in convincing himself, he had no success whatever
in convincing her. He had been inclined to look down
upon her a little for the business-like manner in which she
had "gone into butter," but when he ventured to express

some of the surprise which he felt, she tranquilly unfolded enough of her plans to him to make him feel, for once, thoroughly ashamed of himself. She was very hopeful, for, since the purchase of the second horse, and the chaise, which Edith insisted upon regarding as common property, she had been able to send her butter directly to her customers. The list of these was lengthening, and she was able to command a price somewhat higher than that given at the stores. Less than half of her earnings sufficed to keep the table comfortably supplied with "extras," and to add, from time to time, fresh comforts and conveniences to the house. Her first design—in which her mother fully concurred—was to employ a thoroughly competent governess to instruct the younger girls. She realized the difficulties which attended their teaching by different members of the family, and she did not feel that she was competent to give them either music or drawing lessons, when they should be a little more advanced. The expense of a governess who could teach all three would be much less than that of sending them to school, even should Mrs. Stanley feel willing to part with them. May had always been fragile, and would need constant care and supervision while her education was going on, for her enthusiastic temperament often led her beyond her strength. No one appreciated more highly than did Mrs. Stanley the delights and benefits of a thorough education, but she appreciated also the impossibility of using to the fullest extent the intellectual powers, if they were dragged down by a weak and ailing body.

Elizabeth felt no hesitation in unfolding this much of her scheme to Randolph, and he could not help contrasting himself, for a moment, with her and with Roderick. He had been an affectionately interested listener to the discussion which had followed Mr. Stanley's invitation to Isabel, so long as it remained general, and no specific economy, which should enable them to accept it for her, had been touched upon, but he had somehow been absent when Colonel and Mrs. Peyton decided to sell a handsome young horse which was just broken for their own especial driving, and even had he been present, it is doubtful if it would have occurred to him that he was called upon for any sacrifice—what could he give up ? He indulged in no luxuries, according to his own belief. He noticed once or twice, in the course of the winter, with a feeling of dissatisfaction, that the table was rather more simply provided for than it had been before Isabel went away, but he agreed with himself to think that it was her dainty cooking which was missing, and the loss of which made the difference. But he was not so lost in self-indulgence as not to feel for Elizabeth even greater reverence than he had felt before, for the sacrifice—which he naturally, from his point of view, overestimated—that she was making for her younger sisters.

The work, however, really occupied less of her time now than it had done at first, for she had it thoroughly systematized, and whatever could be, without detriment to the result, was delegated. There was none of the conscious martyr about this true hearted woman. She took life cheerfully, glad of all the little comforts and pleasures which sprang up along her path, provided always that they had no root in selfishness. The ridiculously small sum which sufficed to hire a boy to do all the churning, set her conscience quite at rest about that branch of the business, and when this was regularly done, Aunt Judy often had time to work the butter. She did it much more quickly, although not more thoroughly, than Elizabeth could as yet, but the latter always attended to the printing and moulding herself, for the dainty little prints and balls helped the sale wonderfully. Several of her orders, every week, were for these, but she was becoming more and more dexterous with her tools, and had learned

the wisdom of accomplishing her work in the very early
morning, before heat added a difficulty—for the mornings and
evenings, even in the warmest weather, were almost always
delightfully cool. So on butter days, which came twice a
week now, Elizabeth would " get up over night," as Arnold
expressed it, and have her work entirely over by breakfast,
insisting, when her mother rather anxiously questioned the
wisdom of her plan, that her afternoon naps, on those two
days, were such Oriental luxuries, that they more than made
up for the slight sacrifice involved. But she soon found the
churner was not to be relied upon for these unearthly hours,
and that it was hard upon Aunt Judy to begin her day so
early; also, that the fresh butter was difficult to mould—so
a slight change of programme was made; the butter was
churned and worked in the afternoon, and by the next
morning was in fine condition for moulding. She liked, too,
the solitude and silence which this arrangement gave her.
In the busy and merry household, where appeals to her for
help and sympathy came—as she loved them to come—so
frequently, she had little time for quiet thought. But, with
her hands mechanically employed, while "all the lave were
sleeping," her mind was free; and her best thinking, that
summer, was done in her cool and pleasant little dairy.

Randolph Peyton smiled indulgently, but also incredu-
lously, when she told him this. Part of the curse of slavery
still clung, and would always cling, to him—the belief that
honest work of any kind could be degrading. If Edith
had not appeared upon the scene, he would doubtless, by
this time, have imagined himself hopelessly in love with
Elizabeth, in spite of the latter's calm friendliness, more discouraging than any amount of coldness. Edith's natural
coquetry made her treat him capriciously; whenever he
appeared to be particularly attracted by Elizabeth, Edith
could not, or did not, resist the temptation to try to draw

him away, and in doing this she more than once gave him
reason to think that, should he resolve to devote himself
entirely to her, he would meet with no discouragement. She
would have been both horrified and indignant, had she
known this. He amused her, and that was all, and it did
not occur to her that a tremulous smile in return for an
implied compliment, a look of reproach when he had seemed
unconscious of her presence, an imploring glance when she
begged him to stay a little longer, and other small weapons
of a like sort, tried in succession purely for the fun of seeing
their effect, could be treasured up by him, and construed as
manifesting a tender interest on her part. Kitty, whose
sight was keen, and whose ideas, at least, upon matters of
this kind, were highly sensible, even when she was not
exactly carrying them out, had more than once warned
Edith, that, if she "didn't look out," she would convince
Mr. Peyton of her undying affection for him ; but Edith, on
these occasions, always routed her with scorn, and amused
herself, at the next opportunity, by treating her victim with
a gentle dignity, which made him wonder, and sometimes
ask, how he had been so unfortunate as to offend her. She
had not been particularly delighted when she learned that
he proposed to act as Isabel's escort. Kitty's remarks had
lodged to an extent which would have filled her with
triumph, had she known about it, and Edith feared that
Mr. Peyton's visit might mean more than mere friendship.
It did, for after balancing the pros and cons for some time,
he had decided that, as his mind was so equally divided that
he really could not be certain whether he preferred Elizabeth
or her cousin, it would be the part of wisdom to try his fate
first with Edith. Should her father be brought to consent,
there need be no delay on the score of poverty, for surely
a man so rich as Mr. Stanley evidently was, would not be
exacting as to the wealth of her husband. He succeeded, at

last, in convincing himself that Edith would have been his choice, had her circumstances and Elizabeth's been reversed, and he felt much more at peace with himself after this conviction became settled in his mind.

But, cordially as Edith welcomed him when he arrived with Isabel, on Wednesday evening, her manner made him think that he must have been mistaken in fancying that she meant to give him any "encouragement." He mentioned, accidentally, that he intended returning to Rivermouth the next day, and was sorry afterward that he had done so, for he tried in vain during the evening for a chance to have a quiet talk with Edith. There did not seem to be any design in it, upon her part; she was full of pleasure over Isabel's arrival, and anxiety for her comfort; and he managed to say, in low tones, as Edith bade him good-night:

"You make me wish that I were Isabel!"

"You wouldn't wish so long," she answered, quite aloud, and smiling as she spoke; "Isabel is going to work very hard this winter."

He felt his face flushing with annoyance, and wished her good-night rather abruptly. It was just the same the next day, although he accepted Mr. Stanley's invitation to return to lunch before starting on his journey, in the hope that Edith might relent at the last, and give him a chance to speak to her. But his farewell to her, instead of being the tender and touching affair which he had pictured it, was said in the most common-place manner in the presence of his sister, and he went home thoroughly vexed, both with himself and Edith, and rather doubtful about again attempting the attack.

Isabel's delight in and gratitude for the preparations which had been made for her were pleasant to see and hear. But Edith found that she shrank a good deal from the prospect of her first day at the fashionable school, not only because of her very moderate estimate of her own powers and attainments, but because of her dread of meeting strange people in general and her conviction that her wardrobe was at least a year behind the times. Her simple and pretty traveling dress was new and very suitable for a school-dress until cold weather should come, and Edith, who had a natural gift for millinery and dress-making, promised to look her things over and make whatever changes were needed.

"That is," she said, "I will do the arranging, and it will be a charity to give the sewing to our seamstress. Papa will make me keep one, because he says I shall not sew while I am studying, and I find her reading novels whenever I go up to the sewing-room unexpectedly."

Isabel hesitated. She did not wish to wound Edith's feelings, but it seemed to her that she had already incurred so large an obligation that she shrank from accepting anything more.

"What is it?" said Edith, laughing at her perplexed face. "Are you afraid we shall not make you sufficiently fashionable, Miss Peyton? Would you rather go to a 'real' dressmaker?"

"Oh no! How could you think such a thing?" she replied, so earnestly that Edith laughed again, and pronounced her "almost equal to Polly."

"You *know* that isn't it," she continued; "but Edith, indeed, if I take your sewing-woman's time, you must let me pay——"

"Now see here, young woman," said Edith, placing her hand gently, but firmly, over Isabel's mouth, "I did hope to be allowed, this winter, to live in the delusive belief that you are my sister; but if you are going to begin dispelling the illusion at this early date, and at this rate, I may as well give it up. That creature will remain here, whether she does your sewing or not, and I tell you honestly she hasn't enough to do to keep her out of mischief. If you are going to be so disagreeable, I shall simply buy two or three pieces of muslin and linen and set her at work on my trousseau, to satisfy my conscience about her; it is wicked to allow her to remain in idleness."

"Your trousseau!" said Isabel, eagerly. "Oh, Edith! are you going to be married? when? to whom? Why didn't you tell me before?"

"I don't know the answer to any of those questions," said Edith, seriously; "but it is quite probable that I shall marry somebody if I live long enough, and if I remain single and live long enough I can give it away, you know. But you'll surely not drive me into such extravagance as that, dear? We'll look over your things this afternoon after school, and very probably we shall not find much to do to them, after all."

Isabel knew that Edith was quite capable of carrying out her threat about the "trousseau," and so yielded, although she would greatly have preferred not to incur the obligation. But she already loved Edith dearly, and she tried to see that what seemed so much in taking was really very little in giving.

The much dreaded first day at school was an agreeable disappointment. She was pleasantly welcomed for the sake of Edith, who was very popular; and the teachers, although somewhat awe inspiring, were kind and considerate. Mr. Stanley had called to see "Madame," and to arrange for the course of study which Isabel desired, and, after a little demur at the unusualness of the proceeding, she had graciously consented.

Isabel passed a far better examination for her classes than Edith, judging from her very modest statements as to her attainments, had thought probable. The music-teacher

praised her touch, and the singing-teacher her voice, and
both girls went home in high spirits, Edith insisting that
she should add a postscript to Isabel's first letter to her
mother, telling all the flattering things which had been
said, which she knew Isabel would be too modest to tell
herself.

Mr. Stanley's pleasure almost equaled theirs, and as he
looked at Edith's bright, animated face, and heard her happy
laugh, he congratulated himself upon the success of the
" new departure."

CHAPTER XVIII.

Kitty to Edith.

GREEN POINT, Sept. 20, 18—.

YOUR letter, my dear Edith, was received with rapture, and read aloud to the assembled multitude, the reading being frequently interrupted by flattering bursts of applause. We are all so glad about Isabel—it is such a chance for her, and you would have been so horribly lonely, turning from the "feast of reason and perfect freshet of soul" which you have just enjoyed, to the mild smiles and meek suggestions of the Duenna. Did I assert that we were *all* glad about Isabel? Perhaps I should have qualified that assertion, for have I not observed a pensive shade upon the brow of my venerated elder brother since she left these parts? I may be wrong in connecting it with her departure —he insisted with the calmness of despair, the day after she went, upon eating a cucumber salad, after having partaken freely of soft-shelled clams—so we will give him the benefit of the doubt, and admit that "that confounded cucumber" may have been alone responsible! But you needn't talk of cucumbers, when it comes to the heir of Rivermouth! He has been nothing but a doleful willowwaly-oh! since his return from B——. He has a sweet, touching, if-you-knew-

how-wretched-I-am-your-heart-would-bleed-for-me expression.
I try to comfort him when I have a chance, but he does not
seem to appreciate my well meant efforts. Yet surely it
should please him to learn how popular you are in B——;
and that after you settle here, extra boats will probably have
to run to accommodate your visitors. He did everything but
ask me to show him your letter, but I remained serenely
unconscious of his meaning. That's enough about him—
for the present, anyhow.

I think Arnold and Ernest were very much disappointed
that they could not finish their work of darkness in the car-
riage-house (!) before you went away—it is done now, and
they are so proud of it that the Estate will hardly hold
them, and it really is a highly ingenious and creditable performance. They sawed off the posts of their wreck even
with the body of it, at the back, and to the same height in
front; then, with the best of the curtains, they covered a
sort of dashboard, rigged between the front posts, and gave
the whole thing several coats of black varnish. They then
took Betty into their confidence, to the extent of begging
from her her old blue cloth riding-skirt, which, as such, is
done for, and of this they made cushions, using the old cur-
tain-stuff for the under side, and stuffing them with chopped
hay. They are not exactly luxurious, but you would really
be surprised to see how well the old thing looks—it's a sort
of compromise between an open buggy and a dog-cart;
but we have decided to call it a "village-cart"—it is sheer
nonsense to pretend that there is nothing in a name, and we
think this will keep up its self-respect, and make it last
longer. I have invented a coat of arms, and painted it on
one side of the vehicle. You are quite welcome to share this
coat of arms, if you would like to, with our branch of the
family, though I don't think you have any right to it—it is
a cow rampant, on a green ·field, supported by a very small

darky couchant. It is not large enough to be conspicuous, but we, at least, shall "all know it's there."

We are all well, excepting Rod, who maintains that he is "only tired," but looks badly, and is working too hard. He has had even more engagements for the thresher than he expected to have—some of them so far away that he could not even come home to sleep. Arnold and Ernest are taking turns in going with him, and enjoying it hugely. Arnold is keeping a journal, which he intends to use, he says, in his "Work on Delaware." He is a queer boy, and I like to see the way in which he devotes himself to mamma and Betty. I don't expect him to do it to me—we are too nearly of an age, and somehow my character does not, as a rule, seem to inspire reverence, but we are good friends, generally speaking, and he never will laugh at Polly, no matter how delightful she is.

By the way, your sins have found you out! When Polly went to cut out her gingham gown, she was bewildered to find that there was enough for two of her! She thought first that she ought to take half of it back to the store, for she was certain "the man" had made a mistake; being dissuaded from this course of action, she then proposed to send you the other half, or at least write and tell you of her startling discovery, whereupon Arnold announced that he had been requested, in case of "a fuss," to mention that the other half was for me. I am ever so much obliged to you, for Polly's comfort in her new gown that would wash was sadly marred by the fact that I hadn't one to match, as she then supposed. You know we have always dressed alike, in essentials, and she is a sentimental child.

You will think that there is a great deal of this, considering how little I have to tell, but I really think that the less I have to say, the more I write. Oh, I nearly didn't tell you about the recent tragedy! You know about those turkeys,

the pride of May's heart, and the foundation of a princely
fortune? One of them has committed suicide, and with an
ingenuity with which I would not have credited a turkey—
you know how they go mincing about, saying " Oh la!" to
each other about everything. The boys had been using some
gas tar, and had heated it in an immense kettle. They left
it out to cool, when they were done with it, before putting
it away in the barn, and when they went to get it, the head
of a turkey was feebly bobbing about on top of it, uttering
plaintive little squawks. The stuff was not hot, only warm,
and they fished the poor wretch out, and spread him on a
board, and scraped him with sticks, and rubbed him with
grease, but all in vain; he was tarred and feathered all too
effectually, and he was at rest before sunset. Poor May was
broken-hearted, and she has been asking all of us, at intervals, ever since, if we *really* supposed it hurt to be all
covered with gas tar? And last night, when she went to
bed, mamma found a large black spot on her hand, which
she explained as follows:

" I couldn't find out any other way, mamma, if it hurt, so
I put some on my hand, and I'm so glad I did it, for it
doesn't hurt a bit—it only feels sort of stiff and funny!"

I don't mean to ask you to write often, my dear, for I
know how busy you expected to be, but I needn't tell you
how glad we always are to hear from you. Our lessons have
begun again too, but with a slight alleviation—Mr. Kendall
is teaching us Latin and mathematics, twice a week, in the
evening. He wished to do it "free gracious," but mamma
had a friendly talk with him, and brought him to terms. I
enclose a sketch of his face, when he found Betty didn't
belong to the class. His is a diaphanous character.

We all send a great deal of love to you and to uncle, and
as many of us as can do so with propriety send our love to
Isabel.

You might manage a French postal card now and then, if you can't find time for a letter—you could regard it as an exercise, you know.   I will reply in Latin.

Very affectionately yours,

KATHARINE STANLEY.

The arrangement with Mr. Kendall, of which Kitty wrote to Edith, was only temporary.   Elizabeth thought it safest not to engage a governess for the girls, until she had at least six months' salary laid by.   Her mother and Roderick had talked the matter of the education of the younger ones over with her, and they had agreed in thinking that it was a disadvantage to them to be taught, as they had been, by different members of the family, all of whom had other duties, which made it impossible for the school to be held in the morning.   Kitty especially fretted and chafed at having her time "cut up" in this way, and a governess, if they could secure one, could give her whole time and attention to the lessons during the morning, and leave the children free for the afternoon.   Had no other way been possible, Mrs. Stanley would have enforced the present arrangement, and as it was, she hesitated a little about using the money which was so largely Elizabeth's earning for this purpose.   But when she spoke of this, and suggested that Elizabeth ought to have the benefit of the sum which remained after the wants and even the wishes of the family concerning the table were provided for, the oldest daughter of the house 'asked her why a similar course of reasoning should not be applied to Roderick.

"He gives three-fourths of his time to the farm, mamma," she said, "but all he makes goes for the benefit of the whole family.   Arnold and Ernest work as hard, considering their ages, as he does, but they don't think of charging for their time, and you know how hard it was to make Arnold keep

even a small share of the butter money. Why should there
be a different rule for me? The butter occupies a few hours
of my time, on two days of the week, but it does not keep
me from reading, or studying, or practising, and if I were
not here, you or Kitty or Polly could do my share of the
work quite as well as I do it."

"We may say something like that of almost any one's
work," replied her mother, "for if it were not so, the world
would have come to a stand-still long ago; but the fact
remains that it is you, and not Kitty or Polly or myself,
who attend to the work regularly and successfully, not to
mention that you, in the first place, built up the business.
Still, I can sympathize with your preference for not spending
the money on yourself—'there is that scattereth, and yet
increaseth,' and I will not try to hinder you. We can't all
be helpers, but we can, at least, all keep from being
hinderers."

"You must not talk so, mamma," said Elizabeth, springing up to kiss her. "Why, you are the mainspring, the
Great Wheel, the motive power for all of us! We should fly
apart like a wheel without a tire, if it were not for you."

"It is pleasant to be told so, darling," and her mother
held her fast for a moment; "but I don't mean to be one of
those dreadful old people who think the world will come to
a stand-still if they stop pushing."

By the middle of October, Elizabeth had a sum laid by
which made her feel justified in advertising for the governess.
She would have preferred some other way of finding her, but,
"remote from cities" as they lived, it seemed the only plan.
It was evening, and the family was gathered about the
parlor-table, when she undertook to write the advertisement,
and as soon as she mentioned what she was doing, she was
overwhelmed with offers of help.

"I am so afraid," she said, "of writing as if I expected

the services of a model of all the virtues for two hundred
dollars a year, and yet I must say what we want."

"She must not be very young," said Kitty, decisively, " or
I shall not respect her in the least. I'm not sure that I
shall anyhow. I have a feeling sense that we are about to
exchange King Log for King Stork."

"That's a gracefully turned compliment to those people
who have done everything short of trepanning you, to put a
few useful ideas into your head," said Arnold, with fine
sarcasm, to which she replied, soothingly—

"Don't be literal, dear! I was quoting from Æsop's fables,
and I didn't really mean that mamma and Betty and Rod
and Mr. Kendall were logs, any more than I really expect
the coming woman to be a stork."

" I hope she won't be one of those stiff, prim, very straight-
backed old maids, who are always the governesses in stories,"
said Polly, plaintively. "I'm afraid I shall be afraid of her,
and if I am, I shall never know a single one of my lessons."

" I should insist upon her being pretty," said Arnold, with
an air which set them all laughing; "if she will only be
young and pretty, and an orphan in deep mourning, with
helpless little ways, and Rod will fall in love with her, I can
write a novel without going off the premises."

" I should be glad to accommodate you," said Roderick,
seriously; "but I am afraid I shall not have time. Couldn't
you manage to do it yourself, and so get your sensations at
first hand ? "

"That's not a bad idea," said Arnold, approvingly; "I'll
see about it—but she will have to be *very* young and charming, if I do."

Elizabeth had been writing, regardless of these and other
equally sensible remarks which were flying around her, and
now she said suddenly—

" Will this do ?   'Wanted, in the country——' "

"'Forty miles from any town,'" interpolated Arnold, softly.

"'A governess,'" continued Elizabeth, "'who can teach the common English branches, French, German and music. Address, stating terms, E. S., Green Point, —— Co., Del.' Will that do, or is it asking for too much?"

"It isn't asking for enough," said Arnold. "You've omitted an important 'extra.'"

"Well, I did think of saying Latin, too," said Elizabeth, innocently; "but I was afraid of making it too formidable, and I thought I would risk that."

"I didn't mean Latin," said Arnold, "I meant washing —'French, music, and washing extra,' you know."

"Do you call that a joke, young man?" said Kitty, compassionately; whereupon May clapped her hands in high delight, and said, "Oh Kitty! It's in 'Alice in Wonderland,' and you laughed like everything when you read it to me!"

"That showed my amiability," said Kitty, nowise abashed; "I knew you'd be disappointed if I didn't."

"Do try to stop being funny for a minute, children." said Elizabeth; "I want to finish this thing. Mamma—Rod—do you think it will do?"

"Why, yes, I suppose so," said Mrs. Stanley, a little doubtfully; "it somehow doesn't *sound* as advertisements usually do, but I can't tell what is the matter with it, if anything is."

"I should think it would do," said Roderick. "Of course you would engage no one without some farther correspondence, and references."

"I don't see how I can make it any better," said Elizabeth, with such a hopeless expression, that everybody laughed again. "I've tried three or four different ways, but none of them seem to come right."

"Alice again!" said Arnold. "''Tis the voice of the lobster, I heard him declare——'"

"I don't wonder your wits desert you in this Babel," said Mrs. Stanley, laughing; "wait until some of these rioters have gone to bed, and then try again."

"But we want to hear what she says, mamma," said Kitty. "Come, children, come out in the dining-room, and give her a chance—it's like playing 'proverbs.'"

They trooped out, but in a few minutes there was a sound as of a heavy fall, followed by shouts of laughter.

"Nobody hurt, or they wouldn't be yelling like that," said Roderick, stretching out a detaining hand to his mother, who sprang up at the sound of the fall.

"Somebody will be, I'm afraid," she said, gently releasing herself, "if I don't go and read the riot act."

She found the two younger boys stretched upon the floor, too weak with laughing to get up.

"What *is* the matter?" she asked; "and who made that earthquake just now?"

"They fell, mamma," said May, in tones of apology; "they were practising one of their 'feats of strength and agility,' and Arnold's foot slipped."

"Likewise my head," said Ernest, sitting up suddenly; "you see, mamma, this particular feat requires me to stand on my own head and Arnold's at the same time, but it isn't so difficult as it sounds, for he stretches out his hands—so— and I rest mine on them—that makes it much easier to balance. After a while—when we are quite perfect in it that way—we are going to chalk our heads, and do it with our arms folded."

"You have my best wishes for your success," said Mrs. Stanley, laughing heartily at the picture conjured up by his words; "but I must beg you to practice out-of-doors, in future—you will find the grass so much softer than a floor, to fall upon."

"All right, mamma," said Arnold, cheerfully; "we generally take the haymow, or do it when we're in swimming; we only tried it here to-night by special request."

"You may come back now," said Elizabeth, appearing at the dining-room door; "I have it done—Rod helped me. He thinks it will be better not to be so definite until the answers come; here it is:

"'Wanted, a governess for three pupils between eight and sixteen years of age, living in the country. Address, stating terms and qualifications, E. S., Green Point, —— Co., Del.'"

"But that's so 'horribly vague,'" said Kitty.

"I know it is," replied Elizabeth; "but were I to be ever so explicit, I should need to have some correspondence with her before the thing is entirely settled, and it will be so much easier to write a letter about it, than to go into particulars in an advertisement."

The rest of the family agreed with her, so the advertisement in its second form was directed and sent.

Elizabeth had been speculating as to the next best thing to do, should no replies be received; but she speculated the other way, as Arnold said, on the third day after the advertisement was inserted. Over a dozen letters were received, and this continued for several days, but three out of every dozen would have amply covered all that were worth answering. Some were ungrammatical, others misspelled, and a few were both, and the promising ones only led to disappointment; either the candidates were lacking in some of the requisites, or, being amply qualified, according to their own statements, not only for this, but for far more difficult situations, they demanded a higher salary than Elizabeth could possibly undertake to pay. She was almost discouraged, when a letter at last came which seemed more hopeful than any which had yet been received. It was dated Philadelphia, and signed "Winifred Neale." It was very straight-forward and business-like, coming at once to the point, and mentioning that the writer was twenty-five years old, was a graduate of a well-known college, the name of which she mentioned, referring to the Principal, who would, she said, willingly testify to her qualifications. She would undertake to teach all the common English branches, and also, if desired, German, French, Italian, Latin, music and singing. This was almost too good to be true, but it was counterbalanced by the price asked for it; this "seeming paragon" demanded three hundred dollars a year for her services, and a vacation of two months in the summer, and two weeks at Christmas time. Elizabeth deliberated awhile, and then, by Roderick's advice, offered her two hundred and fifty dollars; it was quite probable that the three hundred could be made up, but it would not do to run any risk about it. They were rather surprised by the promptness with which the offer was accepted, but, as she referred them to a clergyman in B—— with whom they were slightly acquainted, and as the reference proved highly satisfactory, they congratulated themselves upon their good fortune—all but Kitty, who maintained that she was not going to like Miss Neale, if she could possibly help it. Roderick heard her make this declaration, and gently suggested to her that it would be a poor return for Elizabeth's kindness, should she refuse to profit by it.

"I am misunderstood, as usual," she said, resignedly. "Who said anything about not profiting by it, I should like to know? Can't your eagle-eye discern, my chief, that if I don't like her, I shall work a great deal harder for her than if I do? I would not give her the satisfaction of finding fault with me. I don't know why people, as a rule, should treat their relatives and friends inversely to the square of their regard for them—that's a figure of speech, dear, and you needn't analyze it—but I think they generally do. And you needn't worry about my studying, anyhow. I had a faint hope that I should grow up pretty, but it is blighting daily; so now I mean to go in for cleverness, and perhaps even set up for a genius!"

Absurd as this speech was, there was a foundation in fact for it. Kitty was an ardent admirer of beauty, and it was a real affliction to her that she did not possess it, partly because she felt it to be a power; and power, in any shape, was very dear to her. She was far prettier than she imagined, for, although her features were irregular, her bright and ever-changing expression prevented her face from being thought "plain," as it certainly was when it was in repose. She disliked, and hurried through, her dressing and hair-arranging, and it was no wonder that she considered unattractive, and even ugly, the face which she saw reflected while she was thus engaged. Power in some shape she was determined to possess, and, disappointed in her face, she resolved to cultivate her mind. She had never spoken so openly on the subject before, but her mother, who watched for all indications which might help her to help her children, had interpreted pretty correctly the sudden interest manifested by Kitty in her lessons. She had always slipped through her music-lessons with as little practising as possible, although she had a good deal of talent, and a very sweet and flexible voice; but of late she had practised indefatigably, and given Elizabeth real pleasure by her attention to this, and to all her lessons, and the older sister never, if she could possibly avoid it, refused to practise with her. Their voices harmonized remarkably well, Kitty singing alto to Elizabeth's soprano, and the "parlor concerts" had improved greatly in quality since the awakening of Kitty's zeal. Mrs. Stanley said nothing, as yet—she knew that the best seed will not take root in ground unprepared to receive it, and she always patiently waited her opportunity for a "word in season."

When Mrs. Peyton heard about the expected governess, she ask· if Louise might be allowed to share the lessons of the two older girls, and insisted, if this were permitted, upon sharing the expense. This was a welcome proposal, from all points of view—Kitty and Polly would probably study with more interest for having Louise's companionship, and even the small sum which was all that the Stanleys considered fair for Mrs. Peyton to pay, would make Elizabeth's undertaking easier.

As soon as Elizabeth had unfolded her plan, Roderick had sent for a mason, and had one of the larger garret rooms plastered. It was a very pleasant room, with a deep dormer-window, with a broad seat, in the roof, and a good-sized window at one end. Roderick had intended appropriating this room himself, but the boys were fairly clamorous for it, and when he found that they really preferred it, he was very willing to resign in their favor. They could scarcely be induced to wait till the plaster was dry, before moving up, and they made an afternoon's frolic of the moving, ably assisted by Kitty, Polly and May, and winding up with an oyster supper, cooked in their own chimney.

CHAPTER XIX.

"Not always is the heart unwise,
  Nor pity idly born."—WORDSWORTH.

"I FEEL exactly as if I were going to have a tooth out!" said Kitty, making a wonderful face, as she stood by the window, watching for the "phaeton," which had been sent to meet Miss Neale.

"I imagine Miss Neale feels as if she were going to have several out," said Elizabeth, smiling at Kitty's wry face; "I don't pity you at all, by comparison! Just fancy yourself going, alone and undefended——"

"Tautology," from Arnold.

"Into a family of eight perfectly strange people, after having admitted that you are competent to teach 'the common English branches' and two or three languages!"

"Well," said Kitty, defiantly, "she did it of her own accord! We didn't ask her to answer our advertisement, did we?"

"So did you go to the dentist 'of your own accord,'" put in Ernest, "just before we came here, but you made just as much fuss about it as if somebody had sent you."

Kitty joined in the laugh which this unexpected defence of the governess raised, and forgot her ill-humor—so that, when the "phaeton" at last returned from the landing, bringing the stranger, the "eight perfectly strange people" were all looking pleasant enough to disarm the most timid governess of her fears.

There was a general and quickly repressed murmur of surprise as Roderick, who had driven to meet her, sprang to the ground and helped her to alight. She was but little taller than May, very slight, and looking all the slighter for the deep mourning in which she was dressed. Her face was pale, but very pretty, and when she took off her bonnet they saw that she had soft, light hair. Mrs. Stanley and Elizabeth exchanged dismayed glances—she did not look a day over seventeen! yet there was nothing childish about her face. It looked careworn and sad, and her eyes were heavy. A feeling of pity for her took possession of them all, and Elizabeth said kindly—

"Let me take you to your room; you must be very tired from your journey, and you will have time for a nice rest before tea."

"Thank you," she replied, rising with alacrity from the chair upon which she had dropped as soon as she entered the room; "I *am* tired; I have not slept for two nights, and I feel as if I could comprehend nothing until I am a little rested."

She seemed surprised when Elizabeth ushered her into the pretty room which had been made ready for her. A fire sparkled on the hearth; Polly had put a bunch of autumn leaves in a vase on the high mantel-piece, and the white bedspread, window curtains, and bureau cover gave the room a cheerful look. The floor was matted, but two or three rugs prevented any feeling of chilliness. A few water-colors hung on the walls, as well as a small set of book-shelves—home-made, but neat and pretty.

"Is this for me?" she said, looking about her as if she thought there must be some mistake. "Why, how *very* nice it is—am I really to have it all to myself?"

"All to yourself," said Elizabeth, smiling, "and I hope you will feel quite at home in it. Here is a closet; I will lay your bonnet on this shelf for the present, and then I want you to curl up on the bed and not stir until I call you, which I will do half an hour before tea. Your trunk will be here soon, but I will not have it sent up until I call you."

Her eyes filled with tears, and she tried twice to speak before she succeeded.

"How kind you are!" she faltered. "I did not think—I did not expect—oh, you will think me very foolish and weak, but when I saw your mother, and you all seemed so bright and happy, and I remembered——"

Her voice was lost in a passion of sobbing. Elizabeth took her in her arms and soothed her as if she had been a child, saying gently—

"You are tired out, you poor little thing, and I don't believe you have had anything to eat all day. Come, lie down, and I will bring you something; you shall not wait till tea-time."

She submitted, as if she were glad to be taken out of her own hands, and Elizabeth, after arranging her comfortably on the bed, went to Aunt Judy for tea and toast.

"Better take her some dat soup we had for dinner, honey," said the old lady, after listening with much sympathy to Elizabeth's account; "do her heap more good den tea; you go back upstairs, and you'll have it mos' as soon's you git dar."

Aunt Judy was as good as her word, and she smiled all over her broad face, as she watched the effect of her prescription, and saw the deadly pallor of the young girl's cheeks replaced by a faint color.

"She was all done out, Miss 'Lizabeth," said the kind-hearted old servant, as she took the tray, stopping to stroke gently the hand which lay listlessly on the counterpane. "Tuck her up nice in de Yafghan, and leave her to sleep till de tea-bell rings."

"I think Aunt Judy's advice is good," said Elizabeth,

smiling as she "tucked her up nice"; "so we will follow it, and if you don't feel rested by tea-time you shall have your tea up here, and then go right to bed. You will feel very differently in the morning, dear."

Miss Neale threw her arms impulsively around Elizabeth, and held her fast, saying softly—

"You are so good, so *very* good to me that I must tell you —I can't deceive you—I never tried to deceive anybody before, and I only did it now because aunt said I must——"

She stopped to catch her breath, and Elizabeth listened in dismay; what dreadful secret was about to be disclosed?

"I said I was twenty-five," the trembling voice went on, "but it was not true; I am only nineteen."

The relief was so great, and the climax, after Elizabeth's vague fears, so absurd, that she could hardly repress a smile; yet she could not help feeling troubled at the deceit which had been practised, and this feeling kept her silent.

"But the rest is all true," continued Miss Neale, eagerly; "it is indeed! I have my diploma and my prizes and my certificates from the singing and music teachers all with me, and aunt persuaded me—or tried to persuade me—that as I was quite competent to take the situation, and knew as much as if I really were twenty-five, it would be no harm. She said I was *more* competent, for I had not had time to forget anything. I was getting desperate; I had applied for dozens of situations in schools and in private families, and wherever I went they just looked at me and told me I was quite too young, without asking me a single question about what I knew or looking at my diploma, or anything. So when I saw your advertisement, and found you lived so far away, it seemed like a last chance; for I hoped that, if I once came here, you would at least give me a trial before sending me back; and oh, you will, will you not?"

"I must speak to mamma about it, dear, before I can give

you an answer," said Elizabeth, gently; "your being young is no matter, if you can make the children respect you, and really work for you as they would for an older person ; but I wish very much that you had frankly told us the true state of the case; I don't think it would have stopped us from engaging you, for we had so few applicants who seemed at all what we wanted."

"I wish so too, with all my heart," said Miss Neale, sadly, "for it would have been quite impossible to keep on pretending that I am twenty-five, when you are so kind. I never tried to deceive any one before, and I am quite sure that I shall never wish to do it again."

"Indeed, you must rest now," said Elizabeth; "I ought not to have let you talk when you were so tired. Don't come down to tea, if you would rather not—Aunt Judy will like to bring your tea up, and fuss over you."

"No," said Miss Neale, with decision, "I would rather come down, and get it over—it will be even harder, if I wait till morning. And I *will* try to go to sleep now, if you will call me in time."

"Very well," replied Elizabeth; "you will have more than an hour, and I will call you if you prefer it."

She put more wood on the fire, and then left the room, and hastened down-stairs to the eager group in the parlor, to be assailed by all manner of questions:

"What in the world kept you so long?"

"Why didn't she come down with you?"

"Is she really and truly twenty-five years old?"

"Has she been telling you her romantic history?"

"Is she a princess in desguise?"

Elizabeth waited in smiling silence till the clamor ceased, and then she repeated to her mother the substance of what Miss Neale had said to her. She knew that, even had it been right or expedient to do so, it would have been quite

impossible to conceal from the rest of the family the young
girl's misstatement about her age, and she thought it best to
have the matter settled at once.

"The poor little thing seems to have done it under very
heavy pressure," concluded Elizabeth, "and she certainly is
not artful, or she would not have betrayed herself so quickly,
and before anything at all had been said which could lead
her to think we suspected her of not telling the truth."

"But don't you see, Betty," said Kitty, before any one
else could speak, "that she must have known she could not
pass for twenty-five, after we had once seen her, and that it
was better policy to be frank, and get the credit of it?"

"Dear child," said Mrs. Stanley, softly, to Kitty, "is that
the 'charity' that 'thinketh no evil?'"

Kitty was silent, but she looked ashamed, and took no
farther share in the discussion

"It seems to me," said Mrs. Stanley, "that it would be
cruel to send her back without letting her make a trial. If
she does her work faithfully and well, and is as well qualified
for it as she claims to be, her age will not matter, and I am
only sorry that any amount of pressure should have succeeded
in making her say what was not true about it. Her having
done so would make me hesitate about receiving her into the
family, if I did not feel such thorough confidence as I do in
all my children. I don't think I need fear concealment from
any of you, my dear ones."

The result of this appeal was somewhat startling. Roderick stooped to kiss his mother's hand, and as Elizabeth at
the same moment leaned forward to kiss her cheek, their
heads came together with an audible bump, while the others,
who had likewise started forward to show their allegiance,
became so thoroughly entangled that they fell in a heap at
her feet.

The laughing struggle was at its height, when the door

was quietly opened, and Miss Neale appeared. She had quite regained her composure, and she went through the introductions which followed with a quiet dignity which pleased Mrs. Stanley very much. She made no comment on the uproar which had been going on when she entered the room, and which she could not have failed to hear, although it had subsided as soon as the rioters became aware of her presence, and they had disentangled themselves as speedily and silently as they could. The tea-bell rang a few minutes after she came down, and she ate with sufficient relish to satisfy Aunt Judy, who made one of her usual pretexts to take a share in the waiting. She seemed much brighter after tea, and took her part in the talk pleasantly enough, describing her journey, and telling one or two amusing incidents which had enlivened it, in a way which secured the attention of the younger children, as well as their elders.

"We'll try her with the Alice books to-morrow, May," said Ernest, in a low voice, to his little sister, as they sat side by side on the rug in front of the fire; "she doesn't look literal, but there's no telling. It would be mean to go at her to-night, when she's so tired."

"How funny it will be, if she does stay and teach us!" May whispered back. "It seems to me she keeps getting younger all the time."

Prayers were over; the younger children, including Kitty and Polly, had all gone to their rooms, and Mrs. Stanley was about to ask Miss Neale if she did not feel like following their example, when the latter said suddenly—

"I know I have no right to ask anything of you, Mrs. Stanley, but I am going to do it. Will you try me for a week, as you would any hired servant, and then, if I satisfy your requirements, will you forgive the deceit I tried to practice upon you, and let me stay?"

The deep and evident anxiety with which she asked this

question touched Mrs. Stanley to the heart; it was impossible
to believe that the young and innocent face before her was
that of a person habitually deceitful.   The mother glanced
quickly from one of her children to the other, and saw the
confirmation of her thought in their eyes.   She took the
young girl's hand in hers, saying kindly—

"I will do what you ask, my dear, and if all goes well in
other respects, your age, or your youth rather, shall not be
considered an objection.   I cannot believe that you will
deceive us about anything else, and I can believe that you
were not wholly responsible for that deceit."

"Oh, thank you very much!" she said, fervently; "it
is so lovely here—it seems to me that after awhile I might
even be happy again, here.   Will you let me tell you a little
about myself?   I think it will make you see how greatly I
was tempted, before I said—that.   No, don't go away,
please," as she saw Elizabeth and Roderick quietly rising;
"I want you all to be my friends, if you will, and I should
like you to hear, if you don't mind; I will not keep you
long.   But perhaps it is your bed-time?   I will wait till to-
morrow if it is."

"It is only a little after ten," said Mrs. Stanley, "and we
three heads of the family seldom go before eleven—but you
yourself, my dear child?   Ought you not to go to bed early
to-night, after your tiresome journey and loss of rest?"

"I think I shall sleep better if you will let me tell you
first," she replied; "it has weighed upon my heart so."   She
paused a moment, as if to collect her thoughts, and then
went on, in a quiet, controlled voice, as if determined not to
give way to her feelings:

"I had just graduated from —— College when my father
died, a little more than a year ago.   I had no idea that I
should ever be obliged to teach, or do anything for my living,
but he always said that he wished me to be able to support

myself, in case our money should be lost, when he was no
longer with us. He failed a few months before he died. It
was not his fault ; some one whom he trusted deceived him,
and the doctors said it was anxiety and overwork, trying to
bring things straight, so that no one but himself should lose
by his failure, that caused his death. He had one stroke of
paralysis after another, until he died ; but he was ill for
three months, and my mother, who was never very strong,
nursed him nearly all the time. I could hardly make her
leave him, either to sleep or eat; and after he died, I thought
for a while that she would die too. But she did not ; she began to get better, at last, and people were very kind. I never
knew, for six months after my father died, that we had
nothing at all left. My aunt, who owned the small house in
which she lived, and who had a moderate income, enough to
support her comfortably, if she were careful, took us home
immediately after my father died, and helped me to take
care of mother. I did not think about board at first, but
when I did, I told her she must let us pay her what it cost
to have us there. She said it cost very little—that my
mother ate scarcely anything, and I but little more, and that
she loved to have us; that I helped her a great deal about
the house—she only kept one servant. But when I persisted,
she said I might pay her five dollars a week, if it would
make me feel any more comfortable. I never thought of
putting the two things together, but after that she used to
hand me every Saturday a yellow envelope, directed in a
queer, crooked hand, and say—

"'This came for you to-day, my dear,' and it always had
six dollars in it. I was so foolish—you see I knew nothing
about business—that I thought it came from the lawyer who
had been so often at our house before my father died. He
had said he would let me know if he found that there was
anything left, and I supposed he had, and I thought how

16

fortunate it was that there should be just enough to pay
Aunt Sarah what it cost her to have us there. I wanted her
to take it all, but she never would; so I used to buy little
things for mother with the other dollar, for the table was
very plain, and she had no appetite. I wondered sometimes
what made Aunt Sarah so anxious about every cent that was
spent, for I knew she had enough to live upon, before we
came, and I thought the five dollars ought to cover our
expenses. It was mother who guessed it first; when she
grew strong enough to sit up, and take an interest in anything, I told her about the money, for I thought it would
be a comfort to her to know it. She sat thinking for
several minutes, and then she said—

"'There is some mistake, my child; there was absolutely
nothing left.'

"'But it comes every week,' I persisted, 'in a yellow
envelope, directed in a strange hand, and who *could* it be
but the lawyer? Might he not have found, afterward, that
there was a little left—enough to make this much a week?'

"Mother asked to see one of the envelopes; one had just
come that day, so that I could show it to her. She looked
at it a moment and said—

"'Dear Winny, that is your aunt's writing; she has tried
to disguise it, but I would know it anywhere! How fearfully she must have pinched and contrived to do this!'

"I went to my room, and cried and cried. I don't believe
I can make you understand how I felt, but it seemed to me
that every grumbling thought I had had about the management of the house, and Aunt Sarah's anxiety about money,
turned into an accusing angel. I felt as if I could never
forgive myself. But when I tried to tell her something
about it, she was so distressed that we had found her out,
that I was obliged to stop. Then I begged her to send away
the servant and let me do all the work, but she would not

listen to that; she said that if I did anything, it must be what my father had thought of; she had no doubt that, with my 'splendid education,' I could find plenty to do, and receive a large salary. She said I must not fret for a moment about mother—that it made her so happy to have some one in the house, and that I could go with an easy mind, for they would keep each other from being lonely. I was afraid to speak of it to mother, but when I did, she said I was quite right—that we must not let Aunt Sarah deny herself as she had been doing, and that she should look for something to do as soon as she was a little stronger. But she saw this made us both so wretched, that she promised not to do it, if I succeeded in finding a good situation, with a salary large enough to permit my paying her board—that was why I asked so much at first, but I would have come for almost anything, for, as I said, I was desperate.

"Aunt Sarah insisted, at first, upon paying for an advertisement for me, but it cost so much, and all the people who answered would not have me when they found how young I was, so I stopped putting it in at the end of a week, and began to watch the papers and answer advertisements instead. I would hardly believe it myself, if I had not kept a careful record, but in a month I had tried ninety places just in Philadelphia! I offered to go as nursery-governess, as companion, and even—though only mother knew about this—as lady's-maid to one person, and child's-nurse to another. I think the one who wanted a maid would have taken me; she said I was too young, as they all did, but that she liked my face, and just as I thought it was all settled, she asked me if I knew how to dress hair. I said no, that I had never arranged anybody's hair but my own and mother's since she had been ill, but that I thought I could very soon learn. But she said she could not think of taking any one who was not a good hair-dresser, and that before I applied for another

situation as lady's-maid, I had better take lessons. The one
who wanted a child's-nurse almost engaged me, but she said
I must leave off my mourning and dress cheerfully for the
sake of the children, and I could not do that so soon. I
never told Aunt Sarah about these two attempts—it would
have made her really angry, I am afraid.

"It was just after the second had failed, that I saw your
advertisement, and somehow I felt hopeful about it, as soon
as I had read it. I showed it to mother and Aunt Sarah,
and they both said it would be better for me to be in the
country; and mother did not say a word, as I had been
afraid she would, about its being so far away. But just as I
sat down to answer it, Aunt Sarah came to me, and told me
it would be like all the rest, if they found out beforehand
how young I was. She said she thought the suspense and
anxiety were wearing upon mother, and keeping her from
gaining strength; that it was not a deceit which would
harm any one, and that, when I was once settled, I could
confess it, and tell my reason for pretending to be older than
I was. She could not have made me do it, if she had not
said that about mother, but I saw that it was true—mother
would grow feverish and restless every morning when it was
time for the paper to come; and whenever the postman rang,
she was excited until the letters were read, and sometimes
long afterward. I did not dare to pray about it, for in the
bottom of my heart I knew I was wrong; but I dashed off
the letter while she sat there reasoning with me, and she
took it from me and had it posted before I had time to
change my mind. I was wretched enough afterward, but
just then the doctor's bill came in, and I was obliged to go
and ask him to wait. I had never done such a thing before,
and I hope I may never have to again. He was very kind, but
I could see that he was disappointed; and he asked me how
soon I thought I could settle it. I told him it all depended

upon my finding a situation, and he said he hoped I would
find one soon, for he had lost a number of bills of late.
Something in his manner made me think that he believed
we could pay him if we would, and when I found your letter
at home, making a definite offer, I wrote at once and accepted
it, and then, after the letter was gone, I remembered my watch
—it was a very beautiful and costly one, with a heavy chain
and charms; my father had given it to me when I graduated.
Fortunately, the jeweler from whom it was bought had
known us for years; he was a good man, and when he saw
the watch was in perfect order, he gave me very nearly what
had been paid for it, and a little silver watch beside, for he
said if I meant to be a teacher, it would never do for me to
be without a watch of some kind. I had told him that I
was looking for a place, because I thought he might hear of
one among some of our old acquaintances. But it was
worst of all when I took the money to the doctor—I had
more than enough, and I was so glad, for I could not have
borne to ask Aunt Sarah for money to bring me down here.
He smiled in a way that made my blood boil, and said I had
been fortunate in being permitted to anticipate my salary!
I was so angry that I told him I had sold a valuable watch,
one of my father's last gifts to me, rather than remain in
debt, and then I turned and went away, before he could say
another word; but the next day I received a note from him,
containing his receipted bill, and a very humble apology. I
told mother how I had paid him, but not the rest—it would
have troubled her too much. But all this only made me feel
more and more that I *must* find something to do; and Aunt
Sarah kept encouraging me, and telling me that, under the
circumstances, it really was no harm—that it would all come
out right, when you found that I was competent to fill the
place. I knew this was not true, though I tried to believe
it, and the worst of it all was, that I did not dare to tell

mother what I had done. I knew she would have made me
write at once, and tell you the truth, and then, I felt certain,
you would not let me come. I thought the worst was over,
when that last sleepless night at home was gone through
with, and I had said good-by, but the next night, on the
boat, was far worse. Nothing would have tempted me to
keep on, if I could possibly have turned back, and I dreaded
meeting you all, inexpressibly. I fancied that Mr. Stanley
looked surprised the moment he saw me, and I knew, although I was so tired that I could hardly see, that all the
rest of you did. For a few minutes, I thought I would let
things take their course—I was so frightened—and that
perhaps, if I said nothing, you would only think I looked
young for my age. I had arranged my hair very plainly,
and I am so pale and thin that it seems to me I must look
older than I am. But it was only for a few minutes—when
I remembered how many times I might have to tell what
was not true, and how easily I could be found out, it seemed
like utter folly, and I knew I should not have a happy
moment until you knew the truth, so now you know it, and
I cannot expect you to trust me for awhile, even if you keep
me; but, indeed, it has been a very bitter lesson, and one
which I shall never forget."

She had risen as she finished speaking, and held out her
hand to Mrs. Stanley, to say good-night. Her eyes were full
of tears, and she looked so childlike and helpless that all
their hearts were touched with compassion, and Mrs. Stanley
took the slight form into her motherly arms and kissed the
trembling lips, saying: "I don't believe you will, my poor
child, and I will trust you freely. My children and I have
no secrets from each other, and you must come to me now
as if you were one of them; you will have to be much more
incompetent than I think you are, if you do not stay with
us, but the first use I shall make of my authority will be to

send you straight to bed—it is striking eleven, and you are quite worn out. Good-night," and she kissed her again.

Elizabeth and Roderick shook hands with her, with cordial kindness, and she went up to her pretty room "not a little comforted," to find Aunt Judy asleep on her hearth, so near the fire that she was almost singeing, and with one hand stretched out in a protecting manner toward a covered bowl of beef tea. The old dame awoke with a start and a snort, as the door opened, but was up and alert before Miss Neale had crossed the room, and she offered the beef tea as if she were asking rather than bestowing a favor, saying, coaxingly, as she did so—

"You'll drink dis for aunty, honey? We can't have nobody 'bout here wid such white little faces! Dare! Now go to sleep like a lamb, and aunty'll bring you brekfus 'fore you gits dressed; don't you stir till she comes!"

The weary girl tried to speak her thanks, but tears came instead of words. Aunt Judy undressed her as if she had been a baby, "tucked her up" in the white bed, covered the fire, and left her self-appointed charge with a fervent "good-night and pleasant dreams, you pore little lamb, you!" But she chuckled all the way down-stairs, breaking out at short intervals, as she wound up her affairs for the night—

"So dat's a guberness? Oh my laws! Looks like she couldn't gubern her own se'f, let alone them uproysterous gals and boys!"

CHAPTER XX.

"How poor a thing is pride! when all, as slaves,
Differ but in their fetters, not their graves."—DANIEL.

MRS. STANLEY called a meeting of her children before breakfast the next morning, and told them briefly the sad story which Winifred Neale had told her the night before, dwelling on the penitence which had so quickly followed the error.

"I do not mean," she said, "to make light of her deceit about her age, but only to show you how sorely she was tried, and how voluntary her confession was. Now we must try to forget that it ever happened; for, if I thought there were any danger of her being habitually deceitful, you know quite well that I would not let her stay, truly as I trust you all, and painful as it would be to me to disappoint her. She will be sensitive about it for awhile, and we must try to let nothing remind her of it, and to be so unobtrusively kind, that she may feel that we trust her. I believe that we shall find her fully competent to teach you, my girls, and her staying with us will depend upon you, after all, unless I am very greatly deceived in her, which I do not think I am."

Boys and girls alike promised allegiance to the mother's wishes; even Kitty was touched, and resolved that she would not scorn her governess's youthfulness, "unless she should turn out to be dreadfully silly."

"What did mamma mean, Kitty," said Polly, after breakfast, drawing her double into a corner, as she spoke, "by saying that Miss Neale's staying would depend upon us? I should think it would depend upon her being a good teacher, shouldn't you?"

"Why, don't you see, Miss Goose," said Kitty, in the superior manner which she was too apt to assume when she spoke to Polly, "that no matter how good a teacher she may be, it will make no difference if we make light of her, and don't mind her because she is so young? You needn't open your eyes at me like that—I mean to study for her just as well as I should if she were ninety, and I nine, unless she turns out very silly and disagreeable, and I don't think she will."

"Of course she won't," said Polly, warmly. "She has one of the sweetest faces I ever saw, and I do hope she will like me! I mean to learn all my lessons *perfectly*, and I won't even make a fuss about compositions, if she thinks we ought to write them."

"But suppose she tells us to write French and German compositions?" said Kitty, mischievously.

Polly groaned, but said, loyally—

"Well, I shall try my best even then, and she can't expect more than that, can she?"

"Neither she nor any one else, my dear," said Roderick, stopping to kiss her, for in her earnestness she had spoken quite aloud. Her face flushed with pleasure, as it always did for praise or petting, which, to her humble mind, seemed undeserved.

Mrs. Stanley wished Miss Neale to rest for the remainder of the week, and not begin school regularly until the following Monday; but she seemed anxious to go to work, and disappointed Aunt Judy, the morning after her arrival, by coming down-stairs when the rest of the family assembled for prayers and breakfast. She had slept soundly and sweetly, and looked so much better already, that Mrs. Stanley made

no further remonstrance, when she begged that her duties
might begin at once.

There had been a lively discussion before she came, as to
which room had better be used as a school-room.   It would
be inconvenient, now that school hours were to be in the
morning, and no longer irregular or uncertain, to give up
the dining-room, and although callers before dinner were
not very frequent in their arrivals, still, they came occasionally, and the girls, apart from this reason, disliked the idea
of subjecting their pretty parlor to the wear and tear inevitable in a school-room.   Roderick was sorry that he had not
"stretched a point," while the mason was at work, and
had another of the large garret-rooms plastered and made
habitable ; he resolved to do it yet, with the first money
he could spare from the running expenses, and meantime he
solved the difficulty by suggesting that his "study" was
quite at their service ; they hesitated about appropriating it,
but as school hours were to be from nine to one, and the
study hour from three to four, he assured them that they
would not interfere with him in the least, as he was always
busy, either about the farm or in the workshop, at those hours.

"But you won't be, Rod, in a little while, when the fall
work is over," suggested Kitty, "and we made this room
just on purpose for you."

"I know you did, dear," he replied, "and I am very proud
of it, but it will give me pleasure to lend it for so worthy an
object—for I am not *giving* it, mind that, you children!
and before I shall need it again in the day-time, I fully expect to have another of the garrets plastered and fitted up for
a beautiful school-room.   I will have the chimney finished
like the one in the boys' room, and we must keep our eyes
open for another pair of andirons—I am sorry, now, that I
did not get one of those which 'sold for a song' at that
famous sale."

Arnold and Ernest had, through Mr. Stanley's assistance, disposed of those they had bought at a handsome profit, but they both exclaimed—

" Why, you could have had a pair of ours, if we'd known you wanted them ! "

Kitty was still dissatisfied with the appropriation of the " study," but she saw that it would be useless to say anything more, and so, for a wonder, said nothing.

The boys, with a little assistance from Roderick, had made four desks for the school-room, plain, and rather heavy, but convenient. They rejoiced greatly in the nearness of the saw-mill, and the cheapness of lumber, but they cherished a secret project which, to them, was of such vast dimensions that they did not yet dare to make it known. They meant, one day, to have, not a " treadmill," but a sawmill " of their own," on the creek, within a convenient distance of the house. Curiously enough, Roderick was revolving in his mind the same project. The work done by the mill from which they obtained their lumber was often poorly and carelessly done, and any one leaving an order there might make up his mind to submit to needless and exasperating delays. The men who ran the mill had only the most superficial knowledge of the qualities of different kinds of lumber, and took no interest in the subject whatever, as Roderick had discovered when he tried to get some information from them to guide his first purchases, and it had more than once occurred to him that the business might be made very profitable, if it were conducted with intelligence and spirit. But, for several good reasons, he kept his thoughts on the subject to himself—he knew how wildly the boys, and the girls too, for that matter, would advocate the plan, if it were once mentioned, and he was not yet in a position to carry it out. He knew too, that Mr. Stanley, should the subject reach his ears, would insist upon advancing the money at once, and nothing but the direst necessity, he was firmly resolved, should put them again under the yoke of a debt, were it ever so small.   No; the plan must wait till "the way opened," and Roderick derived much comfort at this time from the old nursery rhyme concerning the "dog who went to Dover," not by lightning-express, or in frantic jumps, but "leg over leg," soberly, "unhasting and unresting."

But all this is a long digression, for which the school-room desks are responsible ! To return to them—they were things of beauty in the eyes of the younger boys, because they were stained with a composition which, like the White Knight's helmet, was "an invention of their own." The process of manufacture was a profound secret, because, as they declared, they meant to apply for a patent. But it had transpired that walnut leaves and white-oak bark, in large quantities, went to its manufacture, and "something sticky" which would not wash out of their clothes without much previous greasing, and which was suspected of being home-made turpentine.   Edith had applied for the position of purchasing agent for them, and all their chemicals were sent by her, according to their order. Whatever money they made was pretty sure to go in this direction, and neither Mrs. Stanley nor Roderick interfered, or questioned them. This confidence made them careful, as no amount of sur-veillance would have done, and any experiment of an explo-sive nature was always carried on at a "laboratory" which they had erected on a shady bank of the creek, at some dis-tance from the house. Their mother had begged them always to be careful about their hands and faces, and espe-cially their eyes; and the result of this suggestion was a set of frightful looking masks and gauntlets, made, as Ernest loftily proclaimed, of "a substitute for asbestos, which *we* invented!"

They had good reason to be pleased with the "invention," which turned the white pine desks into something which really looked somewhat like walnut, if one did not examine it too closely, and which, in spite of Kitty's dark and freely-expressed forebodings, did not "come off on everything, and stick everybody together." They had offered to make benches, as well as desks, but Mrs. Stanley, while thanking them in an appreciative manner, declined the offer—she meant the five chairs in the school-room to be the most comfortable the house afforded, short of absolute lounging-chairs, for she had a vivid recollection of the weary hours spent on backless benches, in her own school-days, and she knew that it is hard enough for a young and active body to keep still for an hour at a time, under the most favorable circumstances. More than an hour at a time she would not permit ; then five minutes were to be spent in exercising with light dumb-bells, or the trapezes which hung from the boughs of the elm-tree, as the girls might choose. This rule Mrs. Stanley explained to Miss Neale, in the little talk which they had, before the latter took possession of the school-room and the scholars, and she was pleased with the ready and intelligent assent which the young governess gave.

"I should have been so thankful," she said, "if such a rule as that had been enforced at the College. The session lasted from nine till two, with a short intermission in the middle of the time, and sometimes I would feel so heavy and drowsy, before it was over, that I could hardly fix my mind upon what I was doing. My feet and hands would grow numb, too, and I would feel stiff from keeping one position so long."

Breakfast took place early on "the Estate"—at six in summer, and now, when the days were shortening, at seven; this was necessary for the accomplishment of the various work which filled the day; later, when the mornings should be dark, and the pressure of summer and fall work over, Mrs. Stanley had no intention of sacrificing comfort to theory, and the hour would be changed to eight.

As it was, there was plenty of time to send Moses to River-mouth for Louise, and she came back with him in the "phaeton," Randolph having promised to bring her horse for her at one o'clock, for the return trip. The girls—or at least the Stanley girls—had expected Miss Neale to be "flustered" when the time came for facing them all, and opening school, but their expectation was not fulfilled. She was very pale—as pale as she had been when she first arrived, the evening before—but perfectly composed and dignified.

When they had taken their seats, she said, quietly—

"I should like, if you are willing, to begin every morning by reading a chapter from the New Testament."

And she read, in a low, clear voice, the first chapter of St. John's Gospel. Then she began, in a business-like manner, to examine them as to their proficiency in the different studies which they were to take up, and they were all pleased to find that, in most of them, Louise and the twins could be classed together. This made little May rather mournful, but Miss Neale's gentle, encouraging manner soon reassured her, and she decided that it would not be so very dreadful to be "the only one in the class." It had not yet been arranged when Louise was to take her vocal and instrumental music lessons, but Miss Neale suggested that, if her mother approved, Louise should come four times a week at eight o'clock instead of nine, twice for the piano, and twice for the singing lessons. When the days grew too short for this, some other arrangement would have to be made, but for the present this seemed best, as it avoided the dinner-hour, and Mrs. Peyton was quite satisfied with it. She called a day or two after Miss Neale's arrival, and had a pleasant talk with her about Louise, but Mrs. Stanley was

pained to see how unconsciously the old lady assumed that
she and Miss Neale belonged to such widely separated
" classes" that they could have nothing in common. There
was no arrogance in her manner; the distinction she evidently made was like an impalpable mist, fine and penetra-
ting, and the young girl only showed that she felt it by an
additional gravity and dignity, and by excusing herself as
soon as she perceived that Mrs. Peyton had finished talking
about Louise.

"A very sweet girl, and evidently well-informed," said
Mrs. Peyton, turning to Mrs. Stanley as the door closed upon
Miss Neale; "but, dear Mrs. Stanley, is she not entirely too
young for the situation? I was given to understand that
she was twenty-five, but surely there must have been some
mistake."

"There was," said Mrs. Stanley, quietly—she saw no
necessity for explaining about the deception which had been
attempted, outside of her own immediate family, but she
wished Mrs. Peyton to know about the sad circumstances
which had driven Miss Neale out into the world so early to
battle for herself, so she added—

"Miss Neale is only nineteen, but she has brought with
her ample proof that she has received a very thorough and
comprehensive education, and I am quite satisfied from what
I have seen, and from what my children tell me, that she
will teach as thoroughly as she has learned."

Mrs. Stanley went on to tell, in as few words as possible,
the pitiful history which she had heard the night before,
and Mrs. Peyton's kind heart was deeply touched. All
thought of questioning the fitness of the young governess
for her position was lost in compassion for her, and the
wish to help her, and when Mrs. Stanley said, in conclusion—

"I do not know her mother personally, but she comes of

an excellent Philadelphia family, cultured and refined, as you may judge from her language and manner."

Mrs. Peyton looked a little embarrassed, and said ruefully—

"My dear, that makes it all the harder for her. She will understand the distinction of class which separates the employer from the employee far more painfully than she possibly could if she had been brought up in the rank to which she has been obliged to descend."

Mrs. Stanley found it difficult not to manifest something of the impatience and annoyance which she felt, but she succeeded in saying calmly, and without apparent irritation—

"When I heard her story, it seemed to me that she had risen immeasurably, rather than descended. You surely would not respect her more, if she had lived in idleness, at the expense of all comfort to her aunt and mother?"

Mrs. Peyton's shoulders gave an involuntary and scarcely perceptible shrug.

"Of course I should not; her conduct has been most praiseworthy; but, if you will pardon me for saying so, that has nothing to do with the question. These distinctions must be maintained, even if an individual here and there be sacrificed in maintaining them; there is entirely too much of the leveling tendency in this country now, and it is increasing rapidly, I am sorry to say. You surely would not wish centuries of hereditary culture and refinement to go for nothing—to be held utterly valueless?"

"They never will, and never can be," replied Mrs. Stanley; "but ought not those who have this great privilege to try to raise others to their level, instead of treading them down?"

Mrs. Peyton was silent, and Mrs. Stanley continued—regretting afterward that she had done so—

"If I am not mistaken, Isabel intends teaching as soon as

she feels that she is well qualified for it; shall you be willing to apply, and have applied, to her, this cruel standard, with its total disregard of intrinsic worth?"

The fair old face flushed warmly, as Mrs. Peyton replied, in tones which told her displeasure at the turn the conversation had taken—

"That is merely a fancy of Isabel's, and I am extremely annoyed that she has been so foolish as to talk of it outside her family; or, indeed, even to me. We should, of course, never permit such a thing, and she would not defy our authority in this or in anything."

Mrs. Stanley felt at a loss for a reply, and was thankful for the opportune return of the Colonel, who had, as usual when he visited Green Point, been going about the place with Roderick, full of kindly interest in what had been done, and approval and shrewd suggestions for what was projected. Also, as usual, he had one of the twins on each arm and May dancing in front of him, complaining that there was no arm for her. He declared that he had "adopted" them all, and he was, beyond doubt, their most welcome visitor. He came in cheerily, quite unconscious of the dangerous state of the atmosphere, and the danger vanished at his entrance; both Mrs. Peyton and Mrs. Stanley were thankful for the diversion, and both resolved that in future the subject under discussion should be carefully avoided.

"The girls have just introduced me to the little governess," said the Colonel, as soon as he had shaken hands with Mrs. Stanley, "and she looks younger than any of them, except the May-blossom here. Still, from Louise's report of her proceedings I should think she would know how to govern her kingdom—no insurrections tolerated—eh, Miss Kitty? I had a little talk with her, thinking all the time that I must have met her before, but it was not till she turned away and left me that it all came to me in a flash.

17

She said her name was Neale, and I do believe she's the daughter of a college friend of mine—the prince of good fellows when I knew him, and of merchants afterward. I saw his death in the paper about a year ago, and when I have a quiet chance I want to ask her to tell me all about him. Poor fellow! it's hard that his daughter should be driven to teaching for her living, after the way in which she must have been brought up."

Mrs. Stanley repeated to the Colonel the outline of Miss Neale's story, and he listened with deep interest and a look of pity on his kind face. But when the story was finished he shook his head, saying—

"What were all the young fellows in Philadelphia about, I wonder, to let the poor child go off teaching, when she'd have made one of them such a sweet little wife? It's a terrible pity—teachers are pretty sure to turn into old maids, and she's far too pretty for such a fate! You'd better look out for your son, Mrs. Stanley; there's nothing like propinquity for leveling distinctions and making matches."

The two mothers exchanged an involuntary, conscious glance; nothing had ever been said about Roderick's preference for Isabel; but each knew, from that time, that the other had noticed it. Mrs. Stanley was about to reply—

"I do not admit the distinction——" but she stopped in time. Nothing would be gained by renewing the discussion, for if "a man convinced against his will is of the same opinion still," a woman is even more so; so she merely smiled, and replied—

"I am not at all uneasy about my boy; I can trust him to do nothing which would wound his mother. Did the boys show you their beehives?"

"Indeed they did," said the Colonel, with hearty interest, and accepting the hint—for although the younger girls were no longer in the room, Elizabeth was there, and he feared he had been imprudent—"indeed they did, and I was astonished at the cleverness with which they were made. Arnold's arrangement for taking the honey is capital; I expect to see those fellows invent the coming substitute for steam before I die!"

"I hardly look for that," said Mrs. Stanley, laughing; "but a new patent for any sort of farming machinery or utensil will not surprise me—that is, if they do not first succeed in blowing themselves up; their free time is pretty equally divided between the carpenter's bench and the 'laboratories,' as they call one end of the workshop, and the hut they have built by the creek."

"But do you really allow them to make chemical experiments?" asked Mrs. Peyton, in astonishment. "Is there not great danger of their hurting themselves?"

"A little, perhaps, but not much, I think," replied Mrs. Stanley. "Roderick has a sort of general supervision, and they never send their list of chemicals to be filled without first consulting him. There must be some little danger in whatever a really boyish boy undertakes, and I want to give them all the freedom I can, so long as their pursuits are innocent."

"You are quite right, madam," said the Colonel, emphatically. "A boy should never be tied to a woman's apron-string, or made into a milksop—your boys are the most manly—yes, and the most gentlemanly—little fellows for their age, that I have ever seen; your confidence in them is well rewarded already, and as for my friend Roderick—but I will not say what I think of him, to his mother, or she might accuse me of flattery."

The visit ended pleasantly, and neither Mrs. Peyton or Mrs. Stanley alluded again to the "bone of contention"; but when, a few weeks afterward, an invitation came—as it often did—to Mrs. Stanley and her family, to dine at River-

mouth the next day, a postscript to the note, written, as
Kitty asserted, by Louise, said:

"Pray, bring Miss Neale with you—we shall be delighted
to see her, if she will favor us."

It was no doubt considered a great concession to Mrs.
Stanley's feelings, but Winifred quietly declined the honor,
saying—

"It is very kind in Mrs. Peyton, but I have made no formal visits yet," and she glanced at her black dress, adding,
"Should I write a separate note, or will you make my
excuses in yours?"

"I think you had better write a little note to go in mine,
dear," replied Mrs. Stanley, "and one of us will stay with
you—it will be too lonesome for you to be here more than
half the day by yourself."

"Oh, please don't let anybody stay for me!" she exclaimed, looking very much distressed; "indeed, I do not
mind being alone, at all. I shall write to mother, and read
the new magazines, and not be in the least lonely."

Mrs. Stanley saw that it would be kinder to take her at her
word, so the invitation was accepted, and she was left alone.
Mrs. Peyton, after having received several "regrets" from
the younger members of the family to these general invitations, on the score of their school hours, had at last hit upon
the plan of always naming Saturday, and, as she took care
to mention that no other guests were to be invited, Mrs.
Stanley generally allowed the younger ones to go with their
elders.

Mrs. Stanley's views concerning her girls and society were
variously estimated, in the neighborhood, as "stiffness,"
"pride," or "exclusiveness," according to the views of the
estimator; but Mrs. Peyton fully agreed with her, and it
came to be understood, after awhile, that where the daughters
of these two families were wanted, the mothers must also be

invited. Louise did not, as yet, go to any very large or general entertainments, and Elizabeth, although she was a good deal sought after, and very popular among her young neighbors, cared very little for dancing, and frequently excused herself from the dancing parties to which she was invited.

The Stanleys had been a good deal surprised by the number of "neighbors," living anywhere from five to fifteen miles away, who had called on them; they had fancied that in coming to Green Point they were leaving the world behind them, and, in a certain sense, they were ; but in another it was very much the reverse. The young people of the neighborhood were gay enough to have satisfied the liveliest "girl of the period," during the fall and winter months, and as soon as the evenings began perceptibly to lengthen, invitations began to come in, sometimes at the rate of three or four in a week, and, although Elizabeth did not know it, many more would have come but for Mrs. Stanley's so-called "strictness," and Elizabeth's frequent refusals to those which she received. Kitty grumbled freely to Polly because all invitations to anything like a "party" which had come for them had been courteously declined by their mother, until they ceased to come.

"I don't see why mamma need keep us from *everything*," she said, moodily, after a particularly tempting invitation to a large "Hallow-e'en party" had shared the fate of the rest. "I could stand it, I suppose, if she only refused the dances and supper parties, but I do think she might let us go to things like this! Why, the Trevor girls go to everything, and two of them are younger than we are ; and the Hustons are as nice as can be, and their mother lets them go to ever so many small parties, and all the sociables. and they're only a year or two older than we are, if they're that much !"

"I don't think you ought to talk like that about mamma,

behind her back, Kitty," said Polly, with a most unusual
display of warmth ; "I should believe she knew best—yes,
and Betty and Rod, too—if they were to ask us to walk into
the fire, and I can't bear to hear you say such things—it's
being like a traitor, and you know it is ! "

Polly's words ended in the quaver which always struck her
voice when she was much excited—it had cost her a great
effort to speak so boldly to her "superior officer," as the
boys had dubbed Kitty. The rebel opened her mouth to
give a sharp retort, but suddenly closed it again, seized the
astonished Polly in her arms, whirled her about the floor
until she was dizzy, then set her down suddenly, kissed her
with needless force, and left the room with that startling
abruptness which characterized so many of her words and
actions, and to which the unfortunate Polly could never become accustomed.

CHAPTER XXI.

" A poor blind spinner in the sun,
    I tread my days ;
I know that all the threads will run
    Appointed ways.
I know each day will bring its task,
And, being blind, no more I ask."—H. H.

RODERICK had worked early and late, while any threshing remained to be done, and Arnold had worked faithfully beside him, excepting on the few occasions when Ernest had been allowed to take a turn. The little fellow had begged to go in Arnold's place much oftener than he had been permitted to; for, although the help which Roderick required, beside that of the man whom he had hired for the threshing season, and who always went with him, involved no very heavy work, it kept the boy on his feet all day, and Roderick had a great fear of overworking either of his brothers. It would have been well had he extended this fear to himself; but as May once said of him, "he seemed to forget that he had any himself," and he turned without pausing, when the threshing was over, to the farm-work which he had deferred for it, hiring one or two extra hands to make up the time—for he had found, by a slight calculation, that this would be more profitable than to let any of the threshing escape him—but working himself as if he were the only "hand" on the place. He had set his heart upon laying aside the money for the saw-mill, and had at last confided the plan to his family—he wanted so to talk it over, and make it seem a possible, if not a probable thing,

that he resolved to risk the impatience of the boys. Their
delight at finding their vision considered even remotely practicable was so great, that they readily promised to be patient,
and "not bother" about it until the money for it was
actually in hand. But they racked their brains for projects
which might help to swell the fund which was begun and
slowly increasing, and they had never come so near rebelling·
against their mother's and Roderick's wishes as they were
when school opened, and they found they were expected to
begin their attendance again. To their great joy, the opening had been delayed until early in October, because of
some badly needed repairs to the school-house, which, according to the custom of the country, had been put off till
the last moment, and then kept back by the dilatoriness of
the workmen.

The threshing was finished by that time; so the boys had
not that for an excuse, but they begged for another month—
a week, then three days? It was so unusual for them to
withstand their mother's wishes, that she was surprised as
well as troubled by their persistence, but she remained
quietly firm about it, and they soon saw that resistance was
useless, and unconditionally surrendered. But the first trip
of the season to the school-house was anything but a cheerful one, and Mr. Kendall, seeing their mournful counte-
nances, inquired anxiously, at recess, if any one were ill?

"Oh no, thank you, Mr. Kendall," replied Arnold,
smiling for the first time that day; "she's—I mean we're all
quite well, but the fact is, Ernest and I had so much on
hand that we didn't see how we could afford to go to school
this term, before Christmas, anyhow, but we couldn't convince the mother and Rod—so here we are!"

"No, I don't think you are," said Mr. Kendall, promptly.
"Ernest's performance at the blackboard, and yours in the
Latin class, were enough to convince me that you had left

the best part of yourselves at home, and to-morrow I should
like you to bring it! Your business, just at present, is to
grow, mentally and physically, and it will be your own
faults if your growth is stunted, either way, for I can see
nothing about you which will prevent your attainment of
full growth."

"But don't you think, Mr. Kendall," said Arnold, who
dearly loved an argument, "that if we were allowed to get
things off our minds, as it were, between this and Christmas,
that we should make up for lost time between then and
spring, or summer, rather?"

"Not in the least!" he replied, with much decision. "By
the time the Christmas holidays were over, you would have
other projects on hand, fully as important and fascinating as
those which are absorbing you now. And that is not all.
You would have rebelled against 'constituted authority,'
which it is always a bad thing to do. It is well to learn the
lesson of obedience early—I don't mean a blind and lazy
submission to everything and everybody—not at all! But
as you go through life, you will be obliged to submit to a
great many things which you would gladly change if you
could, and your manner of submitting will have a great deal
to do with your own happiness, and that of those about you.
Come now, be honest, and tell me if you do not think it
would be just as hard to begin school again after Christmas,
as it is now?"

"I am afraid it would," said Arnold, with reluctant
candor; "we are all the time thinking of new things, and
of course we shall keep on at it."

"I *know* it would," said Ernest, decisively. "Indeed, I
think it might be harder, for mamma and Rod, and perhaps
some of the others, have promised to give us some things we
want very badly in the laboratory, for our Christmas presents,
and after we get them we shall want to stay there all the time."

"That's honestly spoken," said Mr. Kendall, smiling; "and now I want you to act honestly too. Give the whole of your minds to your lessons, while you are in school, and as long, when you are at home, as you find necessary for their thorough mastery—you will work all the better, and play the more heartily in your free time. When I was a small boy, I read a fairy story which made a lasting impression on me—somebody was set to catch a flock of fairy geese, but he failed again and again, because he tried for one and another of the flock *beyond* the nearest one. He only succeeded when he took the nearest one first. The 'moral' is obvious. You can do a great many things, as you grow older, which you cannot do now, but certain other things in the way of discipline and training to mind and muscles you can do now, but never hereafter. Am I preaching? If I am, you see it is a short sermon, for I must ring the bell now; I am sorry to have robbed you of your intermission—I did not think I had talked so long."

"*We* are not sorry at all," said Arnold, heartily, "and I think we'll remember about the geese—perhaps they were the same geese as the ones who saved Rome."

"Oh no, they couldn't have been!" said Ernest. "Those Roman geese had quite too much sense to allow themselves to be caught, in any way, first or last."

The boys had been very much touched with Miss Neale's sad story, and they manifested their pity by many little quiet acts of attention which were a constant pleasure to her. In return, she interested herself in their plans and experiments, and sometimes gave them valuable hints and helps. She liked chemistry nearly as well as they did, and was better posted as to modern experiments and discoveries than Elizabeth, or even Roderick, for she had recently enjoyed the benefits of the fine laboratory and illustrated lectures at the college from which she had graduated. When the boys dis-

covered this, they listened to her remarks with much deference, and they were greatly flattered and delighted when she
asked them, "quite of her own accord," as they proudly proclaimed, to make her a mask and gauntlets similar to their
own, out of the "substitute for asbestos." They agreed
that, as she knew so much, and talked so little "except when
she really had something to say," it would be safe to take
her into their confidence about all the projected patents.
This mark of their friendship she seemed fully to appreciate,
and she frequently made valuable suggestions. She drew
remarkably well, and her pencil was always at their service
to make plans of their various brilliant ideas. Her offer to
give them drawing lessons was joyfully accepted. She had
consulted Mrs. Stanley before making it, and the latter had
acceded to the plan with much pleasure, only objecting on
the score of the additional work and loss of her free time,
which it would entail upon Miss Neale, and hinting that an
addition should be made to her salary on account of it.

"Oh, please don't say anything like that, dear Mrs. Stanley," she replied, earnestly. "I am here to do all that I
can—all that you would like to have me do, and I wish you
would believe that I don't want any 'free time,' excepting
enough to write a few letters every week. I like to be busy
all day, and then I can sleep all night ; if I am idle even for
a little while, I find I am going over and over the last happy
year at home, until it seems as if I could not bear it—as if
I *must* be with mother, no matter what work I do, or what
we go without."

"My poor little girl, I am very sorry for you," said Mrs.
Stanley, kissing her as tenderly as her mother could have
done; "but you must try to believe that if that happiness
had been better for you, you would have been allowed to
keep it. I feel so sure of my ignorance and blindness, and
my Father's love and clear sight, and so uncertain of every-

thing else, that I try to live just a day at a time, 'forgetting
those things which are behind, and reaching forth unto those
things which are before.' We shall know all about it after
awhile, and meantime we must be patient."

" I will try to be," said Winifred, humbly, "and indeed,
I ought to be happy here, you are all so good, so very good
to me. But *please*, don't say anything more about increasing my salary—you know you are giving me more than you
expected to give, as it is, and you must just let me do whatever I can find that needs doing, and not dream that I shall
ever consider myself 'put upon.' Why," she added, smiling,
" I expected all sorts of dreadful things—to be snubbed, and
slighted, and 'kept in my place,' and to have a forlorn room,
probably in the garret, and you have treated me, from the
first, as if I were a favored guest. All I can ever do will not
make up for that."

Mrs. Stanley was very glad to see the growing friendship
between her boys and Miss Neale. They were just coming
to the "hobbledehoy" age, when awkwardness and bashfulness are too apt to have uncouth and noisy manifestations,
but she had never "seen the necessity" for the roughness
and selfishness of half-grown boys, which is so often con-
doned with indulgent allusions to the "awkward age."

Roderick had grown from a manly and gentle boy into a
manly gentleman, without being a scourge in the transit,
and she welcomed all influences which should help the
younger boys in a similar development. They never remembered when they were taught to bring a chair when a lady
entered the room, and to open a door for her when she left
it—never to let their mother or sisters lift or carry anything
in their presence, without themselves assuming the burden,
or to ask their sisters to "run upstairs" for this and that,
instead of offering to run themselves, whenever they saw an
opportunity ; but if they did not remember, it was because

the lessons began when they were so young, and took root so early. And their courtesy to their sisters was met and rewarded by the cheerful performance of all the many little loving offices which sisters should perform for brothers. They never were obliged to ask twice for the bits of sewing and mending which are so often wanted in desperate haste by active boys; their tastes and likings were consulted in the manufacture of cake and desserts, and no meddling fingers interfered with the half finished work which they sometimes left about; if it chanced to be too much "about" for the comfort of the family, a gentle word from the mother gave them the chance to put it away themselves. There is no happier community than a family of boys and girls living on these terms, and the memory of such a home is a tower of strength, in after years, to men and women hard pushed in the battle of life.

A few days after Mr. Kendall had talked with the boys at recess, Ernest suddenly paused in his drawing to say—

"Miss Neale, if I ask you to do something for me, will you tell me, really and truly, if you had rather not?"

"I will," she replied, smiling at his serious face; "but I don't believe I shall be under any such painful necessity— you have come to me with no unreasonable requests, so far; or, yes, there was one, and you know I refused it."

"Oh, when we asked you to test those fire-proof gloves on our hands? It isn't anything like that—it will be a good deal of trouble, I'm afraid. We want you to make us a little picture for the laboratory."

"That I will do with pleasure," she answered, brightly. "Had you any particular subject in view?"

"Yes, that was why we wanted you to do it—Arnold and I. We have lots of pictures pasted and tacked about the workshop and both laboratories, cut from the Graphics and things that Uncle George sends—that English Graphic has

beautiful things, you know—but we couldn't find exactly
this picture that we want, though at first we thought we
could.   It's just a flock of wild geese, flying past a window
of some sort."

"I can easily draw that for you," she said.   "You know
I am very fond of drawing birds, and have a number of
studies in my portfolio.   How large did you wish the picture to be?"

"We had not fixed upon any size," he answered; "we
thought we would leave that quite to you.   You see, it's as
a sort of reminder that we want it.   Mr. Kendall said something the other day.   Arnold and I tried to beg off from
school until after Christmas; we might have known better
than to try, for of course mamma was not going to back
down—she never does, after she has said a thing, and I
think that must be one reason why she's so careful only to
say right things.   But the first day we went to school, we
didn't go exactly cheerfully, and we were dreadfully stupid
about our lessons and examples.   Mr. Kendall saw something was wrong, so he talked to us at recess, and we told
him all about it, and then he told us about a fairy story he
had read when he was a boy, of a flock of geese that could
only be caught by catching the nearest one first—if the person who was trying to catch them reached over for the one
beyond the nearest, he didn't catch any at all.   I can't remember all he said exactly, but what he meant was, that
our education was the nearest goose just at present, and that
we shouldn't really make anything by trying to skip it.   I
didn't want to think he was right, but I'm afraid he is, and
so is Arnold, and we thought it would be sort of encouraging
to have a picture of the geese where we could look at it
when we had to leave the laboratory and go to school."

"I think it will be an excellent idea," said Miss Neale.
"Shall you frame it, or tack it up against the wall?"

"Oh, we shall frame it, of course! We've had some real walnut wood cut up and drying for some time—we mean to have a jig-saw before long, and do some Christmas-work if we have time—and we can make it either of that or the yellow pine with the shellac varnish. Which do you think will be prettier?"

"I don't know till I see them. Here, I will give you the dimensions, and then suppose you make one of each, and see which you like best—you can use the other for something else, you know. I will take one of these pieces of paper. Have you your measure—oh, of course you have! Thank you—the frame must be eighteen by twelve."

"Oh, will you make it so large as that?—that will be jolly. We can each make a frame, and then you shall choose, and perhaps Arnold will have a drawing good enough for the other, before long. He learns so much faster than I do."

Arnold had been silently drawing during this conversation, but he raised his head now to say, "You mean I *draw* faster. If I'm not mistaken, you'll come out ahead at the end of six months—don't you think so, Miss Neale?"

"It is almost too soon to tell yet," she replied; "but I see what you mean, Ernest very rarely has any erasing to do."

"That's a mild and flattering way of putting it," said Arnold; "I think I use my eraser quite as much as I do my pencil, and sometimes I tear things up, and begin all over again."

"There is a proverb which I like, perhaps because of my remote Irish ancestor," she said. "It would make a good motto for you, Arnold—'Fair and asy goes far in a day.'"

The boys both laughed at the genuine Irish accent which she gave it, and Arnold said—

"I'm afraid I shall be a good while learning that proverb,

Miss Neale; and really, now, don't you think it sounds just a little lazy, as well as 'asy'?"

"It may sound lazy," she said, "but it isn't in reality. Fair—that is, giving its due time to each piece of work, not slighting one for another, or omitting what we don't like; and 'asy'—not hurrying through one work, as if it were something to be gone through with anyhow at all, but deliberately, as if we liked it."

"But it's so hard to do that with work we don't like," said Ernest. "I always rush through the things I dislike to do, to have them over and done with, and then, when I am doing anything I like, I linger, and fuss, and polish up, and don't wish to let it out of my hands."

"You will have to divide yourself a little more evenly," she replied. "It is well to know when a thing is done; decision is, I think, almost the same thing as genius."

"But about doing what we don't like as if we did like it," said Arnold, "I do not believe I shall *ever* be able to do that! Miss Neale, may I ask you a searching question?"

"You may—but I must reserve the right not to answer it, if it is too searching."

"Of course! Here goes, then—Do you really and truly like teaching?"

She paused a moment, and than said slowly—

"Perhaps I should assert my right, and refuse to answer —but then, perhaps it will help you if I do. I do not like teaching, Arnold—'really and truly.'"

"I thought you didn't," said Arnold, triumphantly, "as soon as you said we ought to do what we disliked, as if we liked it. Before you said that, I supposed you were very fond of it—you do it so thoroughly, and throw in so much."

"Throw in so much?" she repeated, questioningly; "I don't think I quite understand."

"I mean," said Arnold, "you do so much more than you

really need do. I saw you helping May to learn her verb,
yesterday, and Kitty says you often stop after school hours
to show her about her examples, and — I can't think of everything now, but you know what I mean."

"Yes, I imagine I do," she answered, smiling, but color-
ing brightly, too; "if I really loved teaching, naturally, I
should not always be afraid of doing too little—I don't suppose I should think about it at all, in that way. But knowing I did not like it, when I began, I felt that I must be very
careful not to slight or neglect it in any way. And you
must not regard me as a martyr, dear Arnold—I have found
it much more easy than I expected to, and I am really
beginning to think that I shall like it, after awhile. If you
had all been stupid and disagreeable, and had not cared to
learn, I should probably have hated it cordially, by this time;
but you all work so heartily and honestly, that I am more
and more encouraged every day."

She could have said nothing which would so effectually
have spurred the boys on to continued exertion, as this.
They fervently resolved that she should never have any
reason to hate teaching on their account.

The lesson was over, but Arnold lingered.

"What is it?" she asked. "Do you want any more directions about your drawing, so that you may finish it? I am
in no hurry."

"No, thank you," he replied. "I wanted to ask you if
you would mind, if I were to tell the girls what we have
been talking about this afternoon?"

"No, I don't think I should," she answered, thoughtfully, "if you will be careful not to give them too strong
an impression of my dislike for teaching, and remember
that it was a theoretical dislike, which is yielding to treatment."

18

CHAPTER XXII.

"There's no way to make sorrow light
But in the noble bearing."—W. Rowley.

AS the pressure of the fall work subsided, Roderick's mother first, and then his brothers and sisters, began to notice that he seemed tired all the time. He slept later than usual, several mornings in succession, and seemed more vexed about it than the occasion warranted. He was generally wide awake and bright in the evening, no matter how busy he had been through the day, but now he grew drowsy before nine o'clock, and, to his great annoyance, actually fell asleep once or twice in his chair. His appetite, too, had failed a good deal, and it seemed to require an effort for him to interest himself in what was going on around him. When things came to this pass, his mother begged him to see the doctor, and, after putting her off once or twice, he consented to do so. He went on horseback, and came home looking so pale and tired that Mrs. Stanley reproached herself for not having kept him at home, and sent one of the younger boys to bring the doctor to him. She asked him anxiously what Dr. West had told him, and he replied, with weary indifference—

"Oh, he said something about malaria, and gave me a lot of quinine and one or two other things—I'll be all right in a day or two, little mother—don't worry, I've only been working rather too hard."

He lay down on the sofa, and fell at once into a heavy sleep, from which he was roused with difficulty at tea-time. He came to the table, but Kitty said presently—

"We might as well have let you sleep, Rod, if you aren't going to eat any supper. Wouldn't you like Aunt Judy to make you a piece of toast? She'd be proud and happy to do it."

"No thank you, dear," he said, heavily; "I believe I am not hungry, and if you'll all excuse me, I think I will go to bed—the sun was hot, and the ride tired me."

They exchanged troubled glances—the afternoon had been cloudy, with a fresh breeze blowing from the bay.

He half rose from his chair, and then sank down again, saying in the same drowsy voice—

"I think I'll have a cup of tea before I go, mother; the room feels chilly."

The room was anything but chilly, for Clara, with more zeal than discretion, had thrown on the fire an armful of "pine kindlin's" just before the tea-bell rang. Mrs. Stanley poured out the tea, and Roderick drank it in silence, and then once more excused himself and went upstairs.

"I *wish* I had not let him take that ride," said Mrs. Stanley, anxiously. "I did ask him to let one of the boys go, but he laughed, and said he only wanted a little quinine, and he was quite able to go for it. He has a burning fever; his hands and lips felt like fire."

"Hark!" said Kitty, nervously; "what was that?"

Arnold was out of the room, and half-way upstairs, while she was speaking. Roderick's room was directly over the dining-room, and the sound which they had all heard was that of a heavy fall. They were all about to rush upstairs, but Mrs. Stanley kept them back.

"Stay here, all of you," she said quietly, although her voice trembled, "except Elizabeth; come, dear, we will see what is the matter."

The children obeyed reluctantly, and Mrs. Stanley and Elizabeth went out together. They found Arnold trying to

lift Roderick, who had fallen to the floor, his head just missing the sharp corner of a chair.   He was insensible, and it
was quite beyond Arnold's strength to lift him alone, but
together they managed to raise him and lay him on the bed.

"You must go at once for Dr. West, Arnold," said Mrs.
Stanley, hurriedly, "and if he is not at home, follow him
till you find him.   Take the horse that has not been out to-
day—not the one Rod had.   And be as quick as you can."

Arnold only waited for her to finish speaking, and in less
than five minutes they heard the sound of the horse's hoofs,
as he galloped away.

"Mamma, what can we do?" asked Elizabeth, in a trembling voice.   "We *can't* wait till the doctor comes; it will
be so long."

"Run quickly and see if Moses is here yet," replied Mrs.
Stanley, "and tell him to bring up the largest tub and fill it
with hot water.   I think he and Ernest and I can manage to
get Rod into it."

Moses was still in the kitchen, and in a very few minutes
he and Aunt Judy had a large tub filled with water by the
bedside.   The rigid look was passing away from Roderick's
face, and he was put into the warm bath without much difficulty, and then wrapped in heated blankets.   Aunt Judy
had been busy meanwhile; she had made a journey to the
corner of the yard where her herb-bed grew, and now she
came back to the room with rue steeped in vinegar, which
she bound upon Roderick's wrists and ankles.   The doctor,
on being told afterward of this, and that the convulsive
shivers which had been shaking his frame stopped almost
immediately after this application, smiled indulgently, and
said it was a "coincidence"; but happily for her serenity of
mind, Aunt Judy did not hear his verdict, and would not
have understood it had she heard.

Arnold was so fortunate as to find Dr. West at home, and

they returned together, the doctor riding instead of driving for the sake of greater speed. He questioned Arnold closely, as they rode along, about Roderick's recent doings, and especially as to whether he had been out-of-doors much after sunset. Arnold said that he had—that several times, when they had been out together with the threshing-machine, Roderick had returned home late in the evening, fearing his mother would be anxious about him, but that on these occasions he had always insisted upon leaving him, Arnold, to follow in the morning.

"He's been out late while he was sowing the wheat, too," added the boy, "although he would make Ernest and me come in at sunset; and when we asked him why we should come in if he didn't, he said he was older and stronger, and could stand more than we could."

"I was afraid so," said the doctor; "strangers who come here from the north are nearly always imprudent. I don't suppose the night air, in itself, would have done him much harm, but he has been over tiring himself; I have seen it for some time. Well, here we are, and now I want you to take a hot drink and a hot bath, and go straight to bed, my boy, or we shall be having you down next."

Anxious as Arnold was to see Roderick again, and to hear the doctor's verdict, he obeyed orders, only begging Ernest to bring him word what Dr. West said the first moment he could.

Aunt Judy was hovering about as they entered the house, and hearing Dr. West's order to Arnold, she hastened to make a bowl of steaming gruel, and Arnold praised it to her heart's content, as he carefully scraped the last drop from the bowl. She tucked him up snugly, and then sat before the hearth "minding" the fire until he fell asleep. She had wondered to herself at his submission to the doctor's wishes, but Arnold had thought more than once about Mr.

Kendall's "sermon" on obedience—he knew that much would now devolve on him, and that it would be a poor beginning to unfit himself for service by a foolish obstinacy. He had hoped to share his mother's watch in Roderick's room that night, but "sober second thought" showed him that Elizabeth could be far more useful there than he could, while she could not take his place, the next day, in the farm-work and errand going. He thought it would be quite impossible for him to sleep, but after a busy day the hurried ride had tired him, and the warm bath, together with Aunt Judy's comforting bowl of gruel, proved all sufficient anodynes. He did not wake when Ernest came to bed, and when Elizabeth softly called him in the morning he asked drowsily—

"Is the doctor gone? What did he say about Rod, Betty?"

Doctor West had stayed until late in the night, and when he at last went home, he promised to call again before noon the next day. He had assured them that Roderick was in no immediate danger now, adding—

"He has had a pretty sharp congestive chill, and I am afraid he is in for a tedious attack of malarial fever—he ought to have come to me sooner. You must find some beef somewhere, and give him beef tea and milk as often as he can take it—he is very much run down."

So Arnold's first errand in the morning was an expedition in search of beef. He went to Colonel Peyton's first, by his mother's advice, for fresh meat was found oftener there than elsewhere in the neighborhood, and if the Colonel should not happen to have any just now, he would probably know who had. He was full of kindly sympathy, and delighted to be able to supply Mrs. Stanley's need.

"It's the most fortunate thing that you should have needed it just now," he said, earnestly. "No; I don't

mean that—of course I don't. I mean it is most fortunate
that I actually had a quarter all ready for you—I was going
to send it over to your mother this very morning. But come
in—come in and have some lunch while the boy is getting it
out of the ice-house. Mrs. Peyton will want to see you, and
hear all about Roderick. He's a fine fellow, if ever there
was one, but he ought to take better care of himself; he
really ought, when so much depends on him."

Mrs. Peyton was full of loving sympathy, which took—as
her sympathy always did—a practical form, for when the
"boy" came in with the beef, she secured the basket, and
filled up the chinks with whatever she could find in her
pantry, which she thought would be useful to patient or
nurses.

"Give my love to your dear mother, my boy," she said, as
she forced the lid of the basket down, and tied it for better
security, "and tell her the grape wine is for her and Elizabeth—it's quite pure, and I keep it for sickness, for it is un-
fermented wine, and the best wine I know of. They must
keep their strength up by all means. And the white wine is
for wine-whey for dear Roderick—ask the doctor if he may
have it, of course, but I know he may! And I'm so thankful I made calves'-foot jelly yesterday—I don't make it out
of that dreadful gluey stuff they call gelatine, but out of the
genuine calves' feet. I'd have put in another bowl, but the
basket will not hold it, so I will send it over to-morrow, by
Louise. I filled up the chinks with those seed-cakes you all
like so much—poor children, you'll want Aunt Judy for
other things beside baking. There, I won't keep you, dear,
for I know you want to be off with the beef—put these
cookies in your pocket, to eat as you go home."

The dear old face was beaming with loving kindness, and
Arnold, obeying an impulse, threw his arms around her
neck and kissed her, for a sudden lump in his throat kept

him from speaking. Was Rod going to die, he wondered, that her heart was so touched?

She seemed to understand his thought, for she hugged him as if he had been her own boy, and said, cheerfully—

"There, my dear, there! You mustn't be frightened about Rod; he has youth on his side, and a splendid constitution, and he will have the best of nursing—and all our prayers."

Arnold kissed her again, and rode away without trusting himself to speak. If Rod were not in danger, he thought, she would not talk in this way.

As he went rapidly home, it seemed to him that everything he had ever said or done to Roderick, which he would have wished unsaid and undone, forced itself into his mind. It was very seldom that the harmony between them was marred, but they were too near each other in age to keep from all friction, when their wills crossed, and the younger boys sometimes resented Roderick's attempts to control them, carefully as these attempts were always made.

One particular instance weighed most heavily on Arnold's conscience. He and Ernest had sometimes lingered at Mr. Joyce's store, listening to the stories told by two or three lazy, good tempered fellows, who professed to earn their living by fishing and crabbing, but who spent most of their time at the "corner," exchanging narratives of their own supposititious experiences and exploits. There was a sort of dry humor about these recitals which, with the effort which each one always made to "cap" the last story told, greatly tickled the boys, and they often amused themselves with trying to imitate the dialect, and the inimitable drawl, of the narrators. But they admitted to Roderick that the stories were often coarse, and always more or less sprinkled with profanity, and he begged them earnestly never to listen to another, but to leave the store promptly when their errands were done. They had both grumbled at this, and Arnold had argued the point at some length.

"It's all nonsense, Rod," he said, angrily, when he found that Roderick remained firm; "we're not babies, as you seem to think we are, and surely we can enjoy the fun without taking any harm from it—we needn't remember all we hear."

"Very well," replied Roderick, quietly; "I have no authority over you, of course, but since you are so sure of your ground, you will not object to stating the case fairly to mother, and abiding by her decision. She, at least, has a right to advise you."

Ernest had yielded, as he always did when he saw that he was wrong, with perfect frankness and good temper; but Arnold had turned sullenly away, and "sulked" more or less for the remainder of the day—a most unusual proceeding for him. He appealed to his mother for a final decision of the case, although he knew quite well in his inmost heart what that decision would be, and that he would be obliged to abide by it; she was hurt and grieved that he should have resisted Roderick's advice in the matter, and she told him that, until he could submit cheerfully, and because he knew that it was right, to her wishes about it, she would send Moses on the necessary errands. It was several days before he unconditionally surrendered, but when he did, he was very penitent. His apology to Roderick was met with cordial affection, and the whole affair was immediately and totally ignored. Mrs. Stanley almost invented an errand to the store, that afternoon, at a time when Arnold was the only one at liberty to go, and in a few days nearly every one but himself had forgotten about it.

It came back to him now, exaggerated by his grief and remorse. How noble Rod had looked, as he said those few strong words about keeping the memory pure from evil words, which live in it so often against the will! How small, how contemptible, he himself must have appeared, strutting and crowing by way of asserting his manly dignity!

"Oh, if Rod will only live!" he said to himself, while his eyes were blinded with hot tears, "I'll show him what I think of him as I never have done before. "

The house soon settled into the dreary routine which a tedious illness involves, for before many days Roderick's fever was unmistakably typhoid in its character, and the doctor recommended, both for Roderick's sake and that of the others, that no one should be admitted to his room but those who were engaged in nursing him. These were Mrs. Stanley and Elizabeth; Kitty and Polly begged, with many tears, to be allowed to take their share of the nursing, but their mother thought it best not to allow it, for although the doctor would not say that the disease was exactly infectious, or even contagious, he said there was no use in exposing the younger ones to the atmosphere of the sick-room, at a season when "fall fevers" were more or less prevalent. The girls at first were inconsolable, and especially when their mother insisted that the daily lessons, with the exception of music, should go on as usual.

"I can't do it!" sobbed Kitty, dropping suddenly on the floor, as her mother left the room, and burying her head in Miss Neale's lap; "I can't keep my mind on lessons and things, when I know that Rod is lying there burning up with fever, and maybe will not get well. I think mamma *might* let us help her with him, and I don't see how she can imagine we can attend to our lessons now."

Polly was crying quietly at her desk. She had no idea of rebelling, but she felt the impossibility of thinking of anything but Rod, quite as keenly as Kitty did.

It was curious to see how Miss Neale's gentle dignity, and the knowledge of her talents and attainments, had conquered

Kitty's respect, and gradually made the difference in their ages seem much greater than it really was. Kitty was rapidly becoming interested in her studies in a manner which made her forget the unworthy ambition that had governed her a few weeks before, and her really fine mind took constant pleasure in the sympathy and appreciation of her teacher.

Winifred stroked the bowed head, saying, gently—

"Dear, you must not think I am preaching if I say something to you—we can all help, but we must not try to do it in our own way. I have thought of a great many things we can do, to make it easier for your mother and sister ; may I tell you some of them—you and Polly ? "

"Oh, how can you ask ? " cried Kitty, starting up suddenly, and dashing the tears from her eyes, while Polly came out of her corner, and listened with eager attention.

"Perhaps you may think them stupid ways," said Winifred, smiling, "but listen patiently, at any rate. You and I, Kitty, can attend to the butter, if Aunt Judy will show us a little, and we can all three take turns in washing the breakfast things, and keeping the parlor and bedrooms dusted, and in nice order. We can count the wash, and put the clothes away, and do all the little things that your mother and sister do about the house, so that, when they are not with your brother, they may have perfect rest. Then I am going to ask you to take my room for the school-room, for the present—you see, the little room, with its comfortable lounge, will be just the place for the one who is not watching to rest in—it is so near Mr. Stanley's room, and yet in such a quiet part of the house. We shall find other things that we can do, I think. If we keep the spirit lamp always in order, and see that the tea or coffee is freshly made the last thing in the evening, then it will be sure to be ready when they need it in the night. When I took care of mother in her illness, I found that the time when I felt like sinking was always early in the night, between twelve and one o'clock; if I could get past that, I was safe for the night—so I used to drink some tea or coffee, and force myself to eat something, as soon as I began to feel faint, and I know they will do it too, if we arrange things so that it will give them no thought or trouble. And another thing—I think we had better make the beef-tea ourselves. Aunt Judy would do it joyfully, but her sight is not very good, you know, and so much depends on cutting the beef fine, and taking out every bit of fat—you know beef-tea is like the 'little girl who had the little curl right in the middle of her forehead—when it is good, it's very, very good, and when it is bad, it's horrid.'"

The girls had listened with eager attention, and now they both laughed, as she meant they should, and Kitty seized her hands, exclaiming—

"You are simply an angel! I knew all the time that I shouldn't make a good nurse, but it seemed to me I should die if I couldn't do something for Rod, and now I see there are lots of things, but I should never have seen them if you hadn't pointed them out. I am like that pitcher of Gail Hamilton's that was so easily upset, and was 'made foolish, anyhow.'"

"No, you weren't 'made foolish,'" said Winifred; "you can't plead that excuse truthfully; if you would give yourself time to think, once in awhile, you would be a very valuable member of society."

"But *do* you think we can possibly study, and say our lessons, at any rate, before Rod begins to get better?" asked Kitty, not so desperately as before, but very mournfully.

"I do," replied Winifred, with decision; "I think you would be far more wretched, if you were to allow yourself any idle time. The busier you keep, the more rapidly these

days of suspense will go by, and you will find the very effort
you have to make will be good for you—it will have the effect
of a tonic on your mind."

" We'll try then," said Kitty, speaking, as she so often
did, with perfect confidence for both of them; "my mind
needs a tonic, dear knows! But trying isn't succeeding, you
know."

" It goes a long way toward it," said Winifred; "and one
thing I will promise you—if I find that the lessons are really
interfering with our services to your mother and sister, I
will petition to have them shortened, or even omitted, should
it seem necessary. But I shall not consider that they do
really interfere, if we fail to arrange our work to the best
advantage."

" What a rigorous person you are!" said Kitty, half-smil-
ing and half-pouting; "and the worst of it is, you are harder
on yourself than you are on any one else, so that all our
complaints fall to the ground."

" But you know they are groundless, Kitty," said Polly,
perfectly unconscious of her feeble pun, and Kitty, in spite
of her grief and anxiety, could not resist the laugh and whirl
about the room with her victim, to which one of Polly's unintentional jokes always excited her.

CHAPTER XXIII.

"Oh friends, I pray to-night,
Keep not your kisses for my dead, cold brow.
The way is lonely ; let me feel them now.
Think gently of me ; I am travel-worn.
My faltering feet are pierced with many a thorn.
Forgive ! oh, hearts estranged, forgive, I plead !
When dreamless rest is mine, I shall not need
The tenderness for which I long to-night."

KITTY and Polly were obliged to admit, in the course of a few days, that their mother and Miss Neale were right. The regular hours and well filled time helped them through those long days of anxiety and dread as nothing else could have done, and Mrs. Stanley and Elizabeth, with their hands upheld by everything which loving forethought could devise, bore the strain far better than the rest of the family feared they would. The kindest offers of help came from all quarters. The nearest acquaintances came to ask with real interest how the patient was progressing, and if they could not do something, anything to help his family. By some of these, the non-acceptance of their offers to watch with Roderick at night was taken very much amiss, and set down to the score of the same "pride" and "exclusiveness" to which other refusals had been attributed, and this, notwithstanding the careful explanation which was always made, that the doctor did not permit him to see any one but his mother and elder sister.

"It's my belief he has small-pox, or something ketchin'," remarked one offended dame, as she drove away, "and *I* sha'n't go where I am not wanted any more—you girls can do as you please about it, but I hope I have a little spirit!"

"But mother," said one of the "girls," who had no desire for any coolness between herself and the Stanleys, "you know we asked the doctor, and he said it was only a fall-fever, and Miss Kitty says even she and her younger sisters don't go into the room, and that everything depends on his not being excited."

"I've set up with sick people before he was born, I reckon," said "mother," unappeased, "and it was always the way to have the neighbors come in and help, two fresh watchers every night, and begin and go round again, if it lasted that long."

"Well," said the daughter, persisting in her defence, "I hope you'll have it different when I need watching with—I think about three nights of entertaining company when I wasn't able to lift my head would finish me up—the doctor always said it was that that ran little Johnny Hadden into brain fever, when he only had intermittent. I heard him say myself, that two old women talking across you all night was enough to lay you up if you was well to begin with."

"The doctor had better keep a civil tongue in his head," said "mother," sharply, "and not be so sure he's smart just because he's new fashioned."

Most of the neighbors and acquaintances, however, were quite satisfied when they heard that Roderick was not allowed even to see all of his family, and contented themselves with frequent inquiries, and offerings of any and everything they could make, or find on their places, which they thought might be suitable for the invalid or his care-takers.

Some of these were very funny, and if Roderick had taken a quarter of the infallible cures for chills and fever, tonics and composing draughts, compounded of various herbs, roots and "simples," which were brought to him, his case would have been hopeless. But the warm good will and neighborly feeling of which these and the more judicious offerings were manifestations, were valued by the sorrowing family at their full worth.   It was Kitty who conceived the idea of saving all the notes of condolence and inquiry, to show to Roderick as soon as he should be able to read them, and, strange to say, she had no thought of amusement in doing so, although some of them, from a literary standpoint, were amusing enough, were it only for the various devices resorted to, for the spelling of Roderick's name.   But the valuable part of Kitty's character, which, as a usual thing, was not so apparent as the other side, was developing rapidly under this trial.   She was far gentler and more docile than she had ever been before.   She no longer felt that "fun" was worth the sacrifices of better things which she had frequently made for it, and under Winifred's gentle and almost unfelt guidance, she was learning a quick and loving appreciation of the rights and needs of those about her.

Polly was just the same loving and lovable Polly under trouble as she was when skies were fair; but even she was learning more fully the spirit of that sacrifice which gives life, only to find a fuller and more beautiful life awaiting it.

The doctor had said that it might be six weeks before the fever would have run its course, though he had a faint hope of breaking it sooner than this.   Roderick lay most of the time in a stupor, from which he was with difficulty roused sufficiently to take medicine and food.   At first he seemed to know, for a few minutes at a time, who was waiting on him ; but very soon it was evident that when he was conscious of the presence of any one, he had no idea who the person was.   He was sometimes wildly delirious at night, and his delirium always took the form of self-reproach. The debt to his uncle, the fear that he was mismanaging the farm or the boys, or that he was letting himself murmur about the deferring of his studies, about all these things he would mutter and moan, while his mother or Elizabeth sat in silent grief at his bedside. Often he would start up, thinking he had overslept himself, and it would require all their strength to keep him on the bed, while they coaxed and soothed him back to quietness, which, in a few minutes, would sink again to the heavy stupor.

Dr. West told Mrs. Stanley, after two weeks had passed in this way, that while he was so entirely unconscious of their presence would be a good time for them to let some one relieve guard, and allow them to gain fresh strength by taking their much needed rest.

"You can be close at hand," he said, "so that, if he should suddenly recover consciousness—which I do not think he will do, however—you can be called, and your aid can disappear. I know you don't like the idea, my dear madam, and it is quite natural that you should not; but just fancy for a moment what the consequences would be, if you or Miss Stanley, or both, should be added to the sick-list!"

Mrs. Stanley tried to fancy it, and the result was, that when Mr. Kendall and Randolph Peyton called, one in the evening, and the other the next morning, and once more asked earnestly if they could not do something to help, she told them they could, and engaged each for a night's watch —two nights, she felt sure, would suffice to give renewed strength to herself and Elizabeth, and for more than two she could not bring herself to resign her place.

The doctor expressed his satisfaction when she told him what she had done, but added, by way of warning: "And don't try to sleep with one eye and ear open—engage your substitute—make him promise to call you instantly if any change should occur beside that from stupor to delirium, and back again, and when you have done this, try to go honestly to sleep, as if you had nothing else to do. I see Miss Stanley thinks I am talking nonsense—here, give me a

19

bottle—I shall leave you each a good dose of bromide, and I
trust to your honor to take it; I should give you something
stronger and surer if you were quite certain not to be called,
but, worn out as you are, this ought to settle you, and no
great harm will come if your sleep is interrupted."

No change took place on the two nights when Mrs. Stanley and Elizabeth resigned their charge to other hands; they
slept quietly, after having cast their care upon Him, who, as
they felt very sure, was caring for them, and felt renewed
strength for the struggle.

They would not allow Mr. Kendall to repeat his kindness
for awhile, because, busy as he was nearly all day, he had
little chance to make up the lost sleep; but when Randolph
Peyton begged earnestly to be allowed to come at least twice
a week, until some change in Roderick's condition took
place, Mrs. Stanley gratefully accepted his offer. She would,
perhaps, had she not been so thoroughly absorbed by one subject, have seen that this was not wise. Randolph had freely
expressed his admiration for the "little governess," as he
condescendingly called Miss Neale, and her more than indifference to him piqued his vanity into trying to interest
her. Coming as he now did into the household, when so
large a share of the housekeeping had insensibly passed into
her willing hands, their acquaintance ripened into friendship
with a rapidity which would have been impossible under
ordinary circumstances. Beside this, he showed to far better
advantage, in this short time of trial, than if she had seen
him only when he was leading his home life of busy idleness.
He sincerely liked and admired Roderick, and was heartily
glad to be of service; but he had offered his help with more
alacrity, because of the presence of the "little governess."
He had no idea of really making love to her—he merely
wished to see if her indifference to him was—as, in his
vanity, he suspected it of being—assumed rather than

genuine, and to amuse himself with a mild flirtation, such as he had had on hand with one or another of the girls in the neighborhood, ever since he could remember. It was no wonder that he was vain—his indolent acts of attention had met with such flattering response, his invitations to drive or ride had been so invariably accepted, so frequently angled-for, that a stronger minded man than he was, moving in a like narrow circle, might have been pardoned for over-estimating his consequence. He had sufficient tact, as a general thing, to conceal, or at least not to obtrude, his vanity and that gently deferential manner—the deference of conscious strength to acknowledged weakness—which many women consider attractive. He soon saw that the sort of admiration which he was accustomed to finding effective would produce no impression on Winifred, or rather, that the impression it would make would be quite the reverse of that which he wished to convey. She seemed covertly amused by pretty speeches and telling glances; and to be obliged to explain a tender allusion, somehow robs it of its charm.

So he started on a new tack. He skilfully led her to talk of herself, until by degrees she had told him of the events which had brought her to the necessity of working for herself and her mother, and, as by this time his interest in her began to be genuine, she was more touched by the few words of real sympathy which he spoke when she had finished, than by all his previous compliments. He was well read on many subjects which interested her, and he began to consult her opinions with a deference which was the most delicate flattery possible. He managed to have a few minutes' talk with her now whenever he came, and generally another as he was going, always beginning about Roderick, and skilfully leading her on to talk of other things, until sometimes, after he had gone, she reproached

herself for heartlessness, as she recalled the fact that, while
they talked, she had forgotten the trouble in the house, and
felt a pleasure keener than she had believed herself capable
of feeling again. With the exception of one very humble
person, no one noticed what was going on, unless it in some
way related to Roderick. To Kitty and Polly it seemed perfectly right and natural that, when Mr. Peyton was to watch
with Roderick, he should have a good deal to say to Miss
Neale, who now filled Elizabeth's place in the household,
besides acting as medium between those in the sick-room
and the rest of the family. At one time Kitty would have
violently resented the idea of having any one outside the
family set above her in this way; but Kitty, too, was learning the lesson of obedience. She saw that Winifred's experience, and thoughtful, unselfish character fitted her for
the post, while she knew very well that she could not depend upon herself never to forget, and always to do the
right thing at the right time. Indeed, she had been humbled
to the dust, once or twice, by her forgetfulness of things
which she had voluntarily undertaken to do. Whenever
she had happened upon one of Mr. Peyton's prolonged greetings with, or leavetakings of, Miss Neale, she had heard
nothing more sentimental than—

"You are sure there is ice enough to last till to-morrow?
Mother bade me ask, particularly, and I drove over instead
of riding, so that Pete might take a message back." Or,
"Pray do not trouble yourself about the spirit-lamp to-night
—I assure you I like the tea even better cold—I will put ice
in it, and it will keep me awake more effectually."

It required some dexterity on Mr. Peyton's part, sometimes, to have one of these practical remarks in progress by
the time they were interrupted; but, being gifted with quick
sight and hearing, he always managed to do it, and Winifred, who was herself wholly free from guile, did not readily

suspect it in others. She would instantly have taken alarm, had he not adopted the tone of respectful friendship; this put her entirely at ease with him, and she began to think that she had misjudged him—that the silly flatteries which he had at first addressed to her, were the natural result of association with foolish girls, to whom such tributes were welcome; he had seen that they were distasteful to her, and was offering her the tribute of an equal friendship. Farther than this she did not choose to let herself think. As for him, he very soon acknowledged to himself that he loved her—that his fancy that he had loved either Elizabeth or Edith was a total mistake, and he felt an honest shame at the remembrance of his views concerning Edith's fortune. He had precisely the same ideas about "caste" and "class" as those held by his mother and father, but, like most of his ideas, they were loosely held, and he soon succeeded in persuading himself that, in this case, they did not apply—Winifred's present position was a mere accident, which marriage with him would repair, by restoring her to her proper sphere. Even his mother had admitted that she came of an excellent family, and that it was a sad pity she had not waited and considered a little before stepping down from her own rank to a lower one! It was Aunt Judy alone, of all the household, who had discovered "Mass' Randolph's" secret, and highly delighted she was by the discovery. She loved Winifred already nearly as much as she did "her own young ladies," and what fate, she thought, would be more delightful for her, than to be snatched from the drudgery of teaching to be the wife of a handsome young man, and live in one of the "big houses" of the neighborhood? She had settled it in her own mind that "Mass' Randolph" must be very rich, because he seemed to have no business of any kind, and yet he always wore "good clothes," and rode a fine horse; besides, did he not seem to have unlimited "change" in his pocket, ready to be slipped into the hand of any servant who was so fortunate as to wait upon him?

Roderick's illness had declared itself late in October, and it proved to be a case of "old-fashioned typhoid," as the doctor said, running six weeks before the decisive change took place. That this change was for the better, instead of the worse, was due, as Dr. West frankly avowed, far more to the "perfect nursing" which his patient had had, than to his own attendance. Mrs. Stanley and Elizabeth had saved their strength in every possible way, taking rest whenever it was possible without detriment to their charge, and food regularly, whether they wanted it or not. It is scarcely probable that Elizabeth would have done this, if she had been left to herself—excitement would, perhaps, have kept her up until the strain was over, and then she, too, would have sunk under the weight of work beyond her strength. But her mother's quiet influence and example made it seem only natural and right that they should take care of themselves, in order that they might take care of Roderick.

"You know, dear," Mrs. Stanley had said, when Elizabeth at first refused to eat or rest, "to do good work we must have the right tools. I am rested now, and can readily take your place; but if you keep up until we are both tired out, Rod will be the sufferer, as well as yourself. So now let me see you eat this soup, and then go and lie down, and I promise to call you at the right time."

Elizabeth had yielded to her mother's wishes simply as a matter of obedience, but in a few days she fully appreciated the wisdom of the system. It was hard to resist her impulses in the matter, but she found that this was the real, and the only valuable, self-sacrifice.

When at last, to all those loving hearts waiting so anxiously, the day came on which Roderick fell into a deep sleep, calm and natural, and awoke, almost too weak to utter

a word, but free from fever, and entirely conscious, his two
nurses, instead of being prostrated by the revulsion of feeling, felt new strength for the many days which must yet
elapse before their work would be over, for all would now
depend upon the most watchful and intelligent care.

"If anybody would come to hear me," said Dr. West,
on the evening of that happy day, as he sat at the tea-table
enjoying the bright faces around him and Aunt Judy's
muffins at the same time, "I would give a course of lectures on Nursing at the Court-house."

"Oh, *we'd* all come, Dr. West," said Kitty, demurely;
"and we should make quite a good-sized audience—we
should fill at least half the benches."

"You're the very ones I don't want, ma'am, saving your
presence," he replied. "It is the delightful contrast which
this family has presented to all other families, which inspires
me with the idea of enlightening the rest. You know I have
eyes in the back of my head, as well as the front—a doctor
is obliged to—and you needn't think I haven't seen how
things have been managed. Here are your mother and Miss
Elizabeth, after six weeks of nursing and anxiety, not quite
as fresh as daisies, but good for another six weeks, if they're
needed. Why? Because they've been decently waited on,
and had that rarest of all gifts in a—keep cool, Miss Kitty,
—in anybody, common-sense. Do you suppose that, if they
had been obliged to go up and down-stairs half-a-dozen times
a day, and fidget over the beef-teas, and milk-punches, and
worry about the housekeeping, and the butter-making, and
the mending, that they could have stood it as they have?
Not for a week! Your mother has known that everything,
down to the lessons and the lamps, has kept right on in the
beaten path—bless all you dear hearts, there isn't an eye-
servant or a shirk among you. As for this boy," and he laid
his arm across the shoulders of Arnold, who sat next to

him, " I should wonder where he found the old head he's
been carrying on his young shoulders for the last six weeks,
if I hadn't the honor of being a friend of his mother's. Rod
will find no dropped stitches to mourn over, when he gets
out and about again."

" If he doesn't," said Arnold, with a little tremble in his
voice, " it will be chiefly because he set me the pattern. I
never really knew what Rod was till—till——" he stopped
abruptly.

" Doctor West," said Kitty suddenly, and with assumed
sauciness—for she saw that her sister and brothers were painfully excited— " if you mean to toast us all in turn, you'd
better have your cup filled—it's entirely empty. And Aunt
Judy has been standing at your elbow for the last five
minutes, with a plate of muffins which were hot when they
came in—I suppose you're letting them cool because you
told me hot bread was an invention of the evil one."

" What I tell you officially, Miss Katherine, is one thing—
my course of action as a private citizen, with the digestion
of an ostrich, is quite another. I never get such muffins as
these anywhere else, and Aunt Judy knows it—there is an
article called by that name, with a hard, shiny back, which
always reminds me of a small mud-turtle, but is to *these*
muffins as moonlight unto sunlight, and as water unto wine!"

The doctor buttered his muffin as he spoke, and Aunt Judy
went to bake some more, feeling that this was a compliment
indeed, for she could not understand more than half of it!

Doctor West was at least twenty years older than Kitty,
and had long been pronounced "a confirmed old bachelor,"
the "confirmed" being varied, occasionally, by such adjec-
tives as "crusty," "cranky," and even "cantankerous."
They never met without exchanging shots, and nothing enter-
tained the doctor more than Mrs. Stanley's look of anxiety,
and gentle intervention, when—as she nearly always did—

she feared the sparring in jest would end in sparring in earnest. There was little danger of this, for Kitty, under all her bantering manner to the doctor, felt a very great respect and liking for him, and he—well, he was beginning to call himself "an old idiot!" But he was very careful to give no one else the opportunity of calling him one. With his gray hair—which was unusually gray for a man of his age, and had, moreover, totally deserted a good-sized round spot on top of his head—his near-sighted glasses, and the two heavy wrinkles between his eyes, he looked at least ten years older than he really was, and Kitty treated him very much as she treated Mr. Stanley, occasionally apologizing meekly to him when their war of words had led her on to speak "disrespectfully." He sedulously concealed the irritation which these apologies always caused him, but he would go away muttering to himself angrily—

"The child behaves as if I were her respected grandfather. And so I am, to all intents and purposes—I think it must be second childhood that is coming over me!"

He ran up once more to Roderick's room, before leaving the house, to assure himself that all was still going well, and to reiterate his charges about frequent nourishment for both patient and nurses. "If you two come out of this without breaking down," he said, "you will serve as illustrations to my lecture, to the end of the chapter—so don't you dare to disappoint me!"

CHAPTER XXIV.

RODERICK'S health improved rapidly, when once "the turn" was past, and as soon as the doctor allowed him solid food, he developed an appetite which Kitty said was worthy of the giant Blunderbore, and slept peacefully much of the time when he was not eating.

A few days after permission had been given him to sit up for a few minutes, and to go on increasing the time by five minutes every day, the boys entered his room in triumph, with a structure which they dignified with the name of a "reclining-chair." In appearance, it was something between a cot-bed and a stretcher, but it was really a marvel of ingenuity; it was made on the plan of a steamer-chair, and they had drawn on their memories for the model. The seat and back were made of bagging, which Aunt Judy had cheerfully washed and bleached for the purpose; the foot-rest was covered with one of the soft knitted rugs which the girls had manufactured some months before, and the back could be arranged at any angle, by means of hinges and ratchets. Roderick, after trying it, declared that it was the nearest approach to Oriental luxury he had ever been privileged to attain to, and that when he was well again they had better hide it in the daytime, or he should be tempted to live in it. The young faces beamed with pleasure, and the really hard work which it had cost them, "seemed as nothing" to them when they saw how well it had succeeded.

Randolph Peyton's visits became more frequent, as Roderick's convalescence progressed. He read aloud most agreeably, and he beguiled Roderick of many a tedious afternoon in this way, especially after the invalid had begun to be carried into the parlor, that he might have a thorough change from his sick-room. The family was not given to afternoon naps, and was generally to be found, between dinner and tea-time, gathered together in the parlor, with various employments, while some one read aloud. Arnold and Ernest were often absent at one of the "laboratories," or in the workshop, especially as Christmas drew near, and Winifred was sometimes with them; but Randolph seemed to know by intuition when she would be with the rest of the family, and to time his visits accordingly, and when he did find that she was absent, he was too, in a different sense. Several times she had been reading aloud when he entered, and, as he had insisted upon not interrupting the proceedings, she had gone on. It was on the first of these occasions that Mrs. Stanley had begun to suspect the truth. Winifred, with her eyes fastened upon the book, was quite unconscious of his fixed, admiring gaze, and it did not seem to occur to him that any one else would observe it.

Mrs. Stanley felt uneasy; Winifred was under her care; she loved the young girl sincerely, and she knew that, although Randolph Peyton had many fine qualities, he lacked the steadiness of purpose without which other gifts are of little avail. She would have been deeply distressed had she seen any signs of a growing attachment between him and one of her own daughters, or Edith, and her feelings were but little less acute concerning Winifred. It was out of the question that she should say anything, while no overt advances were made, and she knew the young man quite well enough to believe that any opposition, no matter how quietly and unobtrusively it was manifested, would only act as a spur to his inclination. Winifred, she felt sure, was quite unconscious of the direction which affairs were taking, and she comforted herself with thinking that a girl so immeasurably superior to Randolph Peyton as she was, would fail to find any real attraction in him. But she did not allow for the fact that, situated as Winifred was, the prospect of a settled home, with some one pledged to care for her, would be far more attractive than it would have been were she more happily circumstanced, and would incline her to over-estimate the person who offered it to her. He would be a hero of romance—a modern King Cophetua, a second Lord Ronald.

As it often happens with weak people, Randolph was excitable and impetuous, and, provided the strain did not last long, was capable of both exertion and endurance. Every day increased his affection for Winifred and his determination to marry her—with the consent of his parents, if possible; if not, without it. But he had little doubt of obtaining their consent—he did not think it possible that they could refuse him anything which would involve the happiness of his whole life, as he firmly believed his love for Winifred would.

As it was, Colonel and Mrs. Peyton never dreamed of what was going on—even the possibility of it did not cross their minds. On the contrary, they imagined that if Randolph's sudden devotion to Roderick had any secondary cause, Elizabeth was responsible for it, and this idea gave them extreme pleasure. They acknowledged to each other that Randolph was a little lacking in ambition and stability, but they were quite persuaded that, were he to marry such a woman as Elizabeth, he would immediately "settle" and become all that their hearts could wish. So they seconded, in every

way, his intimacy with the Stanleys; if he showed no signs of
going there in the course of the day, Mrs. Peyton was almost
sure to devise some errand which made his going imperative,
or at least advisable. When Roderick began to go about
again, and no longer needed the close attention which he
had so long required, Mrs. Peyton insisted that Elizabeth
should come and stay at least a week at Rivermouth, that
she might have change of scene and perfect rest. She went
very willingly, for she was tired enough to enjoy the easy-
going life, and absence of all care and responsibility which
she would have there, and, at so short a distance from her
home, she could be immediately recalled, were she needed.

Randolph would have been highly amused had he known
how largely his mother's wish to further his supposed plans
had influenced her in giving the invitation, and how, without the least intention of misleading her, he convinced her
that her supposition was correct. He really liked Elizabeth,
and, even had he not done so, he would have considered
himself bound to be courteous to her, while she was a guest
in his father's house. Besides, although she was not the
rose, she was living with the rose, and, with the skill of an
able tactician, he managed, no matter where the conversation began, to lead it around to Winifred. This was not
difficult to do, for Elizabeth, as well as all the rest of the
family, felt lovingly grateful for the good offices which had
so lightened their burdens; she was never weary of praising
the young girl, and was quite unsuspicious of the fact that
it was generally Randolph who gave the key-note to their
talk. It was no wonder that Mrs. Peyton, seeing their faces
without hearing their words, as she frequently did when
they talked, was misled by Elizabeth's earnest look and
Randolph's rapt expression. Any one less single-minded
than Elizabeth would have guessed his secret long before the
week was over—indeed, he began to be a little provoked

that she did not. He did not quite "see his way clear" to
confiding in her, because he was by no means sure of her
approval ; he had judged correctly as to her opinion of him,
and he doubted very much whether she would think marriage with him an advisable or advantageous thing for Winifred.   Still, it was possible that she might approve, and if
she did, she might be a valuable ally, and he wished she
would guess his intention, without giving him the trouble
of explaining it. She did not, but she liked him better than
she had ever done before.   The unselfishness of his love was
refining him.   All his dreams about Winifred were of the
leisure she should enjoy after the toilsome life she was now
leading, which to him seemed far more toilsome and unendurable than it did to her—of the love and care with which
he would surround her, going without the small luxuries to
which he was accustomed, that she might "fare delicately."
He was ashamed to remember how he had tried to convince
himself that he loved Edith, seeing, as he now did, how
much he had been influenced by interested motives.

Dr. West continued his visits, if not quite so frequently,
certainly with unnecessary frequency, after Roderick came
down-stairs, and even after he began to go out, asserting
that, if he did not keep a sharp eye upon his late patient, he
should be disgraced by a relapse yet.

"You see, Miss Katharine," he said one afternoon, when
he had dropped in, as he so often did, toward tea-time,
"when I am attending one of these tranquil natives, who
wouldn't hurry if the house were on fire, my mind is quite
easy on the score of over exertion, but with a family of live
Yankees, who are never idle excepting when they are asleep
or ill, and then are industrious in their dreams, it is quite
different.   I caught Rod at the barn this very afternoon—
he *said* he wasn't going to pitch down the hay for the cows,
but he was in suspicious proximity to a pitch-fork, **and**

I distinctly saw the Alderney wink at me, when he said it."

"I've never been able to make up my mind, Dr. West," replied Kitty, "as to whether you are a Yankee or a Southerner — you have one or two strongly marked Southern traits——"

"Such as——"

"Letting the fire go out, rather than put a stick of wood on it;" and she stooped and lifted a large log to the andirons before he could interfere, rising with cheeks flushed by the exertion, and mischief sparkling in her eyes. "I've seen Colonel Peyton sit in front of a dying fire, and call for the 'boy' to bring some wood, when it was piled up in the entry, ten steps from where he sat."

"Anything more?"

"An inability to tie a reliable knot," and Kitty, trying to repress the laughter which was overcoming her, pointed down the road, where the doctor's white horse was just discernible, as he made the best of his way home.

"I'll bet my hat you saw him untie himself," said the doctor, savagely.

Kitty nodded, tried to speak, and then broke into a peal of laughter.

"Kitty! Kitty!" said Mrs. Stanley, in tones of gentle reproof. "Indeed, you must excuse her, Dr. West; I don't think she *meant* to be rude."

Kitty "went off" again at this, and the doctor said—

"I shall punish her by staying to tea, if you will have me, Mrs. Stanley."

There was a chorus of "Of course we will!" and Kitty started up as if to leave the room.

"You needn't go away, Miss Katharine," said the doctor; "you can stay, if you'll behave yourself, and stop giggling."

"I don't giggle," said Kitty, loftily, "and I'm only going

to tell Aunt Judy to be sure and bake muffins for tea—she doesn't know you're here."

" Come back this instant, miss," said the doctor, sternly. " Do you suppose that my sole object in coming to Green Point is a muffin supper? "

" Oh no," she replied, demurely ; " not your *sole* object, Dr. West, but Aunt Judy nearly always has some ' sot,' to use her own expression, and you may just as well have them as not."

" And Shakspere had the face to ask what was in a name," said the doctor, " and then answered with a heroine named Katharine! Why, there is a shrew——"

" Dr. West ! "

" Don't annihilate me—I was about to say, there is a shrewd, spicy flavor about the name which at once suggests——"

But Kitty had disappeared, and remained invisible until just before tea was announced, when she returned, looking alarmingly meek and amiable, and remarking, as she entered the room—

" Rod, Aunt Judy says there are horse thieves in the neighborhood—they tried the Dutchman's stable last night, but the dogs frightened them away before they got it open."

" Then how did he know they were there?" promptly, from the doctor.

" He found their footprints in the mud this morning, Aunt Judy says," replied Kitty, seriously; " and Rod, don't you think Moses had better stay and sleep in the stable to-night? He hasn't gone home yet—shall I tell him ? "

" No, dear, I don't think it is worth while," said Roderick; " the dogs are very watchful, and there's a good lock on the stable-door."

Polly had been listening intently, and now she exclaimed, as Kitty expected she would—

"Oh, Dr. West, I *hope* they won't catch Lady! Do you suppose there is any danger?"

"Not the least," said the doctor tranquilly. "And they'd have their hands full, if they did. Lady has a bad trick of kicking, when she is handled in a way that doesn't suit her, and besides, I don't believe they were horse thieves, Polly: they were probably some neighborhood darkies, in search of a Christmas turkey, and the Dutchman's fears have magnified their footsteps—which is quite unnecessary, for some of the colored gentry about here have fully a quarter of their length turned up in feet."

"That's just what Moses said," interposed May, who had followed Kitty out, and returned with her; "I don't mean about the feet, but about the thieves—he says he doesn't believe they are horse thieves at all, but that we'd better keep a sharp look-out after the chickens. I do *wish* my turkeys could be made to understand that they ought to roost in the chicken-house, instead of in the apple-trees. Do you know of any way to make them, Dr. West?"

"Feed them just inside the door of the chicken-house, dear, for two or three evenings, about the time when the chickens go to roost, and then shut them in," said the doctor, kindly; "or," he added, with twinkling eyes, "engage your sister Katharine to talk to them about chicken thieves, and convince them of their danger."

"They wouldn't understand the talking," said May, laughing, "but I wonder I didn't think of feeding them in the chicken-house myself, greedy things! They'd go anywhere for corn. I'll go do it now—they're not quite settled, for I heard them fussing about when I was in the kitchen."

"No, I'll go, Pussy," and Arnold put her back in her chair with gentle force, and went in her stead—it was too damp, he told her, for her to be out-of-doors.

20

He came back just as the tea-bell was ringing, and May asked, eagerly—

"Well, did they go, Arnold, or had they gone to sleep?"

"They all went like lambs," he replied, "except the old gobbler, the pride of your heart, my dear. The others were on the lower limbs, and came down as soon as they saw the corn, and I had no trouble enticing them into the chicken-house; but the chickens have my sincere sympathy—I don't believe the turkeys will let them sleep a wink."

"And *wouldn't* the gobbler go?" asked May, mournfully. "Did you coax him?"

"I coaxed him," answered Arnold, "not only with corn, but with a bean-pole, and he disdainfully flew up out of my reach, and gobbled at me. I am afraid he'll have to take his chance."

The history of May's turkeys was becoming painfully like that of the Ten Little Indian Boys.

The suicide by gas tar had been the first victim; then a rash member of the family had ventured out into the road, and a stray dog had made off with it; a third had investigated a mole-trap, and paid for his spirit of inquiry with his neck; a fourth had simply and unaccountably "turned up missin'," as Aunt Judy announced, and poor May, with her hopes and ambitions so lamentably reduced, expected every day to hear of a fresh catastrophe, and mourned over her blighted hopes more bitterly as Christmas drew near. It was time now, Aunt Judy said, to "put up" the remaining six turkeys, for it wanted barely two weeks of Christmas. May decided to run no more risks, and the evening after the conversation about horse and chicken thieves took place, she and Ernest watched until the turkeys began to gather about the tree which they had selected for their roosting-place, and then, by spreading corn along the path, enticed them into the large coop which the two boys had made ready for

DUKE'S TROPHY.

them. But, alas! only four appeared, and among the absentees was the lordly gobbler.

" Perhaps he and the other one will come back when it is darker, Pussy," said Ernest, hopefully ; " I'll come out after tea, and if they are in the tree, I'll go up and catch them, and put them in the coop with the rest."

May thanked him warmly, and resolved not to despair until after dark. But the lost ones did not return, and nothing more was seen of them—at that time.

May said she was "very thankful" that four were saved— one should go to Uncle George, one for their own Christmas-dinner, and the remaining pair she was still resolved to keep, as founders of a future family. Moses advised her to let them remain in the coop until after Christmas, saying—

" Dere's some dese niggahs 'bout heah, little missy, what can't help deyselves, dawgs or no dawgs, ef it's mos' Christmas, and de tukkey ain't perwided for de fambly, and dey happens to light on one. But our dawgs won't let 'em stop to open no coops—dey'd find deir legs chawed up befo' dey knowed it."

It was evident that Moses knew what he was talking about, for on more than one night, as Christmas drew near, the family was awakened by the angry barking of the dogs, sometimes accompanied by sounds of scuffling, and on one night by a prolonged howl. At this sound, Arnold rushed into his clothes, and out of the house, fearing one of the dogs had been killed, or at least badly injured, but he found them both safe and sound, and in a state of wild excitement, Nero "pointing" to a place in the fence where a rail had been thrown off, and Duke angrily shaking something which proved, upon investigation, to be the lower half of the leg— not of the marauder exactly, but certainly of his trowsers. Arnold secured the trophy, patted and praised the dogs, and went back to bed, and there were no more disturbances that night, nor for several weeks to come. The next morning, Aunt Judy positively identified the fraction of a garment as belonging to the colored neighbor who rejoiced in a brick-chimney, and had such faith in the force of the wind, and she was highly indignant.

"But how can you be sure, Aunt Judy?" asked Arnold, laughing at the epithets which she heaped upon the culprit. "It's only a piece of gray cloth, or cloth that was gray, and it might have belonged to any of them."

"Some young folks is mighty fond of teachin' deir grannies how to suck eggs!" said Aunt Judy, with a scornful toss of her turbaned head. "Mass' Randolph Peyton wore dem pants less'n two years ago, and why he gib 'em to dat no 'count niggah, when my ole man was workin' for him at dat 'dentical time, is bes' knowed to hesef, but dat he did, I'll stan' to! But I ain't got no time to fool wid ole man Knowall dis mornin'," and she turned disdainfully away.

Arnold made an errand to the house with the brick chimney, in the course of the morning, and found the proprietor limping about the premises.

"What's the matter with your leg, Uncle Jake?" asked Arnold, gravely.

"Rheumatics, young marster, de wors' kind! You'll know all 'bout it, some dese days, when you's old and rheumaticky you'se'f!"

"I've something here that will perhaps help your leg," said Arnold, handing him the trophy, neatly wrapped in paper.

Jake took the roll with profuse thanks, and unwrapped it with lively curiosity, which changed to dismay, when he discovered what it contained.

"Ef here ain't my——" he began, unguardedly, and then, with a look of childlike innocence, continued—"ole granny's berry notion! She allus said to wrap up de place in worsted. Dis off'n your ole trowsis, young marster?"

Arnold had been using his eyes while they were talking, and now he pounced upon a bundle which had been jammed under the eaves of the porch, unrolling it before Uncle Jake could interfere. It was the gray trowsers, minus about half of one leg.

"I think you'll find it will fit here, Uncle Jake," said Arnold, holding up the dismembered trowsers; "but I wouldn't advise you to give Duke another chance—he might go deeper next time, and we always keep the shot-gun handy, with a charge of number six shot in it—you wouldn't enjoy picking that out of your poor legs, would you?"

"Now what young marster *kin* mean, by dis kind joking, beats me right out!" and Uncle Jake scratched his head with a look of puzzled innocence. "Dem ole trowsis was gib me dis mornin' specially fur crabbin', and I des tore off one leg to show de ole woman how short dey was to be cut! If young marster's dawg foun' de piece, and shuk it like he 'pears to have shukken it, I doan' mind—I didn' *want* de piece, de Lawd knows!"

Arnold was indignant for a moment, but the audacity of the lie was so astounding that, in spite of himself, he found his indignation giving way to amusement, and, determined not to let Uncle Jake see him laugh, he turned abruptly away, Uncle Jake calling after him—

"I hope young marster doan' doubt my word. And I'll keep de piece fur Cindy's kyarpet-rags!"

CHAPTER XXV.

"Be not with honor's gilded baits beguil'd,
    Nor think ambition wise, because 'tis brave;
For though we like it, as a forward child,
    'Tis so unsound, her cradle is her grave."—W. DAVENANT.

IT must not be supposed that Mr. Stanley and Edith had
remained silent and indifferent during Roderick's illness—the former had twice come for a night, at no little
inconvenience to himself, and Kitty had sent a daily bulle-
tin, so long as there was any fear about the termination of
the illness. Besides this, a hamper had come once a week,
packed by Mrs. Crawford's careful hands with everything of
which either father or daughter could think, for the comfort
of the patient and his nurses, or indeed, any of the family,
for Edith made it the excuse for sending all sorts of delicacies, from choice tea and other fine groceries to the best confectionery. Remonstrances were ignored, and the hampers
continued to come, even after Roderick was down-stairs again.

Nothing short of the high pressure under which she was
working for the next year's examination, and for the report
which she meant to bring away of her last year, could have
kept Edith from going with her father and remaining at
Green Point until the crisis was past, but her ambition was
thoroughly roused; Isabel's had taken fire from hers, and
the two girls worked together with an ardor and pleasure
which neither had ever felt before. Mr. Stanley sometimes
was uneasy, when he found how closely Edith was applying
herself, but he insisted upon her walking to and from school,

whenever the weather was even moderately good, and upon
her going to bed regularly at ten o'clock, excepting on the
rare occasions when he took both girls to a concert or lecture.   He had adopted this measure, because he found that
whenever they became especially interested in their studies,
they sat up till twelve or one o'clock, and were listless and
dull the next day.   They made no secret of it, and after one
or two gentle admonitions, he laid down the law.   Edith
entreated in vain to have the matter left to their discretion,
promising to be very discreet indeed.

"You know, papa dear," she said, coaxingly, "it doesn't
matter if we sit up a little late Friday and Saturday nights,
because we can make up our sleep in the morning, on Saturday and Sunday."

"My little daughter," he said, "if one of your window-
plants had seven blossoms on it, and I were to ask you for
one, would you pick out the smallest and least beautiful for
me?"

"Why, you *know* I wouldn't, papa!" she replied warmly,
not catching his meaning.

"Our Father asks us to give one day to Him," continued
Mr. Stanley; "shall we shorten it wilfully for our own
pleasure or convenience?   Most of us would hesitate to act
towards an earthly father, even in a small matter, as we too
often do towards our Heavenly Father in this matter, which
He thought worthy of a special command."

"I didn't think of it in that way, papa," said Edith, humbly; "but I will try to remember, after this, and get my
work done early on Saturday, so that I may be rested for
Sunday."

Nothing more was said about the early bed-time Mr. Stanley had fixed, but he knew that Edith would obey him, and
that Isabel would not try to make it more difficult for her
by refusing to follow his wishes.

They talked it over, as they did many things, while they were undressing that night, and Isabel, whose sweet and honest nature was a constant pleasure to Edith, said penitently—

"I never thought of it before in that light, but your father is right, Edith. We seem to grudge that one day and to be always devising ways to keep part of it for ourselves, without exactly seeming to, and now that I look at it squarely, how contemptibly mean that is! I do believe it is quite as bad as openly disregarding it—worse, as far as we ourselves are concerned, and for other people too, if they find it out. I always used to sleep a great deal later at home, and go to bed earlier, and often take a nap in the afternoon besides. But I mean to turn over a new leaf now, and it will be much easier to do it here than at home, for we can always go to church twice, and you have so many nice Sunday books in your library, beside the papers and magazines which your father takes."

"I've been much more inexcusable than you have," said Edith, "for I've always had all these helps, and you haven't. It must be rather hard to get through a Sunday respectably, with neither reading nor church to help one."

"I could always have gone once a day, if I had wished to," replied Isabel, too honest to accept the excuse, "and I dare say I could find good reading if I would take the trouble to hunt it up; papa has ever so many old books in the library, of which I don't even remember the names, and beside, the servants are always delighted if any one will read to them; no, I have no excuse, my dear, and I feel ashamed of myself, but I will try to do better after this."

Isabel was far less excitable than Edith was, and found no difficulty in falling asleep almost as soon as her head touched the pillow, no matter how animated the discussion had just been, or how hard she had been studying, but with Edith it

was different. The train of thought once started, could not
be stopped, and after the new regulation had been in effect
for about a week, she said to him one morning as they sat
at breakfast—

" Papa, I begin to go to bed like a lamb every night when
the ancestral clock that I bought at the sale strikes ten, but
I'm like the love-stricken Irishman—

> 'There's no use at all
> In my going to bed,
> For 'tis dhrames, and not sleep,
> That comes into my head,'

and it's generally at least two hours before the 'dhrames'
even come."

Mr. Stanley looked distressed.

" Dear child," he said, "cannot you manage to finish your
lessons before dinner, and then spend the evening in some
way which will not excite you? "

" Not *possibly*, little father ! You see we don't get home
until half-past two ; then lunch takes half an hour, and
nearly always something turns up which keeps me from
getting to work until at least half-past three, and at half-
past five I must stop to dress—that gives me only two hours,
and I spent the whole of it yesterday, for example, over my
Ancient History, and barely knew it then, and that pushed
all the rest into the evening, and then I was cruelly cut
short at ten, and that obliged me to ask the Monument to
call me at five—she did it, with heart searching faithfulness,
for she stood there while I 'fell asleep in her face' three
times, and each time she gave me a gentle shake, and
repeated in precisely the same tones—'Miss Edith, my
dear, you requested me to call you at five.'"

" My dear child," exclaimed her father, "you might better have missed your Ancient History for once than to have
cut short your much needed sleep. I must positively for-

tid your being called before seven after this—you see what a Turk you are obliging me to become!"

"Oh, papa!" she said, beseechingly; "don't say that I mayn't get up when I like, please! I haven't had one mark yet below the highest, and it would break my heart to have one now. *Please* take that back!"

And to his utter consternation, she began to sob, she who always spoke with such unmixed disdain of "crying women."

"My darling," he said, taking her in his arms and soothing her as if she were a child, "I did not mean to be harsh or severe—it is your own good that I am seeking; your health will be ruined if this strain keeps on. There, there, don't cry any more—I will compromise ; you may be called as early as six, if you find it really necessary, but not every day ; if it comes to that, I shall take you from school and send you to the south of France for the rest of the winter."

"Take me, you mean, dear!" she said, succeeding at last in her effort to stop sobbing and smile ; "you know quite well that nothing would make me go there without you. But indeed, you mustn't worry about me so; just see how well we look, and Isabel is studying just as hard as I am."

"No, Edith ; I don't think I am," said Isabel ; "you know I only have about half the number of lessons that you have, and although some of them are pretty difficult, I have plenty of time to learn them—I am almost always done before nine o'clock. And even if I were, I sleep so soundly that I always wake up in the morning feeling ready for anything."

Isabel was looking well, but Edith was not. She was thinner than she had been when school began, and, when her cheeks were not flushed with excitement, as they usually were in the evening, she looked pale and languid.

Mr. Stanley was greatly perplexed as to the best course to pursue. The least suggestion that she should give up graduating seemed to irritate her more and more, and he feared that, were he to insist upon it, she would fret herself ill. On the other hand, it was quite evident that, whatever might be the effect upon the rest of Madame's scholars, Edith was unequal to the mental strain which the last year before graduation involved. He resolved to consult the family doctor, and did so, but he did not obtain much satisfaction, for Dr. Bronson was sceptical on the subject of nervous ailments—perhaps with some excuse—and smiled as he said—

"Don't alarm yourself, my dear sir! All school-girls are whimsical, and more or less hysterical. Miss Stanley probably needs a tonic; here," and he rapidly wrote a prescription, "have this put up, and see that she takes it three times a day, and she had better take beef-tea at bed-time, and when she wakes in the morning, before rising—don't get the extract, have it made at home, strong, and of good fresh beef. You say she has no local ailment? No headache, or soreness of the spine? Ah well, she'll soon regain her tone, if she obeys orders. If I remember rightly, she was a remarkably healthy child."

Mr. Stanley saw to it that she did obey orders, and Mrs. Crawford was in her element, attending to the making of the beef-tea, and with her usual trustworthiness, bringing it to Edith with her own hands, morning and evening. The tonic, which should more properly have been called a stimulant, delighted her so with its effects, that she did not rebel against it, after taking one or two doses, and the fictitious strength which it imparted, together with the real but temporary good effect of the beef-tea, produced such a marked improvement, in a few days, that her father concluded not to remove her from her school, unless the symptoms which had caused him such uneasiness should return.

He looked forward hopefully to the Christmas holidays, for, now that it was quite impossible for his sister and her family to come to him, he had consented to bring Edith to

Green Point, and, after himself spending Christmas Day with them, leave her there for the remainder of the holidays. Isabel was delighted with this decision, for she had never yet spent a Christmas anywhere but at home, and had been fearing that it would be considered best for her not to take the journey for so short a time as the vacation. It was, of course, not until Roderick's recovery was assured, and progressing rapidly, that this arrangement was proposed and decided upon, and after it was, Edith spent a whole Saturday in her Christmas shopping, learning her lessons on Friday afternoon and evening, that she might be free. She and her father had held an earnest consultation about Isabel—Mr. Stanley wished very much to provide her with the means of taking home gifts to her family, of more intrinsic value than the pretty things with which her skillful fingers had been busy ever since she came, but he feared to wound her pride. They at last devised a plan which Edith carried out with little trouble—the door between their rooms was nearly always open, and while Isabel's trunk was in process of packing, Edith handed her a small parcel, saying—

"Papa and I want to give you our Christmas gifts now, dear, for we shall not be together on Christmas Day, you know. Please consider the love that goes with it, and even if you don't like it, accept it for the love's sake—you know papa and you agreed to be uncle and niece, the other day."

"I shall be sure to like it!" said Isabel, warmly, and quite unsuspiciously; "but you can't expect me to wait till Christmas Day to open it—may I look now?"

"Since you are so curious—yes," said Edith, leaving the room as she spoke.

Edith's gift was a beautiful purse, or pocket-book, rather, for it was of Russia leather, with a silver frame and clasp, and a small silver plate on the side, with Isabel's name engraved upon it. Inside were three double-eagles, fresh from

the mint, wrapped in white paper, on which was written :
"My new niece must spare her lazy old uncle the trouble of
choosing her present, and take the enclosed from him, with
best love and wishes."

Whether the gift be large or small, "love is the whole,"
and while Isabel would have proudly refused money from
Mr. Stanley, had it been less delicately given, she could not
wound his feelings by returning the shining coins which had
come in such a wrapper. But when she thanked him that
evening, she said—

"I somehow don't think you will be angry with me, *uncle*,
if I do not spend the whole contents of my lovely new
pocket-book on myself—will you ?"

"I shall not be angry with you, whatever you do, my
dear," he replied ; "for I know you could do nothing to
make me angry."

So Isabel went with Edith on the shopping expedition,
and they thoroughly enjoyed it, Edith's superior knowledge
of the "tricks and manners" of city shopkeepers being of
great assistance to Isabel, while Isabel's frankly expressed
wonder at, and admiration of, much that she saw, gave
Edith a fresh pleasure in many things which were no longer
novelties to her. Each of them made valuable suggestions
to the other, and they returned at dusk, in the highest
spirits, to find such an alarming array of parcels in the hall,
that Mr. Stanley, who was waiting for them in the library,
threatened to go either the day before, or the day after, that
which had been fixed upon for the journey.

The dinner that night was "an unusually brilliant affair,"
as Edith asserted when they rose from table, and her father,
looking fondly at her flushed cheeks and sparkling eyes,
blessed the doctor in his heart—she was his gay little girl
again, and his fears of a few weeks ago seemed absurd.

The evening was spent in cheerful talk over the various

purchases.   Mr. Stanley had been only too delighted with
the opportunity for giving to his sister and her children all
that he could think of, or that Edith could devise, either for
pleasure or use, and had commissioned her to make several
of his purchases for him, which she had done, in a manner
so sensible, and so entirely to his liking, that he praised her
warmly, as package after package was unwrapped and in-
spected.   An oil painting, and some beautiful engravings
for Mrs. Stanley's parlor, were the most important of the
purchases, so far as the selection went, but the music for
Elizabeth, the books for Roderick, the color-box and other
art-equipments for Kitty, the thoroughly furnished writing-
desk for Polly, the printing-press and camera—no mere
toys, but both capable of doing good work—for Arnold and
Ernest, and the yard-long doll, beautiful as the most imagi-
native child's vision of a doll could be, for May, were all
chosen with good judgment as well as good taste.

Edith's own gifts were less costly, for she had begged that,
this year, she might have no special Christmas-money given
her, but might rely, instead, upon what she could save from
her ample allowance—that, she said, would be more like real
giving, and her father wisely agreed to her wish, much as he
longed to put into her hands a sum which should more
nearly carry out her warm hearted impulses.   But Edith had
begun to realize that a great deal which she had been accustomed to regard as generosity, or at least liberality, in herself, had been merely a careless lavishness with that which it
cost her no sacrifice to give, and she enjoyed spending the
comparatively moderate sum which she had gained by real
self-denial, more than she had ever enjoyed lavishing the
money which she had carelessly asked, and thoughtlessly
accepted.   Her father saw with a glad heart the look of
deeper thought, of finer feeling, which was giving a higher
beauty to her already beautiful face, and he trembled as he

realized how closely his heart-strings were twined about this one precious life—a life in which the lost wife and mother almost seemed to live again.

The exhibiting, and discussing, and planning—for a mighty hamper was still to be made ready—made the hours fly, and it was striking eleven as they said good-night.

"Why, surely," said Mr. Stanley, pulling out his watch; "that clock is—no it isn't, either! You scamps! not another minute, another good-night! You have taken shameful advantage of a helpless old man."

"Papa, you shall *not* call yourself an old man!" said Edith, indignantly, and turning back for another kiss, "he grows younger and handsomer every day, doesn't he, Isabel?"

And Isabel answered merrily—

"Of course he does!"

CHAPTER XXVI.

"Look not mournfully into the past; it comes not back again. Wisely improve the present; it is thine. Go forth to meet the shadowy future without fear, and with a manly heart."

MEANWHILE, at Green Point, preparations for "the approaching festivities," as Mrs. Crawford would have said, filled the mansion. From Mrs. Stanley, who gave the final touches to the mince-meat, and mixed the puff-paste as she only could mix it, down to May, who tied evergreens until her fingers were brown with turpentine, every member of the family, excepting Roderick, added his or her share to the cheerful bustle, and even he, generally "sat upon," as he good-humoredly complained of being. if he so much as attempted to put a stick upon the fire or draw a glass of fresh water for himself, did not look as if he were suffering under his oppressors. The tranquil gladness of escape from danger and returning health brightened his face, and repressed all fretful thoughts about his unfulfilled plans, and helplessness where all the rest were so helpful. He had made a great advance in the lesson which all must learn, if they would not be a burden to themselves and others—the lesson of cheerful and unquestioning patience. And it would indeed have been a thankless heart which could have fretted, surrounded as he was with a joyful devotion which showed how great the fear had been. He was not utterly helpless. May graciously permitted him to "bunch" for her, as she tied her wreaths, until she fancied he looked weary, when, with a pretty air of authority, she

would take her greenery from his hands and lead him to the
"reclining-chair," tucking the Afghan round him, and arranging the pillow under his head, as if he were her favorite
doll. He was allowed to read to his family when it was
assembled in the afternoon and evenings, "if he would stop
the minute he felt the least bit tired," and even to hold
skeins of silk and worsted, and to give his opinion upon
sundry and various of the mysterious works which were going on about him—works involving wild and sudden flights
from the room, and only saved from discovery, sometimes,
by the good offices of the recently popular apron. He often,
afterward, looked back to that peaceful time, free from care
and responsibility, and made happy by the love of so many
loyal hearts, and gathered fresh strength from the memory.
It was a good time, too, for thinking, and often, as he lay
there in twilight and firelight, and they stepped and spoke
softly about him, thinking him asleep, his mind was busy
with the past and the future, with the two mistakes he had
made, and the best way to avoid them in future. Over-
anxiety, at first, had made light things heavy, and clouded
not only his own spirits, but the spirits of those about him.
In shaking this off, he had unwarily fallen into another pit-
fall, and in trying to do more than his rightful share of the
world's work he had, to a certain extent, succeeded, but
with what result? The balance had been more than struck
by the fact that for weeks his work had been laid upon the
shoulders of others, and not only that, but heavy duties had
fallen on some of his best beloved, as a result of that "zeal"
of his, which had surely not been "according to knowledge."

He remembered how Colonel Peyton and others among
the neighbors had warned him of the probable result of im-
prudence, especially to an unacclimated person, and he resolved, in the future, to temper his valor with discretion.
He realized, as he had never done before, that "no man

21

liveth to himself alone," and that there may even be a selfish form of unselfishness.   But, though he was looking
searchingly, he was not looking mournfully into the past.
There is no penance exacted by Him who, while we are
saying, "I have sinned," answers, "Thy sins are forgiven
thee."

Mr. Kendall was looking forward to his Christmas holidays with curiously mingled feelings.   He had not been
home for nearly a year, and he was naturally eager to see
his mother and sisters once more; but how devoutly he
wished that it had been possible to reverse the order of
things, and bring them to spend the holidays with him.   He
actually caught himself estimating what it would cost, and
arranging which rooms in his commodious but by no means
elegant boarding-house could most easily be made ready for
them.   And then he called himself an idiot, and resolutely
packed his trunk.

Kitty and Polly openly lamented his departure, "just
before the fun began."   He was a decided favorite with them,
although Kitty evinced her partiality chiefly by a wicked
propensity toward making him miserable, a work in which
she was only too successful, and was often unconsciously
seconded by Polly, in a manner doubly effective from its
very unconsciousness.

"All roads lead to Rome," and it never occurred to him
that, with Elizabeth in the house, Mr. Peyton could have
any other object in making such frequent visits as, from
the remarks dropped by Kitty and Polly, he too evidently
made.

"You can tell us, Mr. Kendall," Kitty would begin, "if
that historical novel we are reading has its facts straight.   I
contend that it hasn't, but Mr. Peyton was saying—was it
when he was here yesterday, Polly?"

"No, the day before," Polly would reply, innocently;

" you know we got to talking yesterday until it was too late
to read."

And so on, while Kitty's victim soliloquized, as she meant
he should—

" I do believe that fellow is here every day ! "

Kitty never deviated a hair's breadth from the truth, with
which sophistry she consoled herself when her conscience
accused her of conveying a false impression. Upon one
excuse or another, there was seldom a day now when Mr.
Peyton did not come to Green Point, were it only for a few
minutes, and his attachment to Winifred was an open secret,
although nothing was ever said about it, and it was still
unsuspected by his own family. He developed a brilliant
ingenuity, manifested solely in devices to secure a few words
with Winifred, apart from the rest, were it only at a distant
window, or in the hall, as he came or went. She must have
been deaf and blind not to have discovered his love for her,
but so far he had said absolutely nothing which demanded
any answer from her. He seemed content if he could be
near her and win a few words or a smile before they parted,
addressed to himself alone. She was of far too grateful and
loving a disposition not to be touched and pleased by a love
so disinterested as, it seemed to her, his must surely be. She
did not love him—yet, but it seemed very probable that,
should nothing happen to break the spell he was weaving
about her, she might come to fancy that she did, for, excepting where a principle was involved, she was very easily influenced, and even this exception, as we have seen, did not
always hold good when a strong will tried to dominate hers,
and her affections played the traitor in the camp. She felt
dimly conscious of the way in which circumstances were
drifting her, and she was glad of the opportunity for quiet
consideration of the matter which her holiday would give
her ; in her aunt's peaceful home, with nothing to distract

her thoughts, she could tell better what would be the wisest course for her to pursue. Kitty and Polly tried laughingly to persuade her that she had much better remain with them for the holidays.

"Just think, dear," said Kitty, persuasively, "how much more you will realize that you are having a holiday here than you possibly can at home, where you have never taught anybody. You can lie on the rug before your fire and read magazines and things, and come down late to breakfast, and learn all the new stitches of art embroidery, and hear us make mistakes without being obliged to correct us, and burn yourself up at the 'laboratories' all day, if you wish to, and take that ride you and Arnold are always talking of, and never taking, and——"

"What would my mother say to my even listening to such a treasonable suggestion?" interrupted Winifred, laughing. "Don't you suppose she is counting the hours now till she sees her only daughter again? There are four of you, but you must remember that there is only one of me."

"I am not likely to forget it," said Kitty, gravely, but with mischief in her eyes, and she went out of the room humming—"Rose of all the world to me!"

Thursday would be Christmas Day, and arrivals and departures were arranged accordingly.

Mr. Kendall started for his distant home on the previous Monday, having given a two weeks' holiday. He succeeded in making his adieux at Green Point without saying anything to Elizabeth more ardent than his good-byes and good wishes to the rest of the family. It would be impossible to tell how often he had argued the matter with himself and decided that, until he had something to offer the woman of his choice beside a faithful heart and an empty hand, he was bound in honor to be silent. Even should he be phenomenally successful in his chosen profession, it must still be

two or three years, at least, before he could provide for her
the humblest home ; he was not confident that he could win
her love, and, if he had been, he would still have hesitated
about binding her to an indefinitely long engagement.

But as the distance between them lengthened, his arguments all seemed to turn about and face the other way.
With what invincible strength and courage could he go on,
if he were only sure that she loved him!   What an idiot he
had been to risk everything by his silence! surely he might
have said a few words, which, while they would bind her to
nothing, ask no promise of her, would yet let her see how
wholly he was hers, if she would but have the patience to
wait for him.   And if that most successful of all match-
makers, propinquity, should plead Randolph Peyton's cause
successfully—the thought was intolerable to him, and he resolved to write to her as soon as he reached home.   But long
before that time he had succeeded in again convincing himself that he had no right to do this—that he must patiently
wait, and only try, by every means in his power, to shorten
this painful probation.

As for Elizabeth, she did not see in every man of her acquaintance a possible lover. She liked Mr. Kendall heartily,
and with a liking very different from that which she accorded
to Randolph Peyton, and she never wearied of his society, as
she sometimes did of that of the latter, and that, so far as she
knew, was all there was about it.

Miss Neale took her departure on Tuesday, with a mysterious package in the corner of her trunk, which she was
on no account to open till Thursday.   Each of the girls, as
well as Arnold and Ernest, had made her a Christmas present,
and she, in turn, had been busily employing all her spare
time, for many weeks past, with making a drawing for each
of them.   She had long ago finished the flock of geese for
the "laboratory," but she drew a second, idealizing the sub-

ject, turning the geese into swans, and stationing the "little foot-page," who was trying to catch them as they sailed majestically past, on a mediæval tower. It was really a beautiful picture, and Arnold's delight was great when he discovered it among his presents, with an affectionate note from the artist, suggesting that it be hung in the indoor laboratory, and the first one on the same subject in the outdoor.

Mr. Stanley, Edith, and Isabel were to arrive on Wednesday, but, at Mrs. Crawford's suggestion, the hamper was sent early in the week.

" For you see, my dear," said the housekeeper, in her even, sensible tones, "it would be a pity for your aunt to provide for her Christmas dinner, before the arrival of the hamper— it could not fail to occasion waste, and besides, situated as I understand you to say she is, remote from all trade centres, it will doubtless be a relief to her mind to know that the delicacies which you have provided are in the house, and she can make her other arrangements accordingly. You are *sure* that it is best not to include a turkey?"

"Oh yes," said Edith, confidently; " May's feelings would be deeply wounded, for she has been raising a flock of turkeys with special reference to Christmas, and I know she meant to send us one—so we shall probably have one at each end of the dinner-table."

A few days before Christmas, Arnold rushed into the parlor in a state of great excitement.

"Rod, will you lend me your gun?" he asked, eagerly; " I'll be very careful of it. I've just seen two wild turkeys in the wood-lot—perfect whoppers, a cock and a hen, and I *must* get them; they're the first I've seen here."

" I'll lend you my gun, with pleasure," said Roderick; "but are you quite sure? I think I heard Colonel Peyton say that there are none left about here."

" Oh, I'm *perfectly* sure!" replied Arnold; "I heard

them gobble, and caught glimpses of them through the bushes beside. Thank you, old fellow—I suppose it isn't loaded?"

"Of course it isn't," said Roderick; "and, see here, don't load too heavily—it wants cleaning, and will be very apt to kick you. I wish I could go with you."

"I wish so too," said Arnold, darting out of the room as he spoke. The gun was a handsome little double-barreled fowling-piece, as light as it could be made to be strong and serviceable, and had been given to Roderick by his father, shortly before the death of the latter. Roderick had himself taught the boys to fire at a mark with it, until they were both pretty good shots, and he had already lent it to Arnold several times for rabbit shooting, without having had any cause to regret doing so, for Arnold, though sometimes careless with his own things, was invariably careful with the property of other people. Roderick watched him from the window, as long as he was in sight, and heard, a few minutes after he disappeared in the wood, two shots fired in rapid succession, and shortly afterward he reappeared with the gun in one hand and the two birds dangling by their long necks from the other. With all the enthusiasm of a sportsman, Roderick raised the window as he came near, and shouted—

"Well done, old fellow! You're a pupil to be proud of! Fetch them in, and let me see them, won't you?"

Arnold nodded; but it struck Roderick that he did not look enthusiastic, an impression which deepened as Arnold entered the room with his game.

"What's the matter?" said Roderick, a little anxiously. "Did the old gun kick you?"

"No," replied Arnold, "not at all; but I wish that it, or somebody else had, before I fired it! Oh, Rod! Can't you *see* what I've done? It's May's special gobbler, and one of her hens!" He had no chance to say anything more, for Roderick interrupted him with a perfect explosion of laughter.

"It's a shame to laugh, I know," he said, as soon as he could speak, "but I really couldn't help it! And I don't think May will care at all, dear boy; it has happened just in time to keep her from sacrificing two of her prisoners in the coop, and if these two had not been captured in this way, she would probably never have seen them again—the only wonder is that they have managed to escape Uncle Jake so long."

Arnold was much consoled by this view of the case, and saying—

"I only hope May will take your highly rational view of the affair," he started to find her, and get the confession of his unintentional trespass off his mind. To his great relief, the little sister, instead of blaming him, went even farther in philosophy than Roderick had gone.

"Why, it's like a story!" she exclaimed, when Arnold had told his "horrible tale"; "and I don't see how you could *think* I would be angry, Arnold dear. Don't you see that if you hadn't shot them, Uncle Jake or somebody would have done it, and we'd never have got them back at all, and now none of those dear things in the coop will have to be killed. I don't mind telling you now, that I cried, only last night, because Aunt Judy said one wouldn't be enough for such a large family, and that we must have the one I meant to send uncle, and tell him it was his; they have grown so tame, that it made me think of that lovely turkey in the 'New Year's Bargain,' that walked all around the dinner-table on Christmas Day, instead of being on it; but I knew that wouldn't do this time, and so I cried; and now I shall keep all four, and raise hundreds next year, and we'll have the big gobbler roasted, and the hen boiled, with oyster sauce, just as Aunt Judy said."

" You're a dear little soul!" said Arnold, with a sigh of relief, and he gave her an emphatic hug and kiss. " But," he added, anxiously, " this is only Monday—do you think they will keep clear till Thursday ? "

" Oh yes ! " replied May, with an air of womanly wisdom ; " Aunt Judy was going to ask Moses to kill the others to-night—just think what a narrow escape the poor things have had—because it makes them tender to be hung out for two or three days. You know there's a heavy frost every night now. Come, we'll take them to her, and when Moses has finished at the barn he can pick them."

Arnold's relief that the tragedy had terminated in this cheerful manner was so great, that he could not help telling the whole story to Ernest, and it soon passed into a family joke, of which there was a large and ever increasing store. Polly furnished a good share, but all contributed more or less.

Mrs. Stanley had tried so to arrange matters, that all might be in readiness for the Christmas dinner before the arrival of Edith and her father, and had in great measure succeeded ; but Aunt Judy's easy-going nature had made it impossible for her to fully fall in with this arrangement, and, as a matter of course, part of her share in the preparations was postponed till the last possible moment. The hamper had afforded, as Mrs. Crawford predicted, much relief to Mrs. Stanley's mind ; both dinner and tea-table would now be prettily as well as abundantly set forth, and she no longer felt " tried " that it had been an utter impossibility to procure any fresh meat. The generous tin of English plum-pudding, duly mixed and brought blazing to the table, with its branch of holly in the middle, would ably support the mince pies and pretty dish of fruit and confectionery—the " epergne," which the girls regarded as a triumph of art.

"Now would you ever guess, Rod," said Kitty, at the "private view" with which the invalid was favored, "that it is made of a plate, and two glass dishes, and a goblet, and a flower vase?"

"Never!" said Roderick, with the most gratifying promptness; "it looks as if it had been made at a single casting, and does equal credit to your heads and hearts, my dear."

Inspired by this generous praise, Kitty could not refrain from farther confidences.

"You must not breathe it," she said, "but the croquettes are made of corned-beef."

"Impossible!" ejaculated Roderick. "I was favored with one for my lunch, and there was not a hint, not a suspicion of the pickling tub about it."

"No, I don't suppose there was," said Kitty, complacently, "for we soaked the beef for three days, changing the water twice a day, and then boiled it in two waters after that, and Aunt Judy chopped it till it was like dust, and then we used the richest cream, and lots of things beside, to disguise it."

"It is equal to one of Augustine's, made of the springiest spring-chicken," said Roderick; "but, by the way, if I may be allowed to inquire, why was not a chicken sacrificed, to save all that work and trouble with the corned-beef?"

"*A* chicken!" repeated Kitty, with gentle scorn. "My dear boy, we allowed four croquettes apiece for the boys, and two for every one else, and half-a-dozen for manners'; you see that makes thirty; now even you, in your ignorance, can't fancy making thirty croquettes out of one chicken. No, we talked it all over, and decided that we couldn't spare more than half-a-dozen chickens altogether—it's too much like killing the goose that laid the golden eggs to kill those dear hens who are simply frantic to hatch out spring-chickens for us—and it was Betty who thought of the corned-beef as a substitute. That leaves us the chickens to broil and roast, you see.

Roderick put his arm around her as they walked back to the parlor—for in her pride she had led him to the pantry, to see the great dish of croquettes standing ready to be fried —not "flat," but "deep."

"Perhaps it is because I never doubted your cleverness, my dear," he said, "but somehow, certain recent manifestations, which I need not specify, have given me more pleasure than your bright wit ever did—which is saying much."

Kitty caught him in an alarmingly sudden hug, saying as she released him—

"When you talk to me like that, Rod, you make me feel very small, but as if I might possibly grow."

CHAPTER XXVII.

"Evenings we know happy as this
Fond hearts and true, gentle and just—
*   *   *   *   *   *   *   *
Peace to their dust, we sing 'round the tree."

THE boats had been taken off a month ago, although there had been no cold weather then—indeed, it would be an unusually severe winter, should ice enough form in the creeks and little rivers, to interfere with their passage, but the company feared that there would not be enough passengers, through the fall and winter, to pay the running expenses, and stopped them in November, promising that they should resume their trips in May. This, of course, made it necessary for the travelers to come by rail, and Colonel Peyton asked to be allowed to send for all three, on the plea that the long cold drive could be more comfortably accomplished in the old-fashioned coach, than in Roderick's more open vehicle. Mrs. Stanley gladly accepted the offer, only stipulating that, as Moses would be obliged to take the cart for Edith's baggage, and to pass Rivermouth on his return, he should bring Isabel's as well. Arnold walked to Rivermouth in time to go in the coach to the station, and Randolph went with him to meet his sister. They had a merry drive home, but Edith was struck with the change which was manifest in Randolph since their last meeting. He seemed frankly glad to meet her again, and was all that was courteous and polite, but the air of devotion which he had assumed at their last meeting was entirely gone. With the whimsicality which so often overcame her better qualities, Edith was piqued by this, though, of course, she carefully concealed the feeling, and seemed in rather gayer spirits than usual.

When the carriage stopped to let the brother and sister out at Rivermouth, Edith leaned forward to say earnestly—

"You must bring Isabel to Green Point very soon, Mr. Peyton—you can't imagine how I shall miss her."

"I can form some slight idea, from the extent to which we have missed her," he said, with a bright smile, judiciously divided between Edith and his sister, "and you may be sure she will not be separated from you long."

With this, and a cavalier-like bow, Edith was obliged to be content, and her father could scarcely repress a smile, as he saw the little pout with which she turned away, as the carriage resumed its journey. At the same time, he resolved to say a few words to her at the first opportunity, which should prevent her from doing for her amusement anything which might give pain. She was heedless, though not heartless, and the state of repressed excitement which seemed just now to be her chronic condition, behooved him to be doubly watchful both for and of her. The fact that she was to have her aunt's motherly care over her for two weeks was a great comfort to him; she dearly loved Mrs. Stanley, and a change for the better was always perceptible in Edith after they had been much together.

An impatient group waited in the parlor for the carriage, and Kitty, Polly, and Ernest kept flying to the windows with false alarms for at least an hour before anything but a pair of "fast trotters" could have accomplished the long drive from the station, since the arrival of the train. Everything was in readiness, to the setting of the tea table. The house was a perfect bower of green. Wreaths adorned every picture and looking-glass, and framed every door and window. Even the balusters were twined with a slender wreath of ground-

pine. A heavy festoon of cedar and holly hung from each
corner of parlor and dining-room, looped up in the center
of the ceiling. Arnold and Ernest had manufactured in the
workshop, weeks before, a tall step-ladder, with a special
view to the Christmas decorations, and later, the light frames
for stars, crosses, and mottoes. The mother's taste and
judgment had governed the decorations, but she had said
nothing to limit them, excepting an occasional gentle reminder that other work must not be slighted or neglected
for them. The house had been in a sort of glad bustle ever
since Roderick had begun to come down-stairs, and it was
surprising, considering his weak condition, to observe, as his
mother and Elizabeth had silently done, to how many of the
enterprises he had "lent a helping hand."

"You know I'm a gentleman of elegant leisure," he
had said to the younger ones, "so you must bring me any of
your small affairs with which a feeble-minded, but well-
meaning person can be safely trusted."

He had held skeins of worsted and silk, and disentangled
knots, and picked out mistakes, and given an interested
opinion on matters of color and form, until, in his wander-
ings from bedroom to parlor, and from parlor to library, he
was followed by an echo of "Where's Rod?"

"I should think it would aggravate you dreadfully, you
darling," Kitty had said to him one day, as he held a bright
skein for her winding, "to be helping us all to finish our
things, when you've been so utterly cut off about your own
affairs."

"I dare say it would have provoked me—before," he
answered, "but now it seems to me so good just to be alive,
and among you all once more, with strength coming back to
me every hour, that I don't feel as if I could complain about
anything."

He had had a number of plans for Christmas, all depending on his own work, for he would not spend any money for himself yet, beyond what was absolutely necessary; but by the time he was able to handle his various tools again, even for an hour or two at a time, it was quite too late to make a beginning. It would be the first Christmas which had ever found him unprepared with gifts for those he loved best, but Elizabeth had vainly urged him to make free use of her little store of butter-money, saying coaxingly—

"It is really no more mine than yours, dear, for I don't pay board for the cows, you know."

"And are you going to help yourself to Christmas-money out of it, ma'am?" he asked.

"Oh no," she replied, "I took a few dollars to buy some working materials, but I would not take much, for there will soon be enough to buy another cow—at least, *pretty soon*—and then we can send butter to the city-market."

"Then you can't blame me for following your example, my best of business-women, even granting that I have a right to part of your hoard," he said, laughing at her for the guileless manner in which she had furnished him with an argument; "I will borrow two or three dollars of you, and write to Edith to invest it in cards for me, and they must be accepted by my family as promissory notes, due next Christmas with compound interest."

With this compromise she was obliged to be content, and she did not guess that it was granted far more for her gratification than for his own.

The boys had made a special expedition to the woods, accompanied by Moses with the horse and cart, for a tree which should make enormous "back-logs" for each chimney, and an extra supply of light-wood for the blazing fires they all loved to surround at twilight. They had gone on a clear, bright, frosty day, and May had begged so hard to join the party, and her brothers had promised so faithfully to take care of her, that she had been allowed to go with them, and had amused herself, while they were busy with the enormous tree, by gathering dead boughs of fantastic shapes from the ground, and throwing them into the cart, and when she tired of this, she picked up pine-cones, and made tiny faggots of pine-needles and dead leaves, carefully storing her treasures, when they reached home, for the Christmas fires. Aunt Judy had entered into every plan with the wildest enthusiasm—she had seen no such preparation for "a reg'lar, ole-fashioned Christmas," since "befo' de wah," when she was a slave in a more southern State, and Mrs. Stanley had to exercise her gentle authority many times a day, to keep the old body from "flyin' off'n de handle," as she herself put it. She would leave her cooking at the most critical point, if she were not watched, to follow the sounds of pounding, talking, and laughing made by the decorators, or to listen at the door as the family practised a Christmas carol which Edith had sent them. But when Mrs. Stanley gave her leave to follow her own devices, for the Christmas-Eve supper, so far as the resources of "the Estate" would permit, there was "no more foolin' for her," as she solemnly announced. Mr. Stanley and Miss Edith had praised her muffins, but they were not fully aware of her capabilities when it came to "Sally Lunn," and pone, and rice batter cakes, and waffles. They had tasted her fried chicken, but not such fried chicken as she would give them this time—and *had* she ever made an omelet for them? She couldn't "rightly" remember, but if she had, she would make one now light enough to fly away with all their recollections of omelets! She was so full of her plans, that she could not help imparting some of them to Elizabeth, who mildly suggested that it would be a pity to have so many kinds of delightful hot bread at once, as some of it must needs be wasted.

"Doan' you worry honey," she answered, nodding her

In the Woods.

head wisely. "Dey'll take deir choices, some one kind, some 'nudder kind, and I sha'n't mix much of no kind, 'cep'in it's muffins, and all dey doan' eat dat night, I'll fry for 'em nex' mornin', like de queen did—dey's all de better nex' mornin', now de cold nights has come, and dey doan' sour."

So when at last—just when it was due—the carriage appeared, and the hall door was flung joyfully open, a mingled and indescribably festive odor, which had crept subtly through the house from the kitchen, greeted the travelers first of all.

Winifred's empty room had made it easy to arrange for the accommodation of the guests, for Kitty and Polly were so very sure that Edith would not wish to sleep anywhere but in their room, that Mrs. Stanley agreed to let her sleep there, at least for the two nights while her father remained, and then, if she preferred it, she might take possession of the vacant place. But the girls' faith was justified—Edith scorned the idea of exchanging her lively quarters for a peaceful solitude, and Mrs. Stanley's gentle—

"Not any more noise to-night, dears," was in nightly requisition for the two weeks of her stay.

Mr. Stanley grasped one of Roderick's hands and Edith the other, when they entered the parlor, which he had been sternly forbidden to leave, and for a moment neither spoke. All three were remembering that when uncle and nephew had last met, the latter had lain helpless, unconscious, and, as many hearts had feared, dying. He was given back to them, almost from the dead, and words seemed very weak and meaningless to tell what they felt.

It was Kitty, as usual, who broke the spell. Her aversion to any public manifestation of feeling was very great, and she managed to raise first a smile and then a laugh, and to whisk Edith off upstairs before the crisis, which she dreaded, came.

22

It was five o'clock, and both Mr. Stanley and Edith announced themselves to be ravenously hungry, having had "nothing but a lunch basketful" since breakfast; so Aunt Jady was told to set forth the feast as soon as she could, without injury to it, regardless of the regular supper hour, which was half-past six. But the old dame had made her calculations, and was not to be hurried, and the two sufferers sternly refused to impair two such magnificent appetites as they boasted by "piecing."

"If I were among strangers," said Mr. Stanley, in reply to the offers made him of a sandwich, a piece of bread and butter, a ginger-snap, a cracker, "then I should be only too glad, if I could do it privately, to 'take a snack by way of a damper,' for I should not dare to eat as I now expect to; but in the bosom of my family, with muffins—I am confident that I smell muffins in process of baking, and other things which blend in an odor as of Araby the Blest—why, my *dear* children, you must think that I have dropped into my second childhood since you saw me last!"

The entrance of Dr. West, at about six o'clock, afforded a welcome diversion. Mr. Stanley had been most favorably impressed by him, and was glad to meet him again, and to introduce him to Edith, who had not yet seen him. The doctor did not wait for a second invitation to take off his overcoat and stay to tea; he frankly acknowledged that he had come with that intention, and should have been much disappointed if they had failed to invite him, or done it in such a perfunctory manner that he would have felt obliged to decline.

"There is a sixth sense," said Kitty, in a generally audible aside to Polly, "with which some—not all—people are blessed; it enables them to tell when their friends are going to have muffins for tea."

"Why, they can tell by smelling," said Polly, "of course

they can! Smelling is one of the five senses; what *do* you
mean, Kitty?"

"Don't ask her, my dear," said the doctor, sitting down by
Polly and patting her hand; "there is nothing so painful,
as I know by experience, as being asked to explain a joke."

"Then in future," said Kitty, benevolently, "I will always laugh at your jokes, doctor, when I see that you intend·
one, whether I see the point or not; but you must try, at
least, to make it plain that you intend one."

"Kitty! Kitty!" said Mrs. Stanley, softly, and the doctor replied for her—

"Oh, I don't mind her, Mrs. Stanley, I assure you I don't
—she amuses me!"

He insisted upon sitting next to her at the tea-table, but
declared that, with such a supper before him, he could not
waste time in quarreling with her.

Aunt Judy was in her glory, and a particularly brilliant
turban, the latter put on and tied at the side with the
science peculiar to a colored aristocrat. Clara vainly tried
to imitate that arrangement, and especially the knot, meeting at times with derision on the subject which tried her
soul. Aunt Judy's effect that evening was meteoric—she
could leave her baking for but a moment at a time, but she
could not bring herself to lose the compliments which she felt
to be her due, and which greeted her every time she entered
with a fresh supply of hot cakes, or fried chicken, or oysters,
or clam fritters. The doctor noticed, with silent approval,
that none of Mrs. Stanley's children were drinking tea or
coffee; and that the younger ones made their supper of
stewed oysters and bread, or toast and butter, declining the
array of tempting hot cakes and bread, without any apparent
sign from their mother. That question had been settled
long ago—Mrs. Stanley had told her younger children that
if they preferred not to be tempted by food which she did

not wish them to have while they were growing boys and girls, they could have their meals before the rest of the family had theirs, but that she would be much happier with all of them at the table at the same time; they had all chosen the latter arrangement, and had learned to control their wishes in this respect, until now the effort was very slight. Kitty, whose nature it was to grow more persistent in the face of opposition, had more than once been trouble-some about it, but two or three solitary meals had always brought her to order again; the pleasure of rebellion, she found, did not equal that which she was losing.

Bright talk and happy laughter lengthened out the supper-hour, but at last they returned to the parlor and gathered about the fire, which was so brilliant with May's treasures that every one voted for the banishment of the lamp, and they sat in the glow of the firelight, gradually "quieting down," until Edith exclaimed—

"Why does a wood fire on andirons strike everybody dumb?"

"Is that a riddle, dear?" inquired Kitty.

"If it is," said Edith, "it's like that disagreeable Wonder-land riddle, the answer of which the asker did not know. But I have noticed it often, since I had the chimney at home opened and set up my fire on andirons—people begin to gaze into it, and gradually subside as if they were under a spell."

"It's like watching the clouds," said Polly; "it seems to take all sorts of shapes—there, Kitty, what do you see *there?*" and she pointed to a glowing cavern in the centre of the fire, strewn with fantastic shapes in blackened coals.

"It looks like a witch's cavern," said Kitty, after silently gazing for a moment; "and see"—pointing to where little tongues of flame crept in at the corner—"there are the three witches, peeping in and drawing back, afraid of their own spells."

"What a grewsome idea!" said Elizabeth; "it looks to me like a beautiful grotto under the sea, with curious moss, and wonderful shells, and sea-sprites weaving their charms and spells."

There was a general laugh, and Arnold exclaimed—

"She's dropped into poetry! Go on, Betty dear, it's beautiful!"

"Why, what did I say?" asked Elizabeth, perplexed, and Arnold repeated her impromptu to her, with proper pauses and emphasis, and she laughed with the rest.

"Go on, doctor, it's your turn next," said Kitty; "see if you can improve upon Betty's lofty strain."

"I would not dare aspire so high," said the doctor, meekly; "you may have heard that 'a man can't make himself a poet, no more'n a sheep can make himself a go-at'; you will perhaps be shocked, but it looks to me like a black-smith's forge; see, there is the anvil, and there are the horseshoes, hanging up in a row. By the way, Miss Kitty, you've never asked after Lady—did you receive the message I sent when I returned Rod's horse the next morning?"

"The man said you found her waiting for you," said Kitty; "was that it?"

"I told him to tell you that I found her at the door of the chicken-house, as if she had somehow mistaken it for the stable."

"Why, I always thought you considered Lady very intelligent," replied Kitty. "Doesn't that look a little 'like she was' stupid?"

"By no means," said the doctor, gravely. "The brightest minds are often coupled with the most erratic imaginations."

"Oh!" said Kitty.

"Have you any more pine-cones and fairy-faggots, Pussy?" asked Roderick, as the blaze began to die down, and Ernest drew the basket containing her store from a shady corner, and handed it to her. She daintily picked out cones and splinters of light-wood, and tiny faggots, adding them from time to time where she thought they would be most effective. The piny odor was fragrant as incense, without its power to cloy, and the great log at the back was gradually taking the fire to its heart, and turning to a mass of glowing red.

"It is beautiful," said Edith, looking dreamily into the heart of the fire; "but when I look at a great log like that, burning away to nothing in a few hours, it always makes me feel sorry to see—

'Half a century's silent growth
Go up in cheery flame and smoke.'

Think of the years it has stood, the storms it has trembled under, the sunshine and dew and rain it has absorbed, and all for—this!"

And she pointed to the crumbling log, as, with a sound like a low sigh, it fell apart.

"It does not seem to me a sad or ignoble fate," said Mrs. Stanley; "it has put a lovely picture into many a heart, while it was growing, and 'a thing of beauty is a joy forever'—we can always turn back to look at it—and now it is passing away, diffusing warmth, and light, and fragrance, and pleasant thoughts, as it goes. Surely that is a fate to be coveted, from beginning to end."

"Your eyes see deeper than mine do, Aunt Louise," said Edith, gently; "you catch the sentiment, while I stop at the sentimentality, of things."

"My eyes are older than yours, my darling," said Mrs. Stanley, "and have learned to look through many things which they once only looked at.

'A man that looks on glass,
On it may stay his eye,
Or, if he pleaseth, through it pass,
And then the Heaven espy.'

I can see the joyful ending, now, to many sorrowful ways."

They were all silent for a few minutes; those whose way stretched longest behind them looking back, the others looking forward.

The clock on the mantel-piece took this opportunity to strike ten, and Dr. West sprang up, exclaiming—

" Bless me! I had no idea it was so late. I had meant to pay another call this evening; are you sure that clock is right, Mrs. Stanley ? "

Three or four watches were pulled out in defence of the clock, and the doctor, declaring that Aunt Judy must have bewitched the waffles, and drugged the muffins, began to look for his coat, but Kitty laid a detaining hand on it, when, having found it in the corner where he had thrown it, he was about to put it on.

"Oh, wait five minutes, please," she said ; "I am going to ask Betty to play the accompaniment, for us to sing ' While shepherds watched their flocks by night,' and we want your tenor—*please* wait !"

"I will," said the doctor, meekly, and resigning his coat to her as he spoke; " but I did think you were going to be civil to me at last, and for once, and say that you wanted *me !* "

"Why, of course we want you," said Kitty ; and this time she spoke without her usual sauciness, adding, softly—

"Do you think we can forget so soon that but for you, Rod——" and she stopped and turned away, but as she turned, he saw the fire-light glitter from a tear.

But her voice rose clear and sweet in the hymn, and when she said good-night, she asked him to give her love to Lady, and tell her she'd better keep away from the chicken-house!

CHAPTER XXVIII.

"Is there a leaf that greenly grows
Where summer meadows bloom
But gathereth the winter snows,
And changeth to the hue of those,
If lasting till they come?"—MRS. BROWNING.

THE business of the evening began as soon as the doctor was gone; he drove off lingeringly, looking back at the windows through which the firelight gleamed, crossed by shadows of swiftly passing figures, and muttered to himself—

"'In happy homes he saw the light
Of household fires gleam warm and bright,
Above——'

What an old idiot I am! I've sung that thing too many times with a tiger chorus to reclaim it for sentiment now. With what filial respect she looks up at me, when she isn't chaffing me!

"'You are old, Father William, the young man said,
The few hairs that are left you are white,
And yet you incessantly stand on your head—
Do you think, at your age, it is right?'

I'm well aware that it isn't—it's like measles, like measles—having it once is no protection—older you are, harder it goes with you! Only contagious when the system's predisposed; take a chill on it, and it strikes in; no danger when it comes out freely! If it had been Miss Elizabeth now, Stephen, I would't have blamed you. She's a good deal younger than you are, but there's nothing foolish about her, and she'd help you immensely with the old women and babies—*if* she saw fit to have you. But—that Limb! What a woman

she'll make, when some of the nonsense—not all—is taken
out of her, and she gives herself to some one, for better or
worse! But I think I shall 'pull up my stakes and migrate
to Dahomey,' or somewhere equally distant and inaccessible,
before that day comes. Get up, Dandy! Are you going to
sleep?"

And he rattled home to his cheerless boarding-place,
built a roaring fire on his cold hearth, lit his pipe, and wrote
an essay on contagious diseases for a medical journal to
which he occasionally contributed.

Meantime, preparations for the next morning went
rapidly on at "the Mansion." Edith had marked all her
parcels before packing them, which saved a great deal of
time and trouble now. May had petitioned to hang up her
stocking, promising not to investigate it until after breakfast, when, it had been decided, the others were to receive
their presents. But she said she wanted to put out her
hand and feel it, when she first woke up, so it was hung on
her bed-post, and, after she was asleep, it was filled, and a
pillow-case, containing the rest of her presents, was hung
beside it.

At Kitty's suggestion, the pillow-case idea was adopted for
the rest of the family, and a row of chairs, with one pinned
to the back of each, and duly labeled, was ranged at a safe
distance from the parlor hearth—the chairs could receive
anything too heavy or unwieldy for the pillow-cases.

To her great delight, Aunt Judy was called ; a large basket
was filled with the consignment for each chair, and Ernest
went with her to read the names. as his own chair came last,
and she could be trusted to fill it alone, without making any
mistakes.

Prayers had been read before May's departure ; Mrs. Stanley was taking Roderick's place, until he should be stronger,
but when Mr. Stanley was there, she preferred to yield it to

him, and to-night he had added to other words of thanks-giving, "We also bless Thy holy Name for all Thy servants departed this life in Thy faith and fear," and all the older children's hearts turned with loving remembrance to their father; May alone could not remember him, but the words recalled the regret which she so often felt, because she could not. Edith stole her hand into Mrs. Stanley's. It seemed to her that she missed the gentle young mother who had so early left her, more and more with each advancing year. But none of them "sorrowed as without hope," and if there was less laughter and merriment, after their thoughts had been called to the beloved dead, there was no lack of quiet happiness. Roderick was banished soon after May's depart-ure, for he was still under orders, and by his obedience to them he saved much trouble, and materially hastened his recovery. Kitty wasted a good deal of compassion on him for various things which would have gone hardly with her, but which faith and patience made easily endurable to him.

Mr. Stanley and Edith had both been tempted, in their glad revulsion of feeling about him, to make his share of the Christmas presents, like Benjamin's mess, "five times so great" as any of the others, but Edith had suggested that this would give him pain, rather than pleasure, and they had tried to make no apparent difference.

It was nearly twelve o'clock when Aunt Judy made her last and solitary trip into the parlor with her laden basket, but no one seemed apprehensive that the family would over-sleep itself next morning, although breakfast was to be as usual at eight o'clock, in order to give time for the "dona-tion party" before church.

Aunt Judy, for once, did not feel slighted because the meal was dispatched more quickly than usual—her own curiosity was on tip-toe, not only about the array of parcels in the parlor, but because she felt very certain that, in the general distribution, she would not be left out in the cold—a feeling which Clara and Moses fully shared, and their faith was quite justified by events.

The parlor was full of joyous clamor for almost an hour. Mrs. Stanley was seated on the "throne," and her gifts were brought to her by her loyal subjects; then Mr. Stanley was similarly honored, then Elizabeth was led to her collection, to find the chair removed, and its place supplied by a beautiful Davenport, her uncle's gift.

"We didn't bring it in small pieces, in our pockets, dear, and put it together in the night," said Edith, smiling at Elizabeth's wondering face; "the magic was of a very simple nature—it came with our luggage yesterday, but papa was on hand as the cart came to the barn, and helped Moses to hide it there, and then to bring it in this morning—he felt like a traitor coming in 'unbeknownst,' but he was careful to look at nothing but the floor."

The boys went into such wild ecstasies over the printing-press and camera that their mother recommended them to run two or three times around the house *outside*, to relieve their overcharged feelings, which they promptly did, returning sufficiently calm to look at the rest of their presents, among which steel skates shone conspicuous.

May had with difficulty brought down her pillow-case, wondering what it could be that was so long as to stick up out of the top, and so wide as to nearly fill it. Her French ladyship had been carefully wrapped in many papers, but when at last the lovely blonde head, with its dark blue eyes, emerged from the last concealing fold of tissue-paper, and the eyes softly closed, as the head chanced to be turned downward, May gave a little shriek of delight, and held the treasure on her lap, as she looked at her other things, saying, when it was time to make ready for church—

"Don't you *think* she might go, mamma? She *must* be alive—and she will be sure to sit still."

"I am afraid her little mother would not be quite so sure, darling," said Mrs. Stanley, smiling, "and you know Whose house a church is—you must not grudge an hour or two out of your happy day to Him."

"Oh mamma!" she exclaimed, "I didn't think of it that way—you must stay at home, darling, but your mother will put you where you can see her the moment she comes back."

So mademoiselle was carefully propped up in one of the wide window seats, where she sat in great apparent content, gazing out with her lovely blue eyes with real eyelashes!

Aunt Judy paid several wondering visits to her, in the course of the morning, returning to her kitchen each time with a puzzled shake of her head, muttering—

"Nebber seed no doll like dat! Hope it ain't nuffin to bewitch little missy, but she better be keerful. Eyes follers you 'roun' like dey was alive, sho' 'nuff, and shets up when she lies down. Doll! Dat ain't no doll!"

She watched May closely for days, and finally decided that if there was any "charm" about the mysterious stranger, it was one for working good instead of harm. But she never wearied of seeing the blue eyes close as May laid her treasure down, and open again when it was picked up.

The "carry-all" driven by Moses, and well supplied with warm wraps, took all the party, with the exception of Roderick, to church. Each in turn begged to be left with him, but he insisted upon it that he would have none of them—that the quiet rest would do him good after the excitement he had just passed through, and that Aunt Judy would watch over him like a mother. They yielded, finding that it would please him better, and after reading awhile, he retired to his special chair, where they found him peacefully sleeping on their return.

The church was a bower of greenery, lit up by holly boughs laden with berries, and the good old minister preached to them on thankfulness, with a wise brevity which left the impression of his few well chosen words on many hearts. The music was not ambitiously chosen, but was very sweet. All the young Stanleys, excepting May, had been gathered into the choir, and Elizabeth's refined taste and good judgment had more influence in the selections that were made than she was herself aware of. Roderick's voice was missed, and there was great jubilation over the announcement that he would probably take his place again in ten days or two weeks.

Hearty greetings were exchanged with friends and neighbors, as they left the church, and kind messages sent to Roderick. Colonel and Mrs. Peyton were there, with all their family, but Randolph gave to Edith the same cordial salutation which he bestowed upon the rest, neither more nor less. By this time, however, light had begun to dawn upon his behavior to her. Kitty and Polly, in their innocent talk the night before, had expatiated largely upon the loveliness of their governess, and, in quite a separate connection, upon Mr. Peyton's great kindness to Roderick.

"Two and two do sometimes make four," said Edith to herself, and, as her interest in Mr. Peyton had never gone below the merest surface, she resolved to waste no more thought upon him.

The slighted breakfast predisposed everybody to do justice to Aunt Judy's dinner, which was a brilliant success, from the immense raw oysters on the half-shell, to the blazing holly-crowned pudding, and tiny cups of coffee, handed in Aunt Judy's best style, and Clara's careful imitation of it.

May had been unable to refrain from telling Edith the

turkey story, and she in turn had told it to her father, who
insisted, as he helped himself to a second slice of the gobbler, that there was a certain wild-turkey flavor about him,
for which no amount of "yarbs" could account.   He asked
for a second "chicken croquette," remarking on their deli-
cacy as he did so, and Kitty shot a triumphant glance at
Roderick.

The weather was brilliantly beautiful, with just enough
frost in the air to make it exhilarating, so a walking party
was organized, at a respectful interval after dinner, including
every one but Mrs. and Mr. Stanley, Roderick and Elizabeth.
These four gathered around the fire, and spent the rest of
the afternoon in pleasant talk, partly a grateful recapitula-
tion of events since the farming enterprise was taken in
hand, and partly of plans and suggestions for the future.
Roderick hoped soon to be "out and about" again, and he
was planning an arrangement for an ice-house on a small
scale, which he thought that the boys and himself, with
Moses to do the heavier work, could manage to construct.
Colonel Peyton had showed him, on his own farm, the ice-
pond which had been made by clearing out a gully where
the soil was chiefly gravel, and damming it at the lower end,
just as the winter rains began, so making a shallow sheet of
water, which froze much more readily than a deeper one
would.   His ice-house was built so near this place, that no
carting was necessary—two men with wheelbarrows were all-
sufficient to bring the ice to the door of the ice-house, where
two more received and packed it.   Roderick knew that it
would be impossible to have an ice-house built this winter,
and the success of his plan would depend entirely upon the
weather, but he thought it worth trying.   There was a sort
of small gulch not far from the creek, in one corner of
the farm, that would do very well for the pond; across
the outlet of this a dam had been made, and on the high

gravel bank above, far enough from the edge to avoid all
danger of caving in, but not farther than this, Moses was
digging a square cellar-like pit. The bottom of it was to
slope slightly toward the gulch, and that side was to be
pierced through close to the floor, from the steep bank of
the gulch, and a long earthen draining-pipe inserted. The
inner walls were to be thickly lined with hay, kept in place
by boards and stakes, and, when the pit was filled with ice,
it was to be covered with hay and loose boards. The site for
it had been chosen under the shade of two or three good-
sized trees, and, although Mr. Stanley laughed a little, and
called Roderick the White Knight, he admitted that, if the
pond would obligingly fill and freeze, he did not see why the
plan should not succeed, at least to the extent of providing
ice for the dairy, which was the chief object of the scheme.
The new house came in for its share of discussion also. The
cellar had been dug, and the foundation wall laid, while
Roderick was ill, and Arnold had faithfully taken his place
as supervisor. The architect had been in doubt about some
of the details, and lively discussions had taken place between
Edith, Mr. Stanley and himself, the upshot of which was,
that he had asked permission to go and see the situation of
the house before finally deciding about certain windows and
verandas. He was to come during Edith's visit, and Mr.
Stanley regretted that he himself could not also be present.
At the same time, he said, he had no doubt that Edith would
make her wishes quite clearly understood, and he asked Mrs.
Stanley to act as moderator at the meeting, as the architect
seemed to understand his business, and must be allowed to
have the decisive vote in the matters in dispute. Mr. Stanley inquired if Mr. Brook—the architect—could find lodging
anywhere in the neighborhood, as it would be impossible for
him to go from and return to B—— in one day; Mrs. Stanley knew of none, and said she should be happy to have him

stay at Green Point, to which, after a little demur, her
brother agreed, saying that he knew Mr. Brook well, and
considered him a very fine fellow, adding, with a smile—

"He has had serious difficulties to contend with—he has
money enough to live on, in his own right, and is, beside,
the only child of a rich father, but he has worked at his profession as if his whole living depended upon his success in it,
and he is succeeding. His worst faults, I think, are on the
surface—his manner is a little too superlatively elegant, and
he has an unnecessarily high regard for his own beliefs and
opinion; but things on the surface can be rubbed off, you
know, and I fancy I begin already to see the good effect of
friction. He has an exasperating habit of drawling when he
speaks, and if I did not feel morally sure of offending him, I
should ask him to leave it off, and depend upon his natural
voice, which is very good. It amuses me to see him with
Edith—she knows him so slightly that she is obliged to curb
her impatience over his deliberateness, but it requires a severe
struggle. I think you will like him, Louise, and, as he has no
mother, poor fellow, you can mother him a little while he is
with you—it's very good of you to be willing to take him in ;
but then, you are always good, you dear woman!"

"It is pleasant to receive such large returns for the small
investments which I make in the way of goodness," replied
Mrs. Stanley, smiling, "and I shall be quite curious to see
your *rara avis*, as a man unspoiled by prosperity certainly is.
Hark! Do you not hear singing? Yes, it is a Christmas
carol, and I recognize the voices of the waits."

The children had crept quietly up to the parlor window,
and now, standing outside in the twilight, and the light of
the moon, they gave first the new carol, and then two or
three of the old ones, until their mother raised the window,
and invited them in. They came at once, but Kitty said,
regretfully—

"Oh, mamma! we wanted to sing one more, and there's no danger of malaria now, after all the frost we've had."

"But people can catch cold," said Mrs. Stanley, "even when they are above catching malaria, and you know you can't afford to lose any time in the holidays, and above all, while my extra daughter is here."

The extra daughter drew a low chair to her mother's side, and took possession of a hand, with the eager response which she always made to any "mothering" from Mrs. Stanley.

"I should like to know," said Mr. Stanley, when wraps were taken off and put away, and the enlarged circle—or rather half-circle—had once more settled itself about the fire, "why we can't have that 'one more' as well inside as outside the windows. You don't sing so shockingly as to make distance necessary to enchantment."

"After such a whole-souled, generous compliment as that," responded Kitty, "it would be base to refuse—come on, children!" and she led the way with "Christmas Day in the Morning," the rest at once falling in.

Carols and songs followed in quick succession, as one and another called for some favorite, and twilight deepened into night, but no light was wanted beyond that of the glowing fire.

Mrs. Stanley had directed Aunt Judy to postpone supper for half-an-hour beyond the usual time, in consideration of the late hour at which they had finished dinner; but when the bell rang, Mr. Stanley gave a little groan, and said—

"'Must I leave thee, Paradise?' This chair is so comfortable, and I ate so much dinner—where is the use of having supper anyhow!"

"What a monster of selfishness!" cried Edith; "*we* took a three-mile walk, and we are quite ready for our supper—and you'll have to buy a rowing-machine, or a pair of dumb-bells, or something, papa, for you grow stouter and lazier

23

every day; you'll be wanting to roll instead of walk, before
long."

"Why don't you box her ears, Uncle George?" cried
Kitty, springing up. "I'll do it with pleasure, if you'll only
give me authority—now don't get up, any of you—I have a
brilliant idea—I don't believe you, or mamma, or Betty, or
Rod, really do want much supper, and so——"

"You want four of us to eat their suppers for them, and
leave them in peace?" interrupted Arnold. "I'm your man
—I'll take Uncle George's!"

"Don't be stupid, dear," said Kitty. "Mamma, may we
bring in some of the things, and have a handed tea? We'll
arrange the parlor as if it were quite a grand affair—may we?"

"I have not the least objection," said Mrs. Stanley, smiling,
"if you can make your grand arrangements in half an hour
—there's nothing to get cold, for I knew no one would want
a hot supper to-night, and Aunt Judy need not begin baking
till you are ready—don't scald the tea until everything else
is done, dear."

"Mamma! what do you take me for? No, Betty, you sit
still—you four elderly people are the distinguished guests!
Come on, girls!"

"And boys?" said Ernest, insinuatingly; "they always
have men-waiters at swell affairs you know, Kitty, and you
can lend us white aprons. It will be much more aristocratic."

"Very well," said Kitty graciously; "only you know
I'm the head-waiter, and you must mind me! Now the rest
of you must converse, and pretend that you don't know anything is going on."

"Kitty," said Mr. Stanley, drowsily, "come here and kiss
me first, or before the evening is over I shall be caught
kissing a pretty waiter-girl!"

"Papa, you shock us!" said Edith, severely. "I wouldn't
go, Kitty, if I were you!"

"That you never can be," said Kitty, giving the kiss as she spoke, and then marshaling her subordinates out of the room.

There was much flitting to and fro in the twilight, before the preparations were complete ; the two " men-waiters," each with a long white towel pinned on apron-wise, first brought in a small table and three or four candlestands, disposing the latter conveniently near the distinguished guests. Then the headwaiter appeared with a table-cloth, which she spread upon the small table while the two other "pretty waiter-girls" brought in cups and saucers and plates, dainty ham-sandwiches and buttered rolls, baskets of cake and pitchers of milk and cream. When all was in readiness, Aunt Judy appeared, in her best turban and most voluminous white apron, bearing aloft the urn, and chuckling audibly as she set it down. She was immediately dismissed, and shortly afterward two shadowy forms could be discerned in the hall, near the other door of the parlor, and a sound of subdued giggling came from time to time through the half-open doorway, as the feast progressed. Edith, by special request, presided at the urn, while the others stole softly about the room, deferentially attending to the wants of the distinguished ones, who discovered that, under such fascinating circumstances, they could eat a little supper after all.

" Papa, do you really think you ought to eat any more sandwiches ? " asked Edith, gravely, as Mr. Stanley took the last but one from the plate beside him ; " there were eight on that plate, to my certain knowledge."

" You are forgetting your place, young woman," he replied, with dignity ; "and as for the sandwiches, it would take about a dozen of them to make one respectable slice of bread, cut as I like it cut."

When "the quality" positively declined to eat or drink anything more, Edith sprang up and began " clearing off " with frantic haste. Aunt Judy and Clara made their appearance, and assisted, unforbidden ; in fact, the head-waiter was heard to say—

"You'd better cut some more cold ham, Aunt Judy—oh, and some cold turkey, too, and I don't believe those escalloped oysters would be bad cold, you might put them on, anyhow! What are you replete people laughing at?" turning suddenly upon them, "haven't we walked about two miles more, waiting on you? That makes five! *We* have earned both our appetites and our suppers !"

They departed, and "there was a sound of revelry by night," until the meeting was broken up by the recollection that Mr. Stanley was to leave them in the morning, and that they were losing too much of his society.

"It's a little mean, anyhow," said Edith, "for me to stay here and leave him desolate for nearly two weeks; I wish he would wind up his business, or retire, or something; it's always in the way!"

CHAPTER XXIX.

"O spirits gay, and kindly heart!
Precious the blessings ye impart!"—J. BAILLIE.

MR. STANLEY went the next morning, much lamented over by his family, and also by himself.

"I wonder I come here at all!" he said mournfully. "I always go away coveting your whole tribe, Louise, and if you were a truly benevolent woman, you would give me at least one of these superfluous boys."

"I will—when I find them superfluous," she answered, smiling; "but be patient, my dear brother—you will have all you want of them next summer, and if you have more than you want, I shall just read you a lesson on covetousness."

Arnold drove Mr. Stanley to the station, leaving Moses to finish the "ice-house," for there was a rise in temperature, and a general gathering of clouds, which promised rain, and the preparations for catching it were by no means complete. Kitty suggested allowing the hole to fill with water, undrained, and then freezing it "with the hartshorn bottle and garden-hose," but as she declined to go into farther particulars concerning the manufacture of artificial ice, her project was not considered.

Edith and Kitty, Polly and Ernest, all offered their escort to the station, and their offer was accepted in the most flattering manner. Roderick had advised Arnold to take the "carry-all"—as the market wagon purchased at the sale had

come to be called—at all events, for it could be made
weather-tight, should the rain overtake them, which was the
case with none of the other vehicles.

They had a merry drive, waiting at the station until the
train carried Mr. Stanley off, and coming home through a
pouring rain, which had begun soon after they turned
homeward.

Arnold put on the oil-skin coat which was the common
property of all three of the brothers, and which being long
enough for Roderick had, as Kitty said, "a demi-train on
Arnold and a full court train on Ernest," and rushed out
to see if the dam was holding and the pond filling. He
came in exultant, reporting "two feet of water in the hold,
and rising every minute, and the dam as firm as a rock."

" Now, *if* the water doesn't all leak out of the bottom of
the pond before it freezes," said Kitty, teasingly, "and *if*
it will only freeze hard for four or five nights in succession
while the water is there, the ice crop is a sure thing, whatever other crops fail. I wonder if it would pay to convert
the Estate into an ice farm? There's an idea for somebody!
Instead of working in spring-fever time, and blazing July,
and glorious October, all the work would be done in cold
weather when it's so much easier to be industrious, and in
summer we might keep a swimming-school in part of the
pond and hire boats on the rest. We will reserve a small
patch of ground for raising pea-nuts ; and we can make
ginger-ale and sassafras-beer, and ginger-cakes without any
spice in them, and we will take turns in selling them
through the kitchen window."

" It is a great comfort to have such a resource in view, if
all other crops should fail," said Roderick, gravely, "but
you must give me a fair trial with my wheat crop first—that
has the advantage of being already in the ground, you
know."

The rain continued all that day and, with an occasional let-up, till Tuesday night, but nobody complained of being dull. Arnold and Ernest, rejoicing in their freedom from school, were making alternate experiments with the printing-press, the camera, and the fresh supply of chemicals which, according to their request, had been among their gifts, and the days seemed all too short. New books abounded, and sewing, with reading aloud to sweeten it, went briskly on among the girls, Roderick acting as reader most of the time. Mrs. Stanley was busy restoring the house to its wonted order, choosing May for her assistant, who carried her waxen lady from room to room, and carefully arranged her " so that she could see " what was going on. Sunday was of necessity spent at home, but the family afforded a good-sized congregation, to which Mrs. Stanley read service, and there was a " choir-meeting " in the evening, which shortened it amazingly.

The family had just sat down to tea, on the fourth rainy evening, when they were startled by the sudden sound of knocking at the front door—the old-fashioned brass knocker having never been replaced by a bell.

It was so unusual for any one but the doctor, who generally knocked and came in, to call in such weather, and at this hour, that Mrs. Stanley started up anxiously, saying—

" I hope it is no bad news—I have not heard from your Aunt Mary for more than a week."

Arnold instantly arose, saying—

" I'll go and see, mamma—I do believe Aunt Judy and Clara are both afraid to go; you stay here till you know who it is, please."

He returned in a few minutes, laughing silently until he had closed the door behind him, when his laughter became audible.

" It's your architect, Edith," he said ; " it is, really and truly! The poor wretch has walked all the way from the station, and is wringing himself out in the hall, with many apologies. He's about a foot taller than you are, Rod, and I am reveling in the anticipation of seeing him in your clothes.'

"I'll take him to my room at once," said Roderick, rising as he spoke.

"Now please to stay where you are," said Arnold, entreatingly; "it will give you cold only to look at him, and I know you'd insist upon shaking hands with him. I'll do the honors—mayn't I give him your dress-suit? It's a little short in the trousers for you, you know——"

"Arnold!" said his mother, gently.

"I beg your pardon, mamma," and he stooped to kiss her. "I wasn't in earnest—I will not take advantage of a helpless stranger! Which was the last suit you had made, Rod?"

"The gray cassimere," replied Roderick; "but perhaps that will be too thin—you can give him his choice between that and the brown cloth."

Arnold hastened back to the "helpless stranger," and escorted him to Roderick's room, heaping fresh wood on the fire, lighting the lamp, and getting out dry garments with good-natured zeal.

"You'll be glad to hear that we had only just sat down to supper, Mr. Brook," he said, when all was ready; "for you must be starved as well as drenched; I'll wait for you in the hall—you're sure you wouldn't like some hot water?"

"Quite sure, thanks," said Mr. Brook; "you're very good; but don't let me keep you in the hall. I dare say I can find my way down."

"Oh, that's all right!" said Arnold, cheerfully; "I'll take a book—don't hurry yourself."

He borrowed a candle from his mother's room, and sat down on the top stair with the book he had taken from

Roderick's table ; but he had not much more than begun reading, when Mr. Brook appeared, looking so utterly ludicrous that Arnold had hard work to control his laughter. The architect was a man of unusual height, but so well proportioned that his size was not conspicuous, except by contrast with other men. Roderick was five feet eleven ; but the effect of his clothes upon Mr. Brook was to make the latter look like an overgrown school-boy. The coat was far too tight to button ; the waistcoat had been induced to meet by letting out the buckle in the back, but had a sort of precarious look about the buttons as if the wearer had better not sigh. The trousers had the graceful effect of candle-moulds, and left a wide expanse of ankle visible. Mr. Brook was not exactly vain of his small hands and feet, but he had always been glad that they were small, and he was particularly glad upon this occasion, for he found that by a slight exertion he could put on Roderick's shoes. But they were uncomfortably tight, and this obliged him to exchange his usually free and graceful movements for a mincing gait, which, as Kitty afterward declared, was the "cap-sheaf." If he had really been the vain fop which he so often seemed to be, he would have declined to appear before he could do so in his own clothes, but this would have necessitated the sending up of his supper, and he preferred being laughed at to being "discourteous."

Mr. Stanley had with some difficulty induced him to accept Mrs. Stanley's hospitality, and he was not going to open proceedings by behaving as if he imagined himself at an inn. He watched Arnold's struggle for a moment with grim satisfaction, and then himself burst into hearty laughter, saying—

"Do you imagine I did not look at myself in the glass ? I have not seen anything so funny since the last time I was at a pantomime."

"See here!" said Arnold, delighted with this beginning; "try to get your face straight before we go into the dining-room; look unconscious while my cousin introduces you to mamma and all of them, and see what they will do—they will not dare to laugh, if mamma doesn't, and I am pretty sure she will not."

"It is a rather cruel thing to do," he replied, with a sudden gleam of mischief in his dark eyes, "but I will try it, and I will bet you anything you please to nothing, that they will all break down before Miss Stanley has finished her introduction—you see your uncle has told me a good deal about you all incidentally."

"Come on!" said Arnold, gleefully, and they entered the dining-room with sober faces.

Mr. Brook advanced to where Edith was sitting, and held out his hand, his coat sleeve coyly retreating as he did so. She rose to greet him, took in his appearance at a glance, made a mighty effort, and said cordially, with only the proper amount of smiling—

"I am very glad to see you, Mr. Brook—allow me to introduce you to my aunt, Mrs. Stanley—to Miss Stanley, Miss Katharine, Miss Pauline, Miss Mary, Mr. Stanley, and Ernest—Arnold you have already met. Here is your seat—you must be quite ready for your supper, after such a walk as you have had."

There was a slight quiver in her voice, which increased as she neared the end of her speech, and as bow after bow from Mr. Brook made the short-comings in his raiment more apparent, but she kept courageously on, and succeeded in finishing without breaking down.

Mrs. Stanley expressed kind regrets about the long wet walk, and wondered why Mr. Stanley had not written them to meet Mr. Brook. Her voice, too, was slightly tremulous, and the others, not daring to speak, took refuge in an

ominous silence, except Roderick, who hospitably urged
their guest to eat and drink—but in short and detached
sentences.

Arnold seemed in a fair way to win his "anything," when
a faint and suppressed giggle from the kitchen door proved
the last straw—Mr. Brook broke into irrepressible laughter,
and one after another joined him, Mrs. Stanley and
Elizabeth yielding last, and gasping out apologies as they
did so.

It was impossible, after this, for anything like stiffness to
supervene, and Mr. Brook had never shown to such advantage—in Edith's eyes, at least—as he showed during the evening which followed. Aunt Judy took possession of his wet
garments, and restored them to him not only dry, but
smooth, before nine o'clock, and the transformation they
made in him was wonderful; but by that time he was talking
with the different members of the family, and they with
him, as if he were an old acquaintance. It transpired that
he belonged to a glee club, and he joined, without urging,
in the music which almost always formed part of the evening's entertainment, to its great advantage. The genuine
simplicity and absence of all affectation by which he was
surrounded seemed to make him for the time forget the
mannerisms which so often concealed his real character, and
the evening was almost gone before the business upon which
he had come was alluded to. When it was, a warm dispute
between Edith and himself ensued—a dispute which could
only be settled, he said, on the site of the house. Upon
which Mrs. Stanley gently suggested that all farther argument
concerning it had better be postponed till the next day,
when, if the weather would permit, the combatants could
resort to this means of arbitration. Edith "subsided," with
the parting shot, "I wish there might be a law obliging
architects to live for one year in every house of their own

planning! We'd see, then, if they were so penurious as to bay-windows and balconies."

But when the next day came, the proposed "arbitration" was simply impossible; the rain had increased to a steady pour, and mud and mud-puddles, too formidable for Edith's fording, lay between the "Mansion" and the site of the new house. Mr. Brook exhibited a praiseworthy amount of patience under this dispensation, and when Mrs. Stanley cordially invited him to remain with them until the weather should permit them to reach Mr. Stanley's lot without fording puddles and braving the storm, he gratefully accepted her invitation, remarking that business was dull during the holidays, and that he did not think it would suffer for his absence.

A little of the affectation which was so distasteful to Edith had returned, but he was still agreeable enough to afford a welcome diversion, for they were all beginning to tire of their imprisonment, being used to taking a good deal of exercise.

The boys were delighted to find that he was well-informed on their favorite subject, and carried him off to the indoor-laboratory, to give his opinion on their latest experiments, returning shortly to invite the girls to join them, as there was to be an exhibition of chemical fireworks. After that, no amount of affectation, or even priggishness, could have shaken the allegiance of Arnold and Ernest to their new friend.

The rain continued to pour steadily all day, but just before sunset the west wind cleared a space above the horizon, into which the sun seemed to drop, like a ball of fire in depths of clear water—a double rainbow spanned the black clouds which were rolling sullenly down the eastern sky; every twig on trees and bushes seemed suddenly strung with jewels, and a chorus from the birds thrilled through the air.

There was a rush to the front door, and then every one stood still—the exquisite beauty which lay before them, heightened by the sound of the bird notes, was almost painful.

Some impulse made Mr. Brook turn from the pageant before him to look at Edith's face; there was a noble beauty in it which he had never seen before; her lips were trembling, and her eyes bright with tears.

The sun sank below the horizon; the rainbows faded, first the shadowy duplicate, and then the solid arch of color, which looked, while it lasted, strong enough to bear the weight of an adventurous climber; the joyous bird notes sank into sleepy good-night songs, and the growing dampness warned the spectators in. Roderick had been banished after the "one good look" which had been graciously permitted him.

" Now, when we have the veranda with the enclosed porch in the middle," he said, " we can sit and enjoy sunsets at our ease, and in the course of time, we can run it all around the house, with another porch at the back, so that we may have the benefit of the moonrisings as well. The view from the back is almost as good as that from the front."

Mr. Brook inquired why the enclosed porch was a necessity, and was enlightened as to the dangers of night-air; whereupon he suggested mildly to Edith, that, if sitting in the moonlight were an impossibility, he could not see any motive for the balconies upon which her heart was set, adding deferentially—

" You never heard, I am sure, Miss Stanley, of any balcony which was considered attractive in broad day-light—did you ? "

"I shall have striped awnings over them," replied Edith, in her most matter-of-fact tones, " and I shall keep a kerosene stove for the express purpose of drying the air on them whenever I wish to spend an evening looking at the moon.

If that is insufficient as a safeguard, I heard Aunt Judy say the other day that nobody can 'ketch de shakes' while holding a peppermint-lozenge in the mouth, and I shall try that!"

There was a general laugh at the vision which Edith's words conjured up, and Arnold murmured—

"'Lozenges I gave my love'—fancy Romeo saying, 'Sweets to the sweet!' and handing his Juliet a paper of peppermint-lozenges."

Mr. Brook shuddered visibly.

"I have nothing more to say on the subject of balconies," he said, resignedly. "The house shall bristle with them, if you please, Miss Stanley, without regard to their visible or invisible means of support, to the laws of architecture, or even to symmetry."

"I hope you all heard that," said Edith, triumphantly; "I may need some of you as witnesses, so please 'make a note of' it."

The next morning was faultless as to weather, and Edith persuaded the whole family to join her expedition, saying that she would probably need their moral support, as well as their testimony. The light and somewhat sandy soil had absorbed most of the puddles, and with overshoes the expedition could easily be made, even by Mrs. Stanley. The site which had been chosen for the house was about a quarter of a mile from the "Mansion," and Roderick for the first time rebelled a little against his tyrants.

"I'm sure that much of a walk, in this bracing air, would do me good rather than harm," he said, "and I really don't think Dr. West meant me to stay in the house forever, when he said I must be careful at first—I shall be obliged to appeal to him, I am afraid."

"Peace, perturbed spirit!" said Arnold, soothingly; "you shall go—I have thought of a way—possess your soul in patience for ten minutes. Mamma, will you marshal your hosts and lead them to victory? You stay with Rod till I come back, Ernest," and he ran quickly around the house.

Mrs. Stanley did as she was requested to do, only stopping to say to Roderick—

"You will do nothing imprudent, my son?"

"Not a thing, dear," he answered cheerfully, "if you'll forgive my grumbling. I won't attempt to walk there."

Arnold returned before the ten minutes were up, with the large wheel-barrow, which he had carefully brushed out, lined with a rug, and supplied with cushions from Roderick's lounge. He had provided a rope, with which he "hitched" Ernest to the back of the barrow, directing him to "go ahead and steer."

Roderick entered into the joke with spirit, and disposed himself as gracefully as he could in his stately coach, asking Arnold deferentially whether he would prefer his passenger to sit tailor-fashion, or let his legs hang down in front, or out over the back.

Arnold begged him to consult his own comfort, without reference to appearances, and Roderick said he would assume the attitude highest in favor at the Turkish court.

"Why, that's the same as tailor-fashion!" said Ernest, looking over his shoulder, as Roderick with some difficulty crossed his long legs in the narrow compass of the wheel-barrow.

"In everything but name, perhaps it is," admitted Roderick, "but there's a great deal in a name, I don't care what Shakspere or any body else says to the contrary!"

"I meant to bring the 'phaeton' at first," said Arnold, as he and Ernest pranced gaily along the edge of the wheatfield; "but I wasn't quite certain I could get it through the wood-lot, even by the fence, so I thought this would be

better.   Can you climb this fence, or shall we pull down a
panel, and wheel you through?"

"I should hope I could climb it," said Roderick, springing up almost as lightly as if no illness had weakened him,
and vaulting over the fence without farther preface or apology.   The wheel-barrow was lifted over, and the mettlesome
steeds made such good time, that they overtook the walking-
party just as it reached the boundary fence between the farm
and Mr. Stanley's lot, producing a sensation which satisfied
even Arnold.

The review of the situation, and the discussion which followed, ended in a compromise.   Edith yielded one balcony,
when she saw that it could not be made perfectly safe without a sacrifice of symmetry, and Mr. Brook gave a reluctant
consent to "put in" the three-story bow-window, continued
into a sort of tower, or observatory, enclosed in heavy sashes
containing single panes of plate-glass.

"It will look as if a bit of the conservatory had blown up
there," he said, resignedly; "and I must beg that you will
never mention me as the architect who designed this house
— I don't think it would be fair."

"Very well," said Edith, with a gracious smile; "your
wishes shall be regarded, of course, and if I am questioned,
I shall merely say that I designed it myself, with a little
assistance from a professional architect, whose intentions
were good, but who had never been called upon to live in a
house of his own planning.   Will that answer?"

"Perfectly," replied Mr. Brook; "it will amply account
for the—well, we will say the unprofessionalness of the
plan."

There was not so much as a single cloud to be seen, when
the hour arrived for driving Mr. Brook to the train, and although he was courteously invited to remain longer, he fancied
that it would have created some little surprise had he accepted

the invitation. His face brightened, however, when Mrs. Stanley told him with evident sincerity, that should business again call him to their neighborhood, she hoped he would consider their house his home, and he assured her earnestly that she had given him every reason to do so and that he would! It is needless to say that he cherished an inward conviction that business would call him there again—if not sooner, certainly not later, than the approaching summer.

Arnold and Ernest escorted him to the station on their own special vehicle, for the sun was warm, if the air was frosty again, and Mr. Brook clinched their regard for him, by the remark that driving in an open carriage nearly equaled riding. There was no intangible—or tangible—restraint in their hearty invitation to him to "come again as soon as ever he could, and stay longer the next time," and they parted with mutual good-will.

Mr. Brook hastened to report to Mr. Stanley, on his return, touching lightly on his forced march in the pouring rain, and speaking in the warmest terms of Mrs. Stanley, and all the family. It was an ideal home, he said, such as he had never before been privileged to enter.

"But do you mean to say," said Mr. Stanley, with a puzzled look, at the first pause, "that you *walked* all that distance from the station? How was it that they failed to meet you? I am certain that I wrote them of your intended coming."

"They had evidently received no intimation of it," said Mr. Brook. "The mails at this season are crowded, and perhaps——"

He was interrupted by a sudden exclamation of "Bless me!" from Mr. Stanley, who had been feeling in the pocket where he kept his letter case, and had drawn thence the "intimation," which he had certainly written, but as certainly never sent.

24

"I remember all about it now," he said, remorsefully. "I wrote it at home, and happened to have no stamps in my pocket, so I brought it down town with me, and something occurred which took all my thoughts for a few hours; when I did think of it again, I was under the impression that I had mailed it. My dear fellow, I don't know how to apologize to you!"

"Then pray do not attempt it," said Mr. Brook, with a most forgiving smile. "I assure you that I often take a walk of that length merely for exercise and pleasure, and in this case I should have been amply repaid for a far more arduous undertaking."

"It is very good of you to say so," said Mr. Stanley, gratefully.

"Would he continue to hold that opinion, if I were to say a little more on the subject, I wonder?" murmured Mr. Brook to himself as he returned to his neglected office.

CHAPTER XXX.

"Death is the port where all may refuge find,
The end of labor, entry unto rest."
EARL OF STERLINE.

A FEW days after Christmas, Randolph Peyton was idly turning over a newspaper which had just been sent to his mother from Philadelphia. A vague idea that he might chance to see something connected with Miss Neale made him smile at his own folly, but he started violently, and gave a sudden ejaculation of dismay, at sight of the name in the column of deaths. He was thankful that he happened to be alone in the room, for he felt his hands trembling as he tried to hold the paper steadily enough either to verify or contradict his fears. Another glance sufficed to do the latter; the death was, indeed, that of a "Winifred Neale," but "wife of the late Stuart Neale." It was, undoubtedly, Winifred's mother. He had never chanced to learn the street and number of Miss Neale's city home, and had been unable, when he parted from her last, to frame an excuse for asking a point-blank question; he only knew that Mrs. Neale lived with a sister-in-law. But he could not believe that this was merely a coincidence—the funeral was to be "from the residence of Miss Sarah Neale," on the very day upon which he was reading of the death, and he felt no doubt whatever on the subject. His first impulse was to go at once to Philadelphia, and he did not wait for it to cool, but here the weak side of his nature intervened; he was determined to go, and to let no arguments or considerations detain him, but he could not bring himself frankly to announce his reason for going. He had discovered the delusion about Elizabeth and himself, which was pleasing his parents, and that added to the shrinking which he felt from declaring the truth. There was still the same tone of gentle superiority, when his mother spoke to or of Miss Neale, which he would, not so long ago, have thought perfectly appropriate and correct, but which now nearly maddened him. He could not, he argued with himself, take the time for an explanation now, when, if he did not act promptly, he should be delayed for at least another twenty-four hours. He must devise some excuse—some reason which he could truthfully give for his sudden departure, and then, when he returned, he would have no more concealment about the matter, but would assert his intention, and take the consequences, should there be any of an unpleasant nature, which, he tried to persuade himself, was quite improbable, for surely his mother could not resist the arguments he could heap up in his favor.

He looked at his watch—he had only an hour left before he must start, if he would catch that day's train. He racked his brain for a reason which should sound plausible, and at last remembered that an old friend of his father's, an architect of high standing, had been interested in and for him, some years ago, and had cordially invited him to make use of their acquaintance, should he ever wish to settle in Philadelphia. He would go to this Mr. Lansing; and he hastily resolved that his going should not be a mere pretense, that if Winifred would give him the slightest encouragement, he would resume his studies in earnest, and settle in Philadelphia if he could find any promise of business there. All this he rapidly arranged in his mind, as he packed a valise, and ordered his horse and light carriage. Then he went to find his mother; his father he knew, was not at home, and on this he secretly congratulated himself—still more on the fact that he had a day or two before received the small quarterly payment of interest on his money.

His quiet answers to his mother's astonishment and hurried questions gave her the impression that his plan was the result of days of thought and deliberation, and her pride in him—which had been faltering of late—rose again as he unfolded his plan, or rather, the one of his plans which had been arranged to shield the other. She insisted upon adding a ten-dollar bill from her private store to the sum which he already had on hand, and upon examining his valise, to see if he had everything which he ought to have. When he returned to the parlor, with his preparations all made, and fifteen or twenty minutes yet to wait, before it should be time to start, he found Louise with the Philadelphia paper in her hand.

"O Randolph," she said, looking up with a shocked face, as he entered the room, "there is a death here which I am certain is Miss Neale's mother—it is the street and number which she told me, when I happened to ask one day whereabout in Philadelphia they lived."

"Are you sure it is the same?" asked Randolph, with an assumed indifference which completely misled both his sister and mother; "you know it is not at all an uncommon name, and you may not have remembered the street and number correctly."

"Yes, I have," said Louise, very positively; "and oh, how I pity her! It will nearly break her heart that she has been away from her mother all these weeks, when she must have been dying."

"It is very sad," said Mrs. Peyton, compassionately; "I have the highest regard for that young girl—she seems to be truly conscientious, and remarkably well-informed. You have never enjoyed your studies so much, I think, Louise, as you have since she took charge of them, and your improvement in music is something remarkable. I hope this will not interfere with her return to Mrs. Stanley's."

"Mamma!" cried Louise, impetuously, and with tears starting from her eyes as she spoke; "how *can* you talk so indifferently about it—as if she were somebody in another world? She is the sweetest, the loveliest girl, with more refinement in her little finger, than there is in the whole of the girls I visit, and am expected to treat as my equals. I shall always be ashamed of the fine-lady airs I put on when I first met her, although she has never, by word or look, let me see that she noticed them."

Before Mrs. Peyton could reply to this sudden charge, which filled her with astonishment, Randolph drew Louise to his side, and kissed her tenderly.

"Good-by, my brave little sister," he said, with a look of affection which delighted her heart; "I shall come to you when I need a champion."

"Oh, Randolph!" she said, detaining him, "*won't* you go and see her, and give her my dear love, and tell her how very, very sorry I am ?"

"I will, my dear," he said promptly, "and I will love you better from to-day than I ever did before. Good-by, mother —tell father good-by for me, please—I will write you what day to send to the station for me."

"My boy, I meant no unkindness to Miss Neale," she said, hurriedly; "if you see her, give her my love and sincere sympathy, and do not think hardly of me for an imagination of Louise's. Good-by—write and let me know that you made the journey safely, my dear son."

His resentment vanished as she looked in his eyes with anxious love, and he kissed the beautiful old face with a tenderness deepened by compunction. Surely he need have had no concealment from her, even if it were necessary with others.

He did not feel especially proud of himself, as he drove away. He knew perfectly well, in his inmost heart, that he should have denounced his conduct as cowardly and sneaking, had it been that of any one else, and he was glad to make conversation with Pete, to beguile the drive, and to lose himself in a novel, which he hastened to purchase from the train boy, as the train sped on, and he felt that the question of his going was settled.

Winifred had made the same journey a few days before, with a light heart and joyous anticipations. She had not been able, in her letters, she felt sure, to convey to her mother and aunt any real knowledge of her happy situation —she could spend days in describing the Stanleys, the house, the neighborhood, the people she had chanced to meet. Safe in her purse was her salary for the time of her stay at Green Point—she had meant only to ask for enough to pay her passage home and back, but Mrs. Stanley, before Winifred found an opportunity to do this, had handed her the whole amount. In her trunk were the pretty presents, long ago finished, for her mother and aunt—a beautiful water-color of the house at Green Point, in a neat ebonized frame which Arnold had surprised her with, having accidentally learned about the drawing. This was for her mother ; for her aunt she had knitted a soft white shawl, large enough to be really useful, but feathery-light. She did not care to read—her mind was full of thoughts far pleasanter than anything she could find in a book. How thankful, and yet how humble, she felt, as she remembered the tears and bitterness of heart which had attended her departure, and thought of the abounding charity which had met her repentance, forgetting as well as forgiving. She had never been able to bring herself to write about it, but she could tell her mother the whole story, sure of loving sympathy.

The journey seemed far shorter than it had seemed in

going, and she did not even feel tired when she reached her aunt's door. The meeting was as joyful as the anticipation had been, and she was delighted to see how much better her mother was looking than when they had parted. Her eyes were bright, there was a faint color in her cheeks, and she was dressed with a care and taste which made Winifred glad —she must surely be a great deal stronger than she was three months ago, when it exhausted her to dress in a simple wrapper. But as the evening advanced, and the first excitement of the meeting wore off, Winifred's joy began to change to an anxious foreboding. Not only had the pretty color left her mother's face, but a peculiar pallor, such as Winifred had never before seen there, had taken its place. She talked very little, and moved with a sort of deliberate slowness which puzzled her daughter. Shortly after nine o'clock in the evening Mrs. Neale rose, and said playfully that it was her bed-time, but that Winifred might come and sit with her until she was ready to go to sleep, and might act as lady's-maid, even though she were ignorant of the art of hair-dressing! Mrs. Neale's feebleness became more and more apparent, as she made the slight exertion which was all her daughter's loving care allowed, and she seemed too exhausted to speak, when her head sunk upon the pillow. Winifred waited, holding the thin hand closely clasped in her own, until she felt sure that her mother slept; then she hastened to find her aunt. Miss Neale had gone to her room, but she opened the door and called Winifred in, whispering as she did so—

"Is your mother asleep, dear? Did she take her wine? I left it all poured out, on the little stand."

"Yes, she took it, aunty," replied Winifred, closing the door, "but oh, what is it? What has happened? Tell me all the truth about mamma."

Miss Neale's kind eyes filled with tears. "My dear," she

faltered, "there is very little to tell; your dear mother suffers no pain, none at all, I assure you; but—she is very weak, and the excitement of your coming has probably been too much for her. She will be better to-morrow; but we must induce her to keep quiet, and not to exert herself to dress, as she did to-day. It was too much for her."

"Aunt Sarah," said Winifred, taking the old lady's hands, and looking steadily in her eyes, "you are concealing something from me. You mean it kindly, but it is not kind. Tell me the whole truth, please."

Miss Neale stood silent, with quivering lips.

"Is mamma—dying?" asked Winifred, controlling her voice by a mighty effort.

Miss Neale nodded silently—she could not speak without crying, and she was determined not to cry, but the look in Winifred's eyes overcame her resolution, and she dropped her head on her niece's shoulder, sobbing bitterly. Winifred stood silent, with her arm about her aunt, until the sobs ceased, and then she said quietly—

"Now, come sit down, dear, and tell me all about it—you see I am very still—I will not make any noise, or disturb mother."

"I noticed the change in her color soon after you went away," said Miss Neale, trying to speak steadily. "I couldn't love her more, Winny, if she were my sister twice over—so brave, so patient, so helpful, in all her weakness and distress. She is a mother to be proud of, my darling! I sent for a doctor at once—not that vulgar man who made you sell your watch, but a *gentleman*, and one who knows his business, too. I never saw anybody gentler and kinder than he was. He stayed an hour, though he's overrun with practice, and cuts most people short, I hear; but he told me he knew my brother well, and that a more honorable man never lived; and he treated your mother as if she were a

duchess—or no, not that, either, for they say he snubs the
ones who think they ought to be treated that way. At any
rate, he just talked with her, easily and kindly and cheerfully, for I heard her laugh, which she had not done for
many a day. I sat at the other end of the parlor, so that I
couldn't hear half he said, but I saw that he asked her a
question every once in a while, and that he was watching
her like a hawk ; and from a word here and there, I guessed
that he had led her on to tell him all about you. When he
got up to go, he said he should not say good-by, for he was
coming again soon, to talk over old times with her—he and
your father went to school together, it seems. I went out of
the other door, while he was shaking hands with your
mother, and nabbed him in the hall; he didn't wait for me
to ask—he just took my hand, and said,

"'There is no need to agitate your sister—I think she is
ready for any change that may come, but *you* ought to know
that she has a disease of the heart which may end her life at
any moment.'" Miss Neale's voice quivered into silence
with the last word, but Winifred said quietly—

"Did he say nothing more ?"

"Yes," returned her aunt, with an effort. "He said that
she must be kept free from all exertion and anxiety and
excitement, and that she might live for several years, but
that she might—go—at any time."

"How long ago was this ?"

"I don't remember exactly, dear ; it was soon after you
went."

"Why have you never told me of it ? Didn't you *know*
that I would rather have gone out as a servant, begged,
even, than to have been parted from her if I had known the
truth ?"

"My dear, my dear, don't look at me so ! It was she
herself who said that you must not be told—she made the

doctor tell her all about it, when he came again, a few days afterward; he found she had pretty nearly guessed the truth, and that she was perfectly composed about it. She asked if there would probably be any warning, and he said yes, that the breathless feeling would, he thought, increase just before the end, but he couldn't be positively certain, although in most cases it did. So then she said that not a word of it must be written to you unless you asked some question which could not be evaded; that you were happier, she could see by your letters, than you had any hope of being, and that you must not be disturbed, unless she should have the warning of which the doctor spoke; then, she said, you should be sent for at once."

"You ought not to have obeyed her—you should have written to me at all hazards."

"My dear," said Miss Neale, piteously, "you are unkind! You would have rushed home at once, if I had written, and there would have been a scene, and she would have been all shaken up, and very likely not have lived another day, and now you blame me, when the Lord knows—I don't say it irreverently—that I prayed, and cried, and thought over it all, all day, and often half the night. But it's always the way!"

"Oh aunty, forgive me, forgive me!" entreated Winifred, taking the sobbing woman in her arms. "I hardly know what I am saying—it all seems so dreadful, so impossible! You have been everything kind and good—oh, please say that you forgive me!"

"Of course I do, you poor child," and Miss Neale stopped crying that she might comfort Winifred. "Say any thing you please, I shall not mind it at all, if it'll do you any good."

"Do you think," asked Winifred, fearfully, "that she seemed worse than usual to-night? I helped her to undress in every way, but she could not speak when she first laid down, and her breathing was more like panting."

"I am afraid she is," said Miss Neale, drawing her niece closer as she spoke; "I noticed yesterday that she could only say a few words at a time; and last night, when I helped her to bed, she said to me, smiling, too—

"'Winny will be in time, Sarah, but not much more, I think.'

"Yet she would dress for you this afternoon, though she was more than an hour doing it, for she said she wished you to be told quietly, not to find it out the minute you saw her face."

"I must go back," said Winifred, rising hastily; "she may want something."

"She did not seem to wish me to sleep in the room," said Miss Neale, "though I do believe, now, that it was because she was afraid of disturbing me—so I arranged a bell to ring in my room, and always left the handle of the cord close by her on her little table, but she never has rung for me yet. She asked me to put you in the spare room, dear; it's all ready for you, and I'll call you in a minute, if she rings."

"I can't go, aunty; I *can't.* Give me a quilt or blanket, and I will creep in and lie on the lounge; she will not hear me, and then I can listen—perhaps she might want us and not have strength to pull the bell."

"Very well, dear," replied her aunt; "I don't wonder you feel so—here, you shall have my warm wrapper, and do try to sleep—you must be tired out after your journey."

"No, I slept a good deal on the cars—don't make me too comfortable, aunty, or I may fall asleep without knowing it."

She managed to steal unperceived into her mother's room, and saw, by the faintly-burning light, that Mrs. Neale was sleeping peacefully, so she lay down upon the lounge, sure of not closing her eyes. But she was more tired than she knew, and dazed and bewildered with sudden grief besides, and it seemed to her but a few minutes after she entered the room when she woke to find it full of sunshine, and her mother bending over her.

"Mother!" she said, springing up as she saw the loving smile on her mother's face; "did I dream—it isn't true?" she stopped bewildered, and her mother said gently—

"A happy Christmas to you, my darling! It is almost breakfast time, and we must not keep Aunt Sarah waiting."

She paused a few minutes, and then added—

"After breakfast we will talk—now, will you help me a little before you dress yourself?"

She made no comment upon having found Winifred upon the lounge, and spoke but little while they dressed, or at the breakfast-table, but she was calm and cheerful, and Winifred did her best to talk and smile as usual.

"Shall you go to church, dear?" Mrs. Neale inquired, when breakfast was over.

"No, mother, I don't think I shall," replied Winifred; "I should grudge the time spent away from you—you know my holiday will slip away before we know it, and there is so much talking to do."

"Very well, darling," said her mother; "I am only too glad to keep you, and you will not lose the whole service— Mr. Young has been very attentive and kind, and he promised to come this evening and give me the communion."

"I am very glad," said Winifred, controlling her voice with an effort; "you must not try to go to church until you are stronger, darling."

Mrs. Neale was as much delighted with Winifred's gift as her daughter had hoped she would be, and seemed especially touched and pleased with the history of the frame.

Miss Neale kept the pretty shawl on her lap nearly all day, stroking it at intervals as if it had been a kitten, and wondering how and when her niece found time to make it. She gave Winifred a quaintly set opal ring, which had been stored away among her treasures for many years, overruling all remonstrances with—

"I've nobody but you and your mother, child—you'll have it one day, and why shouldn't *I* have the pleasure of seeing you wear it?"

Mrs. Neale's gift was some delicate embroidery, done at intervals, as her strength had permitted, since Winifred went away.

"I have nothing but my work and my love to give you, darling," she said; "but I know you will value both beyond their worth."

She seemed tranquilly happy all day, and not very much exhausted by the service which Mr. Young held, towards evening, in the parlor. He stayed awhile after it was concluded, talking gently with her, and leaving them with that beautiful benediction—

"The peace of God, which passeth all understanding, keep your hearts and minds in the knowledge and love of God; and the blessing of God Almighty, the Father, the Son, and the Holy Ghost be amongst you and remain with you always. Amen."

Winifred begged her mother to go to bed before tea, and have it brought to her, but Mrs. Neale said she would rather come to the table, and that she would go to bed soon afterward. By this time Winifred began to think that perhaps her fears of any immediate danger were exaggerated, but she again took her place on the lounge, and her mother made no objection.

She had only slept an hour, when her mother's voice waked her, and she sprang to the bedside.

"Dear, lift me up," said Mrs. Neale, pausing for breath between every two words; and Winifred raised her gently, at the same time pulling the bell. Mrs. Neale fixed her eyes on her daughter's face with a loving smile.

"Kiss me, darling," she whispered; "you have been very brave, very good. There shall be no night——" Her voice ceased, and even while Winifred listened breathlessly for the next word, she was "away."

CHAPTER XXXI.

"Madness and anger differ but in this,
This is short madness, that long anger is."—CHARLES ALEYN.

WHEN Randolph Peyton rang the bell of Miss Neale's house the day but one after the funeral, he meant to be very calm, very prudent. But when Winifred entered the parlor and came toward him, pale and silent, with a pitiful attempt at a smile upon her face, everything was forgotten, save her trouble and his love.

"My poor darling," he said, and had her in his arms as he spoke. She did not resist, but, with her head upon his shoulder, "cried her heart out" for the first time since her mother's death. A very few words, as she grew quiet, sealed the bond between them. As has been said, her character, with all its beauty, lacked strength, and now when she was crushed with a hopeless sorrow it did not seem to her possible to refuse the comfort of his love. Nothing was said about the future for several days, and in the meantime Randolph had called upon Mr. Lansing, and met with the kindest encouragement. No allusion was made to the months of wasted time which had passed since the latter made his offer—it was renewed with gratifying promptness. Randolph displayed two or three drawings, which he had taken the precaution to bring with him, and the successful architect, whose business was beginning to weigh upon him a little too heavily, offered the young man a small salary at once, to be increased with his proficiency, and even hinted something about "taking him into the concern one of these days."

Highly elated, Randolph formed a sudden and rash resolution. He wrote a hurried note to his mother, telling her of his success, and asking to have the carriage sent to meet him the third day from that on which he wrote. It would of course, he said, be necessary for him to live in Philadelphia, at least for the present, but he would first return for his clothes and books, and for a less hurried and unsatisfactory farewell.

Then he went to Winifred, and, for the first time since their engagement, asked her if she had made any plans.

"Yes," she answered, sadly; "it was necessary that I should. I discovered that Aunt Sarah has for some time had a good offer for this house, and I am quite sure she would have accepted it, but for—us. I will not let her lose another day about it, for fear it should be withdrawn, so I shall go back to Mrs. Stanley next week—it is the only thing for me to do, and no doubt the best thing. I shall have less time for thinking."

"But you cannot, you shall not, go back to that drudgery!" said Randolph, warmly. "It was bad enough before, but now! No, Winifred, listen to me. You know I have a small income—almost enough for us to live upon, if we are very careful, and Mr. Lansing has promised me three hundred a year, to begin with, and more, as my services become more valuable—he even hinted about taking me into the firm some day. So it is very plain what you must do. We must be married at once—to-morrow at the latest—and then I will take you home with me, and present you as my wife, before they can say anything about prudence, and economy, and waiting till I am fairly started. Why, I am fairly started!"

"That is not all they would say," said Winifred, a bright flush passing over her pale face. "I know what your mother thinks about the difference in our rank, quite as well as if she had told me, and I do not blame her—it is the result of

25

all her traditions—you must first win her consent, dear, and then, I don't care how poor you are, or how we have to contrive, I am ready, for—I love you."

"My darling!" he cried, impatiently. "If you loved me as much as I love you, you could not talk in this cool way. You are not a teacher now—you shall not be again, and when you are my wife, you will take what my mother chooses to consider our 'rank'—— save the mark! You shall *not* go to teaching again! Wait—where is Miss Neale?" and he was gone in search of her before Winifred could remonstrate.

He returned with her in half-an-hour, flushed and triumphant.

"Now talk to this unreasonable woman, Aunt Sarah," he said, leading Miss Neale to the sofa, and seating her beside Winifred; and the gratified old lady, whom, by a little judicious flattery, and his own version of the case—given, as he believed, quite honestly—he had completely won over to his cause, did talk.

"I don't see why you should refuse to do as Mr. Peyton——"

"Randolph, you mean, Aunt Sarah."

"Well, as Randolph wishes, Winny. You say you won't come and board where I am going, though you know I'd love to have you, and you're no more fit than a kitten to go back there and teach, after all you've been through. You needn't shake your head—you're not, and you might just as well marry Mr.—Randolph now, as to keep him on tenterhooks while you wear yourself out with your obstinacy. Now look here—I'll slip round this afternoon, and tell Mr. Young all he need know about it, and to-morrow afternoon you and—Randolph shall just be here quietly in the parlor, with nobody but me, and he shall come and marry you, and you'll not know anything about it hardly, before it's out—over, I mean! Bless me, I must have been thinking of the dentist!

I wouldn't be contrary about it, if I was you. It's all non-sense about his family opposing it, when they sent you such sweet messages, and even begged him to come and see you! Come, deary, be sensible!"

Randolph seized her hand, and bent his face to hers. There was a laughing light in his eyes.

"Darling!" he whispered. "Don't be 'contrary!'"

And Winifred, unequal to opposing them both, as Randolph had guessed that she would be, wavered, faltered—and consented.

Three days afterward the Peyton carriage met them at the station, and Winifred felt herself blushing under the wondering gaze of the old coachman. But she was very pale when she reached Rivermouth; she was beginning to realize all the possibilities which Randolph's specious reasoning had veiled from her.

Randolph was brave with the brief and sudden courage which often comes to a weak nature. He seized her hands as the carriage stopped, and whispered, smiling—

"Don't look so terrified, my darling! It is not a den of ogres that you are entering."

She smiled faintly in return, but there was a choking sensation in her throat which forbade her speaking.

Louise had been standing at the window, and as she saw them alight, she turned with a wondering face to her father and mother, saying—

"Why, there is Miss Neale with Randolph, and she looks like death!"

"Poor thing!" said the Colonel, compassionately; "I am glad she availed herself of his escort, and that he was thoughtful enough to make her stop here and rest a little—we'll send her over to Green Point this evening, or to-morrow. It was very hard on her to have to come back so soon to her teaching."

"But papa!" said Louise, hurriedly; "she wasn't coming till next week——"

"Oh well," said Mrs. Peyton—for the Colonel had gone to meet the travelers—"perhaps she found her aunt was going to give up the house at once, and preferred to come back to Mrs. Stanley—poor child, I don't wonder; it must be awful to have no home!"

Conviction of the truth had flashed through Louise's mind as she saw Randolph lift his wife from the carriage; there was but a moment more——

"Mamma!" she exclaimed, "be kind to her—promise me that, however it is, you'll be kind."

"My child, of course I will!" said Mrs. Peyton, surprised by Louise's vehemence, and before anything more could be said, they were in the parlor, and as Colonel Peyton closed the door after them, Randolph took Winifred's trembling hand, and led her to his mother, saying—

"Mother, I bring you my wife. Father, here is another daughter for you. Louise——"

Louise took Winifred in her arms before any more could be said, and kissed her heartily, exclaiming as she did so—

"I am so glad! Dear Winifred, dear sister, I love you very much!"

But the Colonel's face darkened.

"Louisa, leave the room!" he said, sternly, and Louise dared not disobey him; but as she went, Randolph turned and kissed her fervently, saying—

"God bless you for this, little sister."

"Now tell me what this theatrical performance means," said the Colonel, slowly, and frowning heavily as he spoke.

"I mean exactly what I have said, sir," said Randolph, haughtily, and drawing Winifred to his side; "Miss Neale, at my earnest entreaty, and with the sanction of her aunt, became my wife day before yesterday, and I brought her

home, expecting to be received at least with common courtesy. I see I was mistaken in my estimate of my family—
excepting Louise, God bless her!—and as soon as I can
collect my books and clothing, I will trouble you no more—
come, my darling, you will be safe in my room while I make
my preparations, and Mrs. Stanley will shelter us till to-
morrow—come!"

"Stop!" said the Colonel, his voice falling, instead of
rising, as his anger deepened. " Before you accuse me of
discourtesy, explain, if you can, the duplicity which you
have practised toward your mother and myself. For weeks
past you have been paying marked attention to Miss Stanley.
We believed, and you allowed us to believe, that your atten-
tions were acceptable to her, and that you would ultimately
marry her. You have given not the remotest hint of any
partiality for this—this designing young——"

" I will not listen to this language, even from the man
who calls himself my father!" broke in Randolph, furiously.
"Since my word goes for nothing, ask Elizabeth Stanley,
and she will tell you that all our talk, whenever we met, and
there was the least opportunity, was of the lady who has
honored me by becoming my wife. I never spoke one word
of love to her, nor she to me. It was your own fancy, to
delude yourself into a belief that your wishes were facts.
Now I will hear no more—I will leave you, to return only
when you see fit to apologize for your insulting, your un-
gentlemanly language. Come, Winifred, my darling!"

He caught the trembling girl by the hand, and strode
from the room with her. Mrs. Peyton, who had vainly tried
to stem the torrent of his indignation, and make herself
heard, sprang up to follow them, but the Colonel, thoroughly
aroused, and with all the more deadly effect because of his
usual easy good humor, stood with his back against the
door.

"You will stay where you are, Susan," he said, sternly, "until that puppy and the woman who has made a fool of him have left the house. And after they have left it, you will make no attempt to communicate with them; and if you make any such attempt, I will see that it is frustrated. No woman with any self-respect could have turned from her mother's grave to write a lying letter, and consent to a clandestine marriage with a man whom she dared not attempt to marry openly."

Mrs. Peyton sat silent, stunned, and crushed. She knew that opposition would only make her husband more determined, and, dazed as she was, she was still conscious enough to avoid this danger. She began feebly planning in her mind how she might contrive to see them before they went, next day, hoping as she did so that Louise was with them even now, and that this possibility might not occur to the Colonel. It had occurred to him already, but he had chosen what he considered the least of two evils—Louise had openly sided with the rebels, and her feeble support could do them no good, but, were his wife's joined with it, he would be left in the minority, and he had a fear unacknowledged even to himself, that he might be brought to yield, or at least to compromise. His conscience told him that Randolph had spoken the truth—although much too tardily—that there had been no real ground for their belief about Elizabeth Stanley, or so little that only their earnest wishes had led them to build upon it. It told him also that Winifred was not a designing woman.

He had, from the first, been attracted by her refinement and modesty, and his naturally kind heart smote him, as he recalled her pale and terror-stricken face. He was on the point of yielding—not in his own person, pride was too strong in him to permit that, just yet, but so far as to let his wife go to them; no doubt her tears and entreaties would have their effect upon Randolph, whose moods, of any kind, never lasted long, and—he did not know just how he would act, but perhaps, at any rate, he would permit them to stay long enough to avoid anything like publicity about the affair, and, after their return to Philadelphia, it need only be said that they were married privately, on account of the recent death of Winifred's mother, and that a favorable business-opportunity had induced Randolph to settle in Philadelphia. He had reached this point in his meditations, and his wife, intently watching his face, had understood him almost as well as if he had thought aloud, when the sudden sounds of the closing of the front door, and driving away of the carriage, which Randolph had ordered back to the door before the horses had been taken out, told them both that his relenting had come too late. At the same moment, Louise returned to the parlor, with eyes red from crying, and before they could speak, she exclaimed indignantly—

"You might have believed Randolph, papa! You might have given her a chance to defend herself! She *did* write Mrs. Stanley, the day after her mother died, that she would come back either this week or next, but when Randolph persuaded her to marry him at once, and won her aunt over to help him, and told her, mamma and I had sent our love to her, as we had—you remember we had, mamma—the poor child was so bewildered, and troubled for fear she was doing wrong, that she forgot all about having written the letter, until it was too late to write again. And I don't wonder at all—her aunt's house was to be sold in a few days, and Winifred was obliged either to go straight back to her teaching, or let her aunt, who isn't rich at all, and has been very generous to her, pay her board; and then Randolph came, and you know well enough how he can 'talk the bird off the bush,' when he chooses to try, and he won her aunt over to side with him, and they arranged it all, and just walked her into the parlor and married her, and she loves Randolph so dearly, that all she cares about, now, is that what they have done will hurt him!"

Louise stopped to cry again, and Mrs. Peyton cried with her, while the Colonel, but a moment before ready to yield, stiffened into rage again at Louise's reproachful tone.

"And you uphold this cowardly, underhand proceeding?" he said, sternly. "That woman's teaching and example are bearing fruit already, I perceive! What was there to hinder your brother from coming to me like a man, and telling me of his intention before he left home, instead of hiding behind the pretense of going to see Mr. Lansing?"

"It was not a pretense," said Louise, indignantly. "He has told me all about it, and it was only after Mr. Lansing had offered him three hundred dollars a year, that he asked Winifred to marry him right away."

"Can he, or can you, say truthfully that he had not engaged himself to her before that, or that his chief motive in going to Philadelphia was not to see her?"

Louise was silent.

"Then let me hear no more of the matter," said the Colonel, speaking still more sternly from the disappointment of not being contradicted. "As I said to your mother, so I say to you—you are to hold no communication of any kind with your brother and—that woman, until I shall give you permission to do so; any attempt that you may make will be foiled. You have spoken to me with the utmost disrespect and insubordination. You can go to your room, and remain there till to-morrow morning."

"I shall be *glad* to remain there!" she cried, passionately. "You are unjust, cruel—and oh, I am so glad that Isabel is at the Stanleys; she will read my note, and *she* will believe me, and give Winifred a sister's welcome, and——"

"Go!" said the Colonel, suddenly interrupting her, and Louise, excited as she was, dared not disobey him.

He sat down before his desk, as she left the room, and wrote a hasty note, which he directed to Isabel. Then he rang for one of the "boys" who worked about the stable, and told him to saddle Sultan—Randolph's special riding-horse—and ride as rapidly as he could to Green Point with the note. "If you reach there before the carriage does," he said, "I will give you a dollar, and a whole holiday to-morrow ; but if you fail to do so, bring the note back to me —it will be useless if the carriage arrives there first. I shall not blame you if you fail to pass the carriage," he said, kindly, "but it will be to your own interest to try."

In less than five minutes, the Colonel heard rapid hoof-beats, as Sultan galloped down the road, and he smiled grimly to himself. The carriage-horses were tired with their jour-ney to the station, and Sultan had not been used since Randolph went away.

The note contained only the words :

"I wish you to return at once in the carriage. Any delay that you may make, farther than the few minutes which you find absolutely necessary, will be an act of deliberate dis-obedience to your father."

It was after eight o'clock when the carriage once more drove up to the house, and Isabel alighted from it. She had been spending the day, and had expected to spend the night, at Green Point, and was very much startled by her father's note, the abruptness of which made her fear that some sudden disaster had taken place at home. She made her few preparations in trembling haste, and sat waiting anxiously for the carriage. She had some little time to wait, for Sultan, in wild spirits at being once more upon the road, had needed no urging beyond a free rein, and had easily overtaken and distanced the carriage. When the lat-

ter arrived, and Randolph and Winifred alighted, her first
idea was that which had misled the Colonel—she thought
that her brother, in his compassion for Winifred, had volunteered to escort her on the journey which would otherwise
be so forlornly lonesome.   She greeted Winifred with warm
kindliness, and then stepped hastily into the carriage, waiting impatiently for Randolph to follow her, that she might
question him as to the cause of her summons.   To her utter
astonishment, he thrust a note into her hand, and said,
impatiently—

"Read it, Isabel—there is no such wonderful hurry for
you to go, is there?"

"I must," she said, anxiously.   "Papa has written me not
to delay an unnecessary moment—oh, what has happened,
Randolph?   Why don't you get in, and let us go?"

"Nothing has happened that need affect you," he said
bitterly, closing the carriage-door as he spoke.   "Drive on,
Pete," he added to the coachman, who at once turned his
horses and obeyed, chiefly concerned about his supper, which
he feared he should miss at both ends of the line, and which
he had been flattering himself he should enjoy with Aunt
Judy.

Isabel tore open Louise's note, read it, and cried quietly
all the way home.

Her father said nothing to her, beyond a few brief words
of greeting, until he bade her good-night.   His anger had
subsided by that time to a quiet, but settled displeasure, and
he told her, as he had told her mother and sister, that she
was to have absolutely nothing to do with her brother and.
his wife.   Mrs. Peyton, who was present when he spoke,
noticed, with faint hopefulness, that he did not again speak
of Winifred as "that woman."

"You must not fancy, Isabel," he continued, "that they
are martyrs; your brother will continue to receive the in-

come which has been his, independently of me, since he came of age, and beside that—he says—a salary of three hundred dollars a year, to be increased in time. When he sees fit to apologize to me for the gross deceitfulness of his conduct, and the insolent language which he used to-day, I will try to receive him and his wife as if nothing had been amiss, although I can never regard him with perfect confidence, or her with more than toleration; but until he offers me and your mother the apology which he owes us, of his own free will and accord, I do not wish his name, or that of his wife, mentioned in my presence, and it will be quite useless for any of you to attempt to correspond with them."

Isabel made no reply, but the Colonel was more deeply wounded than any of them imagined by the cold constraint of their manner when they bade him good-night.

Meanwhile, the arrival of Randolph and Winifred at Green Point had created almost as much of a sensation as that occasioned by their advent at Rivermouth. The general impression, at first, was the natural one already twice produced; but Randolph lost no time in correcting this, and appealing to Mrs. Stanley for sympathy. Winifred's white and stricken face made it impossible for any of them to harbor a harsh thought concerning her, and the girls in a body carried her off to pet and comfort, leaving Mrs. Stanley and Randolph alone.

"You must see, Mrs. Stanley," said the latter, pacing the floor in restless excitement as he spoke, "how cruel and unjust my father's conduct has been! You surely cannot blame me for refusing to be the first to attempt a reconciliation. When he chooses to apologize for the insulting language he used to-day, I will accept his apology; but it is the insult to my wife—who is an angel of goodness—which I resent far more than that to myself, and which must be retracted, before I can advance a step toward making peace. Surely you agree with me!" he added, impatiently, as Mrs. Stanley remained silent.

"You must forgive me," she said, gently, "if the frankness with which you have spoken induces me to be equally frank. I admit, freely, that it will be hard for you to forgive, and still harder for you to forget, your father's words to-day; but what I wish you to do is, simply to try to put yourself in his place. He has a keen sense of honor, and is rigidly truthful; whatever the real facts may be—and I do not pretend to judge concerning them—your conduct had the appearance of deceit, and a total want of confidence in your best friends. An open declaration of your intentions might, and probably would, have made him angry, but it could never have wounded him as concealment, or what he believes to be concealment, has done. Can you not see this?"

His answer was consistent with the want of candor which was inherent in him: "All this may be true," he said, gloomily; "but he has no right to make the innocent suffer for the guilty. He spoke of Winifred as if she were an adventuress, who had led me into a marriage, whether I would or no, when he knew—he *must* have known, even from the little he had seen and heard of her—that this could not be true. If he will apologize for that, I am quite willing to overlook what he said to me about myself."

"Then write and tell him so, my dear boy," said Mrs. Stanley, eagerly; "write respectfully, as a son should write to a father whom he has deeply wounded, and apologize for what you know to be wrong in your conduct. State clearly and fully all that you have told me of the persuasions you used, the assertions you made, to induce Winifred to consent to this hasty marriage, which would have been most creditable to your heart, if not your head, had you only spoken openly of it beforehand. Your father is warm-hearted, if he is quick-tempered; and if you tell him, as you told me just now, of the desolation in which you found the poor child, his heart, I know, will be touched. Do this, I beg of you, and then wait patiently here for his reply."

In her earnestness she laid her hand kindly upon Randolph's shoulder. He caught it in his own, and pressed a kiss on it, and she thought he had yielded, but he said —

"You are very kind; I shall always love you for your kindness to my darling and to me, but I cannot do what you ask. I will send my address to you, after we return to Philadelphia, and you can, if you think it best, give it to my father. One line of acknowledgment from him will bring all he could wish from me; but after what he has said to-day, I cannot be the first to speak."

Mrs. Stanley saw that all further remonstrance would be useless, and said nothing more upon the subject. Nor did she in any way reproach Winifred, for she saw how very little the poor child had been to blame. The children, including Elizabeth, Edith, and Roderick would not admit even that little, and parted from Winifred with the warmest good-will, and Mrs. Stanley made no effort to convince them of her view of the matter—the deed was done, past helping, and all the comfort which the poor little wife could gather, before setting out upon her perilous life voyage, would be none too much, Mrs. Stanley thought, and thought rightly.

CHAPTER XXXII.

"The deepest ice that ever froze
Can only o'er the surface close;
The living stream lies quick below,
And flows, and cannot cease to flow."—BYRON.

"I SHOULD just like to know," said Kitty, when the excitement caused by Winifred's marriage had subsided a little, "what we poor orphans are to do for a governess. Shall you advertise again, Betty?"

"I don't know," said Elizabeth, doubtfully, "I feel almost afraid to; if I do, it shall be an 'iron-clad' advertisement, and I will engage nobody without first managing to have a personal interview with her."

"Now why, necessarily, 'her'?" said Kitty, in an argumentative tone; "I personally should ride off on my vaulting ambition in a way that would astonish you, if I might also have the pleasure of astonishing a pleasing tutor. Do not look so righteous, dear Elizabeth; I have no wish for anything but a truly Platonic teacher—a man with his head in the clouds and his heart in the highlands, or anywhere else that he likes. But there is a scope, a strength, about the manly intellect, which is, I fear, not to be found in that of the ordinary governess, and we can't afford any more extraordinary ones, if we wish to preserve the friendship of our neighbors. It is an astonishing thing to me that the Peytons didn't send us to Coventry—it argues well for the height of their minds."

Mrs. Stanley had written a frank and affectionate note to Mrs. Peyton, pleading Winifred's cause, but saying nothing of Randolph which she could well avoid saying. This note Mrs. Peyton had, with many misgivings, handed to the Colonel, who had silently read and returned it; but that evening he had suddenly said, "No blame can justly be imputed to Mrs. Stanley or her family. It was not her place to warn us, and anything she might have said would, in all probability, only have hastened the end. She could not refuse her hospitality, when it was rudely claimed. It is my wish, Susan, that our friendship shall remain unbroken; but it will be better for you to let her know at once that, to this end, the subject of her note must never again be mentioned between us. When she encloses the address of which she speaks, you will instantly burn it, keeping no copy."

Mrs. Peyton wrote from the fulness of her heart to Mrs. Stanley, assuring her that the moment Colonel Peyton relented, she and her daughters would joyfully welcome back both Randolph and his wife; but that, until that time came, it would be worse than useless to agitate the subject.

Isabel returned with Edith to B——, and Louise, cut off from the lessons she had so enjoyed and from the daily intercourse with the friends who had put so much brightness into her life, went sadly about the house, studying and practising fitfully, but without much interest in either books or music.

Kitty, whose mischief-loving mind was never idle, returned to the charge about her imaginary tutor, and, after airing her views on the subject two or three times, exclaimed one day in a tone of settled conviction—

"I have it! It takes me to evolve brilliant ideas from my scintillating inner consciousness. Mr. Kendall is the man for our dear sister's butter-money! We will offer

him what we offered poor dear Winifred, *and* his board—it
is quite as much, I imagine, as the school-committee gives
him, and just think how much better the board will be!
Why don't you all applaud me?   Betty, what do *you* say
to this excellent plan ?"

"That you are a goose, dear," said Elizabeth, smiling, but
not blushing, or looking in the least confused, and continuing to sew tranquilly.

"'Crushed again,'" said Kitty, dramatically; "if I had
not the most elastic, as well as the sweetest of dispositions,
I should have been permanently flattened out, long, long
ago.   But, dear sister, assertion is not argument."

"Why, Kitty!" said Polly, "rising," as Kitty hoped she
would, "the idea of Mr. Kendall going out as a governess!
Why it's perfectly preposterous!".

"You darling! you enchanting little lamb!" cried Kitty,
rapturously; "I shall yet be compelled to educate you for
the stage, and write a few plays for your starring.   You
would bring down the house—the city—the whole world!"

Polly was at last beginning to discover Kitty's designs
upon her, although, so far, she had only made the discovery
after their carrying out, but even this, as Kitty mournfully
declared, was a great deal too much, and might go on to
worse!   So she only said—

"Don't be foolish, Kitty—I see you were joking—of
course, he couldn't do it, really!"

And Kitty, having exploded her joke, let it go, for the
time being, but having failed to produce the effect she had
hoped for with Elizabeth, she took the first opportunity to
"try it on" Mr. Kendall.   She had not long to wait, for he
came to report himself the evening of his return, looking
unusually bright and well.

The subject of Winifred's ill-advised marriage was, of
course, mentioned and discussed, for Mr. Kendall, with the

others, had a warm liking for her. This was Kitty's opportunity.

"It is selfish, of course," she said gravely, when there was an appropriate pause, "but my chief regret is our teacherless condition! We have a slight feeling of doubt as to the advisability of employing another young and pleasing governess, and we shrink from the conventional old stager—there would be danger for Rod, and perhaps even Arnold—so it occurred to me that the real solution of the matter is a tutor. He couldn't possibly marry all four of us, and so might consider himself safe—there is always safety in numbers—and I flatter myself that he would find the situation attractive; a moderate salary, but the privilege of associating with a refined and cultivated family, not to mention Aunt Judy's cooking. Do you know of any one, Mr. Kendall, who could be induced to take the situation? A classical scholar, of course."

Kitty fixed her most innocent gaze upon her victim's face, watching with delight the sudden flush and look of embarrassment which passed over it; but Mrs. Stanley spoke before he could think of a reply.

"You must not mind Kitty's foolish speeches, Mr. Kendall," she said; "I am afraid she sometimes reverses the prescribed order, and speaks twice before she thinks once."

"You do me injustice, mamma," said Kitty, with a little pout; "I have given most earnest thought to this subject, and I don't see why my opinions should be treated so disrespectfully. Now if Elizabeth had proposed a tutor, you would all at least have listened to her, and answered her seriously, but *I* can never obtain an impartial hearing."

Dr. West came in in time to hear the last few words of this harangue, and, after an exchange of cordial greetings, he asked Kitty, with mock sympathy—

"What is your sorrow, Miss Katharine? Is it anything that I can alleviate?"

Kitty once more expounded her "views" on the subject of governesses and tutors, and the doctor, after hearing her patiently, said with perfect gravity—

"I think your idea is an excellent one, and I am inclined to think, also, that I know the very man you want—a professional man, with enough engagements to fill his time agreeably in the intervals of tutoring; a fine classical scholar, a man of much general information, of pleasing address, and old enough to be beyond all youthful follies, while he still retains a warm sympathy for youthful—simpletons. A homeless wanderer, too, to whom the mention of Aunt Judy's cooking, and the prospect of associating with a refined and cultivated family, would be no trifling inducements."

For once Kitty had, as Aunt Judy would have phrased it, "got her come-uppance." She believed the doctor to be quite serious, and she could not doubt that he was speaking of himself, and would drop the thin disguise, should his offer be accepted, or even considered. She had known, from the first, that her proposal was utterly impracticable, and being suddenly taken thus "at the foot of the letter," she was for once in her life at a loss for a reply. The doctor, who could never endure seeing Polly played upon, had given her an audacious wink and smile as he finished speaking, unperceived by Kitty, and she enjoyed being on the inside of a joke, instead of the outside, all the more because of the novelty of the situation. Kitty felt her face burning more and more, as the doctor calmly waited for her reply, and at last she stammered out—

"I dare say—I haven't any doubt he's all you say, and more, but I was only—I wasn't—I didn't mean—I meant it for a joke!"

Arnold and Ernest, who had seen the doctor's aside to Polly, gave a shout of laughter, and loyal Polly, unable to stand her double's discomfiture, burst out with—

"Oh, Kitty! Don't you *see* he's only in fun?"

Kitty gave one quick look at the doctor's repressed smile and twinkling eyes, and then rose and marched indignantly out of the room, entirely disregarding his entreaty that she would stay and forgive him. He sprang up and followed her, overtaking her before she had left the hall, and found, to his utter consternation, that she was crying.

"My dear child," he said, catching her hand to detain her, "I beg your pardon a thousand times! We have had so many tilts, that I never dreamed of really offending you."

"You were very rude," said Kitty, with a little catch in her voice, but not drawing her hand away. "You wanted to make—them all—laugh at me—and it wasn't—kind."

"I know it, I humbly acknowledge it, my dear; but is it any wonder I'm a bear, living as I do? The great wonder to me is that I am as civilized as I am."

"Are you so very lonely?" said Kitty, with her usual inconsequence. "Do you mind living by yourself, and boarding, and—everything?"

"Yes, I mind it," he said, with an unconscious sigh, which went to Kitty's heart. "Some of these days, if you will let me, I want to tell you just why, and just how much I mind it. But what I want now is, to hear you say that you forgive me, and that you'll believe I never mean to be rude, however clumsy I may be."

"I think you're asking a good deal," said Kitty, but the hall lamp revealed the beginning of a smile. "However, I'll try—upon one condition."

"Name it!" said the doctor. "'If it is difficult, it is done already; if it is impossible, it shall be done soon.'"

She looked up in his face, saying—

"I want you to stop calling me 'Miss Katharine.' I know, when you do it, that you're always thinking of that hateful thing that Shakspere invented, and—I don't like it."

"And what may I be permitted to call you?" he inquired, carefully avoiding a meeting of his eyes with hers.

"Why, what all the rest do—Kitty," she said, simply. "You always call Polly, Polly, and why should you make any difference with me?"

"There is no reason—not the slightest—why I should," he said, hurriedly. "So come—Kitty, come back to the parlor—they will think that we are fighting all this time."

"Now mind, it is a bargain," she said, as she turned to obey him. "Shake hands upon it, Dr. West—'fast bind, fast find,' you know."

He took her hand, and dropped it so quickly that she was half-inclined to take offence again, but was disarmed by the gentleness of his voice, as he said—

"I hope you will ask for some real test of my friendship, little girl, if you can ever think of one which you would value."

"Peace, war, or an armed neutrality?" inquired Arnold, as the supposed belligerents returned to the fireside.

"Peace—until farther notice!" said Kitty, composedly, "and a general amnesty to all sympathizers with the enemy."

But after the doctor was gone, she made an opportunity to speak alone with her mother.

"Did you enjoy seeing me cooked in my own sauce to-night, Mrs. Mother?" she asked.

"No, darling," replied Mrs. Stanley, "for I knew you were really distressed, and I can never enjoy that; but I don't think Dr. West would wilfully hurt any one's feelings, and I hope you made friends with him when he apologized."

"Of course I did, mamma—you know I never can stay

angry long, even if people don't apologize and I really want
to. But I can't understand Dr. West at all—sometimes I
think he only likes me because I am one of your daughters,
and Betty's and Polly's and Rod's sister, and then he is so
kind and gentle that I can't help believing that he really
does like me for myself."

"Any one living so alone as he does is in danger of growing a little peculiar," said Mrs. Stanley, who was the most
unsuspicious of women, and who had observed no difference
in the doctor's manner to Kitty, save a tendency to spar with
and tease her.

"That's just what he said himself, mamma," answered
Kitty. "He is almost always laughing and joking, you
know, but he spoke to-night as if some very sad reason had
made him live by himself, and be different from other people,
and he said he would tell me about it some day, if I would
let him—I hope he will not forget."

"Poor man, it is hard for him," said Mrs. Stanley; "he
is the very person to enjoy a home of his own, and to make
it happy, and it must be perfectly forlorn to live as he does
—I wish he would come here to tea oftener—I can never
forget how good and kind he was while Rod was ill, and his
bill was preposterously small for the number of visits he
made."

"It was silly in me to be angry with him, I know," said
Kitty, reverting to the affair of the evening, "but somehow——" and she stopped, as if precisely the right words
did not occur to her.

"Perhaps it will serve to make you think sometimes, dear,"
said her mother, gently, "when you are tempted to what
you call 'fun' at another's expense. Fun of that sort is
too often a repetition of the story of the boys and the frogs.
I have often wondered at the sweetness of nature which
keeps Polly from resenting your attacks, especially when

she feels, as she must, that it is out of her power to return them."

"I never thought of that, mamma," said Kitty, remorsefully. "Why, it's something like a big boy hitting a little one, and I always did despise that."

"A good honest look at ourselves and our actions, as if they belonged to somebody else, is half the battle sometimes," said Mrs. Stanley. "But come, Polly will be in bed and asleep, if you stay any longer, and the fire has gone out and left us."

There was no miraculously sudden change in Kitty, after this talk, but her mother's lovingly watchful eyes soon perceived the small beginnings of a gradual one. She was as gay as ever, but her bright speeches were less apt to be of a personal nature, and she yielded less and less often to the temptation to take advantage of Polly's literalness.

The question concerning a governess was settled in a most unexpected manner, shortly after the above-mentioned discussion of it. Miss Mackenzie wrote, declaring that she would be put off no longer—that it was all nonsense to imagine that she could not be comfortable with them in winter, when it was degrees warmer there than in B——.

"I am quite certain," she continued, "that my health would be much better in a mild climate, and with open chimneys all over the house, than it will ever be in one of these horrid furnace-heated houses, where ventilating means simply freezing. And I do wonder, Louise, what you think I am made of, anyhow! Here it is almost a year since I have seen any of you, and you talk coolly of my waiting till next spring, or next summer! No, unless I hear from you immediately that it will put you to absolute inconvenience to have me—and I don't see how in the world it can—I shall start on Wednesday of next week; so you may just send to meet the afternoon train on Thursday. I'm not so wedded to luxury, I hope, that I can't rough it a little for the sake of being with my family!"

The children were delighted with this intelligence, for Miss Mackenzie was a great favorite with them. There was a strong family resemblance between herself and Polly, who, among her various nicknames, numbered that of "the niece of her aunt!" Miss Mackenzie was a good deal younger than Mrs. Stanley, but her strongly expressed contempt for "cats with kittenish airs" made "her dress and address" those of a much older woman. She had a round, rosy face, with a peculiarly innocent and childish expression, which often misled superficial observers as to her real capabilities. She had received an education which, at the time of her school-going days, was unusually thorough and liberal for a young girl, and, unlike most school-girls, had continued her studies with unabated interest after she left school. She read a great deal, having, as she frankly admitted, an honest aversion to sewing, and more especially to "fancy work," be it the old-fashioned cross-stitch, or the newest idea in "art-embroidery."

"It really makes me feel ill," she had been heard to say, turning from an elaborately wrought fire-screen, where the broken outline, inevitable in the most finished embroidery, marred a copy of a famous engraving. "For what the materials, alone, of that monstrosity cost, they might have bought a perfect engraving or a pair of perfect photographs; and look at that thing—painful enough to look at now, dear knows, and think what it will be when it turns faded and shabby!"

"But surely you don't condemn art-embroidery, and the various pretty kinds of needlework which are in vogue now?" asked a perpetrator of many "companion-pieces" to the unlucky screen.

"Oh, not at all—in their proper place."

" And that is——"

" According to my thinking, it would be an excellent
thing to introduce it into all the schools for feeble-minded
children, as a sort of stepping-stone between nothing, and
something worth while ; they'd discard it as soon as there
was any radical improvement. I should make it a test—their
discarding it, I mean."

There was no difficulty about accommodating Miss Mackenzie. Winifred's vacant room was once more made ready, and
Kitty said to Polly, as they put the finishing touches and
built up an artistic fire of crooked sticks and pine-cones—

" There's a sort of music in the air of this room, my child,
discernible to my acute senses—I 'feel it in my bones,' as
Aunt Judy says, that before Aunt Mary has been here a
month, she will elope with Dr. West."

" But Kitty, Aunt Mary must be ever so much older than
Dr. West!" remonstrated Polly.

" Oh, that makes no difference at all!" replied Kitty,
calmly. " When kindred spirits meet, you know, and all
that kind of thing. I mean to begin to keep a journal,
immediately, and you must help me remember all about Mr.
and Mrs. Randolph Peyton ; if we go on at this rate, by the
time I am twenty-five I shall have nothing to do but make a
fair copy—using fictitious names, of course—and behold, I
shall have a three-volume novel, true to the life. Nothing
shall induce me to part with the copyright, and the fortune of the family will be made. Would you rather travel
first in your own country, Polly, or go 'abroad' and come
home disgusted with the United States before you have seen
anything of them but one small provincial corner ? "

" I'll make up my mind in the meantime," replied Polly,
laughing ; " there's a good deal to be said on both sides of
the question."

The cheerfulness which had been, not dispelled, but

shaded, by Winifred's troubles, was quite restored on the evening of Miss Mackenzie's arrival. She was charmed with everything, but kept breaking off her expressions of admiration to scold them for having taken advantage of her ignorance to keep her away.

" Why, if you'd nothing but bacon and beans and cornbread to live on," she said indignantly, "the atmosphere made by the climate and these open fires would be enough to make up for it. I never knew such a set of hypocrites! Pretending that my third story room at a boarding-house could compare with the room you've given me, or a boarding-house table with Aunt Judy's cooking! If I had any proper pride, I should go back to-morrow; but you've let me see how comfortable you are now, and I shall stay! If I hadn't been half-sick myself, I should have come when I heard Rod was ill, but I was afraid of giving you two people to nurse, instead of one."

"It was not so nice as it is now, just at first, aunty," whispered May, confidentially, "and we were afraid you would be lonesome; but now, when Uncle George and Edith are coming to be our neighbors so soon, and the winter is almost over, I don't believe you will mind it."

In a few days, Miss Mackenzie declared that she felt as if she had lived there all her life.

" I suppose it is the family mansion, and old family-servant, that does it," she said ; " but I can't convince myself that I came here less than a week ago."

She rose at once to a high place in Aunt Judy's favor, by the readiness with which she accepted being waited upon. She was very near-sighted, and rather helpless, physically, and Aunt Judy's prejudice in her favor, from the fact that she was "de moral of Miss Polly," was confirmed by the manner in which it "came natural" to her to have her things picked up for her.

She had not been among them long, of course, before she heard what Kitty called their romance in real life, and the dilemma they were in concerning a governess. She was unusually quiet and thoughtful for a day or two, and then, one day when she was alone with her sister, she said hesitatingly—

"Louise, I never tried teaching, except in Sunday-school, though I always liked it there, but I think I have studied as much as most governesses have, and—would you trust me to teach your girls?"

"Would I trust you!" and Mrs. Stanley sprang up to kiss her sister. "My dear Mary, I don't think there is any one who could make learning more pleasant to them, and you know twice as much as any governess we should be likely to secure. The only question is, whether it would not be too laborious for you."

"I'll let you know in good time if I feel myself sinking under it," she said, highly gratified with her sister's warm reception of the idea, for, like all really learned people, she was very modest about her own acquirements. "But do you think they would study and behave for me as if I were a *real* governess?"

"If you knew my bairns as well as I know them, you would not ask me that," said Mrs. Stanley, smiling. "I think even my mischievous Kitty will see how the great favor you are doing them ought to bind them to their best conduct."

"I wish you'd speak to them about it, and find out what they think, when I'm out of the way," said Miss Mackenzie, doubtfully. "They'd be too polite to object if I were present, and I want their real opinion on the matter."

"Very well," replied Mrs. Stanley, "I will do so. But, Mary dear, you must let me have my say, now. You spoke of paying board here—the idea was very disagreeable to me, but I knew you would prefer it, so I meant to let you pay about half the sum you mentioned; but if you teach the children, you must give up all idea of it—and, indeed, you ought to let Elizabeth give you what she gave poor Winifred —I say Elizabeth, for it was her project, and the money was the result of her butter business. I know very well how often you are obliged to deny yourself things that you really· ought to have, and it would be a great pleasure to Elizabeth."

Miss Mackenzie answered this appeal by beginning to cry, and trying to talk at the same time.

"You are very unkind," she sobbed; "you treat me as if I were an unpleasant stranger. If you talk to me like this I *will* go back, and stay back! As if I would take money for teaching my own nieces! You ought to be ashamed of yourself, Louise Stanley, and you know you ought!"

"And as if I would take board from my own dear sister!" said Mrs. Stanley. "Come, dear, we'll compromise—I will say nothing about your salary, if you'll say nothing about your board. Will that do?"

"I suppose it will have to," said Miss Mackenzie, reluctantly; "but I don't think it is fair, and I've a great mind to go back!"

CHAPTER XXXIII.

"If we love one another
Nothing, in truth, can harm us, whatever
Mischances may happen."—LONGFELLOW.

"I DO believe I have found out what I was intended for," said Miss Mackenzie, a few weeks after her voluntarily assumed duties had begun. "Do you consider that your children are exceptionally bright and well-behaved, Louise?"

"Of course I do! Did you ever know a mother who didn't, my dear?"

"Then I suppose it is scarcely a fair test; but I never should have imagined that I should find teaching as pleasant as learning. I did suppose the older girls would take some pleasure in their lessons, but little May is as bright and as much interested as any of them, and the school-hours seem to slip away like minutes."

Before the winter was over, the new governess had three additional pupils. Louise Peyton, upon hearing of the new arrangement, had begged so earnestly to return to her companions in study, that Miss Mackenzie had overcome the real bashfulness which she felt about taking a scholar who was not related to her, and had given her consent. She liked Louise very much, and, in addition to this, her kind heart was touched by seeing how large a share of the shadow which had fallen on the Peyton household came to the young girl.

There had been a preliminary encounter, which proved to be Greek meeting Greek, before the arrangement was concluded. Mrs. Peyton had insisted upon paying the same sum which she had paid Miss Neale, and Miss Mackenzie had said, as politely as she could manage to say it, but with what was known in the family as " her Bunker Hill manner," that she was teaching for her own pleasure, that she found it a great help and incentive to learning, and that if anything more were said about money, she must decline the whole proposal. To every one's astonishment, Colonel Peyton, who was present at the engagement, acted as mediator, and, what was more astonishing still, he took Miss Mackenzie's part, insisting that, as they were asking a very great favor of her, she had the right to make her own terms. His wife, as usual, yielded without farther question, and Miss Mackenzie, with tears in her eyes, crossed the room to shake hands with him, and assure him that *he* understood her! He had done a most difficult thing—he had gracefully and cordially accepted an obligation instead of asserting his independence, and Miss Mackenzie was his fast friend from that day, veering round, to the no small indignation of the children, from the views which she had perforce adopted about Winifred and Randolph, and asserting that a young man with such a father had no excuse for concealment, for whatever else he might plead excuse.

As has been mentioned, Mr. Kendall returned from his vacation in unusually good spirits. He was not quite certain enough to speak of the hope which encouraged him, until several weeks after his return. Then it became a certainty, and he came to tell his friends at Green Point that, as soon as he could find a substitute, he was going away, that his studies were very nearly completed, and that he had an offer of a position in an office, without any salary as yet, but with ample opportunity to finish his studies, and a prospect of a salaried engagement when they were completed.

He told frankly how, with the small sum which he had

been able to put by, and other small sums which he hoped
to earn by copying and doing extra work, he expected to
"keep afloat" until he began to receive a regular salary,
and the Stanleys listened, and answered, and questioned with
warm and friendly interest, expressing their sincere regret
at the prospect of losing him from the neighborhood.

He stayed unusually late that evening, and after he went,
Miss Mackenzie said—

"What *do* you suppose ailed that poor young man, Louise?
I've always thought him very sensible before this evening,
but I saw him give a little start as if he meant to go, and then
settle back into his chair again at least six times before he
really went. He seemed to have something on his mind he
wished to say, and to be unable to say it."

> "'For it is with feelings as with waters,
> The shallow murmur, but the deep are dumb,'"

said Kitty softly to Elizabeth.

"I think he was very much excited over the news he came
to tell us," said Mrs. Stanley. "He has been exceedingly
patient, and faithful too, but I am quite sure that teaching
that school has been, generally speaking, no small penance,
from what our boys have told me. Most of the scholars are
overgrown, stupid boys, who go in the winter simply because
they are obliged to, and who have no interest whatever in
learning. To a man of Mr. Kendall's attainments, this
must be very trying, almost unbearable."

"I should think so," said Miss Mackenzie. "What
brought him down here, in the first place? He seems out
of his element, somehow."

"It was the first situation he heard of after he found he
must either teach and study together, or give up studying
a profession, and there were some advantages—there was
very little temptation in the neighborhood to take him

away from his books, and I think he believed very firmly that 'a rolling stone gathers no moss.' Then he and Roderick were gratified to find their aims were similar, and they have lent each other books and encouraged, if not actually helped each other. He said to me, some time ago, that any change he might make would not necessarily be an improvement, and that he could stand the annoyances here, because he knew they were only to be temporary."

"I see," said Miss Mackenzie, musingly; "he seems like a very fine fellow, and I hope he will succeed in all his undertakings; but what will the boys do after he goes? Keep on at the school under the new teacher?"

"I don't know," said Mrs. Stanley, looking a little troubled; "I have often thought that, but for the personal influence of Mr. Kendall, which is very strong with them, I should not be justified in exposing them, and more especially Ernest, to the rough surroundings which are inevitable in such a school. We must think it over—we have a week yet before Mr. Kendall goes."

The boys had gone to bed before this talk took place—in fact, every one but Mrs. Stanley, Miss Mackenzie, Elizabeth and Roderick; and Miss Mackenzie said—

"I do believe I could teach those boys, Louise, with a little help now and then from Rod. I wouldn't have said so before I tried the girls, but it is much easier than I thought it would be, and I like it better every day. I should feel lost without it now. Would you let me try if they're willing?"

Mrs. Stanley hesitated a moment before she answered, and her sister said, without the least resentment in tone or manner—

"Don't be afraid to speak—I know people think that boys ought to be taught by men, but I never encountered any boys before who weren't more trouble than their heads were worth, and I thought with them it might be different—they seem to be polite by instinct."

"That is not what I hesitated about, dear," said Mrs. Stanley, "and you must listen, and be sensible. I have no doubt whatever that, if you were to undertake it, you could, with little or no help from Roderick, fit Arnold for the Freshman class in any college; but I am quite unwilling, and so would all my children be, to have you giving time and strength in a way that would ensure you a good living elsewhere, and receiving no return."

"And do you call my home here, and the way you all treat me, and the knowledge that I shall be welcome to stay here forever, no return?" quavered Miss Mackenzie.

"From a business point of view, I do," said Mrs. Stanley. "I gave up about the girls, because I always try, if I don't always succeed, to let people choose their own way of being happy, unless it is a bad way; but I cannot conscientiously give up any farther. Now, as mother used to say, when a knotty question arose, 'Let's sleep on it,' and to-morrow you can ask the boys how they would like to join your flourishing school; perhaps their answer will help you to decide whether or not you will agree to my lowest terms—if you teach the boys, you must accept what Miss Neale accepted for only teaching the girls, and giving the boys drawing-lessons—you see that that will save us their school-bills entirely, and put us hopelessly in your debt; but I am trying to take your view of the matter, and mix it in equal portions with mine, and you must do the same by me."

Miss Mackenzie loved all her nieces and nephews heartily, but the chivalrous politeness, as well as affection, which Arnold and Ernest daily showed her had secured them a very warm corner in her heart, for she secretly dreaded the roughness which she fancied inseparable from boys of their age. She knew that Roderick had been an exception to this rule, but she had always attributed the fact to some happy accident in his own character and disposition. The idea of fitting the two boys for college, or even for a good school, appealed to her ambition, and by the next morning she had decided that, should the boys seem really pleased with the prospect of having her for their teacher, she would accede without further remonstrance to Mrs. Stanley's "lowest terms." Their reception of the proposal was so flattering that she heroically adhered to her resolution. They had dreaded the idea of continuing at the school after Mr. Kendall's departure, for the rudeness, and even coarseness, of many of the scholars was so unpleasant to them, that they suffered far more from petty annoyances and persecutions than their mother was aware of, because of the idea which prevailed that they were "proud" and "stuck-up." Ernest had at first been inclined to complain at home of these things, but Arnold had said to him, "See here, young man, you may observe that Rod doesn't sing out every time he has a finger-ache, and there's no reason why we should. The only thing that could be done would be to take us away from school, and there's no other for us to go to; beside, Mr. Kendall doesn't like it a bit better than we do—I can see that, and he's worth our putting up with something, even if it were worse than it is."

The boys had no fear of compromising their dignity by learning from a woman. They had reason to know that their aunt was quite capable of teaching them all they could learn for several years to come, and her bright and often droll manner of presenting commonplace facts made learning for and with her pleasant work.

So the household settled down under the new dispensation into a tranquilly happy round of duties and pleasures. There was frequent intercourse with the Peytons, but it was difficult to conduct it safely, and in the old cordial spirit, with the

27

tabooed subject always in the minds of both when they met.
The Colonel was greatly changed—" broken," the neighbors
said, and he often sat silent now, rousing himself with an
effort to a sort of spasmodic cheerfulness.   He had given no
sign of relenting, and his wife looked pale and worn, with
traces on her still beautiful face of the many tears which fell
in secret.   Louise had, to a certain extent, recovered her
spirits, for her daily meetings with the Stanleys, and her
interest in her lessons, diverted her mind ; but at home she
was often dull and depressed, and her affection for her father
had lost much of its warmth.

Roderick's recovery, when once he was released from
authority, was rapid and complete.   The building of Mr.
Stanley's house had been delayed awhile by a few weeks of
freezing weather in January, but " it's an ill wind that blows
nobody good," and Roderick, if he had not the satisfaction
of filling his improvised ice-house, had at least that of knowing that it was full.   He listened calmly to many neighborly
predictions that the ice " wouldn't keep a week after warm
weather set in," but their sole effect upon him was to make
him have a load of saw-dust from the saw-mill "dumped"
on top of the boards, by way of extra precaution.   Both he
and the boys took advantage of the early spring, to be early
at work.   With the prospect of the steamboats, to take all
they could spare from the farm to a good market, it was
worth while to try for the high prices which the first vegetables and fruit always command.   So the sheltered places
which had been purposely left when the wheat was sown,
were planted with peas and beans, lettuce, cabbage and corn,
after having been judiciously fertilized.   The light, warm
soil gave promise that the venture would be successful—and
it was, but only after weeks of unceasing watchfulness and
care.

Roderick soon found that it would be necessary to hire

another man, and, after several unsuccessful trials, he succeeded in finding one who was at least honest, if not quite
so industrious and faithful as Moses. The enemies which
attack fruit-trees are many and insidious, but they can, like
most other enemies, be overcome by faithful vigilance, and
the trees in orchard and garden gave promise of a crop of
fruit at least double the size of that of the year before.

Long before they blossomed, Mr. Kendall had made his
farewell visit, and taken his departure. How Miss Mackenzie
contrived that Elizabeth and he should have a five minutes'
tête-à-tête, she hardly knew herself, afterward ; but contrive
it she did, by means of hurriedly sending him back to the
dining-room for her handkerchief, which she had dropped
under the table. Elizabeth had, as usual, remained a few
minutes after the others left the table, to put away whatever belonged in the dining-room pantry, and if she was not
exactly " cutting bread and butter," she was certainly cutting
generous slices of cake for Aunt Judy and Clara, standing
just inside the pantry-door. Mr. Kendall somehow forgot
about the handkerchief, when he saw her, and also, much
to his discomfiture, the few clear and forcible sentences
which he had repeatedly framed, and in which he meant to
set the facts of the case before her, and ask her to " permit
him to hope that, when he was in a position, etc., etc."

What he did say was—but it would be a shabby thing to
repeat the awkward sentences in which this master of syntax
begged for a little hope. Somehow or other, this style of
broken English seems, in some cases, to be more effectual
than the most polished rhetoric, and a very little of it served
to convince Elizabeth that true respect and sincere friendship were no bad stepping-stones to love.

He led her back to her mother with the air of a conqueror
—he, who a few minutes before had been so meek!—and
Mrs. Stanley, comforted by the knowledge that it must be at

least two or three years, before he could take her daughter, her priceless treasure, away from her, gave her consent, when she had recovered from her surprise sufficiently to speak, to their engagement.   Neither Kitty nor the boys appeared any more astonished than Miss Mackenzie seemed to be; Roderick's surprise was ludicrous, and Polly's still more so.

But he went away with the cordially affectionate good wishes of all the family, and a noble forbearance was shown towards Elizabeth on the subject of the post-office—although Kitty remarked to Polly that the Davenport had evidently been given in a spirit of prophecy.   But neither the Davenport nor the post-office were allowed to interfere with Elizabeth's steady performance of her daily duties—duties which somehow seemed to her even lighter than they had ever seemed.

"Her face always made me think of starlight, before," said Dr. West, when the startling intelligence had been confided to him, "but it is more like moonlight now."

Many months passed, after his promise to Kitty, before it was fulfilled, and when he did tell her the story, it was in a few words, with her mother sitting by.

He had been engaged to be married, and his marriage was to have taken place as soon as he had sufficient practice to warrant it.   He had opened an office in a pretty New England town, and was meeting with gratifying success, when the young girl to whom he was engaged was killed by a fall from her horse, dying before he could be summoned.   The place where this blow had fallen upon him, became hateful to him, and happening to hear of an opening in the remote spot where the Stanleys had found him, he had gone there, caring little whether he succeeded or not.   But his interest in his profession revived, after awhile, and he had now a large and increasing practice, of the most toilsome kind, for his various visiting places were miles apart.   He had often been urged by those who knew his ability, to leave his retreat, and take the place which he was capable of filling, but he shrank more and more from contact with the world, and took a quiet pleasure in his long, solitary drives. Not a wild-flower grew in the neighborhood, with which he was not familiar, as his patients had good cause to know, and he never wearied of the beauties of changing seasons, sunsets, and moonrisings.

He boarded with an old pair of "farmer folk" who, in their queer way, adored him, but whose adoration did not take the form of much comfort for him. He visited at few other houses with the frank friendliness which he showed the Stanleys, and they appreciated the distinction accordingly. Kitty had never quite resumed her defiant attitude toward him, since the evening of her defeat; she was still quite enough to keep things from stagnating in her neighborhood, but as Arnold remarked to Ernest, she was "a northwest breeze instead of an out-and-out norther."

The winter "broke up" in February, and Mr. Stanley put an extra force of workmen on his house, determined to have it finished, and ready for occupation, by the following June, for he grew increasingly anxious about Edith, as the winter advanced. She vibrated between the brilliancy of excitement and the dullness of exhaustion, and had gradually increased the quantity of the "tonic" she was taking, until the prescribed dose was nearly doubled. Her sleep was either heavy and exhausting, or broken with feverish dreams, and her appetite was capricious.

Had her mother been living, this state of affairs could not have gone on; but Mr. Stanley, seeing her, as he did, for a few minutes only in the morning, and then not again until just before the excitement came on which evening always brought her, had no idea of her real condition. It was not alone the severe course of study which she was pursuing, for, had she been physically robust, and of a phlegmatic tempera-

ment, she might very readily have passed through the ordeal
unscathed, although even then her powers of endurance
would have been heavily taxed, for with the exception of the
hour reserved for practising, and the time required for her
music and drawing-lessons, almost every minute of her wak-
ing time out of school was spent in study. The examination
preceding the giving of diplomas was to be public, for it was
Madame's boast that there was no clap-trap in the proceedings of her school—that all the world, if it chose to come,
might see that the diplomas presented had been fairly and
honestly earned. It was the prospect of this public examination which had wrought upon Edith's nerves until it had
assumed alarming proportions. She had a horror of failure,
and it became Isabel's daily task to go over the same ground
with her, and argue and soothe away her fears, and any one
less good-tempered and unselfish than Isabel was, would have
grown weary of listening to, and repeating, the same ideas,
in slightly different words, so frequently, and would in turn
have become irritable herself. But Isabel's warm and increasing affection for Edith and Mr. Stanley would have
stood a far harder test than this, and when she found that
her gentle attempts to persuade Edith, even yet, to abandon
the idea of graduating, or at any rate to defer it until the
following year, only brought on paroxysms of nervous
excitement, she stopped remonstrating, and did everything
in her power to remove all obstacles from Edith's path. She
herself was working hard, but within, rather than beyond,
her full ability, and she found a keen enjoyment in her
work. Her determination to teach was fixed, depending
only on the consent of her parents, which she hoped to gain
in time. Mrs. Crawford longed to point out to Mr. Stanley
the danger in which she felt Edith to be, but she had seen
the effect of Isabel's remonstrances, and she did not dare to
interfere where the latter had failed. So she took counsel

with herself, and the result was a series of what Edith laughingly called "petty persecutions," which, however, the victim neither resented nor resisted. Beef-tea appeared at lunch, now, as well as early in the morning, and at bed-time. The good housekeeper racked her brain, and searched through her collection of recipes, to provide dainty little dishes which might tempt the failing appetite. Cream-toast took the place of milk-toast; the stock for the pleasing variety of soups in which the cook had been instructed, was beef-jelly, rather than broth, and having first conscientiously consulted Mr. Stanley—although he gave her *carte blanche* as to the table, trusting her as he did—she substituted the best port she could procure for the light cooking-wine she generally used, in sauces and puddings, and other tempting desserts.

Most of these changes were unnoticed by the rest of the family, but they were not lost upon Edith, and her careless estimate of Mrs. Crawford was undergoing a radical change. She even submitted to a daily dose of a decoction of bitter herbs, which Mrs. Crawford, not trusting the cook, prepared with her own hands, and offered with a timid doubt as to its reception which touched Edith, and induced her to take it as no persuasion could have done. All these helps post-poned, but did not avert, the evil day. Edith woke with a dull headache on the fateful morning, but, by a great effort, she was bright and cheerful at the breakfast-table, and her father tried to be satisfied with this.

"You'll let me have coffee this morning, little father?" she said, coaxingly, and he consented, with the glad feeling that, after this one effort, her time for rest would come, and she would have no need of stimulants. She drank two cups, full strength—and the cook in that establishment was never guilty of weak coffee—without either milk or sugar, and it had all the effect she desired. In half an hour after break-

fast, she felt, as she declared, "ready for anything," all her
nervous fears had vanished, and she laughed and chattered
gaily with Isabel while they dressed in their simple, but
very pretty white dresses, exactly alike. Mr. Stanley had
asked Edith to purchase the material, and then told Isabel
that she must allow her "uncle" the pleasure of seeing his
daughter and niece dressed as if they were sisters, for once.
Edith's dressmaker had made both, and Isabel had never
looked prettier than when, being ready a few minutes
before Edith was, she ran down to show the effect to Mr.
Stanley, who was waiting to go with them, having taken a
whole holiday for the purpose. He was far more nervous,
and apparently excited, than either of the girls, but as
Edith passed triumphantly and calmly through one stage
after another of the ordeal, showing only by the deepening
flush in her cheeks, and the increasing brightness of her
eyes, that the calmness was superficial, he became reassured,
and drew her hand through his arm with smiling pride, as
she at last stepped down from the platform, and friends
crowded about her with warm congratulations and flattering
comments.

A "reception" was to follow in Madame's large and
beautifully furnished parlors, and to this most of the girls
had been eagerly looking forward. But as Mr. Stanley
turned to follow the throng, with Edith still on his arm,
and Isabel at the other side, he felt his daughter's hand
trembling, and she said, hurriedly—

"Papa, I'm so tired that I don't care about the reception
—I'd rather go home. Just put me in the carriage, please,
and then come back to Isabel—she must not be disappointed.

"But I can't let you go home alone, darling," he said,
anxiously, and at that moment they both caught sight of
Mrs. Crawford, smiling benignly on them across a sea of
heads. Edith motioned to her to meet them at the door.

"Now papa," she said, "I'm all right—Mrs. Crawford will go home with me, and take much better care of me than you, in your ignorance, possibly could! See, the carriage is close by—now go on with Isabel, and I'll be quite rested and well by the time you come home."

He saw a refusal would trouble her, and did as she wished, but with a heavy heart, and when, two hours later, he hastened anxiously home, Mrs. Crawford met him with a troubled face, saying—

"Miss Edith fainted on the way home, Mr. Stanley, or I thought it was a faint, but I haven't been able to revive her. The doctor is here," she added, as he rushed upstairs, but he did not hear her.

Dr. Bronson was bending over Edith when her father entered the room, and he turned to speak to Mr. Stanley with so serious a face, that the question the latter had been about to ask died upon his lips, and he could only look it.

"I should have been consulted sooner," said Dr. Bronson, gravely, and in utter forgetfulness of Mr. Stanley's call upon him a few months before; "Miss Stanley could not have reached this state without premonitory symptoms. However, the past is past—we must do all that can be done, now. I should recommend you to send for two thoroughly good nurses—one for the day-work, and one for the night. Here, I will write you a line to send to the Nurse's Home," and he scribbled a hasty line on one of his cards. "The house must be kept perfectly quiet, and as cool as possible—is any other room cooler than this? No? That is very well, it will be better not to move her. Now I want to see your housekeeper—I've had a little talk with her, and she is quite capable of attending to Miss Stanley till the nurses come—a most sensible woman, evidently."

The doctor had drawn Mr. Stanley out of the room, and softly closed the door, as he began to speak, and now turned to go down-stairs. Edith was not alone, for Isabel, who had gone to her own room, had opened the communicating door as soon as the doctor closed the other.

Mr. Stanley laid a detaining hand on the doctor's arm, saying hoarsely—

" What is it ? "

" Meningitis, I fear," said Dr. Bronson, his voice softening as he looked at the father's face, "and it must have been coming on for months. Has she complained of nothing ? "

" Your memory is short," said Mr. Stanley, bitterly; " I came to you, late in the winter, and laid her case, and my apprehensions, before you, and you prescribed—a tonic, or rather, as I now see, a stimulant, and laughed at my fears."

" My dear sir," said the doctor, impatiently, but not un-kindly, "if you had brought Miss Stanley to me instead of coming without her, I should doubtless have prescribed differ-ently. I was guided solely by your report, and the proba-bilities of the case. In a practice so crowded as mine, more than this would have been impossible. But talk of this sort is useless—what we have now to do is to fight the disease with every available weapon. Your daughter is young, and has, I think, a good constitution. There is much to hope as well as something to fear. Far more will depend upon the nursing she receives, than upon my prescriptions. I will call again this evening, and if I do not think the nurses compe-tent, I will tell you so frankly, and ask your housekeeper to take the night-nursing, which is most important. Now I really must go, as soon as I have given my directions."

When Mrs. Crawford understood the state of affairs, she promptly declared her intentions. A good nurse for the day-time met her full approval, but no one but herself should watch with Miss Edith at night. Miss Isabel, with a few suggestions from her, could give the orders, and oversee the housekeeping, thus leaving her free to rest as much as was needful in the day time. This arrangement she announced to Mr. Stanley, with respectful firmness, Isabel being present at the time.

"But my dear child," he said, turning to Isabel as he spoke. "You must not be kept in this hot city, and away from your family, for us. I am sorry you must take the journey alone, but you can easily manage it, being so familiar as you are with the route. Do not hesitate to leave us—Mrs. Crawford's plan assumes too much."

Isabel threw her arms impulsively about his neck.

"And do you really think," she said, "that I would leave you in your trouble, after all the happiness you have given me? Oh, you *can't* think so meanly of me as that! I have already written to say that I am not coming, and I am your daughter, and Edith's sister, as long as there is anything for a daughter and sister to do."

"Then you shall stay, dear child," he said, "and may God bless you for your good heart."

Edith never could remember much of the three weeks which followed, and the few recollections which that time of peril left her were not pleasant. Vain efforts to recall a sentence, or the solution of a problem, haunted her brief intervals of consciousness, together with a terror for which she could not account. But these intervals were mercifully short. Youth and a good constitution, the best medical skill which the city afforded, and care which fully equaled the skill, at last gained the fiercely contested battle, but it was many days, even after the decisive one, before the anxious watchers felt sure of the victory, and many more before it was safe to take the poor little patient to the beautiful new home which they had feared she would never see. As soon as fear gave place to hope, the family at Green Point had joyfully begun to put the finishing touches on the prettily furnished rooms, under Mr. Stanley's directions, for everything of importance had been in readiness weeks before. Mr. Stanley had decided to remove but little from the city house, at least for the present, and had sent down light furniture, suitable for a summer home, with rugs and mattings for the floors, all of which latter were stained and polished. As Edith gained strength, and the doctor expressed his hope that she might safely be removed in a very few weeks, Isabel, who seemed truly like a daughter of the house, arranged for the dispatching of house linen and china, ably seconded by Mrs. Crawford, whose tranquil face beamed upon Edith with a look of proud possession.

"I don't think there's enough of me left to be worth taking to Green Point, papa," said Edith, surveying herself critically, after Mrs. Crawford and Isabel had dressed her for the journey. "The general effect is very much that of the 'wimple and hood' left behind by the lady in the Ingoldsby Legends, who was spirited away to punish her husband for swearing. Do you really think it's worth while to take such a small remnant, dear?"

Mr. Stanley took her in his arms and held her fast, while "the water stood in his eyes."

"My darling," he said, "I have no words in which to tell you what this remnant is worth to me."

CHAPTER XXXIV.

After Five Years.

" 'Tis easier for the generous to forgive
Than for offence to ask it."
                              THOMSON.

FIVE years had passed since the beginning of the experiment, and every year, in passing, had helped to demonstrate its success, bringing changes, indeed, but mainly pleasant ones.

The wide veranda, with its sheltered porches at front and back doors, was a substantial reality. Deep bow-windows, two stories in height, enlarged the dining-room and parlor, and the bedrooms above them, and everywhere running vines and climbing roses seemed trying to conceal the fact that the mansion was whitewashed, instead of painted. A neat summer kitchen, with a covered way connecting it with the house, stood unobtrusively behind a hedge of thrifty cedars, and where the temporary ice-house had successfully demonstrated Roderick's theory, now stood a substantial permanent one. The sound of a saw-mill, coming fitfully from behind a clump of trees, half a mile above the house, testified to the carrying out of another plan, but did not give the information that a grist-mill stood beside it. Rows of healthy looking fruit-trees occupied much of the land of the original farm, but added acres were green with wheat, or, ploughed in even furrows, awaited the spring planting, for it was late in February, and the winter had been unusually

mild, even for that latitude. A large new barn, with a raised
roadway to its main entrance, and stables beneath it, stood
beside, and quite overshadowed, the old one. Plenty and
prosperity were betokened on every side, and it was evident
that the attention to details which had been the foundation
of success had not been suffered to relax as plans and projects
were multiplied and carried out. The tall, broad shouldered
fellow who rode up the lane and sprang lightly from his
horse was undoubtedly Arnold, but so like the Roderick of
five years ago, that his mother often called him by his older
brother's name. The change wrought in Kitty, who opened
the door while he was fastening his horse, was somewhat less
marked. She was but little taller, and her face still sparkled
with life and merriment, but, to a close observer, it was
very different; much gentler and more attractive, than
when the spirit of fun had been paramount to better feelings.

"I meant to take the letters, so that you could ride
straight to the stable, but you were too quick for me," said
Kitty, holding out her hand as Arnold drew a package of
letters and papers from his pocket.

"That's a feather in my cap," he said, making a low bow
as he handed them to her; "it's generally the other way,
isn't it?"

But Kitty was looking over the parcel, and disregarded
this sally.

"'Here's richness!'" she said, gaily. "Betty, Rod, Edith
—everybody but Ernest."

"I've one from him," responded Arnold; "I began to
read it on the way home, but the gates seemed to come so
much oftener than common, that I gave it up. He's thriving, however, and will be down next week—I read that
much."

"Betty's is for mamma," said Kitty. "Come, you've tied

your steed, you might as well come in, and hear and tell, before you put him up."

"All right, ma'am—I am always amenable to reason, you know," and he followed her into the parlor, where Mrs. Stanley, Polly—looking not a day older than she looked at fifteen—and May were gathered about the little fire which was more "for looks" than for warmth.

The letters were read, until all had changed hands, and then the comments began.

"Dear Rod," said Mrs. Stanley, handing Roderick's letter back to Kitty, "how patient he has been! I can hardly believe that his long waiting is over, and that he and Isabel are really to be married in June."

"Now *I* should have said, how patient Isabel has been," said Kitty; "but it's always the men-folks, I notice, who get the credit in such cases—I suppose because women are obliged to be patient, under the most favorable circumstances."

"Such as only being engaged for six months, and seeing the Object from one to three times daily," said Arnold, pinching her arm by way of emphasis.

"Don't be foolish, dear," she said, with an attempt at dignity; but she laughed, and the bright color went over her face like a wave.

"So John's bridge is going to keep them up there in the wilds till the end of May," said Polly, as she laid down Elizabeth's letter; "I do hope it will be finished then— it would be *dreadful* if they couldn't come to Rod's wedding."

"It would be more dreadful still," said Arnold, with a grave face, "if Rod should be kept away by his tunnel."

"Oh, Arnold!" and Polly's face lengthened perceptibly, "you don't really think—you wretch! you're laughing at me."

"You're not half the fun you used to be, my dear," said Arnold regretfully.

"You see Edith has carried her point," said Mrs. Stanley, looking up with a smile from a second glance at Edith's letter. "Dear child, I am very glad the wedding is to be here, instead of in town, and on the same day as Rod's—it will divert my mind a little, after they are all gone, to sympathize with your uncle."

"I thought His Highness would have to give in about it," said Kitty, "especially when he tried for March—the idea of being married in March!"

"Perhaps it's 'better to be married in' March, 'than not to be married at all,'" said Arnold, "and we can't all be married in September, you know, Mrs. Kitty."

Kitty pretended not to hear him.

"Edith couldn't have carried out her plan of having both weddings on the same day," she said, "if Isabel and Rod had been going to have a reception, but the breathless haste with which they are going off as soon as they've said the ceremony, and we've all cried a little, makes it possible. If Isabel weren't sweetness and light itself, she'd never submit to a wedding without a reception, and a bridal trip to an inaccessible tunnel."

"So *much* handier when the groom lives in the immediate neighborhood," murmured Arnold, apparently to himself.

"Then, according to Kitty, Mr. Brook must be 'sweetness and light itself,'" said May, laughing, "for I know he didn't want a reception, and he did want to be married in B——, and he seems to have given up like a lamb, poor man!"

"Ah, that's the way they do beforehand!" said Miss Mackenzie, who had entered while May was speaking. "*That's* the way to be married, my dear, and *that's* the way to keep house."

And she passed her hand lightly over Kitty's face, first down, and then up.

"You skeptic!" cried Kitty, catching the hand and giving it a vigorous squeeze. "You don't deserve to read this pile of choice literature, but I suppose you will, all the same."

"Of course I will," said the skeptic, calmly, as she put on her "near-sight" spectacles, pushing the "far-sight" ones up her forehead, to make room for them.

"It's a great thing for Ernest, to be allowed to help that old professor in his laboratory so much, it seems to me," she said, when she had finished, having saved Ernest's letter for the last.

"Of course it is," said Arnold. "You've reason to be proud of your pupil, aunty—you ought to have heard that same old professor sing his praises, as I did the last time I was in B——; it would have done your heart good."

"I've reason to be proud of my *pupils*," she answered, patting the strong brown hand that was resting on her shoulder; "but if anybody asked me of which I was proudest, I couldn't answer him."

Laughing acknowledgments were made, and then Arnold said suddenly—

"Oh, my family affection made me forget something which promises to be rather good fun — who speaks to go? I can take the carry-all, and there'll be a good-sized moon."

He drew from his pocket as he spoke a torn bill, and read aloud as follows:

28

LAUGH AND BE HAPPY
FOR TWO HOURS OR MORE.

LEONIDAS,
THE GREAT
BANJOIST,

Will appear in one of his

ORIGINAL, REFINED AND UNIQUE ENTERTAINMENTS,

At —— Court-House,

On Monday, Feb. 20th, at 7.30 P. M.

A CARD.—This is a strictly moral performance, and has been witnessed by the first ladies and gentlemen of the South. As a banjoist, Leonidas challenges competition with the world, playing all styles of music with an ease and readiness never accomplished by any other performer.

THE PROGRAMME

Will consist of Violin, Banjo, and Bone Solos, Sentimental and Comic Songs, Local Hits, Burlesque Speeches, Comic Recitations. Ethiopian Eccentricities. Representing the Happy Plantation Darky of By-Gone Days, and many other features too numerous to mention in this bill.

COME AND ENJOY YOURSELVES!
Each Act Announced from the Stage.
FRONT SEATS RESERVED FOR LADIES,
AND GOOD ORDER ENFORCED.
None Ever Leave Dissatisfied.

Admission only...........................25 cents.
Children ....15 cents.
Doors Open at 6 P.M. Performance at 7:30 P.M.

"Oh, mamma! can't we all go?" asked May, eagerly, as he finished reading; "it's this very evening, and it looks as if it would be such fun!"

"What do you think, Arnold?" inquired Mrs. Stanley, a little doubtfully. "Do you suppose the audience will be rude, or the performance vulgar?"

"No madam, to both queries," replied Arnold; "you know it was a very quiet and respectable audience the night the Old Folks sang at the Court-House, and judging from the programme I should think the affair would be quite jolly."

"Very well, then," said his mother; "you may go, Pussy, if Kitty and Polly wish to go——"

"*Of course* we do, mamma!" from the twins.

"But I think I am too old for such light and trifling amusements—I will stay at home, and have some hot chocolate ready for you when you come back."

"Nonsense, Louise," said Miss Mackenzie, decidedly; "*I* want to go too, and you're not going to be left here all alone to cry over Rod's marriage. Aunt Judy can make the chocolate, and go to sleep on the hearth till we come home —we shall be back by eleven at the latest."

"Too late for you, little Puss," said Mrs. Stanley to May; "but excitements seldom occur to us, so I will give you a dispensation for once, only you must stay in bed till I call you to-morrow morning."

"And you *will* go, mamma?" said Polly, coaxingly; "I shall stay with you, if you don't."

"Then I certainly will," replied Mrs. Stanley; "and I dare say I shall enjoy it as much as any of you, but I am growing fat and lazy in my old age."

"Old age, indeed!" said Arnold, kissing her "round and rosy" cheek; "that is barefaced fishing, my queen."

"I wish we could capture Louise, and take her with us

to-night," said Kitty ; "she don't 'laugh and be happy' any too much, poor child."

"She's going," said Arnold, with assumed indifference ; "I met the old Colonel just outside his gate, and showed him the programme, and he said they would all go ; that he should 'insist' upon Mrs. Peyton's going with them, for she had 'seemed a little dull of late,' and when he 'insists,' you know, they don't exactly tremble, but they certainly obey."

"Poor Mrs. Peyton!" said Mrs. Stanley ; "she will not feel much like laughing, no matter how funny Mr. —— Leonidas, was it? may be. Her face makes my heart ache —I don't see how the Colonel can stand it !"

"Did you know that he gave her leave to write, if she could remember the address, last Christmas Eve ?" said Arnold, "Miss Louise told me so the other day ; of course she had remembered it, and she wrote that very night, putting the Colonel's address on the end of the envelope, with 'Return to,' and sure enough it did return in ten days with 'Not there' scribbled across it."

"I never heard that," said Mrs. Stanley ; "but he has changed and softened very much—his face looked so hard and stern just at first. It was a wonderful concession, his letting Isabel teach."

"I think he was afraid she would do it without leave, if he didn't," said Kitty, "and consented, to save his dignity."

"I wish Louise might join her, as she wishes to," said Mrs. Stanley ; "but it would be too utterly forlorn there, without her—I don't think Mrs. Peyton would live long."

There was nothing suggestive of the majesty of the law about the interior of —— Court-House. A small space was railed off at one end, and benches and dilapidated chairs were ranged in front of this space, but there appeared to have been a scarcity even of these, for the seats came suddenly to an end at some distance from the door. A few dingy kerosene lamps hung upon the walls; and a painted pine table, upon which were perched a chair and two tall lamps, was the only suggestion of a stage. A corner of the railed-in space was further secluded by a faded green curtain, behind which a light was burning, when the Stanleys and Peytons, having met outside the door, went into the room together.

The Colonel did a little good-natured growling at the dimness of the lamps, and the fact that several gorgeously-dressed negroes were occupying some of the best seats; Mrs. Peyton was pale and silent, and had evidently come against her will, and for the sake of peace; but Louise, to whom any break in the monotony of her life was welcome, looked quite animated and very pretty, as Arnold engineered his party so that he might sit next to her. She was small and slight, and no one would have guessed the five years' seniority of which she made capital to treat him in an exasperatingly grandmotherly manner.

At exactly half-past seven the curtain was pushed aside, and a tall, slender man with a very red face and bushy, flaxen hair, beard and moustache, marched up to the table, and with the help of a chair, mounted his uncertain throne amid much applause from the audience. He had piercing dark eyes, curiously in contrast with his hair and complexion, for the latter was fair, and his high color was evidently a work of art. As he glanced over the audience, Mrs. Stanley was seized with an uncomfortable consciousness of having seen him before—where, she could not imagine. He bowed gravely, and announced with a perfectly solemn face that the first part of the entertainment would be of a serious nature, consisting chiefly of songs commemorating the " fallen heroes of the South."

Several of these were sung, and loudly applauded ; but something in one of them moved the fickle audience to laughter, and he paused to say, in a tone of grieved remonstrance—

"Ladies and gentlemen, this part of the performance is serious. If you will have a little patience, I hope to afford you ample cause for laughter when we come to the second part."

The "serious part of the performance" lasted fully an hour, and would have been wearisome, but for the growing interest inspired by the performer. His voice was very fine, true, sweet and flexible, and his accompaniments were played with a precision which indicated talent as well as practice. His hands were long, white and supple, and his face thin and refined.

There was a weary and troubled look in the large, dark eyes, which was strangely out of keeping with the high color he had assumed, and he seemed more and more out of harmony with the part he was acting.

When he cautiously descended from his rickety perch, and retired behind the curtain to prepare for the comic part of the entertainment, a lively discussion concerning him took place between the young Stanleys, but the Peytons were silent, and Mrs. Peyton was even paler than when she had entered the hall.

He reappeared in a few minutes, but at first every one doubted his identity. The flaxen wig had been exchanged for a closely fitting skull-cap of black wool ; moustache and beard were gone, and his face and hands were stained a dark coffee-color. He was showing his handsome teeth in an engaging grin, and was altogether a perfect model of the "end-man" in a negro-minstrel troupe. He advanced to the table, playing a rattling air on his banjo, and mounted his perch again with several jokes upon its insecurity, delivered in pure plantation darky dialect. And now his rich voice, accompanied by the banjo, rolled out in negro melodies, and for more than an hour he kept his audience convulsed with laughter, or rapturously applauding. To several remarks made quite audibly by different would-be wits about the hall, he returned droll and ready answers, invariably getting the best of it, and never relaxing his infectious grin. It was only when he was utterly breathless and exhausted that he begged for a few minutes' silence, and with a most light and delicate touch, played a little Spanish dancing tune, which set everybody's head and feet moving in time. He then asked, in a somewhat husky voice, for a glass of water, which was brought him with a jeering comment on its " weakness," and the gratuitous advice to " have something stronger." He rolled up his eyes at the speaker until only the whites of them were visible, remarking amiably—

" You'll 'scuse de gen'leman, ladies—he's done forgot how it tastes."

The red nose and weak eyes of the cup bearer caused this sally to be received with a perfect thunder of applause, amid which he retired, by general invitation, to a "back seat."

" I will now," said the performer, dropping his dialect, " give you my celebrated and unrivaled performance on the bones, for which my assistant will play the accompaniment on his violin. Mr. Baker!"

A tall and exceedingly disgusted looking man emerged from behind the curtain, with a violin, and placed himself beside the table.

" Now, Mr. Baker," proceeded " Leonidas," politely, " will you oblige us by giving ' The Devil's broke loose in Georgia?'"

The saturnine Mr. Baker instantly complied, and " Leonidas," with a pair of bones in each hand, his body swaying in time to the brilliantly played, rollicking tune, and his grin broader than ever, kept up an accompaniment to which no description could do justice, and with which the walls fairly rang. Two or three packs of fire-crackers, set off simultaneously, and timing their reports to a tune, would give a faint and distant idea of this performance, which truly was " unequaled."

The audience was still holding its breath, and had not yet broken into applause, when a little negro boy belonging to the neighboring tavern forced his way up the aisle, and handed a note to Mr. Baker, who glanced at it, and passed it to " Leonidas." The latter hurriedly read it, and springing to his feet, regardless of shaky table and tottering lamps, exclaimed—

" Ladies and gentlemen, you will excuse me—I left my little child very ill at the hotel; he is worse, perhaps dying, and I must go to him at once."

A murmur of sympathy passed like a wave over the audience, and some one shouted—

" There's a doctor here—that fellow with the black beard and big nose—take him along with you."

The person thus politely designated was Dr. West, and he had reached the railing as soon as " Leonidas" was off the table.

" Oh sir," said the latter, grasping Dr. West's hand, " for the love of God come with me—it is our only child!"

Mrs. Peyton's eyes were fixed upon the speaker's face, and now she quietly fainted, while the Colonel said in a hoarse, deep voice—

" What do you mean by this, sir?"

" Leonidas" made no answer, but catching up Mrs. Peyton's limp form as if she had been a feather, called out—

" Make way to the door—this lady has fainted!" and as the aisle was hastily cleared, he strode out of the building.

followed by Dr. West, the Colonel, and Louise. He crossed
the road to the tavern, entered the front door, and flung
open the door of a sitting-room which had been hastily
transformed into a bedroom. Crouching before a newly-
lighted fire was a pale, tired looking woman, with a very
sweet and gentle face; and as her husband entered with his
burden, she had just placed in a tub of steaming water a
lovely baby boy, apparently about two years old. His
rounded limbs were white as marble, and his beautifully-
shaped head was covered with little rings of gold-brown
hair. But the eyes were closed, the jaws set, and every
muscle rigidly convulsed. Dr. West took the command at
once, and the woman obeyed his instructions with intelligence and docility. In a few minutes the rigid form
relaxed, the beautiful dark eyes opened, and the little fellow
sat up in his bath, and began to cry. The Colonel had been
vainly trying to restore his wife to consciousness, but the
baby's wail proved more effectual than cold water and fan-
ning—she sprang from the lounge upon which she had been
laid, saying faintly—

"Mother's coming, darling!" and staggered across the
room. Dr. West gently led her back to the lounge, and after
a long, bewildered look at the different faces about her, she
burst into passionate crying. The Colonel stood for a
moment with his face buried in his hands, and then looked
up, to say hoarsely—

"What, in Heaven's name, does this mean, sir? How
dare you drag your wife and child through such disgrace as
this? If you care nothing for yourself—for us, have at least
some natural feeling for them, and quit this vile buffoonery
and masquerading!"

Randolph—for it was Randolph—still in his absurd disguise, shot a glance of angry defiance at the Colonel, as he
said bitterly—

"It is refreshing to hear you say that! You, who turned me out of your house because I dared to defy your prejudices by choosing for my wife the best and sweetest woman God ever made!

"I will admit my mistake in coming back here, but I assure you, I thought my disguise perfect, and had no intention of declaring myself. I was weak enough to long for some news of my mother and sisters. I am well aware that I have only you to thank for their silence."

While Randolph spoke, the poor weary mother had been rubbing her baby with a coarse towel, and wrapping him in a blanket, and now she turned to lay him on the bed. She was obliged to pass very near the Colonel, and as she did so, the baby, with a weak little crow, freed one hand, and grasped the old gentleman's beard. His mother's low voiced entreaties had no effect—he clutched the tighter, repeating his attempt at a crow. A curious change passed over the Colonel's face; his lips quivered, and he grew very pale. Then, suddenly bowing his gray head to the golden one, he clasped his arms around mother and child.

"God forgive me!" he said, brokenly. "If this little child had died, his blood would have been on my head. You said you would come back when I begged your pardon, Randolph—I beg it now, yours, and your wife's."

It would be impossible to describe the scene which followed. They all, with the exception of Dr. West, began taking each other in their arms, and Winifred said humbly—

"I was to blame—I never should have allowed him———" but the Colonel stopped her with a resounding kiss.

When the engagement was over, and calmness measurably restored, there was an outbreak of hysterical laughter from Louise—Randolph's face, streaked with tears, and wiped in irregular lines, presented an appearance to which words can do no justice; he hastily left the room, and when he returned, all traces of "Leonidas" had vanished. The Stanleys had anxiously waited in the Court-House, unwilling to go home until they saw the doctor again, and heard the fate of Randolph's child—and they all wondered that they had not known it was Randolph, from the moment they saw him, and heard his voice. Dr. West escaped as soon as he could, and in a few words told them what had happened, and then returned to say that if, as he supposed, the Colonel wished to take his family home that night, it could easily be arranged by an exchange of conveyances, and that the baby would take no harm, well wrapped up, and on the back seat of the carry-all.

So the Stanleys merrily compressed themselves into the Peytons' double carriage, while the Peytons took possession of the carry-all, and before midnight Randolph and Winifred had been welcomed back to the home which had seemed so empty to the mother's heart, while her boy was away. He was but little changed; the want of candor and firm principle which had caused himself and others so much sorrow had brought the weary look to his wife's eyes, more than all their reverses. To her he always was, and always would be, gentle and chivalrous, and it had been long before she would acknowledge to herself the fatal defects of his character. He explained to his father, before they slept that night, the gradual descent from comparative comfort to poverty, which had ended at last in his desperately offering his services to the leader of a celebrated minstrel troupe, who was glad to overlook his inexperience for the sake of his fine voice and masterly performance on the banjo. He had found the associates with whom he was thrown so utterly distasteful, and been so annoyed by the submission to the leader which was of course required of him, that he had suddenly formed the idea of asking the one man in the troupe who was not hopelessly vulgar, to travel with him as his business agent and occasional accompanist on the stage; they had been quite successful for nearly a year, and Mr. Baker looked more disgusted than ever when he found that the arrangement was to come to a sudden end, but his countenance brightened a little when Randolph turned over to him their stock-in-trade and the whole of the last night's proceeds.

Dr. West maintained to Kitty, but to no one else, that it was a secret hope of recognition and reconciliation which had brought Randolph so perilously near home, and Mrs. Peyton, though she mentioned it to no one, thought the same.

An attempt to increase his resources by speculation had deprived him of his legacy, and the death of Mr. Lansing, of his situation, and affairs had been desperate indeed when he fell back upon his voice and his banjo playing, for both of which he had had no small local reputation. He slipped back into his old ways at home, as easily as if nothing had happened, assuming the heaviest of the Colonel's duties, writing an occasional story or paper for one of the magazines, which was sometimes accepted and sometimes returned, and earning an occasional fee at his legitimate business, "more by good luck than good management." Winifred was not unhappy, for he was wholly devoted to her and to his boy, and the Colonel and his wife, Isabel and Louise, soon gave her the warm affection which she craved. But her sweet face had a look of unfulfilment, when it was in repose. Her intimacy with the Stanleys was one of her greatest pleasures, and a day seldom passed when some members of the two families did not meet—a fact which was by turns honey and gall to Arnold, who, the more Louise in a gentle and lady-like manner snubbed him, continued the more to manifest his devotion.

CHAPTER XXXV.

After Ten Years.

"To-day a song is on my lips ;
  Earth seems a paradise to me:
For God is good, and lo, my ships
  Are coming home from sea."—George Arnold.

AROUND the mansion has sprung up a group of three pretty cottages, the "Hen and Chicken Colony," as Kitty calls it, not inappositely, for the spreading wings which have from time to time been added to the house seem trying to reach the smaller buildings, and gather them under one roof.

In the one nearest the house live Kitty and her Doctor; he built it for her the summer before that September, five years and more ago, in which they were married. A small Kitty, so like her mother that Mrs. Stanley often forgets that she is not "the original," flits back and forth many times daily, "helping," as she believes, first one household and then the other with her tiny hands. The doctor seems to have grown five years younger, rather than older, and his practice has had an increase, since his marriage, which would bid fair to make his fortune—were it wholly among the fortunate. But he has come to be *the* doctor among all the financially unprofitable patients, for, if he orders "nourishing food," he generally brings it in a basket, at his next call, and his wife's brisk and cheery voice seconds his advice, with patient counsel to ignorant nurses and mothers. In the wide veranda at the end of the house—arranged with movable sashes, so that in winter it takes the form of a modest conservatory—are gathered once a week a dozen or more of the small black girls which abound in the neighboring bush, and Kitty, sometimes alone, and sometimes with volunteer assistants, gives sewing lessons, varied with what she calls "practical instruction in general housework," and her pupils have no difficulty in finding—and keeping—service places, on the strength of her recommendation.

The next of the cottages is Roderick's, but its occupation is fitful and subject to the contracts, yearly growing in magnitude, taken by its owner. It is rarely closed at Christmastime, however, for then no effort is spared to reach it, be it only for a few days. Roderick and Isabel are rather pitied by the more stationary members of the family for their wandering life, but they do not pity themselves, in the least, for they say that, since their marriage, their life has been a "perpetual wedding journey"; perhaps if children had been born to them, they would think differently, but, as it is, they enjoy their travels and adventures with an ever-fresh pleasure, and their brief settlings-down and playings at housekeeping perhaps even more.

The third and last cottage, not quite completed, is Ernest's. It is rather smaller than either of the others, but is built of dark-red brick, instead of wood, with a square tower of hewn stone, three stories high, and with the flat top enclosed by a railing.

The day of which I am writing was that on which, ten years ago, the advance-guard of the family came to take possession of "the Estate"—the "Forefather's Day" of the little colony, when stout hearts and willing hands had begun the battle for independence, and a home in which to enjoy it.

The anniversary had always been more or less observed, but this time Kitty declared that it should be more, and headed the enterprise of gathering all the flock, with its various additions, under the original roof, for one day at least. At first the success of the enterprise seemed doubtful; Roderick and Isabel were in western New York, Elizabeth and John in a Connecticut village, where, they flattered themselves, they were to remain for at least two years. Edith and Mr. Brook were in Florida, where, in spite of her remonstrances, he had taken her for half of February and the whole of March.

"He says I have a cough," she wrote to Kitty just before their departure, "but neither papa nor I can discover it, and so my father and my little Louise and George are to be orphans for at least six weeks, while my tyrant and I eat oranges and lie on pine-needles gazing up into pine-trees—the needles will present their sides to him. their points to me, for how many coughs my darlings may catch in six weeks! Would Aunt Mary allow herself to be borrowed, do you think? If she would, with how much lighter heart should I go! Investigate, negotiate for me, best of Kittys, and barrels of oranges shall attest my undying gratitude!"

Of course, Aunt Mary allowed herself to be borrowed, so she was in B —— with the "orphans," and Ernest, who was for the time being an inmate of his uncle's house. He had passed from Miss Mackenzie's hands into the University at B——, where he graduated with high honors, and then remained for an extra course of lectures on chemistry, maintaining stoutly that the undoubted fact that Professor Hofer had a very pretty daughter, who had been brought up to participate in her father's studies and experiments had nothing to do with his choice of a profession, but that, on the contrary, he was first attracted to Miss Hofer by her intelligent and evidently sincere interest in his favorite study.

"There are lots of girls," said this wise youth, "who profess the deepest interest in a fellow's studies, and I always like to lead them out of their depth, and leave them floundering—

but with Miss Hofer it's another thing; she and I had each chosen what we liked best before we met, and should each stick to it if we were never to meet again; but all the same, I hope we shall continue to meet again, and I mean to ask her to marry me as soon as I am making enough to keep us both in chemicals for our experiments."

This time came sooner than any one but Ernest himself had dreamed of. One or two patented discoveries gave him a moderate income before he had completed his last course of lectures, and soon after that came his opportunity.

Mr. Stanley, who, a few years after the building of his house at Green Point had wound up his affairs and retired from business, soon made the discovery that unlimited leisure had no charms for a man still in the prime of life and in vigorous health; so he looked about him for something, as he said, to keep him out of mischief, and discovered it when a mill property, some three miles away, was offered for sale. The water-power was excellent, but the building was old and dilapidated, and could only be torn away and replaced with a new one. Here he built a paper-mill, and had no lack of employment after that, for other building enterprises followed, as a matter of course—houses for the workmen, a school-house, with a lecture-room above for Sundays, a store, and a wheel-wright and blacksmith shop. All went well so long as he remained at Green Point and exercised a daily supervision, but whenever he absented himself for a few months, or even weeks, he had reason to regret his absence upon his return. He now offered Ernest a partnership in the business, conditional upon his nephew's residence at Green Point, and the offer was joyfully accepted, for Ernest would have still sufficient spare time to pursue the researches in which his heart delighted, and with which he yet hoped to conquer fame, if not fortune, and he longed to institute certain improvements in the machinery and processes in use in the mill, which he was sure would save both time and money. His uncle insisted upon building a cottage for him, according to his own design, and the tower was a laboratory, from the top of which telephonic communication was to be established with the mill.

He was dismayed to find that Miss Hofer remained firm in her belief that her first duty was to her father, whose housekeeper she had been since her mother's death, when she herself was but twelve years old. She frankly admitted that this was her only objection to marrying him, and he forthwith proceeded to work upon the feelings of the professor with a description of the mills, the laboratory-tower, and the unlimited opportunities for study and investigation afforded by a quiet country residence. The upshot of it was, that the professor was persuaded to give up his position at the University, and retire to a well-earned repose at Green Point, rejoicing in the prospect of leisure to perfect many valuable and invaluable discoveries. The house was nearly completed, and Ernest's marriage was to take place on his twenty-first birthday, which came in June.

Mrs. Stanley, Polly, May and Arnold still remained faithful to "the Mansion," and gave proof of the possible success of a difficult and dangerous experiment. Arnold, with the quiet persistency which had won him so many battles on the farm and in the saw-mill, continued his suit to Louise, year after year, until at last she admitted that nothing but the "absurd" difference in their ages made her continue obdurate. After this, of course, victory for him was not far off, and they had been married now for more than a year.

It did not seem to occur to any one that "our Polly" would ever marry, and the suggestion, made by an outsider, that such a thing was quite possible, and even probable, struck dismay to the heart of the community, and was answered with an indignant—

29

" Why, we couldn't *spare* Polly ! The idea !"

For Polly, as one by one her sisters left the home-nest, quietly assumed their duties, trying to keep her mother from feeling their loss too much until now, Kitty said, the chorus in every Green Point family opera was, " Where's Polly?" Some of her affairs she gladly shared with May, now a "bonnie lass" of eighteen, whose rosy cheeks and vigorous, springing step made her difficult to identify with the delicate looking child of ten years ago.

Miss Mackenzie and her brother Arnold had been her only teachers, and she was thoroughly well taught, but learning had always been made a pleasure, rather than a task, to her, and her mother had carefully held her back whenever her naturally excitable disposition had threatened to hurry her forward too much. Under Arnold's instruction she was an accomplished and fearless horsewoman, and her daily ride was taken in almost all weathers. There had never been any of the friction proverbial in such cases, between Louise and her " in-laws," but with this, good management had far more to do than good luck. Mrs. Stanley had insisted upon relinquishing the control of the house entirely to her daughter-in-law ; all orders to the servants were to come from Louise, all doubtful questions to be referred to her. Not that she intended to relinquish all interest and participation in the work of the household, but she knew the usual fate of a family with two or more heads, and this fate she wished to avoid, for her children's sake, as well as her own. Louise had entreated Mrs. Stanley to remain first in authority, and Arnold had joined his entreaties to hers, but Mrs. Stanley had remained firm.

" It is asking much of you, dear child," she said, " to expect you to share your home with a mother-in-law and two sisters-in-law, and perhaps I am selfish to do it, but Arnold has made himself so necessary to me, that I shrink from the idea of even a slight separation from him ; so you must let me take every precaution against it. We shall be far happier and more at our ease, if we begin, and keep on, with a definite understanding.

Time had proved the wisdom of her words, and while none of the "partners" stood upon ceremony about their share of the work, the management of the house was consistently deferred to Louise, and she, in turn, often appealed to Mrs. Stanley's wider experience and more mature judgment.

Dr. West had laughed rather provokingly when Kitty had announced her intention to call a gathering of the clans for the anniversary, and, after she had gained the consent of the family at "the Mansion" to make the attempt, he amused himself with improvising the various refusals she was to receive. But before the invitations had been out more than a week, he saw her on the veranda, as he drove up the lane one afternoon, triumphantly waving something white in each hand, and as soon as she could make him hear, she called in exultant tones—

" You shall have no supper till you've eaten all your skepticisms. They're all coming—*all!*" and she snatched up Kitty the second, and waltzed the length of the veranda and back again while he was tying his horse.

"Did you offer a prize in every biscuit and a diamond ring in the cake ?" he asked, as he captured the little girl and perched her on his shoulder.

" Read, and own yourself mistaken for once," she said gaily, and the doctor meekly read. Elizabeth wrote that John had not been well, that he was overworking himself, and that she rejoiced in the excuse given by Kitty's invitation for a few days' absence from business for him. He had said, at first, that he " could not spare himself," but on seeing how great her disappointment was, had finally consented to " try."

Edith wrote rapturously—

"My best, my most precious of Kittys, how can I thank you? Will we come to the anniversary feast? Of course we will! When I first read your dear letter and handed it to Malcolm, he said, in his once-for-all-est manner, 'It would be delightful, but of course it is out of the question for us— I hope the rest can go.' And then I did what I have never done before, and probably never will again, I cried at him. I do wish you could have seen his face. I could not resist the temptation to peep at him through my fingers, although I really was crying like everything, for I had a vision of you all at the table, with a turkey at each end, and a ham in the middle, and all the rest accordin', and we not there, and it broke my heart. His surrender was, like all he does, dear man, complete. He said he had no idea I cared so much, but *of course* he would go if I did—we could come back to Jacksonville for the rest of March; so then I entered the breach I had made, and told him I had coughed but once since we came here, and that was because I had swallowed the wrong way, and that I was crazy for the children, and would be very careful and wear a chest-protector, and never go out without a lozenge in my pocket, and *couldn't* we just stay at home after the anniversary was over; and he laughed and said we could. Bless you, Kitty! I always did love you, anyhow. We will pick up Aunt Mary and the babes as we come along, and Ernest too, if he has not already gone."

There was a postscript saying—

"Three barrels of oranges started for Green Point yesterday—I hope they'll arrive in time for the feast."

Mr. Stanley entered into the plan with eager delight, which he testified not only by a prompt acceptance of his invitation, but by three successive hampers, sent as different things occurred to him. The last one, which arrived on the eve of the festivity, was filled with flowers, carefully packed in moss, for the table.

Kitty's conservatory had done well that winter, and all the deep window-seats of the dining-room were filled with flowering plants banked up with moss. The idea of a late dinner, made brilliant with lamps and candles, which had tempted them a little, had been abandoned in favor of the children, and three o'clock fixed upon instead of six. Most of the distinguished guests arrived the night before, but Ernest did not appear until the morning of the anniversary, for he brought with him his special friend, Arthur Brook, a younger brother of Malcolm's, and this youth had insisted that being only a "connection" and not a real relation of the family, it would be "intrusive" for him to put himself upon a footing with his brother.

"Bless his sensitive heart!" said Kitty to the doctor, after hearing this. "If he does succeed in capturing May, I hope she will limber him a little, for the benefit of her family."

The long table, bright with pretty china, glass, silver, and flowers, looked brighter still when the happy faces of parents, children, and grandchildren gathered around it. Eager voices questioned and replied—there was so much to tell, to hear, to discuss.

"How little I realized, five years ago," said Dr. West, at the first pause, "that I was marrying into such a distinguished family! I shall begin to write after my signature, 'Brother-in-law of the engineer of the —— river suspension bridge, of the inventor of'—you'll have to give me the names of your inventions, Ernest—'and the author of "Thoughts on Political Economy, by a Practical Farmer," and half-brother-in-law to the architect of'—which of your plans would you prefer me to cite, Malcolm?"

"Oh, the City Hall, doctor!" said Edith, before her husband could speak, while he, scarcely waiting for her to finish, turned cordially to Arnold, with—

"My dear fellow, did you write that book? I couldn't think why so much of it had a familiar sound, but I do not wonder now—we have discussed many of the subjects. It is making no little stir, I can tell you."

"Spare my blushes," said Arnold, "and those of my amanuensis," and he bowed to his wife, "who patiently copied the scrawls which no printer could have deciphered, written, as they always were, in more or less of a hurry."

"A political economist at twenty-two!" exclaimed the doctor. "If these things be done in the green tree, what shall be done in the dry? There's no possible outcome of such an abnormal precocity, but a President in the family."

"Can't be," said Arnold, seriously; "this family has been under the government of an absolute monarchy since, and probably before, my earliest recollection. Where's your grape-wine, Polly? The people who don't even drink Polly's grape-wine, and the children, can fill their glasses with water, for I am about to propose a toast—*the* toast, for I don't believe any one else has one to propose. Are you all ready? Stand up then—

"'The Queen, God bless her,' the mother, to whom, under God, we owe all we are, and all we have, whose love for us, and faith in us, have never faltered, and never will falter— the corner-stone of every household represented here to-day! Long life to her, and all the happiness she so nobly deserves!"

Mrs. Stanley had risen with the rest, and now she looked about her with a puzzled face, as each one said—

"Here's to her!" and they raised their glasses. She put out her hand to take her own, but Kitty, who sat next to her, laughingly drew it away, saying—

" No, no, my liege lady, even the Queen mustn't drink her own health! She must only reply with a neat and appropriate speech."

" Do you all mean me ? " and she looked from one beaming face to the other, with a growing light in her own. " Dear children! It is like you, to think and say such things of me, but I can't make a speech—I can only say, God bless you all, and let the years bring to you as much true happiness as they have brought to me."

" I think that is a beautiful speech," said Kitty the second, and, judging from the smiling faces around her, she " spoke the sense of the meeting."

Is the realm of such a queen a small one ?

THE END.

THE FAMOUS CASTLEMON BOOKS.

BY HARRY CASTLEMON.

Specimen Cover of the Gunboat Series.

No author of the present day has become a greater favorite with boys than "Harry Castlemon;" every book by him is sure to meet with hearty reception by young readers generally. His naturalness and vivacity lead his readers from page to page with breathless interest, and when one volume is finished the fascinated reader, like Oliver Twist, asks "for more."

⁎ Any volume sold separately.

GUNBOAT SERIES. By Harry Castlemon. 6 vols., 12mo. Fully illustrated. Cloth, extra, printed in colors. In box $7 50

Frank, the Young Naturalist 1 25

Frank in the Woods 1 25

Frank on the Prairie 1 25

Frank on a Gunboat 1 25

Frank before Vicksburg 1 25

Frank on the Lower Mississippi 1 25

GO AHEAD SERIES. By Harry Castlemon. 3 vols., 12mo. Fully illustrated. Cloth, extra, printed in colors. In box $3 75

Go Ahead; or, The Fisher Boy's Motto 1 25

No Moss; or, The Career of a Rolling Stone 1 25

Tom Newcombe ; or, The Boy of Bad Habits . .   1 25

ROCKY MOUNTAIN SERIES. By Harry Castlemon. 3 vols., 12mo. Fully illustrated. Cloth, extra, printed in colors. In box $3 75

Frank at Don Carlos' Rancho 1 25

Frank among the Rancheros 1 25

Frank in the Mountains. 1 25

SPORTSMAN'S CLUB SERIES. By Harry Castlemon. 3 vols., 12mo. Fully illustrated. Cloth, extra, printed in colors. In box $3 75

The Sportsman's Club in the Saddle 1 25

The Sportsman's Club Afloat 1 25

The Sportsman's Club among the Trappers .   1 25

FRANK NELSON SERIES. By Harry Castlemon. 3 vols. 12mo. Fully illustrated. Cloth, extra, printed in colors. In box $3 75

Snowed Up ; or, The Sportsman's Club in the Mts. .   1 25

Frank Nelson in the Forecastle ; or, The Sportsman's Club among the Whalers 1 25

The Boy Traders ; or, The Sportsman's Club among the Boers 1 25

BOY TRAPPER SERIES. By Harry Castlemon. 3 vols., 12mo. Fully illustrated. Cloth, extra, printed in colors. In box $3 75

The Buried Treasure ; or, Old Jordan's " Haunt "   1 25

The Boy Trapper · or, How Dave Filled the Order.   1 25

The Mail Carrier 1 25

ROUGHING IT SERIES. By Harry Castlemon.
3 vols., 12mo   Fully illustrated.   Cloth, extra, printed
in colors.   In box $3 75

George in Camp; or, Life on the Plains 1 25

George at the Wheel; or, Life in a Pilot House .   1 25

George at the Fort; or, Life Among the Soldiers .   1 25

ROD AND GUN SERIES. By Harry Castlemon.
3 vols., 12mo.   Fully illustrated.   Cloth, extra, printed
in colors.   In box $3 75

Don Gordon's Shooting Box 1 25

Rod and Gun 1 25

The Young Wild Fowlers 1 25

FOREST AND STREAM SERIES. By Harry
Castlemon.   3 vols., 12mo.   Fully illustrated.   Cloth,
extra, printed in colors.   In box $3 75

Joe Wayring at Home; or, Story of a Fly Rod .   1 25

Snagged and Sunk; or, The Adventures of a Can-
vas Canoe 1 25

Steel Horse; or, The Rambles of a Bicycle 1 25

WAR SERIES. By Harry Castlemon.   4 vols.,
12mo.   Fully illustrated.   Cloth, extra, printed in
colors.   In box 5 00

True to his Colors 1 25

Rodney, the Partisan 1 25

Marcy, the Blockade Runner 1 25

Marcy, the Refugee 1 25

OUR FELLOWS; or, Skirmishes with the Swamp
Dragoons.   By Harry Castlemon.   16mo.   Fully illustrated.   Cloth, extra 1 25

ALGER'S RENOWNED BOOKS.

BY HORATIO ALGER, JR.

Specimen Cover of the Ragged Dick Series.

Horatio Alger, Jr., has attained distinction as one of the most popular writers of books for boys, and the following list comprises all of his best books.

٭*٭ Any volume sold separately.

RAGGED DICK SERIES. By Horatio Alger, Jr. 6 vols., 12mo. Fully illustrated. Cloth, extra, printed in colors. In box $7 50

Ragged Dick; or, Street Life in New York 1 25

Fame and Fortune; or, The Progress of Richard Hunter 1 25

Mark, the Match Boy; or, Richard Hunter's Ward 1 25

Rough and Ready; or, Life among the New York Newsboys 1 25

Ben, the Luggage Boy; or, Among the Wharves . 1 25

Rufus and Rose; or, the Fortunes of Rough and Ready 1 25

TATTERED TOM SERIES. (FIRST SERIES.) By Horatio Alger, Jr. 4 vols., 12mo. Fully illustrated. Cloth, extra, printed in colors. In box . . . 5 00

(4)

Tattered Tom; or, The Story of a Street Arab . . 1 25

Paul, the Peddler; or, The Adventures of a Young
Street Merchant 1 25

Phil, the Fiddler; or, The Young Street Musician . 1 25

Slow and Sure; or, From the Sidewalk to the Shop 1 25

TATTERED TOM SERIES. (SECOND SERIES.)
4 vols., 12mo. Fully illustrated. Cloth, extra, printed
in colors. In box $5 00

Julius; or the Street Boy Out West 1 25

The Young Outlaw; or, Adrift in the World . . . 1 25

Sam's Chance and How He Improved it . . . 1 25

The Telegraph Boy 1 25

LUCK AND PLUCK SERIES. (FIRST SERIES.)
By Horatio Alger, Jr. 4 vols., 12mo. Fully illustrated. Cloth, extra, printed in colors. In box . . . $5 00

Luck and Pluck; or John Oakley's Inheritance . . 1 25

Sink or Swim; or, Harry Raymond's Resolve . . . 1 25

Strong and Steady; or, Paddle Your Own Canoe . 1 25

Strive and Succeed; or, The Progress of Walter
Conrad 1 25

LUCK AND PLUCK SERIES. (SECOND
SERIES.) By Horatio Alger, Jr. 3 vols., 12mo.
Fully illustrated. Cloth, extra, printed in colors. In
box $5 00

Try and Trust; or, The Story of a Bound Boy . . . 1 25

Bound to Rise; or Harry Walton's Motto 1 25

Risen from the Ranks; or, Harry Walton's Success 1 25

Herbert Carter's Legacy; or, The Inventor's Son . 1 25

CAMPAIGN SERIES. By Horatio Alger, Jr. 3
vols., 12mo. Fully illustrated. Cloth, extra, printed
in colors. In box $3 75

Frank's Campaign; or, The Farm and the Camp . 1 25

Paul Prescott's Charge 1 25

Charlie Codman's Cruise 1 25

BRAVE AND BOLD SERIES. By Horatio Alger, Jr. 4 vols., 12mo. Fully illustrated. Cloth, extra, printed in colors. In box $5 00

Brave and Bold; or, The Story of a Factory Boy . . 1 25

Jack's Ward; or, The Boy Guardian 1 25

Shifting for Himself; or, Gilbert Greyson's Fortunes 1 25

Wait and Hope; or, Ben Bradford's Motto 1 25

PACIFIC SERIES. By Horatio Alger, Jr. 4 vols. 12mo. Fully illustrated. Cloth, extra, printed in colors. In box $5 00

The Young Adventurer; or, Tom's Trip Across the Plains 1 25

The Young Miner; or, Tom Nelson in California . 1 25

The Young Explorer; or, Among the Sierras . . 1 25

Ben's Nugget; or, A Boy's Search for Fortune. A Story of the Pacific Coast 1 25

ATLANTIC SERIES. By Horatio Alger, Jr. 4 vols, 12mo. Fully illustrated. Cloth, extra, printed in colors. In box $5 00

The Young Circus Rider; or, The Mystery of Robert Rudd 1 25

Do and Dare; or, A Brave Boy's Fight for Fortune . 1 25

Hector's Inheritance; or, Boys of Smith Institute . 1 25

Helping Himself; or, Grant Thornton's Ambition . 1 25

WAY TO SUCCESS SERIES. By Horatio Alger, Jr 4 vols., 12mo. Fully illustrated. Cloth, extra, printed in colors. In box $5 00

Bob Burton 1 25

The Store Boy 1 25

Luke Walton 1 25

Struggling Upward 1 25

NEW BOOK BY ALGER.

DIGGING FOR GOLD. By Horatio Alger, Jr. Illustrated 12mo. Cloth, black, red and gold . . . 1 25

A
New Series
of Books.

——

ιndian Life
and
Character
Founded on
Historical
Facts.

Specimen Cover of the Wyoming
Series.

By Edward S. Ellis.

•*• Any volume sold separately.

——

BOY PIONEER SERIES. By Edward S. Ellis.
3 vols., 12mo. Fully illustrated. Cloth, extra, printed
in colors. In box $3 75
Ned in the Block House; or, Life on the Frontier. 1 25
Ned in the Woods. A Tale of the Early Days in
the West 1 25
Ned on the River 1 25
DEERFOOT SERIES. By Edward S. Ellis. In
box containing the following. 3 vols., 12mo. Illus-
trated . . . . ' . . . $3 75
Hunters of the Ozark 1 25
Camp in the Mountains 1 25
The Last War Trail 1 25
LOG CABIN SERIES. By Edward S. Ellis.
3 vols., 12mo. Fully illustrated. Cloth, extra, printed
in colors. In box $3 75

Lost Trail $1 25
Camp Fire and Wigwam 1 25
Footprints in the Forest 1 25
WYOMING SERIES. By Edward S. Ellis. 3
vols., 12mo. Fully illustrated. Cloth, extra, printed
in colors. In box $3 75
Wyoming 1 25
Storm Mountain 1 25
Cabin in the Clearing 1 25

NEW BOOKS BY EDWARD S. ELLIS.

Through Forest and Fire. 12mo. Cloth . . . 1 25
On the Trail of the Moose. 12mo. Cloth . . 1 25

By C. A. Stephens.

Rare books for boys—bright, breezy, wholesome and instructive ; full of
adventure and incident, and information upon natural history. They blend
instruction with amusement—contain much useful and valuable information
upon the habits of animals, and plenty of adventure, fun and jollity.

CAMPING OUT SERIES. By C. A. Stephens.
6 vols., 12mo. Fully illustrated. Cloth, extra, printed
in colors. In box $7 50
Camping Out. As recorded by "Kit" 1 25
Left on Labrador; or The Cruise of the Schooner
Yacht "Curfew." As recorded by "Wash" 1 25
Off to the Geysers ; or, The Young Yachters in Ice-
land. As recorded by "Wade" 1 25
Lynx Hunting. From Notes by the author of
"Camping Out" 1 25
Fox Hunting. As recorded by "Raed" 1 25
On the Amazon ; or, The Cruise of the "Rambler."
As recorded by "Wash" 1 25

By J. T. Trowbridge.

These stories will rank among the best of Mr. Trowbridge's books for the
young—and he has written some of the best of our juvenile literature.

JACK HAZARD SERIES. By J. T. Trowbridge.
6 vols., 12mo. Fully Illustrated. Cloth, extra, printed
in colors. In box $7 50

www.ingramcontent.com/pod-product-compliance
Lightning Source LLC
Chambersburg PA
CBHW022012110726
47901CB00006B/1490